LAWLESS
LOVE

ROSANNE
BITTNER

DIVERSIONBOOKS

More from Rosanne Bittner

The Bride Series
Tennessee Bride
Texas Bride
Oregon Bride

Caress
Comanche Sunset
Heart's Surrender
*In the Shadow of the
Mountains*
Indian Summer
Lawless Love
Love's Bounty

Rapture's Gold
Shameless
Sweet Mountain Magic
Tame the Wild Wind
Tender Betrayal
The Forever Tree
Unforgettable
Until Tomorrow

Diversion Books
A Division of Diversion Publishing Corp.
443 Park Avenue South, Suite 1008
New York, New York 10016
www.DiversionBooks.com

For more information, email info@diversionbooks.com

First Diversion Books edition August 2017.
Print ISBN: 978-1-63576-359-1
eBook ISBN: 978-1-68230-329-0

In memory of the once lawless and untamed American West,
where bad men turned good, good men turned bad,
and most couldn't tell the difference.

There is a factor in life called fate, over which we seem to have little control. There are no rules governing it, and there seems to be little we can do to change it. And it can turn around the lives of men and women alike, leading them down pathways from which there is no return.

PART I

Chapter One

1869

Amanda's insides jumped as steam suddenly swooshed from the sides of the Union Pacific engine not far from where she stood. The large, boiling monster hissed and clanged its bell, and Amanda took a deep breath to calm herself. She was determined that her fright at being alone on this long journey would not get the better of her. After all, weren't the nuns back in New York praying for her?

She picked up the carpetbag that sat on the ground beside her and hurried to the passenger car. In her haste she ran headlong into what seemed like a wall, something broad and seemingly immovable. She let out a small, startled scream as her hat was knocked from her head and one of the handles on her carpetbag broke. Someone reached out and grabbed her gently before she could stumble backward.

"Say there, little lady, you're in a might of a hurry, aren't you?" came a deep and somewhat gruff voice. Yet, when she looked up, the gentle brown eyes of the huge man she had run into did not match his voice and size. She quickly looked away in embarrassment.

Amanda's face turned crimson, and all she could manage was to gasp and utter a string of "Oh, mys!" as she brushed herself off. "I dearly beg your pardon, sir!" she finally added in her soft, shy voice. "I was lost in thought."

The man picked up her hat and handed it to her, and it

was only then that she had the courage to face him again. This time their eyes held for a moment, and a strange, inexplicable feeling crept through Amanda's veins, as though running into this man were some kind of omen. He stood a good six feet tall or better, towering over her own five-foot two-inch frame. His dark hair hung nearly to his shoulders, although in neat waves that looked far from untidy. His face was handsome but bearded, which fascinated her, and it struck her that the beard probably hid a face that would be more attractive without its shroud of hair. And although the man wore a black broadcloth suit and a new gray hat, she could only envision him in buckskins, like the pictures of mountain men she had seen in books.

"You'd be best to sit down before you do your thinkin', ma'am," he was telling her with a soft grin. "What if I'd been the train?" His smile was charming, but Amanda couldn't think of a thing to say in return. She only smiled and blushed more. She had seldom talked to any man—and especially not to strangers—in her entire twenty-two years of life. Her eyes began to tear with embarrassment, and she bent down to pick up her carpetbag by the one handle that was still good. She put her other arm around it to support it.

"Ma'am, I could fix that for you. I've got some rawhide on my saddle back there in the storage car."

"No!" she said quickly. "I—it's fine."

"But you can't carry it around like that all the time."

"I'll manage. Excuse me, please." She turned to get into the passenger car. How could she let this stranger fix her carpetbag? What if he found out what was inside it? He was a huge man and looked worldly and experienced. How did she know he wasn't some kind of outlaw? How could she know who to trust?

"Ma'am?" he called out.

She stopped but did not turn around.

"You all right?"

She simply nodded and quickly boarded the train. She found a seat at the front of the car and sat down wearily, setting her carpetbag beside her. She leaned forward and reached around to rub her back a little. She was tired of sitting on trains, but her trip was not even half over. At least now she had something to look forward to, which would keep her mind off of her aching body.

The Union Pacific would head ever westward, and the train personnel had already told her that the scenery would change to raw, rugged country with buffalo, prairie dogs, and coyotes, flat-topped mesas, and the spectacular Rocky Mountains. And then there would be the Nevada desert and Sierras. These were all things she had only read about in books until now, things she had wished she could see—and now she would. She remembered the man she had just run into. She knew at a glance, without really knowing him, that he was a part of that "big sky country," as some authors called it in stories and articles she had read about the West.

The thought of the tall stranger brought a flutter to her chest and a new flush to her cheeks. She felt like a clumsy fool and hoped she would not see him again.

"May I see your ticket, ma'am?" a porter asked, interrupting her thoughts.

"What? Oh, yes," she replied, scrambling through her handbag until she found it. The porter studied it.

"All the way to California? Now that's a mighty big trip for a little lady like you, ma'am. You traveling alone?"

"The Lord is with me," she replied, taking back the ticket after he marked it.

The porter grinned. "That may be so, ma'am. But where you're heading, you'd be better off having a gun-totin' bodyguard along. You watch yourself, ma'am."

He walked on. "Next stop is Rock Island," he announced to everyone on the train. "Then we'll head into Iowa and Nebraska. It's a long trip, but the Union Pacific is bound to please its customers! You people are traveling the nation's latest grand achievement, the transcontinental railroad. We've made a lot of trips already, and we'll get you to the land of golden sunsets without any trouble. You folks rest easy now. We'll be five or six hours getting to Rock Island."

He walked down the aisle and then back, stopping to look at Amanda again. "You have a nice trip now."

"Thank you," she replied, managing a pleasant smile. So far she had done a decent job of keeping her fears hidden. Amanda had grown up behind the sheltered walls of a Catholic home for orphaned girls, seeing few people other than her peers at the orphanage and the nuns who helped raise her. Of men she knew next to nothing, having known only two priests—whom she almost never saw except in church—and the general delivery men who came to the orphanage. And none of them were anything like the tall stranger she had just run into, nor the other types of men she had read and heard about who lived in the West.

It made little difference, as she had no interest in a relationship with any man. She was much too shy and inhibited, and she planned to become a nun, although she had not yet made a final decision. She had already taken most of the necessary steps. But then she got the opportunity to go to California to teach, and she felt she should see more of the real world before taking her final vows.

Amanda was well educated—as far as books go—and she could cook and sew. But she was ill prepared for life outside the walls of the orphanage, so her new job would give her the opportunity to see how other people lived. She was well past the age that most girls left the orphanage and, although it was frightening, she knew she must get out and be on her own. Going all the way to California by herself seemed a bit excessive, but she was needed there, and it was a chance to step out and take hold of life in a brand new land.

At the time the job had been offered to Amanda five months earlier, the transcontinental railroad had just been completed. It seemed everything pointed to her taking the job.

"Your services are needed immediately," the letter from

Father Mitchel said. "Please make an effort to come to California as soon as possible. Teachers are sorely needed."

And so her decision was made and everything was prepared for her journey. But plans were delayed when Amanda became ill with pneumonia, and weeks of slow recuperation had forced her departure all the way into early October. She knew it was risky leaving so late in the year, as everyone claimed snow came early to the Rockies. But she could not allow Father Mitchel to go another winter without help, and she was afraid she would lose the job if she was further delayed. It was unlikely such an opportunity would ever come up again. She had spent many nights dreaming about what it would be like to go west and see things that her friends and the nuns in New York would never see. It would be an adventure—frightening, but an adventure nonetheless.

But the day Amanda boarded the train in New York, her mounting fears dampened her adventuresome spirit. For the first time she would not only be on her own, but she would be traveling nearly three thousand miles away from the orphanage and the kind nuns who had nurtured and protected her. She felt like a foolish child to be so afraid. The loneliness that gripped her as she peered through the window of the train as the sisters waved good-bye reminded her of the day, when she was five years old, that she realized that her parents would never come back to her. Her memory of her mother and father was vague now. Her whole life had been the orphanage and the sisters. She had smiled bravely to them from the train and they blew kisses to her; then they were gone and she was alone.

She brushed more dirt from her dress and put her dark green velvet hat back on her head, feeling with her fingers to be sure it was in place before she pinned it. She was proud of her lovely hat and the matching velvet cape she wore with it; both were gifts from the nuns for her journey. "You must dress warmly and take care of yourself, Amanda. Remember you've just gotten over your pneumonia," the nuns had cautioned.

She reached over and pulled up the broken handle of

her carpetbag, thinking how nice it would be to have it fixed. But she didn't dare trust the tall stranger who had offered to repair it.

In the bottom of her bag she carried money which the nuns had given her for the trip and for clothes when she arrived in California. But more important was the crucifix that was hidden in the bottom of her bag: a crucifix embedded with rubies and diamonds, a gift from the orphanage to the mission school where Amanda was headed. The crucifix worried Amanda, but she was sure that because of her plain clothes and quiet, reserved manner, no one would suspect she would be carrying anything valuable. "The Lord will be with you, Amanda," the nuns had told her. "You've nothing to fear."

The engine hissed again, and a conductor was walking up and down the tracks outside hollering "All aboard!"

She listened quietly to the general conversation behind her.

"Have you ever seen the Rockies?" a man asked another passenger.

"No. But I'm sure looking forward to it," another man's voice replied. "I figure I'll even bag me some buffalo through the window while the train's rolling."

The men chuckled, but Amanda's stomach churned with anger. How cruel to shoot an animal for sport! She felt that the railroad should put a stop to such behavior. But the railroad actually boasted about it, trying to attract more business by offering easy targets to greenhorns from the East so they could call themselves "great hunters."

Her thoughts turned again to the stranger. She was sure he would be against such an act. He struck her as the type who would laugh at such ludicrous hunting. But then it annoyed her that she had even given the man another thought. Why was he on her mind?

"What about the Indians?" someone else asked, "I've heard the Sioux have been raiding in Wyoming, and they've even tried to stop trains."

"They're just tryin' to hang on to what's theirs," came

a deep and familiar voice. It was the stranger! She was sure of it without even turning around to look. She had not seen him board.

"Oh, but it isn't theirs!" an arrogant sounding voice spoke up. "Why should we let savages squat on valuable land? White settlement is a fact they simply have to face, sir. I couldn't care less if the red man was totally eradicated. It's time to rid this country of its riffraff and get on with progress. Out in Council Bluffs, where I reside, we've chased out most of the Indians."

"How? By shootin' them in the back and rapin' and killin' the women and babies?" came the reply. People gasped and Amanda turned to look. The tall stranger was standing, and he towered over the man who had made the haughty remark about eliminating the Indians in Council Bluffs. He looked menacing and angry, not at all like the smiling and courteous man who had kept her from falling.

"I beg your pardon!" the seated man remarked, turning red in the face. The man had an air of prosperity about him.

"Well, you won't get no apologies from me, mister," the tall stranger replied. "Men who root out the Indians without a thought to whether they'll live or die, and men who shoot buffalo out of train windows aren't men at all in my book. And if you was to face an Indian buck and fight him like a man, he'd have your hide stretched out to dry in two minutes flat and be wearin' your scalp from his weapons belt."

Amanda grinned and turned back around. The wealthy man was infuriated.

"You have no call to speak to me that way!" he fumed.

"I've got as much right to speak to you that way as you've got to be braggin' about riddin' Council Bluffs of Indians, mister. You want to do somethin' about it, you come on outside and we'll see how much of a brave Indian fighter you really are."

The wealthy man smiled contemptuously. "I'll not stoop to groveling in the dirt with the likes of you!" he replied.

The stranger chuckled. "That's what I figured. Maybe some other time then."

People whispered as the stranger moved up the aisle, and Amanda felt her heart pound when he took a seat directly across the aisle facing her so that she could not help but see him plainly. She quickly turned to look out the window, not wanting him to know she had been watching him.

"And have you ever fought Indians, mister?" one man asked him.

The locomotive hissed, belched, and lurched forward. The tall stranger sighed and leaned back, putting his feet up on the seat opposite him. He wore knee-high black leather boots with the pants tucked into them.

"I've gone around with a few," he replied, sounding tired.

"And how about the law?" the pompous man asked with a sneer. "Have you gone around with them, too?"

A faint grin passed over the stranger's lips, which Amanda caught out of the corner of her eye. He did not reply, but merely settled down into his seat and pulled the Stetson down over his eyes.

Once his eyes were covered, Amanda dared to glance at him again. The brief view she had had of him earlier told her he must be in his late thirties—and he was not a man to be pushed around. It was more and more obvious he'd had experience in the vast and mysterious West she was about to enter. But what sort of man was he? Was he a lawman? An outlaw? And what had he been doing in Chicago? Again it struck her that he ought to be wearing buckskins and possibly a gun belt, or carrying a rifle, or both. It annoyed her that she should think and wonder about him at all. Not only was she afraid of men in general, but this man apparently came from a world totally alien to the world she knew.

She absentmindedly pulled a small mirror from her handbag and held it up, tugging little curls farther down her forehead. She studied herself briefly. She was not beautiful—not in the way that wealthy, fashionable women are beautiful.

But she did have a simple beauty: a clear complexion and soft green eyes. She never wore make-up—that was considered sinful—and her long, thick, dark brown hair was pulled into a tight bun at the nape of her neck, with only a few strands left to curl about her face. She adjusted her hat again and settled back into her seat as the train began to move a little faster.

The stranger across the aisle shifted. She dared to glance over at him. His hands were resting on his stomach. They were big hands. Had they killed? Could they be gentle? Her excursion into this new and different world brought forward a myriad of questions to her inexperienced mind. She felt a sudden desire to know more about the stranger and his world.

He shifted again, looking uncomfortable. He pushed his hat back and stood up to pull down a pillow from the overhead rack.

"What kind of Indians did you fight, mister?" a curious passenger asked. The stranger did not reply immediately. He sat back down and fixed the pillow behind his head.

"Mostly Sioux," he finally grunted. "A couple of Apache."

"Did you kill them?" the other man asked.

The stranger was adjusting his hat again. He glanced over at Amanda, and it was obvious he just then realized she had been sitting there. His eyes immediately softened, and he smiled.

"So, we meet again. You all right, ma'am?"

She blushed and looked at her lap.

"I'm just fine."

"I'd still like to fix that bag for you."

The remark was so sincere, she hated to be rude.

"I—I'll think about it."

"Good." He frowned. "You alone?" he asked, after looking around. His voice showed his amazement.

She twisted her hands nervously. "The Lord is with me," she answered. He did not reply, and she couldn't help but look over at him. He was studying her with concern, and she felt a warmth flow through her.

"Mmm-hmm," he mumbled. "Well, just in case that's not enough, you give a holler if you need help."

She blushed deeply and swallowed with nervousness.

"Well, thank you," she managed to say. "But I hardly think it will be necessary, sir."

"Then you haven't been around much. You look a little lost and out of place, and you're a right pretty lady, if you don't mind my sayin' so."

She blushed even more. No one had ever told her that. Oh, the nuns had called her pretty. But they said all the girls at the school were pretty. It wasn't the same as this worldly man saying it.

"I'll…be fine," she replied. She quickly turned and took out some knitting from her bag.

"You didn't answer my question, mister," the other man spoke up. "You kill them Indians?"

The stranger looked at the man who had asked the question.

"Mister, when you fight an Indian, you fight to kill. 'Cause that's what he's gonna do to you if you don't get him first. But I've never killed an Indian that didn't attack me first. And I've never met an Indian I didn't respect."

Amanda's mind raced with questions and doubts about this man. He had killed! It was both appalling and fascinating. And he had not replied when asked if he'd had run-ins with the law. She kept to her knitting, determined not to draw any more attention from him nor to converse with him again.

The stranger settled down into his seat again, pulling his hat back down, but leaving it up enough to slyly watch her without her knowing it. She was lovely, and obviously alone and very much afraid. But she was trying very hard not to show it. Her shyness and simple beauty fascinated him. He was curious about her, yet knew that she was not the type who would open up and answer questions, especially when they came from a stranger who probably looked rather menacing to her.

His eyes rested for a moment on the enticing curve of her

bosom, and he wondered if any man had ever touched her. She wore no rings on her hands and she was traveling alone—not likely a married woman. He wondered how old she was and what she was doing alone. The lost and slightly helpless air about her pulled at his insides, and her quiet manner touched a soft side of him that had not been stirred in many years. He closed his eyes and grinned to himself.

"If she knew all about me, she'd jump out of that window while the train was movin'," he thought to himself. *"No woman like that would give the time of day to ole Moss Tucker."*

Chapter Two

The Sioux chief looked across the small fire in his tipi to the white man who had entered the Sioux village.

"Why is it you come here?" the Indian asked impatiently. "Is this another white man's trick? Another offer of trinkets to keep us from more raiding?" His dark eyes glinted with hate, and the white man squirmed.

"I came here to make a deal with you, Raincloud."

The Indian snickered and looked at the white man contemptuously. "Just as I thought. Who sent you? The soldiers? The 'Great White Father' in Washington who steals our land and our buffalo?"

"I came of my own accord. And if I had any bad intentions, do you think I'd have ridden right into your camp?"

The Indian studied him. This man had shifty eyes. He was not to be completely trusted.

"I am listening, white eyes. The deal should be a good one, or you will leave here dragging behind your horse rather than riding on it!"

"I can get you guns, Raincloud—lots of them."

The Indian's eyebrows went up. He leaned forward, and the muscles of his magnificent arms made the white man swallow. This was Raincloud, a rebellious leader who had done much raiding. He was greatly feared by the whites, and very respected by his own men.

"And just how could you get these guns, my friend, and why?"

"The Union Pacific. In a few days a train will be comin' through Wyoming carryin' hundreds of rifles for the army, along with a heavy payroll for the soldiers. I want that payroll.

But I need help. You help me stop the train, you get the guns, I get the money, and we go our separate ways."

The Indian frowned. "How do you know what this train carries?"

"I have connections. I know, that's all. What do you say? Is it a deal?"

"You realize the guns would be used against your own kind?"

"I've learned a man has to look out for himself and that's it. Ain't none of them people ever done nothin' for me, and they'd not appreciate it if I did anything for them. I don't care what you use the guns for. It ain't my affair. I just want the money and then I'll be headin' down to Mexico to spend it on the señoritas. You do whatever you want with the guns."

Raincloud studied the man with disgust. This white man was betraying his own people, something an Indian would never do. The white man's lust for money would be amusing if not for the tragic effect it was having on the Indians.

"When will this train come?" Raincloud finally asked, studying the white man closely.

"About three more days. We'll have to ride down to a place east of Bear River City to intercept the train before it gets there. I've got men comin' down from Hole-in-the-Wall to meet me. After the robbery, we'll go on down to Brown's Park, hole up there for a while, then head for Mexico."

"These places you mention, they are places where white men who go against their own laws hide out, are they not?"

The white man nodded, then lit a cigar while the Indian thought on the idea. Raincloud pondered for a moment. This white man was no good, that was certain.

"How can I be certain the rifles will be on the train?"

"I have a soldier friend who's kept me informed. Once we heist the money, he's joinin' us at Brown's Park. And he's sure the rifles will be there, too."

"And if they are not?"

"They'll be there. You just remember, there'll be a lot

more of you than there will of us. So if I double-cross you, Raincloud, you can use us for target practice if you so choose. If I wasn't sure, I wouldn't be here riskin' my neck like this."

Raincloud rubbed his chin while the white man smoked quietly.

"I will help you," the Indian finally spoke up. "But I think I do not like you very much, my white-eyed friend. It is a bad thing you do, betraying your own people. But the guns will not be used against them if they leave me and my people alone. We need the guns for survival, to hunt the buffalo. And we need them to fight the white men who come and burn our villages and rape our women. The Sioux did not choose this war. Your own people chose it, by breaking their promises."

"I told you I don't give a damn how you use the guns. Just help me stop the train and get the payroll."

"There will not be soldiers on the train?"

"Only a couple. Too many would give it away. They don't want anybody knowin' what the train's carrying. It's billed as strictly a few passengers and their cargo. It'll be an easy take, Raincloud."

The Indian thought another moment, then rose.

"I will do it. We must have the guns." He grinned slyly. "To protect ourselves from men like yourself."

The white man smiled back and threw his cigar down, stepping it out.

"And as I said, we must have them to kill game—game which is becoming more scarce as the white man moves in and kills it needlessly and fences off more property to keep us from getting to the game. The land belongs to all of us. It is not for man to divide into little pieces and call his own!"

The white man shrugged. "Like I said, Raincloud, them things don't matter to me. You just meet me and my men down in Dixie Canyon, day after tomorrow. You know where that is?"

"The Sioux know the land as well as they know their women."

The white man grinned again. "Speakin' of women, you

wouldn't have any squaws you'd like to loan out for a night or two, would you?"

The Indian's eyes blackened with contempt.

"Not for the likes of you, my friend. We have already made our deal, and a squaw was not part of it. And if you like your hair, the guns had better be on the train."

The white man swallowed. "They'll be there." He turned to leave.

"Wait!" Raincloud spoke up. The man turned.

"The Indians do not live in filth as the white man like to make others believe. You will pick up that piece of your smoke from the floor of my dwelling and take it with you."

The white man pressed his lips together in anger. He was in no position to argue. He glowered at the Indian and walked back, bending over to pick up the cigar butt.

"You have not even told me your name," Raincloud told him.

"Barker. Rand Barker."

"Mmmm." The dark eyes studied the tall and unkempt white man. "I will remember your name, Rand Barker. It is the name of a traitor. Be sure it is not I who you betray."

Barker's eyes glinted. "You won't be betrayed. See you in a couple of days." He quickly went out and mounted his horse. When he neared the edge of the village, a small child played there alone. Barker looked down at the tot, who stared up at the white man with large, brown innocent eyes.

"You little vermin!" Barker sneered. He spat on the child and rode off.

Chapter Three

The Union Pacific rattled and chugged across the nearly eight hundred miles between Chicago and Council Bluffs with not a word spoken between Amanda and the man across the aisle from her. She was too shy; he felt she was too much a lady for a man like him to speak to. And so they rode in silence, disembarked at rest stations in silence, ate in silence. Yet each knew the other was watching, she out of curiosity, he out of genuine concern for her safety.

Amanda thought it odd that she was actually glad the man was along and that he always sat near her. And to her surprise, she found herself beginning to fear at each stop that he might get off and not return. Yet each time he boarded again. She wondered just how far he was going, but was too timid to ask. The other passengers changed, some leaving, some staying, new ones boarding. Amanda kept her same seat, and the stranger kept his across from her.

They finally reached Council Bluffs, where it was announced there would be an overnight stay for some repair work on the engine. Amanda's heart tightened. Now she would have to find lodging. How did she know what places would be decent and which ones would not? And how safe would she be? The stranger left the car before she did, and when she exited she could not see him anywhere. She clung to her carpetbag and handbag, and ducked her head as a chilly drizzle stung her face. She would have to find lodging quickly, being frightened of becoming wet and cold after just getting over pneumonia.

"Dear God, help me find a place to stay," she whispered. She hurried away from the station, heading for the log buildings with various signs on them, most of them reading "saloon."

Then she hesitated. Why not just stay on the train? She could sleep in her seat. After all, she'd been doing so up until now. The porter had suggested the passengers find a place to stay so that they could sleep in a real bed for one night. But most of the passengers were men, who didn't have to be choosy about where they slept. Already many of them were heading toward the saloons, laughing and conversing. And she realized that was probably exactly where the stranger had gone.

Her heart fell. She had subconsciously thought he would be nearby and maybe tell her where to go. She was hurrying back toward the train when two men on foot approached her, blocking her path.

"Need a place to spend the night, honey?" one asked. His breath smelled of whiskey and he sported a couple days' growth of beard.

"I—I'm staying on the train," she answered, trying to get by them.

"Oh, you can't do that, little girl. We'll find you a place, won't we, Harvey?" The man took her arm.

"Please let go of me," she pleaded, tears coming to her eyes. "I want to stay on the train!"

One of them laughed. "We've been watchin' you since Rock Island, honey. You're travelin' alone. Where you headed? Goin' to one of them minin' towns out on the coast to set up a brothel, maybe?" He pulled her close, pushing the carpetbag from her hand. "I'd pay a lot for you, little lady. How much you asking?"

She choked back a sob and struggled as the man tried to kiss her. Her first thought was that the other man would run off with her carpetbag and the precious cross inside of it.

"Please! I'm not one of them!" she cried. "Let me go, please!"

Just then there was the click of a rifle, followed by a loud bang that made Amanda scream and cover her ears. The man grabbing her quickly let go and jumped back as dirt flew at his heels, where a bullet hit too close for comfort.

"You gentlemen figurin' on doin' this lady's choosin' for her?" came the deep voice. Amanda knew it was the stranger. She didn't look at him right away. She quickly picked up her carpetbag and stepped back, hanging her head in embarrassment and shame. If this was what men were like, she was glad she had decided not to have anything to do with them.

"Who the hell are you?" one of her attackers asked.

"The name don't matter. What matters is you're puttin' your hands on private property, mister. That lady belongs to herself and nobody else, and I suggest you keep your hands off her."

"It ain't your business, mister!"

"I'm makin' it my business. And I'd be glad if you'd like to argue about it, 'cause it wouldn't bother me at all to fill your brisket with lead, mister. I've done it before, so it's nothin' new to me."

Amanda finally looked at him. He wore a gunbelt low on his hips, and at the moment he held a rifle in his hands and his eyes were cold. The two assailants stood there staring at the man for a moment.

"Lester, he looks mean. I think he's serious," one of them said.

"I am," the tall stranger replied. "And my advice is that you two get yourself some horses and do your travelin' on four legs instead of iron tracks. I don't want to see you gettin' back on the train. It might upset the lady here to see you again."

Amanda sniffed and moved closer to the stranger.

"Now wait just a minute!" the one called Harvey spoke up. "You can't tell us we can't ride the train!"

"I just did. I'm gonna be watchin' in the morning. If I see you try to get on, I'll fracture your jaws and fix you up so you have to stay here till you mend. And if you don't think I can take care of both of you at once, you just try me. I've not been in a good go-round for a long time. Might be kind of fun."

The two men looked at each other and hesitated. Then the stranger cocked the rifle again and they both started running. The stranger watched them until they were far down the muddy street. Then his eyes moved to Amanda's, and for the first time they both stared at each other for several seconds.

"Ma'am, if you'll trust me, I can take you to a safe place to stay where you can sleep in a real bed. The ladies there aren't exactly what somebody like you would be used to, but they're friendly and they're good-hearted. They'd be glad to make you welcome and you'd be safe there."

"I—I don't know, I—"

"No arguing," he told her, coming closer and taking the carpetbag from her. "You're cold and wet and you're gonna be sick if you stand here any longer." He put an arm around her and forced her to walk with him. Her mind was confused with a mixture of relief and apprehension. Yet this man had just saved her from what could have been a fate worse than death, as far as she was concerned. And she was too weary from the long trip and too weak from the ordeal she had just been through to argue.

He led her to a long, rambling log house, barging through the door without knocking. Amanda was immediately enveloped in the lovely warmth put out by a large fire in a roaring, stone fireplace nearby. Four women sat dressed only in night-gowns; as they looked toward the door their faces lit up.

Amanda blushed deeply as all four of them rushed to greet the stranger, squealing and hugging him. He kept an arm around Amanda, but set her carpetbag on the table and used his other arm to hug them one by one.

"Moss Tucker, you old bear! Where in hell have you been!" a redhead bellowed. "My bed hasn't been the same since you left it, you ole gunslinger, you!"

Amanda thought she would faint when they kissed, but then he let go of the woman and put his hand up for silence.

"Hold up there, now, ladies. I want all of you on your best behavior. I didn't come here to do business. I came to ask you to help this little woman I've got with me. She's travelin' alone and she's all lady, in every respect. So watch your mouths and put on some robes."

All four women looked at her, all of them with kindness in their eyes.

"Why, child, you're shivering. Come on over here by the fire, honey," the redhead told her. She pulled Amanda away from the stranger and led her to a big rocker. "Betty, go get a blanket for her," she ordered another girl. "Honey, let's get this cape off you. I'll hang it up to dry."

"Thank you," Amanda said meekly, grateful for the warmth and the seemingly friendly woman. Were these the kind of women she had heard about? They had to be. They wore too much make-up and their gowns were embarrassingly revealing.

"I'm Della," the redhead told her. "That there is Betty, Rosa and Miriam. We, uh, entertain the male train passengers who come through here, you might say." She laughed lightly and looked up at the stranger. "What's her name?"

The man removed his hat and scratched his head. "Well, now, I never even asked," he replied, walking over to Amanda. He knelt down beside her. "What is your name, ma'am?"

Her eyes met his, and she felt the strange warmth again. In his stooped position, his face was close to hers. His brown eyes were gentle.

"Amanda. Amanda Boone," she replied. His eyes roved her body for one brief moment, and she felt flushed.

"That's a real pretty name," he told her. "Amanda. I like that. I'm Moses Tucker, Miss Boone." He put out his hand.

Amanda hesitated, then offered her hand in response. Tucker's big hand closed around hers and held it for a moment.

"Thank you, Mr. Tucker—for what you did out there. I don't know what I'd have done if you hadn't come along. I—"

Her exhaustion, and the delayed shock from the scare the strangers had given her, hit her all at once and to her disgrace she burst into tears. She tried to pull her hand away, but he kept a tight hold of it.

"Miss Boone, don't you be fretting. I happen to be goin' all the way to California, so wherever you get off, I'll be keepin' an eye on you all the way. Only reason I wasn't right there when you got off tonight was 'cause I'd gone back to the baggage car to get my weapons. Now that we're gettin' into more uncivilized territory, I figured it would be best to put them on."

"Oh, I'm so sorry!" she said in a near whisper, wiping at her eyes with her free hand. "I don't generally act so childish!"

"You're just tired, honey," Della spoke up, coming over and patting Amanda's shoulder. "Betty's putting nice fresh sheets on a bed for you, and Miriam's heating water for tea. I'll fix you something to eat and then you can get a good night's sleep." Tucker let go of her hand and stood up.

"I…can't thank you enough for your hospitality," Amanda replied, shaking a little as she took out a hanky to blow her nose.

"Well, anybody Moss tells us to look out for, we look out for," Della replied.

"Moss?" Amanda asked, looking up at the woman.

"Yeah. Didn't you hear us call him that when you came in? That's what everybody calls this big galloot here," Della answered, going over and hugging Tucker around the waist. He had stepped closer to the fireplace and was lighting a cigar. "Short for Moses. Kind of slides out of the mouth easier, I guess."

Moss chuckled and looked at Amanda. "You can call me Moss, too, ma'am. 'Mr. Tucker' don't exactly fit a man like me," he told her with a wink.

Miriam brought the tea, and Moss walked to the table and picked up his hat.

"Reckon I'll be findin' myself a place to stay," he told them all.

"You mean you ain't gonna stay with me?" Della asked, looking very disappointed.

Moss frowned and glanced at Amanda. "I wouldn't feel right, Della. The little gal there is a fine lady. And I'd be obliged if you didn't do no business with other men tonight. They might frighten Miss Boone, or even get into her room by accident and insult her some way. I'll pay you whatever you think you'd lose."

Della smiled. "Nonsense." She walked up closer and whispered, while Miriam was saying something to Amanda. "You got an eye on that little filly?" she asked the man.

Moss chuckled and gave her a hug. "I would if I figured there was a chance. But that one's untouchable—especially by an old jail-bird like me. But I'd appreciate it, Della, if you'd not tell her everything about me. Might make her afraid to trust me, and I want her to trust me, 'cause she's travelin' alone and I intend to look out for her."

"Sure, Moss."

The man kissed the redhead hungrily.

"Thanks," he told her, giving her a squeeze. Amanda had looked their way, and blushed deeply when she saw them kissing. And to her own amazement, she felt an unexpected surge of jealousy! It appalled and annoyed her that she should care, and she vowed to ask the Lord's forgiveness that night for such sinful feelings.

"You sleep real good now, Miss Boone," Moss told her. "I'll be by in the mornin' and escort you back to the train. You're in good hands, so don't be worryin' about nothing. And no more tears, understand?"

Amanda smiled bashfully and looked down at her lap.

"Thank you, Mr. Tucker."

"Call me Moss, remember?"

"I—I would feel better with 'Mr. Tucker.'"

Moss shrugged. "If it suits you, ma'am. Good-night, then."

She turned to face him once more. "Good-night, Mr. Tucker," she said quietly. Their eyes held a moment, and then he quickly left.

Amanda ate gratefully and was led to a room that looked gaudy and haphazard, but the bed the woman offered her was big and comfortable.

"You sleep real good now, Miss Boone," Della told her with a smile. Amanda looked at the woman, full of questions about Moss Tucker. But if she asked them, these women would think she had a personal interest in the man, and that was the last thing she wanted anyone to think. At the same time, none of them seemed eager to tell her anything voluntarily.

"I'm deeply grateful," Amanda told the woman. "I'd like to pay you."

"Forget it. Moss is an old friend. And you're a nice lady. Lord knows none of us is very nice!" She laughed lightly. "We lost our decency a long time ago! It gives us pleasure to be of service to somebody who's still on the right side of the tracks. Maybe the Lord will remember it when we have to face Him and account for the way we've led our lives!" She smiled a little nervously.

"I'm sure He will remember, Della," Amanda replied. "God loves all of us, no matter what side of the tracks we're on. And He only judges what is in our hearts. If you have a good heart, He'll overlook the other things."

The two women stood staring at each other a moment. Della frowned, then actually reddened a little.

"My goodness," she said quietly. "You talk like a nun or something."

"I was raised by nuns," Amanda replied. "And I've taken nearly all the steps needed to become one myself. I'm on my way to California to teach at a mission out there."

Della's eyes widened. "Bless my soul!" she exclaimed. "Does Moss know that?"

"No," Amanda replied, looking down. "We've never even talked, except to say hello—and except for his help tonight."

Della shook her head and grinned a little. "Lord have mercy on us all!" she said quietly. She laughed lightly and went out, closing the door behind her.

Chapter Four

He came the next morning, just as he said he would. Amanda tried to hide her pleasure at seeing him again. She wondered where he had slept, but did not ask. He had coffee with Amanda and the other girls before leaving, but he avoided talk about himself, sticking to talk about the new railroad. He seemed to be avoiding Amanda's eyes, as she in turn avoided his. Then he insisted on fixing the carpetbag. Not knowing how to turn him down again without appearing rude, she went and got the bag. Moss set it on his lap and took a piece of rawhide from his pocket.

"You sleep good, Miss Boone?" he asked as he worked.

"Very well, thank you. Your…lady friends are very hospitable."

Moss glanced at her and grinned. "To say the least," he replied. Amanda blushed deeply. The girls just laughed and began clearing the table.

"I think you were tryin' to trick us, Moss," Della spoke up. "If you left her here much longer, she'd have us all converted. And then what would men like you do when you need a little relief from that long, lonesome train?"

Moss looked at her curiously. "Now how could this quiet little lady convert wild women like you?"

"Oh, we know somethin' about her you don't!" Della replied. Amanda reddened and got up to help the others clear the table. "That pretty little lady is one step away from being a nun!" Della went on, folding her arms in front of her and enjoying the look on Moss's face. "She's on her way to California to teach at a mission. And she was raised by nuns."

Moss stopped his work on the carpetbag, and the surprise

on his face could not be hidden. Amanda turned to meet his eyes.

"That true?" he asked her.

"Yes it is, Mr. Tucker," she replied softly. "And I'm sure the good Lord sent you to help me get to California. I'll be forever indebted to you." She looked down at the floor, and Moss turned his eyes from her to Della, who raised her eyebrows and smiled. She bent close to his ear.

"Kind of discouraging, ain't it?" she whispered.

He scowled, and she chuckled. Moss returned to fixing the carpetbag, feeling defeated. Not only were his chances of a relationship with Amanda Boone completely obliterated, but the heavy responsibility she was bringing him was more than he had expected. This news about her made her close to a saint in his eyes, and if the Lord truly meant for him to protect her, how was the Lord going to deal with Moss Tucker if he failed? His respect and awe of the lovely Amanda Boone suddenly grew, as did the gnawing little pain in his heart. His feelings for her were deepening, against his better sense.

"You're a damned fool, Moss Tucker!" he told himself as he mended the handle. *"Ain't nobody much further from God than you, and nobody much closer than her. You must be losin' your marbles in your old age."*

He finished the handle and rose.

"You ready?" he half growled at Amanda. She looked at him curiously.

"Is something wrong, Mr. Tucker?" she asked innocently. "Weren't you able to fix the bag?"

His eyes moved over her and she suddenly felt very self-conscious.

"I fixed it," he mumbled. "We'd best get to the train now. It will leave soon."

"Of course," she replied, confused by his sudden surliness. "I'm deeply grateful for the mended handle, Mr. Tucker. You're very thoughtful. God will bless you for your kindness."

He sighed, half rolled his eyes and looked at Della. Then he looked back at Amanda.

"Ma'am, there ain't nothin' about me the Lord would want to bless. Now get your things and let's go."

Amanda blinked back tears. "I...beg to differ with you, Mr. Tucker. God loves you...and the ladies here." She swallowed. "If my...background...offends you or upsets you, it isn't necessary that you look out for me any longer, Mr. Tucker. I can take care of myself."

He frowned. "Like you did last night?"

Amanda blushed. "I just don't want you doing something you'd really rather not do, Mr. Tucker."

His eyes suddenly softened again, and he stepped closer.

"Look, uh, don't go gettin' all worried about it, all right? I'm just a grumpy ole bear in the morning, that's all. But there ain't no way I could just turn my head now and let you go on alone. I'm goin' to California myself, so there ain't no reason why I can't kind of watch out for you along the way. I just—well, ma'am, somebody like you, they're pretty special, you know? Me, I ain't special to nobody. And if you knew all about me—"

"I know all I need to know, Mr. Tucker," she interrupted. "You've helped me, and I'm certain the Lord means for me to trust you. I couldn't care less about your past. If you choose to tell me along the way, that's your affair. If not, then I will respect that also. I—I think you're a fine man, Mr. Tucker."

She suddenly blushed deeply at the realization she had probably talked more to this man in the past five minutes than she had talked to any one man in her whole life.

"I'll get my things," she said, hurrying to the room where she had spent the night. Moss watched her walk. He wanted her, and that was the hell of it. He wanted her.

• • •

The train chugged out of Council Bluffs. Amanda had taken her usual seat, but this time the newcomers had crowded the car so much that the only seat left for Moss was directly in front of and facing Amanda.

"You see?" she said softly. "God has arranged it so you must sit near me."

"You think so, do you?" he replied, slinging his own suitcase onto the shelf overhead. "Don't a man have any control over what he does, or does God control every little movement?"

He eased down into the seat in front of her, and she glanced at the fancy gun he wore strapped low on his hip. She smiled at him.

"God doesn't exactly control every little thing we do, Mr. Tucker. He gives us choices. And he gives us talents. You apparently have a talent with a gun, or you wouldn't be wearing it. The choices you have made before now, I know nothing about. But for now, God has given you a choice of either helping me, or not helping me. You choose to help me. It's that simple. And I can't tell you how relieved I am to know the Lord sent you. It means I don't have to be afraid of you."

He studied her a moment, and her heart pounded. She was astounded with herself! Never had she felt so at ease with a near stranger—and a man besides! Why was she babbling this way? What must this man think of her?

"I—I'm afraid I've been a little bold, Mr. Tucker," she said, looking down at her lap. "It's just that…" She looked back at the kind, brown eyes. "It's just that you've no idea how frightened I've been until now. It's just such a relief. I've—I've hardly ever been outside the walls of the orphanage, and—"

"Orphanage?"

"Yes. I told you nuns raised me. They ran the orphanage where I grew up. My parents were both killed in a fire when I was five years old."

"I'm real sorry about that, Miss Boone."

"Thank you. But I was small enough that the memory is quite vague now. At any rate, to be making a trip like this— well, it's been frightening and lonely. It isn't easy for me to strike up a conversation with someone, and I don't know who to trust."

"Well, now you can talk to me and you can trust me," he replied. There was the handsome grin again. Amanda blushed and took out her knitting.

"I—I hope you don't think me too bold," she told him. "It's just so nice to find a friend, although I've never struck up a friendship with a gentleman before." She blushed more and looked down at her knitting. Moss Tucker smiled.

"I could never think of you as too bold, Miss Boone." He looked around at the passengers, and neither of the men who had assaulted her the night before were present—at least not in that particular car. He was glad. Then he noticed two soldiers sitting at the back of the car. He frowned and studied them a moment, then grabbed the porter as he walked by.

"Yes, sir?"

"This train carryin' somethin' besides passengers?" Moss asked quietly. Amanda looked up at them.

"Why, not that I know of, sir. Just passengers and their baggage."

Moss looked over at the soldiers again. "Mmm-hmm," he mumbled. The porter went his way, and Moss took a cigar from his jacket pocket.

"You mind if I smoke, ma'am?"

"Not at all." She looked around nervously. "Is anything wrong, Mr. Tucker? Why did you ask the porter what the train is carrying?"

"Oh, I just had a hunch, that's all. Nothin' for you to worry your pretty little head about."

She went back to her knitting, flustered over his remark. Moss Tucker took another look at the soldiers and wondered.

Chapter Five

The Union Pacific rumbled across the plains of Nebraska, and Moss Tucker slept a good share of the way. Amanda wondered if he had slept much the night before, and she suspected he had spent half the night drinking and gambling in one of the saloons at Council Bluffs. But she could not bring herself to condemn Moss Tucker for whatever his sins might be, though it was likely he had many. He had befriended her, had already helped her out of some difficult predicaments, and he had been nothing but respectful toward her.

"The Lord works in strange ways," she told herself.

Conversation over those next several hours was minimal, consisting of comments about the weather and such. Moss mostly smoked and slept, and Amanda didn't feel it ladylike to press a conversation if he didn't feel like talking. But she wanted to talk. This man fascinated her, and she secretly hoped he would become more talkative once he felt rested. She knitted for what seemed hours, then set the knitting aside and watched the broad, flat, endless plains that never seemed to change in spite of the distance they had traveled.

How different this land was! How vast and seemingly desolate. She strained to see the farthest distance, wishing she could spot some buffalo, but there were none to be seen. She thought about the struggles of pioneers who had gone this route before—their long, aching, slow journey through this monotonous land and how brave they must be. She felt ashamed to be so afraid herself on this trip, considering the relative safety and convenience of the train.

"So, you're gonna teach at a mission in California," Moss spoke up. She turned quickly from the window.

"You're awake again!" she said, smiling softly. "You've slept most of the day, Mr. Tucker."

He rubbed his eyes and sat up straighter. "Yeah, well, I, uh, stayed up a little late last night. Won me some money. Then seein' as how I had to be sure to get up in time to clean up before I come for you, I didn't get too much sleep." He grinned rather shyly and lit another cigar. "What were you lookin' at out that window?" he asked.

"Oh, I—I was just thinking about how it must be for the settlers who come out here by covered wagon, when some of the Indians are still wild and roam the countryside, and there are hardly any towns. I admire their courage."

"Well, it does take courage, but there's plenty that can't afford to travel this way so they still go by wagon. 'Course, most of the Indians are on reservations, you know, but there are plenty left out there makin' trouble." He eyed her admiringly. "You've got courage, too, you know."

"Me?" She blushed and looked at her lap. "Mr. Tucker, I've been so afraid on this journey, I'm ashamed of myself."

"But that's what's so courageous about you. You told me you've hardly ever been outside that orphanage, and you're scared to death. But you're goin' anyway, and you had no idea whether you'd run into any help along the way. I admire you, Miss Boone. You're a brave young lady, puttin' the needs of that mission above your own fears. Where is the mission, anyway?"

Amanda was pleased and flattered at his compliments, and secretly happy that he seemed to want to talk now. It gave her the excuse she needed to converse with him without appearing too forward.

"It's near San Francisco," she replied. "Most of the children there are orphans, as I was."

"Well, it's nice for kids to have a place to go. Me, I was runnin' the streets of Chicago at thirteen."

She frowned. "Oh, I'm sorry, Mr. Tucker. You were an orphan, too then?"

His eyes darkened slightly. "No," he replied, turning to

look out the window. "But I might as well have been." He looked back at her. How she wanted to know more! But already she could see that was all he was going to say. "No more talk about me," he commented. "You, uh, bein' a teacher and all, you must be pretty well educated."

"The nuns taught me well," she replied. She watched him smoke. What a casual, worldly man he was. How she admired him for his courage and sureness, and how her heart ached to know about his apparently tragic past.

"I never had much education," he told her, actually appearing embarrassed about it.

"There are many forms of education, Mr. Tucker. I've had a lot of book learning. But I know little about the real world. You strike me as a person who's probably been many places. Perhaps you'd be kind enough to tell me a little bit about the land where we're headed. Have you been to California before?"

His eyes saddened, and he puffed on the cigar.

"I've been there before," he said quietly. He appeared to want to say more, and Amanda was full of questions, but she forced herself not to ask them. It wouldn't be right to show too much interest. He sighed and shifted in his seat.

"Let's see now...the country where we're headed. Well, ma'am, it's awful pretty—leastways I think it is. That's mostly because there aren't a lot of people out there yet. Oh, it's growing, mind you, but there's still places where a man could ride a hundred miles and not see another livin' soul, where the only sound at night is a coyote singing, and the only movement is the wind itself. There's big, crazy-lookin' rocks that look like somebody painted them. There's all kinds of pine up on the mountains and junipers, sagebrush, and cactus down below. There's weird, cone-shaped mesas with flat tops, canyons, cliffs, lava beds, groves of golden aspen, thunderin' waterfalls, and there's them magnificent Rocky Mountains and the Sierras."

Amanda sat transfixed, watching him as he spoke. His voice was rather melancholy. He stopped to smoke a moment, and she said not a word. She looked out the window for a moment, trying to envision what he'd been describing. The endless prairies of Nebraska continued to fly past the window.

"Oh, and there's jackrabbits and roadrunners, screech owls and gila monsters, mountain lions, bears, buffalo and deer," he went on. Telling her was like entertaining a little girl. He enjoyed her innocence, he loved her innocence—he loved the woman-child he was talking to. He knew it, and knew how foolish it was; he wondered what had happened to his common sense.

"The days are scorchin' hot and the nights are freezin' cold," he went on. "The rain don't come often, and sometimes it comes in torrents and floods everything. And the sound of thunder up in the mountains…it sets a man's flesh to tingling. And out there—out there a man can be his own man. He can—"

He suddenly stopped, reaching over and putting out his cigar and seeming to be disgusted with something.

"Please go on, Mr. Tucker," she said softly. "It sounds wonderful! I was afraid before, but now with you along, and knowing you know so much about the land…"

His eyes met hers, and they were filled with remorse.

"I know the land all right," he told her. "I know it 'cause I've ridden almost every inch of it."

"Oh? What do you do for a living, Mr. Tucker?"

He studied her, and she felt the strange warmth again. She was alarmed by the pleasant but new sensation his eyes stirred deep within her body: an odd, hungry longing. Longing for what? She wasn't sure.

"It's best we don't talk about me," he told her. "Let's just say I'm goin' to California to kind of start a new life."

Their eyes held again. Her heart went out to him. This man was struggling with something.

"Then I will pray for you, Mr. Tucker. Whatever it is you wish to do, whatever your reasons for starting over, I'll ask God to help you."

He smiled light. "Don't waste your time, Miss Boone. You

pray for somebody more deserving. I'll just rely on myself and my gun. That's all I've ever had."

"I don't believe that," she replied.

He reached in his pocket for yet another cigar, and she realized he was getting nervous over this conversation about himself. He cleared his throat.

"Let's, uh, talk about New York," he told her, lighting up. "Tell me about where you're from. Chicago is as far east as I've ever been. I was born and reared there."

"You were? But how did you end up—"

"No more talk about me," he interrupted, waving his hand. "Tell me about the orphanage."

"Well, it's just about all I know. I may be from New York, but I never saw much of the city because I seldom ventured outside the orphanage, Mr. Tucker. And I guess I'd have to say that the busy streets of New York frighten me just about as much as the barren loneliness of the West. I—I guess you must think me awfully childish. I'm twenty-two years old and I act ten."

She blushed and took out her knitting again. When her eyes met his again, she was almost startled at the gentleness and near reverence she saw there.

"I don't think you're childish at all," he told her. "I think you're a beautiful young lady, and you're…" He sighed. "You probably wouldn't understand, 'cause you don't know nothin' about me, and you don't know nothin' about the kind of life I've led, the things I've seen and done—a world completely alien to you, Miss Boone. So you don't understand how refreshing somebody like you is to me. Back there in Chicago I'd been stayin' with…" He hesitated, then took another puff of his cigar. "Well, all I can say is you're sweet and charming, and I aim to see you safely to California, 'cause I wouldn't want to see somebody like you get hurt."

"I'm grateful, Mr. Tucker. I—"

Before she could say more the train suddenly jolted. People cried out and Amanda screamed as she flew forward, while

Moss tried to catch her. Others who had been seated facing the engine of the train also went flying, and the wheels of the train screeched to a halt. People were gasping and cursing, and Moss Tucker sat with his arms around Amanda. She smelled lovely. The velvety cheek that briefly brushed his rugged face brought an ache to his groin.

"My goodness, what's happened?" Amanda asked, her face crimson with embarrassment as she moved away from him. Moss kept hold of her arms and helped her back into her own seat, bending close to her face for a moment.

"You all right, Miss Boone?"

His closeness made her feel light-headed.

"I—I think so," she managed to reply. Never had a man held her, not even by accident. It momentarily flashed through her mind how nice it would be to have someone strong hold her, someone brave to always be around to protect her, someone—oh, but what a foolish, sinful thought!

Never had Moss Tucker had to hold himself back like this. So close she was! So pretty she smelled! How nice it would be to kiss her virgin lips.

"I'll go see what's happened," he told her, anxious to get away from her for a moment. He left, and she waited anxiously. Others disembarked, and men were walking around outside shouting some kind of orders.

It seemed forever before he returned. But finally he reentered the car and sat down across from her again.

"Cattle," he told her. "Happens a lot, they say. The dumb animals get on the tracks and won't move. We hit one."

Amanda jumped when a shot went off.

"What was that?" she asked, her eyes wide.

"They had to shoot the animal—put it out of its misery."

"Oh," she replied, frowning. "How sad."

"You sure you're all right?"

"Yes. I'm sure."

"We'll be rollin' again in a minute." He moved to look out the window for a moment, and she suddenly realized how dependent she was becoming on this man. Was it right? It had to be. Surely the Lord had sent him to help her. If the Lord had sent him, then it was perfectly all right for her to be conversing with him and relying on his advice and protection. But what about the other feelings she was beginning to have? She realized that if he were to leave the train before reaching California, she would be devastated, afraid and lonely, and—worst of all, she would miss the man. Why should she miss someone she hardly knew? Why should it matter? It frightened her somewhat that she no longer wanted this man along just for protection, but more because she wanted to be near him! Her mind whirled with confusion. All of these feelings were things she had never before experienced.

"Just don't think about it!" she told herself. *"When you reach California and the mission, you'll not see him again, and you can get busy with your teaching. And soon you will take your final vows. Higher goals, Amanda! You must strive for higher goals, just as the nuns taught you. God sent this man to see you safely to California, and for no other reason!"*

The train lurched forward again, and Amanda looked out the window at a large herd of cattle. They passed by the dead one, and she crinkled her nose.

"Poor thing," she commented. "It seems so—so violent."

"Violent? Hittin' a cow with a train?" he asked, frowning. "It was just an accident."

She turned her eyes back to his. She studied the rugged face and its lines of experience. He was more handsome than she had realized, perhaps because she was finding it easier to look at him without being embarrassed. There was a tiny scar on his chin where his beard would not grow.

"To me it seems violent," she told him. She closed her eyes. "I can't tell you how glad I am you're here, Mr. Tucker. I hope nothing more than this happens." She opened her eyes again. "Do you—do you think we'll run into Indians?"

"It's possible," he replied, sitting forward and removing his jacket. She studied the broad shoulders. "The Indians are gettin' mighty restless…fed up with the government's broken promises. I can tell you, ma'am, I don't blame the Indians much for anything they do. They've been lied to, cheated on, starved out, burned out, their women violated, and their children murdered." Amanda reddened at the statement about women being violated. But he went on, although stirred by the way she blushed so easily. He wondered how frightened she would be and how much she would blush on her own wedding night. But then there would likely never be a wedding night for a woman such as Amanda Boone. "The Indian is proud," he went on. "And he's a man of his word. He hates the white man's forked tongue, and I can't blame him. There'll be a lot more trouble before it's settled, and I don't reckon the Indian can possibly come out on the winnin' end. It's too bad, but it's a fact of life. The white man will keep coming, and someday the red man will dwindle down to practically nothing."

"I feel sorry for them," she replied. "But at the same time it frightens me. I would hate to be the brunt of their anger when I've never done anything against them."

"It's human nature," he replied. "I know how it feels to hate the world for what just one or two people have done," he added. His eyes had hardened somewhat when he made the statement, and her heart went out to him.

"I'm sorry, Mr. Tucker. You've had a bad experience of your own then?"

He laughed lightly, pretending not to care. "More than one," he told her. "More than one." He sighed. "There aren't many people in this world like you, Miss Boone, people with hearts big enough for everybody, people who really care about others and are full of kindness, people who know nothing of hate, violence, lust, and vengeance. Most people think only of themselves, Miss Boone, and you'd best remember that and watch out for it. I know you like to think the best of folks, but you'd best be wary of them, too. They'll smile and act nice, then turn around and stab you in the back."

She sat and watched him quietly for a moment. Their eyes met again.

"And what about you, Mr. Tucker? Do you plan to stab me in the back?"

His eyes softened again. Then he smiled softly, a handsome and reassuring smile. "No, ma'am. I'd never do that. I didn't mean to turn around and make you afraid of me."

"You didn't." She smiled herself now. "The point is, Mr. Tucker, that violence and hate just breed more violence and hate, and fear. But love and kindness can also be contagious."

He looked her over admiringly, and she blushed again.

"Maybe so," he told her. "But it's easy for somebody like you to say that. I hope nothin' ever happens to you, Miss Boone, that would change your mind. 'Cause them is mighty pretty thoughts. And you're a mighty pretty lady."

She smiled nervously. "I've never...thought about such things much, Mr. Tucker. Vanity is sinful. But thank you for the compliment just the same."

"You really gonna' be a nun?"

"I haven't decided for certain yet."

"Well, pardon my sayin' so, ma'am, but I hope you decide against it."

She looked over at him in surprise. "Being a nun has almost always been my goal, Mr. Tucker. I believe it's what the Lord wants of me, and what better way to serve the Lord?"

He grinned and looked her over again. "Yeah, maybe. But I'd sure hate to see a nice lady like you hide behind convent walls all her life. You'd make a fine wife, a beautiful mother. Did you ever stop to think maybe God would like you to do that instead?"

Now her face was crimson. This man was planting thoughts in her head that she had never seriously considered until now. Was God testing her through this man? Was He deliberately tempting her to think of other things besides being a nun?

"I—I have no such plans, Mr. Tucker," she managed to say.

"Mmm-hmm," he replied thoughtfully. "Well, that's too

bad, Miss Boone. I ain't speakin' for myself, mind you. Man like me—he don't deserve somethin' as special as you. But like I say, you'd make some man mighty proud. You're a fine young woman, and I'll bet you'd raise a fine bunch of kids. But if you really want to be a nun, well, I admire that, too. Fact is, I admire you very much, Miss Boone. I'm glad you're along on this trip. It's real nice havin' somebody to talk to, somebody to look out for."

"Well, then," she replied, blushing and twisting a knitting needle in her hands. "We can help one another in different ways."

He smiled, and she hurriedly got back to her knitting, flustered over his remarks of marriage and children. She could hardly imagine having that kind of relationship with a man. He was confusing her now.

"What are you makin' there?" he asked her.

"Well, I—I thought I'd make you a woolen scarf, Mr. Tucker, for your help. It started out as nothing in particular, but I'd like to make you something. Do you need a scarf?"

"That's mighty nice, ma'am," he replied. "I surely could use one, and I'd surely like to have something from you to always remember you by when this trip's over."

"Good," she told him, trying to act casual in spite of the flutter he kept creating in her chest. "Then a scarf it will be."

He leaned forward, his elbows on his knees. "Tell me something, Miss Boone. How come you cling to that carpetbag like you do? It can't be just the knittin' you're worried about."

She met his eyes. "I—I don't know what you mean."

"Yes you do. You watch that thing like a hawk, and you didn't even want me to touch it at first so I could fix the handle."

Their eyes held again. Why was she so sure she could trust this man?

"All right, Mr. Tucker," she spoke in a barely audible voice. "I'm carrying a crucifix in the bottom of it. It's encrusted with diamonds and rubies. It's a gift from the orphanage in New York to the mission where I am headed. I—I've heard so many tales about outlaws and such out here that I—I just thought it best I not let it out of my sight."

He frowned. Then he sighed almost disgustedly.

"They never should have left somethin' like that in your care. A sweet little thing like you carryin' somethin' valuable like that! What the hell was they thinkin' of!"

"Mr. Tucker! Please don't swear!" she said quietly. "And I have the Lord to protect me."

"The Lord!" He rolled his eyes. "Jesus, woman, do you know what an outlaw would do to get his hands on somethin' like that! Do you think the Lord is gonna come down here with a six-gun and shoot it out with somebody to protect that cross?" His words were whispered but angry.

"Mr. Tucker, please! Don't blaspheme!" she whispered back. "And how on earth would anyone suspect that someone like myself would be carrying anything valuable! And how do you know what an outlaw would do to get his hands on that crucifix!"

His eyes looked pained, as though someone had punched him. He got up from his seat.

"Mr. Tucker?"

"I'm goin' out to stand outside by the railing," he grumbled. He opened the door of the car, and the train's clatter was momentarily much louder. The door closed. She stared at it for a moment, then put down her knitting and went to the door herself. She opened it hesitantly. The clattering wheels and rush of air startled and frightened her. It was so noisy he didn't even realize she'd stepped out behind him. Tucker stood with his back to her, leaning on the railing. She glanced through the window of the door making sure she could see her carpetbag. She swallowed for courage, turning up to look at Moss Tucker again.

"Mr. Tucker?" she spoke up. He turned in surprise and quickly reached out and took her arm.

"You shouldn't be out here," he said with concern. "It's dangerous."

"I'm sorry, Mr. Tucker, if—if I offended you," she told him, grasping the railing. He kept hold of her arm. Her eyes again held that innocent and charmingly childish fear. "I didn't mean to infer that you yourself were an outlaw, Mr. Tucker."

The curls about her face blew every which way as the air rushed past them.

"What if I was?" he asked low. Their eyes held for a very long time, without a word spoken.

"I told you once that whatever lies in your past is not my affair, Mr. Tucker. I know all I need to know about you. I trust you, Mr. Tucker. Please don't get angry and leave the train. I—I'd be very much afraid without you along, Mr. Tucker."

A tear slipped unwantedly down her cheek. He reached out and brushed it away with his fingers, and the gentleness of his big, rough hands surprised her. She didn't know why she stood there and let him touch her, and she didn't care. She only knew she did not want him to leave.

"Ma'am, there's not a thing you could do or say that would keep me from finishin' out this trip with you," he told her. Their eyes continued to hold. He put both hands to her face now, holding it gently between his palms. She felt a strength flow through her at his touch. "I want you to promise me something," he told her.

"What is it, Mr. Tucker?"

"If it ever happens somebody finds that cross and they want it, you let them have it without no fuss."

"Oh, but I couldn't—"

"You do it!" he said firmly. "Promise me! I know how violent men can get when it comes to somethin' like that. If the Lord intends for the cross to get where it's going, He'll find another way to get it there. He'd not expect a little thing like you to risk her life for it. Please promise me, Miss Boone."

She studied him another moment. How wonderful was his touch to her face, how comforting to feel his strength.

"All right, Mr. Tucker. I promise."

He smiled lightly and nodded.

"Good. I don't reckon we'd run into any trouble like that, but just in case. I don't want you worryin' about it, though, understand?"

"I won't worry, Mr. Tucker. Not with you along."

He smiled more now and shook his head.

"You're something, Miss Boone. And you're danged lucky you picked the right person to trust. There's so much you don't know. So much."

"As long as you know, Mr. Tucker, then it doesn't matter. I'll trust anything you say. And I'll see that you're well rewarded when we get to California."

The only reward he wanted was her. How he wanted to hold her right now! To feel her body against his, to taste the sweet, soft mouth and to look upon her naked body lying beneath him and welcoming him inside her.

"I don't need no reward, ma'am," he replied. "You, uh, best get back inside now. The air out here is cool, but it's dry. Your skin is used to the dampness of the East." He held her arm until she went back through the door. He turned and looked out over the Nebraska flatlands, his heart and mind full of her. Why? Why should he have these feelings for the small, quiet woman-child who was practically a nun? Was he crazy? Was it only because she represented everything he always wanted but could never have, a way of life he'd never known? Or was it just her sweetness, her dependence, her innocence?

He leaned on the railing, wondering to himself what she would think of him if she knew everything. And what would she think or say if he told her about his little girl—his daughter—mothered by a prostitute, the child who now waited for him out in California? He wondered what his little girl looked like. The mother was dead. He'd not seen the woman since he'd been arrested more than three years ago in Sacramento. And he'd never seen his daughter.

He felt the burden of two heavy responsibilities. He was falling in love with a woman he could never have. And he was on his way to California to see about the welfare of a tiny daughter he'd never seen. He would have to find a home for her, for a man like Moss Tucker had no business trying to raise an innocent little girl by himself. He sighed and pulled a tiny flask of whiskey from his inner vest pocket. He uncorked it and took a long swig. And he felt his life was suddenly being directed by someone else. It gave him the chills. His little girl needed him, but she'd need a mother. He'd met a beautiful woman who'd make a wonderful mother. He looked up at a passing cloud.

"No. It couldn't be," he said aloud. Then he laughed out loud. He'd had too many disappointments in life to bother thinking it could ever be good to him now. He'd get Miss Amanda Boone to California, and he'd find a home for his daughter, and he would ride out of both their lives, and that was that. Moses Tucker needed no one but himself, and nothing but his whiskey and his gun.

Chapter Six

"You sure Sol's on that train?" Rand Barker asked one of his men.

"Course I'm sure. Hell, the only reason he joined the army was for somethin' like this. Sol's been in charge of the telegraph, knows everything that's goin' on. Soon as we hit the train, he'll join up with us."

Barker spit saliva from his chewing tobacco as he and his men rode south from the Hole-in-the-Wall toward Bear River City. He scratched at his stubble of a beard.

"Soon as this is over, I'm headin' south and lettin' one of them señoritas give me a bath."

"Yeah. They can work wonders with soapy hands," one of the others commented. They all laughed.

"You figure there'll be any women on that train, Rand?" another asked.

"Could be. But I ain't sure I want to drag no woman along."

"You wouldn't have to. I'd take care of her for you," the man replied. "Real good care."

Barker whirled his horse around and faced the man who had made the remark. The others halted their horses.

"You listen to me, Duke Sage!" Barker growled. "I'm the boss of this outfit. If we take a woman, I'll make the decision. And she'll ride with me. If I decide we can all have a turn at her, I get her first. But if she's fresh, ain't nobody touchin' her. Some of them Mexican ranchers will pay plenty for a young white girl. But they don't want no used one. And I don't want to hear no more of your own ideas!" Barker rested a hand on his side arm. "Ain't no way a deal like this can work unless there's only one boss, Sage. You've been talkin' about your own ideas all this way, so let's get things settled right now. You want to be boss, you draw on me, 'cause there ain't no other way it can be!"

Sage swallowed. No one in his right mind drew a gun on Rand Barker and expected to live. And Barker had a high opinion of himself. He didn't like anyone moving in on his territory. He liked being in command, and his fast gun and quick, almost crazy temper kept him in command.

Sage backed up his horse. "It was just a suggestion, Rand," he said, smiling nervously. "I just figured if we could get a woman out of this—"

"That depends on what we find when we get there! The important thing is the money! We'll stop over in Bear River City soon. There's plenty of whores there. And once we get the money, we can head for Mexico, and you can buy all the hot mamas you want. So don't you go grabbin' no woman without my authority!"

"Sure, Rand. Whatever you say."

Rand pulled his horse up next to Sage. In the blink of an eye his gun was out and rested against Sage's throat. Sage gasped and his eyes widened.

"You remember that it's been a while since I killed a man, Sage. I need to kill! So you mind your business and remember who's boss, or I could just think of an excuse to blow your head off!"

"I'm sorry, Rand! You—you know how I am about women. I see a pretty one and I just—I gotta get under her skirts, that's all. I just had women on my mind."

Rand slowly put his gun back. "You've always got women on your mind. But when the day of that robbery comes, you'd best have that and only that on your mind so you don't mess somethin' up, understand?"

"I do, Rand. I won't cause no problems."

Rand Barker turned to look at the others. "That goes for all of you! I know you're all good at what you do, but there's not one of you can take me. So we'll do this my way, or anybody who objects can draw on me right now if he has a mind to."

"We're all behind you, Rand," one of them spoke up. They all stared at each other a moment.

"Let's get movin'," Rand growled. He nudged the sides of his horse and rode on ahead.

There were eight all together, all surly, unkempt men with one goal in mind: the soldiers' payroll and perhaps a woman captive to sell farther south in Mexico—or to have their own fun with. But that would be Rand's decision.

They made their way through the grand Wyoming country, eight men oblivious to the thrilling beauty that surrounded them. They rounded the side of a mesa, their horses picking their way along a rocky, narrow pathway. This was outlaw country: rocks, canyons, and vast hidden valleys that few people knew about or could find. They passed through a particularly narrow opening at the foot of the mesa, so narrow they had to go through one at a time.

First there was Rand Barker himself, forty-five, and their leader. Barker was tall, dark, and would be handsome if he shaved and bathed. But Barker cared little for personal hygiene. His only care was money—easy money—and he got it through any means he could find, mostly by using his gun. He was very good with his gun. He had killed many men with it.

Next came Wade Gillette, fifty-five and graying. His face was leathered from many years of living under the stars. It was hard to say just where Wade got onto the wrong track, but he'd been on it since a teenager. The outlaw life was the only life he'd known. Perhaps it started back when his father beat him and forced him to steal to keep food on the table.

Clyde Monroe followed Gillette. Clyde was forty, and some thought him a little touched in the head. Clyde enjoyed torture, and he laughed too much, especially when he saw someone in pain. Clyde was a small man, but stronger than he looked.

Next came Duke Sage, whose lust for women ran a close second to his lust for money. Duke was already wanted for several rapes, and the thought of finding a nice, innocent young girl on the train brought an ache to his groin. He was forty-five, overweight, and downright ugly. So Duke seldom found a willing woman. And when he couldn't find one, he simply took one, willing or not.

The horses in the lead half-stumbled down a steep embankment, as those behind continued to pass through the narrow opening. The man called Booner followed Duke Sage. Booner was the only name the others knew him by, and he volunteered no information as to his rightful name. And no one asked. Booner didn't like people asking questions. He was a tall, bearded man, about thirty-five, and quiet. Too quiet. Rand Barker didn't care where the buckskin-clad Booner came from or what his real name was. Booner could handle a gun, and he was deadly with a knife. He was a good man to have along.

Henry Derrick followed Booner, and close behind was Manley Higgins. Both Derrick and Higgins were hill boys from Tennessee. They had no education whatsoever, and were dull-witted young men who didn't think of much beyond where their next meal might come from. So they followed along behind Rand Barker, letting Barker do their thinking for them. As for women, both Derrick and Higgins were like animals around them, and even the whores wouldn't usually give them any business.

Last to come through was Dean Taylor. Only twenty, he was a greenhorn fresh from St. Louis out to prove his "manood" by learning to use a gun. Dean liked the power he felt with a gun in his hand. And he looked up to men like Rand Barker, men who stepped out and merely took what they wanted without asking questions. Someday, Dean thought to himself, he would be a leader like Rand. People would listen when he spoke, or he'd blow their guts out.

There was a ninth member of the group, who was already on the train: a soldier by the name of Sollit Weber, a blond man about twenty-five. Sol had one of those innocent, boyish faces that made old ladies want to give him cookies. But there was nothing innocent nor boyish about him. Sol would turn around and slit the throat of a nice old lady if he thought she had any money he could rob. Sol liked money more than any-thing—almost as much as Rand Barker liked money. He liked the power money brought him. And he enjoyed fooling people with his fresh smile and dancing blue eyes. And at the moment, while his friends were making their way south through canyons and over rivers, Sol was riding the Union Pacific, eager for the moment when Rand Barker and his gang would join him. He would enjoy the surprise on everyone's faces.

Sol had already decided the first man to disarm was the tall, dark stranger who wore a six-gun and sat up at the other end of the passenger car Sol rode. He'd learned the man's name was Moses Tucker, and Moses Tucker looked like a man who knew how to use his gun. But Sol was always thinking, always plan-ning. Moses Tucker seemed awfully interested in the woman he was riding with. Perhaps the woman would give Sol the edge he needed when the time came. She was young and seemed easily frightened. And Sol was certain that Moses Tucker would not want anything to happen to that young woman.

The train rumbled and puffed its way west. Rand Barker and his gang rode south to meet it. And Raincloud and his war party came down in a southwesterly direction. Soon, all of them would gather at the same place, the white men to rob the payroll, the Indians to take the guns.

Chapter Seven

"Mr. Tucker, look!" Amanda exclaimed, with the excitement of a child. "Are they buffalo?"

Moss leaned to look out the window with her. He chuckled over her enthusiasm and innocent excitement.

"Yeah. Them are buffalo," he told her. How easy it would be to simply turn and kiss her cheek. But that might destroy her trust in him.

"They're beautiful!" she said in a near whisper. "They're magnificent! And so—so big! I never dreamed they'd be that large!"

The train slowed down as it approached a rambling herd of buffalo, and as it came closer, Amanda could see buffalo all the way to the horizon.

"Why, there must be hundreds and hundreds!" she said, her eyes glued to the window. Moss laughed lightly.

"I expect so," he replied. Just then a shot went off, and Amanda jumped. A large bull not far away slumped to the ground. Cheers went up from the adjoining car, as well as from men in their own car. Windows were opened and more shots were fired. Amanda watched in disbelief, and Moss Tucker's heart went out to her. Her eyes filled with tears as she watched more of the beasts fall, while the train slowly rumbled through the herd and men took pot shots for the sport of it. Some of the animals didn't even appear to be dead when they fell, only wounded.

"No!" Amanda whispered. She swallowed and turned to Moss. "Why are they doing that?" She wiped at her eyes.

Moss frowned. "Because they're more like animals than the ones they're shootin'," he replied coldly. "They come out from the East in their fancy suits and kill a couple of helpless animals and go back and call themselves great hunters who have conquered the West."

More shots went off. Amanda rose. "Someone should stop them!" she whimpered.

"Ma'am, there ain't nothin' you can do. Just sit down and don't look."

She sat down, but only for a moment. Their eyes held, but Moss looked blurry to her through her tears. She suddenly jumped up again and walked two seats back to a wealthy-looking man who was firing a fancy rifle out the window.

"Got him!" the man shouted with glee.

"Please don't shoot any more of them," Amanda spoke up behind him, amazed at her own boldness. "They're—they're helpless out there."

The man turned and looked her up and down.

"Lady, why don't you go back and sit down? What's a few buffalo?"

"They're magnificent animals!" she retorted. "And—and the Indians need them for food and shelter."

"The Indians!" the man laughed. "They ain't even worth as much as the buffalo!" All the men laughed, and Amanda reddened.

"And you're worth less than either!" she snapped. "You come out here and take easy shots from the safety of the train and call yourself a man! You're a fool and a coward!"

The man rose, looking daggers at her.

"Ma'am, it's too bad we aren't alone. If we were, I'd show you just how much of a man I am!"

By then Moss was up and standing beside her.

"Why don't you show me?" he asked, taking Amanda's arm. "It's easy to be brave in front of a woman, mister. How about in front of a man? How about in front of all of us? Why don't you just stop this train and go out there and walk among them buffalo like the Indians do?"

Some of the others snickered, and the man paled. Sollit

Weber, the soldier soon-to-turn outlaw, watched from the other end of the car with interest. Yes. Moses Tucker was totally enamored with the young woman who was now raising a fuss over shooting buffalo. And the young woman abhorred violence. Sol Weber knew exactly what he needed to know to control Moses Tucker when the time came.

"And would you walk among them?" the fancy-dressed man was asking Moss.

"Right now that's just what I intend to do, mister. 'Cause I'm goin' out there to finish off them you left wounded and put them out of their misery."

The others listened even closer now. To watch a man walk among the buffalo would be more exciting than shooting the great beasts.

"You're crazy, mister!" someone spoke up. "Have you seen the size of them things?"

"I've been around buffalo before."

Amanda turned to look up at him. "You don't need to do it, Mr. Tucker. You could get killed."

He studied her sorrowful eyes. "I do need to do it," he replied. "Now you just go back and sit down. I'll be gone a few minutes."

"But, Mr. Tucker—"

He led her to her seat and picked up his rifle, quickly leaving before she could argue any further. One man left to go back into the next car and tell the others not to do any more shooting, as there would be a man out there killing off the wounded buffalo. Moss made his way forward, climbing up and walking along the top of a baggage car, then jumping to the wood box, across that and down to the engine. The engineer turned to look at him.

"Can you stop this thing for a couple minutes?" Moss asked.

"Hell no, mister! We've got a schedule to keep!"

In the next second Moss's rifle barrel rested against the startled engineer's temple.

"Mister, you found time to slow down so the men back there could use them buffalo for target practice. So I expect you can stop for five minutes and let me finish off them that didn't die! You think you could do that?"

The engineer swallowed. "I, uh, I guess so, mister."

"Good. Now stop this damned train!"

The man quickly pulled some levers and in thirty seconds or so the wheels had ground to a halt. Moss lowered his rifle.

"Thanks," he said with a grin. He jumped down and cautiously walked into the herd, which was now growing restless from the train and the gunshots. Many had already run off, but a few stayed, some of them angry bulls that appeared ready to charge the train.

"There he is!" he heard someone shout from the train. He knew he was doing a foolish thing, but he also knew that the sight of the kicking, grunting, half-dead animals would haunt Amanda Boone. And he could not bear seeing her upset.

He paid no attention to the people on the train. He walked down to the fallen animals, and soon shots could be heard, as he finished off those that still struggled and snorted on the ground. More began running, and Amanda's heart pounded with fear.

"He's doing it for you, Amanda," she told herself. *"He probably doesn't care any more than those other men about the wounded buffalo. He'd not shoot them down from the train himself, but—if not for you—he'd not go out there among them just to kill off the wounded ones. It's for you."*

She struggled against it, yet she knew she was falling in love with Moses Tucker, a man whose world was as alien to hers as night and day, a man far removed from the kind she should be setting her sights on. In fact, she had never set her sights on anything but teaching and becoming a nun. There was no room in her life for a man.

Several more shots were fired, while inside the train Amanda struggled with her new feelings. It frightened her. She had never thought much about how it would feel to really love a man, to want a man. Somehow it didn't seem as sinful as she thought it would feel. Was it because God intended this to happen? But how could He? Why would He bring someone like Moses Tucker into her life? Mr. Tucker had all but flat out told her he'd led a sinful life up to now. Perhaps he'd even been an outlaw once. What would the sisters back in New York think if she told them about this man? They'd never understand. How could anyone back there understand without having been here and seen this land—seen its beauty and magnificence, felt its danger, seen its vastness. A big country, filled with big men like Moses Tucker. A woman needed a man in country like this.

"All you need is God," they would tell her. It made her feel ashamed. She quickly closed her eyes and asked forgiveness for practically forgetting about the Lord. But her mind flashed back to Moses when someone shouted.

"He'd better look out! There's a big one headed for him!" somebody yelled. Men hung out windows, shouting to Moss, eagerly awaiting the outcome of the imminent clash. A huge bull buffalo was thundering toward Moss, its head down in a charging position. Moss rose from a bull he'd just shot and turned at the sound of the shouted warnings.

"Moss!" Amanda whispered. By the time Moss turned, the bull was no more than twenty feet from him.

Moss Tucker raised his rifle and fired three quick shots without hesitation, then ducked and rolled out of the way at the last minute. Amanda grasped her throat as the animal rumbled past Tucker and ran on for several feet before stumbling to the ground.

Cheers went up, and Amanda breathed a sigh of relief. Moss got up and ran over to the fallen animal, which lay kicking on the ground. He quickly reloaded and finished off the animal. Then he turned and headed for the train. He waved to the engineer to get rolling, and steam rolled from the engine as the wheels skidded on the tracks, then took hold. Slowly the train began to move again, and inside men laughed and cheered. Moses Tucker had given them a good show. But

Amanda knew he'd had no intentions of putting on an act for them. His only goal had been to put the animals out of their misery, for her sake.

He was walking alongside the train now, and another buffalo was headed for him.

"Hurry up!" somebody shouted. Moss began running, as the train moved faster now, and he quickly grabbed the railing at the front of the car, jumping up and out of reach of the buffalo just in time. The animal's head banged against the side of the car. Then it turned and ran off. Seconds later Moses Tucker came inside.

"Good show!" someone shouted.

"Now, there's a man!" someone else yelled out.

Moss just scowled at them and sat down across from Amanda. He removed his hat and ran a hand through his long, dark hair, then looked at her almost bashfully.

"Thank you, Mr. Tucker," she said softly. Was it love he saw in her eyes? Perhaps. But it was most likely the kind of love Christian people have for everyone, not the kind of love he truly wanted from her. Women like Amanda Boone didn't truly love men like Moss Tucker.

"You're welcome," he said quietly in return.

"I'm glad you're all right, Mr. Tucker," she said. How she wanted to say more! But she didn't know where to begin. This was all too new. She felt foolish and inexperienced. How did a woman such as herself tell a man like Moss Tucker that she thought she loved him? Perhaps he'd even laugh.

The words went unsaid by both parties. Moss Tucker put his head back and sighed, and Amanda returned to her knitting. The Union Pacific thundered onward, and the buffalo disappeared behind them.

Excitement began to build within Sollit Weber. They were nearing Medicine Bow now, in Wyoming Territory. The high peaks of the Rockies were in sight. Tomorrow they would pass through Bitter Creek and Salt Wells. And before they reached Bear River City, Sollit Weber and eight others would be rich men. Raincloud and his warriors would have their rifles. And perhaps they would have a lovely young woman captive who would bring them a good sum of money down in Mexico, or a good share of pleasure on the way.

Chapter Eight

Most of Amanda's time was spent pasted to the window as the train headed into western Wyoming. Never had she seen such a spectacle, and never had she felt closer to God than when she stared at the snow-covered pinnacles of the Rockies and gasped at thousand-foot high walls as the train passed through canyons. Tall, deep green pines stretched to the heavens, and in the background were the endless mountains—gray, purple, white—stalwart and silent. She caught glimpses of antelope and elk, and once she even thought she saw a bear, but could not be sure.

Moss Tucker simply watched and enjoyed. What a treasure she was, such simple innocence and clean beauty. She had relaxed more—so much more than when she first ran into him back in Chicago. Now her questions were endless, like a child's. All of her fear and apprehension seemed to almost disappear, now that she was sure she could trust him. She had put herself fully in his hands, and the burden was heavy. He wondered if he could possibly tell her more about himself now, and about his daughter.

No. Not yet. It was still too soon. Besides, he liked her easiness with him now. If he told her too much, she might again be apprehensive and quiet. He liked her better this way, smiling and talkative.

"Oh, I can't wait to write the sisters in New York!" she chattered. "They'll be so envious of the things I'm seeing. It's just like they say it is in the books. I thought they were exaggerating, but they weren't at all. Oh, Mr. Tucker, this country is so beautiful. So beautiful!"

Then would come more questions: Have you ever seen the

Colorado River? Have you seen a bear up close? Have you ever seen a gold mine? Have you seen the Pacific Ocean? Have you ever ridden through the mountains on a horse?

"Yes," was his reply to everything. He'd even panned for gold once.

"No!" she exclaimed. "And did you find real gold?"

His face seemed to sadden, although he smiled faintly.

"Yeah, I found gold. Even staked a claim. Did pretty good."

She looked him over as though he were a king.

"Are you a rich man, Mr. Tucker?"

Moss laughed. "No, ma'am." He lit another cigar and kept smiling, although it was obvious he was deeply disturbed inside. "I, uh, lost everything to a crooked banker."

"Oh, I'm so sorry, Mr. Tucker!"

His eyes hardened slightly as he studied his cigar.

"Yeah. Well, it was a long time ago, and I was young and stupid, and in love, believe it or not. That's where my trouble started."

Her heart burned with jealousy at the statement, yet her mind instantly filled with curiosity.

"And what happened to the young lady, Mr. Tucker?" she asked cautiously.

His smile dwindled even more. He cleared his throat and looked out the window.

"She, uh, married a lawyer. Lives down in Los Angeles now." He turned to look at her again, and his eyes were filled with pain. "Once she found out I was broke, she decided she didn't love me so much any more." He smiled nervously. "I reckon it's a good thing I found out what she was like before I married her, huh?"

Their eyes held a moment.

"I'm sorry, Mr. Tucker."

"Yeah, well, it's sort of the story of my life. Too bad she wasn't more like you. I don't expect it would make much difference to you how rich a man was."

She reddened and looked down at her knitting.

"It's the quality of people that counts, Mr. Tucker. But in my case there would be no choosing." She met his eyes again. "My life will be at the mission, as a teacher and a nun."

His eyes moved over her for a brief moment, and again she felt the unfamiliar urging deep inside of herself.

"Will it?" he asked.

"Yes, Mr. Tucker," she replied, not sounding at all sure of herself.

"Well, like I said before, that would be a waste in my estimation. But everybody has to do what they think is right."

She swallowed and managed a smile. Moss Tucker had sent her mind awhirl and put her in quite a predicament. She wished she had one of the sisters there to talk with.

"Won't you tell me more about your past, Mr. Tucker?"

He sighed and smiled softly. "I don't think I'd better tell you just yet. Maybe once we get you safely to California, I could come and visit. There's, uh, somebody I'm goin' to see there, somebody special. Maybe I'll introduce the two of you later on. That is, if you'll allow me to come and see you once in a while."

Her mind raced with dread and happiness. Who was the special person—a woman? Yet he'd said he'd like to see her in California.

"Certainly you may come and see me," she replied, trying to hide her disappointment over his mention of someone special. "And who is this special person? A new love, perhaps?"

Moss chuckled, inwardly relieved that she appeared to be upset over the fact that it might be a woman. That was good. Was that jealousy he read in her eyes?

"No. It's no woman. I'd tell you more, Miss Boone, but I can't. Not just yet."

Her relief was obvious.

"Well, whoever it is, you be sure to bring him or her to the mission. I would like Father Mitchel to meet you. He'll be deeply grateful for your help on this trip."

Again their eyes held. So much left unsaid. Yet it was there in the eyes. She returned to her knitting.

"Mr. Tucker, I—I think it would be perfectly fine if you called me Amanda. I mean, I—I wouldn't object." She looked at him again. "I think we're good enough friends for first names."

He smiled broadly. "Well, now, that's just fine with me. You call me Moss, Amanda."

His use of her first name sent tingles through her body.

"All right, Moss." They both smiled.

• • •

At Salt Wells it was announced that the second passenger car on the train would have to be disengaged, and most of its passengers would have to wait overnight for another train that would come through the next day.

"We've found a cracked wheel," the porter announced, amid groans and curses. "There's not much room on the other car, so unless your trip is a dire emergency, you'll all have to stay here in Salt Wells the night and go on tomorrow on the next train. We're sorry for the delay, but it can't be helped. The Union Pacific will pay for your keep. There's a meal house just behind the station where you can eat, on the house."

Although it was a great inconvenience to the passengers, Sollit Weber was overjoyed when he heard the other passenger car would not be going on. It only made his job that much easier. Now there would be only one car full of passengers to be concerned about, and, of course, Moses Tucker. But he knew how he'd handle Tucker. The rest would be easy now. It seemed everything was working in his favor. Only one car full of passengers, and a woman who would provide him with the advantage he needed.

All passengers disembarked, the ones who would have to wait for another train grumbling about the inconvenience.

"It's too bad the others have to wait," Amanda commented to Moss, as he led her to the meal house. "I'm glad it wasn't our car that was delayed. I'm getting out to the mission late enough as it is."

"Well, they'll be picked up tomorrow. That's not so bad. We've got a little time while they unhitch and sort through the baggage and all. You come on in here and sit yourself down and eat. I'll rejoin you soon."

"But where are you going?" she asked.

"Oh, I've got somethin' to do. I won't be long, ma'am." He led her inside the crowded restaurant. "Looks like this is the only place in this little town to eat," he grumbled. There was not a free table to be had. Then a young, handsome soldier seated nearby stood up.

"Ma'am, you're welcome to sit down right here," he spoke up, smiling kindly. His blue eyes shone with congeniality.

"Oh, I wouldn't want to put you out, sir," Amanda replied.

Sollit Weber put his hand out to Moss.

"Oh, that's all right," he said in a friendly fashion. "I'm Sollit Weber. Private Weber. I'm headed for Bear River City, then Fort Bridger." Weber and Moss Tucker shook hands, but there was something about the private that did not ring true to Moss. He was too eager, too friendly, and too fresh-faced. "You, uh, sit right down here, sir, with your young lady. Me and my friend can wait. Oh, this over here is Pvt. Bobby Keller. He's traveling with me."

Moss nodded to Keller, who had an honest face—more honest than Private Weber's. Keller nodded back and started to rise.

"I'm not staying," Moss told the man. "I have an errand to run. You go ahead and sit there, Keller. When you're through I'll probably be back and I can take your place."

Weber pulled out his chair and motioned for Amanda to be seated.

"I'm very grateful, Mr. Weber," Amanda told him. "You really needn't do this."

"Oh, it's my pleasure, ma'am," Weber replied, smiling. "I'll go ahead and order and eat standing up. And the two of us will stay right here with you until your gentleman friend gets back."

"The name is Moses Tucker," Moss told Weber.

"Well, I'm glad to meet you, Mr. Tucker. You go ahead and run your errand, and Private Keller and I will look out for—" He looked at Amanda and smiled a boyish smile. "Ma'am, we don't even know your name."

Amanda looked up from her chair. "Oh, forgive me!" she said, feeling rude. "I'm Miss Amanda Boone."

"Miss?" Weber replied. "Pardon me, ma'am. But I wasn't sure. I thought perhaps you and Mr. Tucker here were married. I mean, you've been traveling together—"

"We're friends," Moss spoke up, a little irritated. This young man seemed to be cleverly trying to find something out. Was it because he had an interest in Amanda? He suddenly realized he was jealous. The soldier was young and handsome, and didn't men in uniform usually turn a young woman's head? Amanda appeared fascinated with the soldiers, but then she'd probably never seen soldiers before. "Miss Boone is a teacher— soon to be a nun," he added, hoping to dispel any interest Private Weber might have. Weber's surprise was evident, and it pleased Moss.

"Well!" he said, smiling nervously. He looked down at Amanda. "A very commendable choice, Miss Boone. I'm honored to be in your presence." Thoughts were racing through the young man's mind. This young woman was single, and likely had never been touched by a man; she'd bring a good price in Mexico. But he was also confused. If she was truly to be a nun, what was Moses Tucker's interest in her? Weber was sure he had not misread Tucker's infatuation with Miss Amanda Boone. Perhaps Tucker knew a relationship was next to impossible; yet that would not necessarily stop him from loving the woman, and it would certainly not stop him from worrying about her welfare. This new information was a surprise, yet it did not really change Weber's plans to any great extent.

"Mr. Tucker has agreed to see me safely to California,"

Amanda told Private Weber, completely trusting his kind blue eyes. "We met by accident, you might say. But I believe the Lord sent him, knowing I'd need help getting through this rather uncivilized territory."

Weber laughed lightly. "Yes, ma'am. It's not good for a pretty young lady like yourself to be traveling alone in these parts. It's very nice that you've run into your Mr. Tucker." He looked at the frowning Moss and smiled. "You go right ahead and run your errand, Mr. Tucker, and we'll keep an eye on your lady friend while you're gone. We won't leave her side until you return."

Moss studied him a moment, still sure Sollit Weber would try to charm Amanda. A jealousy burned inside him that he knew he had no right to be feeling. Then he looked at Private Keller. The men were soldiers and therefore should be trust-worthy. Moss had little choice. His eyes turned to Amanda, just as a woman came to take their order.

"I won't be long, Amanda," he told her.

"And I'll be right here," she replied. Some of his jealousy left him. She appeared to be a little anxious, hopeful that he would come back soon.

"Don't you be payin' for nothin' either," Moss added. "I'll pay for everything when I get back." He looked at Weber. "You keep an eye on her. And you'd best know I've got a temper."

He detected a momentary flash of cold steel in Weber's blue eyes.

"Oh, I'll remember, Mr. Tucker," Weber replied, smiling again. "One thing a soldier must always be is a gentleman around fine ladies such as Miss Boone."

Their eyes held for a moment, both men mentally chal-lenging one another. Moss was certain he did not like the pink-cheeked Private Weber. But nothing could happen in a crowded restaurant, and Private Keller had eyes that Moss trusted.

"I'm sure you're quite the gentleman," Moss replied rather

sarcastically. He looked at Amanda. "You wait right here. Don't you leave this table."

"I won't, Moss," she replied. Their eyes continued to speak the unspoken. Moss smiled softly, then glared at Weber for a moment before he left.

While Moss was gone, Weber and Keller were both talk-ative, relating to Amanda more things about the West, and the Indians, and about Fort Bridger. Amanda was secretly a little confused over the rather rude way Moss had treated Private Weber, but she brushed it off as the reaction of a man who was not prone to trust anyone. She wished she could read people the way Moss could. Sollit Weber seemed to be the epitome of a brave and proud soldier, and a gentleman. The three of them ate; Amanda ordered pie and more coffee, and was nearly finished with that when Moss returned. At first she hardly rec-ognized him. He approached the table and removed his hat, fumbling nervously with it in his hands. Amanda looked up at him. Her eyes lit up with surprise and pleasure.

"Moss?" she asked. He was clean-shaven, except for an attractive mustache, and he'd had his hair cut a little shorter, although it still came to his shirt collar. And to Amanda's plea-sure, Moss Tucker was a strikingly handsome man without his beard. The face was dark and rugged, and there was still the little scar on his chin.

"I, uh, figured it was time I got rid of the beard," he said, actually appearing a little embarrassed and apprehensive. He flashed a handsome grin, and Amanda felt a stirring deep inside herself. Keller got up and offered his chair to Moss, who thanked the man and sat down.

"Moss, you—you look wonderful!" Amanda told him, wondering if her eyes were giving away her feelings. Her emotions were now more confused than ever. Sitting across from her was not only a man she already knew to be brave and skillful, a man of strength and experience, but also a very, very handsome man, who she suspected was also very lonely. The combination was too tempting to a young woman who found it so easy to love others, and who was struggling with decisions as to what to do with her life.

Moss actually reddened a little. "Thanks," he told her. He rubbed at his chin. "Them beards get a little itchy, and I figured you probably didn't like it much. Most women aren't too crazy about beards. I figured if you had to put up with me all the way to California, I'd best get rid of the hair on my face."

She blushed and looked down at her coffee cup. And to her inner shame, she found herself wondering what a man looked like with nothing on. She'd heard they generally had hair on most of their body, even on their chest. It was a sudden and surprising curiosity that came to her out of nowhere, and she immediately decided she'd have to pray for forgiveness for all the sinful thoughts that had lately come to her mind. She almost wished she'd never met Moss Tucker, for her thoughts were becoming more and more confused. What did God expect of her? And what did Moss Tucker expect?

"Well, it—it looks very nice," she told him. "I really didn't mind the beard. But I'm pleased you were considerate enough to shave it off, just because you thought I might not like it." She raised her eyes to meet his. How dark and moving his eyes were! How broad his shoulders were! How dependable he was! Yes, she was growing much too fond of Moses Tucker.

"We'll, uh, be leaving you two now," Sollit Weber spoke up. He was inwardly very pleased that Moses Tucker had shaved off his beard just for Miss Amanda Boone. He'd been right all along. Tucker was infatuated with the woman. That was good. That was very good. And they were down to only one car full of passengers. Everything was working out perfectly! It was only a matter of hours now. The next step was Bear River City, only the train would never get there—not until it was emptied of the soldiers' payroll and its rifles. And perhaps Miss Amanda Boone would also be a part of the bounty. He would enjoy the look on Moses Tucker's face when the man found out Miss Amanda Boone might be in danger. Weber had allowed the robbery to become a personal thing. For there was a growing dislike between him and Moses Tucker, though the two didn't even know each other. It was the challenge: that inner challenge that grows between certain men without any logical reason. It was just something that was there, usually between two men who were proud and strong, and who had goals that would inevitably clash. It was an unexplainable challenge that had led men to battle for centuries. And when Sollit Weber and Moses Tucker looked at each other, both knew there would be a confrontation. But only Sollit Weber understood why. At the moment Moss was simply confused by his feelings.

"I, uh, reckon I ought to thank you," Moss said to Weber and Keller.

"Oh, it was our pleasure!" Weber replied with a smile. "Hope the rest of your trip is a safe one, ma'am," he added, turning his eyes to Amanda. He nodded to her and she blushed.

"Thank you, Mr. Weber. And good luck in your duty with the army."

"We all do our best, ma'am." He winked at her and walked off. Keller also nodded.

"Good-bye, ma'am." He looked at Moss. "Good-bye, sir. It wasn't any trouble watching out for Miss Boone." He turned to leave.

"Keller," Moss spoke up.

"Yes, sir?"

"Weber. What's he like? Is he a good soldier?"

Keller shrugged. "He's a pretty friendly sort. Obeys orders and all, never gives anybody any trouble. Yeah. I guess you could say he's a good soldier. Before we left Fort Kearney he was in charge of the telegraph messages. I'm not sure what he'll be doing when we get to Fort Bridger. Why do you ask?"

Moss ran a hand through his hair. "I don't know myself." He took out a cigar. "Tell me. Is there somethin' bein' hauled on that train we don't know about?"

Keller swallowed. "N-no, sir." His orders were not to mention anything to any passengers about the guns or the money. "What makes you ask that?"

Moss looked at Amanda, pleased at the admiration in her eyes. He was glad he'd shaved. She seemed completely taken with him. It made him forget about Weber.

"I guess I'm just too suspicious," he replied, now smiling. He looked up at Keller. "Thanks for watching out for Miss Boone. You have a good trip now."

"Yes, sir. Thank you. Like Weber said, it was our pleasure." The young man left, and Moss reached into his pocket.

"I, uh, got a little somethin' for you."

Amanda reddened, and her heart pounded. "For me? Now why on earth did you do that?"

He shrugged. "I just wanted to." He handed her a small box, but she didn't take it at first. He set the box in the middle of the table. "Please accept it, Amanda. I want you to have it. Maybe you'll remember me whenever you look at it."

She swallowed and raised her eyes to his. "I'd remember you whether I had a gift from you or not, Mr. Tucker—I mean, Moss."

He reached over and took her hand, gently squeezing it and setting her blood on fire.

"It's been an honor havin' you call me a friend, Amanda," he told her. "A real honor for a man like me." How soft her hand was! She was so small and lovely.

"I—I don't know what to say," she told him in a near whisper. "The sisters always told me a lady should never accept a gift from a gentleman. It's much too bold and suggestive. I don't think—"

"Please, Amanda," he said softly, still holding her hand. "I've never had many friends. And I've never had one as nice as you. I'd be hurt if you didn't take it. You'd be denyin' me a lot of pleasure, 'cause I know you'll like it, and that would please me greatly. You said you owed me for watchin' out for you. So please take the gift for me."

She smiled nervously and pulled her hand away, then picked up the box.

"All right," she said softly, removing the lid carefully.

She stared at the contents: a small, ebony jewelry case that was covered with delicate, hand-painted roses. Her eyes began to tear when she removed the small case from the box in which it had been packed. At first she simply held it, touching the tiny flower designs with her fingers. The case was about five inches long and two inches wide, and had little gold legs on it so that it could be set on a dresser like a tiny chest. She opened the lid, and it was lined with white velvet. It was feminine and exquisite, and obviously very expensive, especially when found in places like Salt Wells.

"I, uh, figured you could use that to maybe put your rosary beads in, or whatever jewelry you might have," Moss told the temporarily speechless Amanda. "I know you probably aren't a woman who would keep much jewelry. But I know Catholics have them prayin' beads, so I figured you must have some. Do you like it?"

She swallowed and looked over at him. "I—I don't know what to say," she told him, blinking back tears. "It's the most beautiful gift I've ever had." She smiled, and one tear slipped down her cheek. Yes. She loved him. How could she not love him? What was she to do now? "It's exquisite, Mr. Tucker—I mean, Moss. Just exquisite." She quickly wiped away the tear. "You really shouldn't have, but I'll treasure it always."

Their eyes held. "I'm glad you like it, Amanda. I—"

"Moss! Moss Tucker!" a man spoke up. Both Moss and Amanda looked up to see a bearded, unkempt man heading for their table, grinning through teeth brown from tobacco stains. "You ole outlaw, you! Where the hell have you been? In jail?" The man laughed, and Moss's face darkened. He rose from his chair.

"Hello, Seeley. It's been a long time," he said, putting out his hand and looking uncomfortable.

"It sure has! Hell, the last time I saw you was—where was we—Hole-in-the-Wall? I think you was askin' me about a buyer for the cattle you rustled, you ole scallawag! What are you doin' sittin' here with a pretty little lady? Hey, is she one of them—"

"Shut up, Seeley!" Moss grumbled, grabbing the man's arm. He all but dragged the man out of the restaurant. Amanda looked through the window and could see them talking outside. Moss looked highly upset and angry, and Amanda's heart was tortured with love and sorrow for him. The man called Seeley had only verified what she'd already suspected. She was not totally surprised, only more curious about Moses Tucker. What things had he done, and why? There must have been reasons; he seemed such a good man at heart. Was she simply naive and stupid? Was she becoming so enamored with the handsome Moses Tucker that she was not thinking reasonably? Should she continue to trust him?

He finally returned and sat back down. "You, uh, ready to go?" he asked, looking at the floor.

"Yes. Aren't you going to eat, Moss?"

He smiled disgustedly, still not facing her. "I'm not hungry. I'll go pay for yours." He got up and walked away. She stood up when he returned, and he reached down and picked up her carpetbag for her. Amanda picked up the ebony box and put it back in its container.

"I'd better put this in my carpetbag," she said quietly.

"Amanda, you don't have to keep that if you don't want to. I'd understand," he told her. She raised her eyes to meet his. All she saw was pain and sorrow—and loneliness.

"That place…The Hole-in-the-Wall," she said softly. "It's one of those places where—where outlaws hide, isn't it? I've read about it."

Their eyes held. "It is," he replied flatly.

She swallowed. "I see." They were lost in each other, oblivious to the people around them, and no one paid any attention to the two of them or to their conversation.

"Moss," she went on softly. "When Christ died on the cross, two men hung on either side of him. Both were criminals, outlaws. He loved them both. And one of them asked Christ to forgive him, minutes before he died. And he was forgiven. If a person wishes to change his life, then God does not hold that person to blame for things in his past. Someone such as I has no right condemning another human being, when Christ does not condemn. I want very much to keep the case, Moss."

She tore her eyes from his and opened the carpetbag while he held it, gently placing the ebony case inside. Moss just watched her, a little dumbfounded.

"Shall we go?" she asked, picking up her gloves.

He wanted to kiss her. He wanted to hug her, feel her close to him, tell her he loved her. Oh, yes, he loved her! But he could not have her. Strangely enough, just to know that she accepted him seemed to be enough for the moment. She had not turned him away. Surely she knew his past had been far from commendable. He felt almost as though he were in competition with God, for Amanda Boone seemed to be perfect material for a nun. Surely that was what her God intended for her. How special she was! How lovely and innocent and special!

"You're a good woman, Amanda Boone," he found himself saying. "And I won't disappoint your trust in me. I promise you that."

"I believe you, Moss." Her ease with this man never ceased to amaze her. When she first left New York, she never dreamed she'd be able to strike up a friendship with a man or converse with one as easily as she did now with Moss Tucker. She studied the dark handsome face, the eyes that held the answers to so many questions. But she would not ask them. If he wanted her to know, he would tell her. He suddenly bent down and lightly kissed her forehead. She blushed deeply, but was not offended.

"Maybe I should apologize," he told her. "But I had to do that, Amanda."

She twisted her gloves in her hand. Never had a man's lips touched her! She felt on fire and hoped she didn't look as flushed as she felt.

"We'd better hurry. We'll miss our train," she replied. She turned and walked to the door, with Moss close behind. She hoped she'd get to the train without falling down, for her legs felt weak. Moss Tucker had kissed her, and her feelings for this man she knew to be a one-time outlaw were becoming more and more uncontrollable.

To her relief she made it to the train without fainting. They boarded and sat down in their same seats. Moss set her carpetbag beside her as always and glanced to the rear of the car. Sollit Weber was watching him. The young man smiled and nodded. Moss scowled and sat down, too engrossed right now in his feelings for Amanda to care about Sollit Weber, whatever sort of man he might be.

Chapter Nine

"Did you know that Moses is a very Biblical name?" Amanda asked, as the train rumbled through a tunnel. Moss grinned, and the car lit up again as it came back out into the sunshine.

"Well, I know there was somebody famous in the Bible called Moses, but I don't know the whole story. And comparin' me to somebody in the Bible..." He chuckled. "Well, let's just say I reckon I'm a far cry from somebody like that!"

Amanda smiled softly. "Perhaps. And yet maybe not. Moses led his people, the Israelites, to freedom. He led them out of the land of Egypt, rescuing them from the people who had enslaved them. And through Moses, God performed many miracles to help them all escape. Even the great Red Sea was parted so that the Israelites could walk through and not drown."

Moss smiled. "Sounds exciting. I think I'd have liked to be that Moses. Lots of adventure."

Amanda laughed lightly, and it was music to his ears. He'd never heard her laugh that hard before. Their eyes held, and then his roamed her body again, making her feel weak.

"You ought to laugh more," he told her. "It sounds nice. I have a feelin' you've never laughed a whole lot."

Amanda blushed. "The nuns are usually rather serious about most things," she replied. "And I'm not so sure it's right for me to be sitting here laughing and talking with a man I've only known for three days."

"Sure it's right," he replied. "There's nothin' wrong with it." He leaned forward, his elbows on his knees. "Tell me something," he went on. "You ever dance, Amanda?"

Her eyes widened. "Dance? Goodness, no!"

"But haven't you ever wanted to? I mean, a pretty, young thing like you—you must have thought about it."

She smiled bashfully. "Our human, sinful side makes us think of such things, Moss. But when that happens, I pray to God to help me eliminate such thoughts from my head."

"But why? What's wrong with dancing?"

"It can lead to other things." She sat up straighter, trying to sound sure of herself. "A girl dances, wears a pretty dress, and she begins to think she's pretty. That leads to vanity. Then perhaps she intentionally—or even unintentionally—flaunts herself in front of men, making them think lustful thoughts, and—"

She suddenly reddened deeply, feeling flushed as his eyes again studied her form. Then he took her hand, and she did not resist.

"Amanda, a woman don't always have to dance for a man to think them thoughts," he told her quietly. "And it's not always wrong if he does. Didn't God create man and woman for a specific purpose?"

"Mr, Tucker, please!" she whispered, withdrawing her hand.

"Oh, so now it's Mr. Tucker," he said. "What are you afraid of, Amanda? You think God's gonna punish you for thinkin' things that are natural for a young girl to think about? And wasn't there a lot of dancin' in the Bible? I mean, I'm no scholar on the Bible, that's for sure. But I've heard tell them Israelites did a lot of dancin' and celebratin' to their God. And one more thing, Amanda," he added, taking her hand again, this time against her will. He squeezed her hand lightly. "Look at me," he told her.

She met his eyes, her face flushed and her eyes seemingly wary now.

"Amanda, just because a man looks at a woman lovingly, it don't mean he's bein' lustful in his thoughts. There's some women a man thinks lustful thoughts about, and there's some women a man only thinks beautiful things about 'cause she's special in his eyes. Very special. And what he thinks about her—it's not wrong, Amanda. And maybe it's even what God intends for him, or for the woman, to think. You have to give some things a chance, Amanda, and you have to understand the difference between lust and love."

Their eyes held a long, quiet moment. What was he telling her? That he loved her? Now she was at a loss for words. This was something new. Her body felt on fire as his hand kept hold of hers. He leaned closer to her, talking quietly so others could not hear the noise of the clattering train and the murmurs of others kept their own conversation private.

"If men and women didn't have certain feelings about each other, there'd never be no marriages and there'd be no more children in the world," he went on, feeling an ache in his groin as she blushed more. "So it can't be all bad. And I reckon maybe God meant for men and women to have them feelings. The secret is respect and love. Those two things make it okay, Amanda."

She finally found her voice. "I…" she swallowed. "I've never had any…experience with such feelings," she replied. "You're confusing me, Moss."

"I'm just tryin' to make you see both sides," he replied, squeezing her hand again. "You can't make no final decision unless you understand both sides, Amanda. And you bein' so inexperienced, like you say, you ought to understand a little bit about men and how they are. There's some women a man don't have much respect for. I've been with them kind, and I'll admit the things them women do and the men, too, are bad things." She blushed even more and looked down at her lap. He kept hold of her hand. "Sure, that's sinful and wrong," he went on. "And I expect I've sinned in just about every way a man can sin. I know I'm no good, Amanda, especially for the likes of you. But at the same time I'm concerned for you, and I want you to be able to make the right decision if some man should come along who loves you. You're the kind of woman a man's got nothin' but respect for, and the feelings he might have for you—they're not wrong."

She raised her eyes to meet his. "You shouldn't say you're no good, Moss. Everyone is good. Sometimes life leads people astray. But they're still good at heart. In God's eyes I'm no better than you, Moss."

A faint smile crossed his lips—lips that wanted very much to taste hers. He suddenly realized with an overpowering jealousy that he wanted to be the one to claim this woman—if she should ever decide to give herself to a man.

"Well, that's nice of you to say. But in my estimation, a man like me don't deserve somethin' like you. And one more thing, for your own protection: it ain't true that everybody is good at heart, Amanda. There's some men who'll never be good at heart—never. There's some that are just downright evil, through and through. I've known men like that. And you'd best be knowin' it's so, honey. Thinkin' everybody is basically good is a bad mistake."

"But how am I to know the difference?"

"Sometimes it's pretty hard."

"And you? Have I made a mistake about you?"

He looked at her silently for a moment. "No," he told her. "I've done some bad things, but certain circumstances led me to it. I wish to hell now that none of it had happened, but it did. I wish I'd have met somebody like you a long time ago. But I guess you could say I was kind of born into sin."

"Born into it?"

He let go of her hand and sat up straighter. "I was born in a brothel, Amanda. My ma was a prostitute, and I never knew my pa. I'm a bastard."

Again she blushed, but her heart ached for him. He sounded almost as though he hated himself—for something he had nothing to do with.

"I'm sorry, Moss."

"No. I'm sorry," he said, scowling. "I shouldn't have told

you that." He sighed, disgusted with himself. "Just forget everything I said."

"Everything?" she asked.

He turned his eyes to meet hers. "You make me say things and think things I ain't got no right sayin' and thinkin'," he told her. "I'm no good, Amanda. I'll see you get to California, and then you'd be best to go on and take them vows and be a nun like you planned."

"That will not be so easy now, Moss," she said quietly. "You've given me things to think about. And you were right. It's necessary that I think about them. I have to be sure."

His heart pounded with love for her. Was she saying she'd actually give consideration to one Moses Tucker? Perhaps that was too much to hope for.

"You want to know something?" he asked her.

"What?"

"There's somethin' I've been wantin' to ask you."

"Then ask me, Moss."

"Well, it's really kind of silly—maybe."

"Then ask me and I'll decide."

"Well, I—I want to call you Mandy."

Her eyebrows went up in surprise. A nickname! No one had ever given her a nickname.

"I mean, it just seems natural," he went on. "I mean, you look and act like a Mandy, you know? You're young, small, and pretty, and Amanda sounds too old for you. Mandy—that sounds nice, like the pretty little girl you are, you know? Only if it offends you, I won't call you that."

She smiled shyly. "I—I'm actually flattered," she told him. "I mean it makes me feel special, different."

He smiled again. "You are special." He took her hand once more. "You're very special, Mandy." Their eyes held, and he squeezed her hand, looking around nervously at the others in the crowded car. "Mandy, I—I wish you'd come out on the platform with me, just for a minute. It's so stuffy in here, and I have somethin' more to tell you."

She felt a lovely warmth surge through her body, and her head swam in confusion. Her better sense told her not to go, told her what he wanted. Yet she found herself rising with him and going through the door of the railroad car and out onto the platform. Cool air hit their faces and she was grateful, for she was sure her cheeks must be embarrassingly flushed. He still had hold of her hand, and he turned then to face her.

"Mandy, I wish—I wish you'd think about maybe—maybe doin' somethin' different with your life. You're so young, so pretty."

She looked down and started to turn away and go, embarrassed and flustered. Then a big arm came across her chest, his hand at her waist. He pinned her against him for a moment, her back to him, and she trembled at the sensation of being held close, at the feel of his power, the touch of his hand at her waist and his arm across her breasts. Her heart pounded. She wanted to run but her legs would not move.

"Mandy," he said softly, seemingly both in desire and near worship. "You're the nicest thing I ever met in my life." He wanted to say he loved her, but was afraid to. He gently forced her to turn, and for the first time in her life her breasts were crushed against a man's chest. She kept her head turned away as one arm remained around her in a firm hold, his big hand pressing into the small of her back. With his right hand he reached over and pulled up her chin. Her eyes begged him not to do this, but her lips were too inviting and he bent to meet them, parting them slightly as he broke in her virgin lips. He was consumed with a burning need to make her his own, with a terrible desire to make her want a man. He felt her respond for just a moment and her lips were sweet and delicious. He heard a light whimper above the noise of the rattling train and he pulled her tighter, kissing her hungrily then, wanting to devour her, invade her. But then she suddenly stiffened and pulled away.

"Moss, please!" she whimpered.

His chest ached with a terrible remorse then. How he

hated himself! What kind of man was he to try to destroy such innocence, to confuse her mind with suggestions of things less honorable than were fit for her. And what made him think that, even if she did take a man, it would be a worthless ex-outlaw with no future. Men like Moses Tucker weren't worth the little finger of someone like Amanda. His throat constricted and he swallowed, still holding her. He shuddered and took a deep breath.

"I—my God, forgive me, Mandy. I'm just a worthless, no-good—"

She gently pulled way, taking his hands but unable to meet his eyes. "No," she interrupted. "It wasn't your fault. I… let you kiss me. It's all my fault. You apparently have feelings for me, and I'm sure they're honorable. And I—I have feelings for you, too, Moss. But I must not let those sinful feelings stop me from doing what I must do. I suppose this is just another barrier the Lord has put in front of me to test me."

She stumbled slightly with the sway of the train, and he caught her hands tighter, then reached out and put an arm around her shoulders, holding her beside him and bracing himself with his other hand against the railing, looking out at the swiftly passing terrain.

"I reckon if God was to use somebody as a tool to put sin in front of you, I'd be the best choice, that's a fact. I'm sorry, Mandy. Truly I am. I need to know you won't hold it against me, won't be afraid of me after this. I won't try it again, I swear on my life. I'll see you get to California."

She touched her lips with her fingers, his kiss still burning her lips. It made her shiver with new feelings she had never before experienced. She felt so safe when he held her, so free from worry, fear, and burdens. It was easy to see how nice it must be to lean on a man for strength and comfort. But she had been taught to lean on no one but God.

"I would never hold it against you, Moss. And I want very much for you to go to California with me. I'd be too frightened without you."

She dared to look up and meet his eyes then, and she saw the pain and remorse there.

"It's all right, Moss. Somehow I knew—knew why you wanted to come out here. And I came anyway, perhaps to find out something for myself."

He studied her eyes. "And what did you find out?"

How handsome and rugged he was! "I—I'm not certain yet. There are so many things I know nothing about. I feel so foolish sometimes." Her head reeled with new thoughts and her body pulsed with new feelings and desires.

He touched her cheek lightly with the back of his hand. "Let's get you back inside."

She smiled lightly for him and nodded. He took her back inside and they took their seats, both lost in thought and in each other. Amanda met his eyes again, and he was looking at her apologetically as Sollit Weber approached them.

"Well!" Weber spoke up, breaking the spell. "Are you having a nice trip, ma'am?"

Amanda looked up, almost startled. Moss scowled, irritated that Weber had interfered with this special moment.

"Oh!" Amanda spoke up, putting her hands to her flushed cheeks and sitting up straighter. "Yes," she went on, blushing. "The scenery in this area is breath-taking."

Weber smiled and winked. "Now you aren't going to tell me you've been watching the scenery!" he said jokingly. "I've seen you two do more looking at each other than out the window!"

Amanda blushed and Moss glowered at Weber.

"I'd say what we're lookin' at isn't your business, mister," he grumbled. Weber laughed and Amanda frowned at Moss.

"Moss, he's just being friendly," she spoke up. "After all, Mr. Weber did help look after me back at Salt Wells."

"That's all right, ma'am. Mr. Tucker is right," Weber said in a friendly fashion. "It wasn't my business. Say, I have something to show you, if you'll allow me."

"Oh?" Amanda asked.

"Yes, ma'am. If you'll let me sit down beside you there for just a minute?"

Amanda looked at Moss, who was still frowning with irritation. He sighed and moved back a little to let Weber through, but only because he knew Amanda would think him rude if he objected. Weber set Amanda's carpetbag on the floor and sat down next to her, still smiling.

"Ma'am, I've got something here." He reached into the side of his coat. "It's called a Colt .45, ma'am." He shoved the steel barrel against her side. Amanda gasped and Moss sat immobile, his mind racing. He instantly hated himself for not acting on his original opinion of Sollit Weber. How could he have been so stupid! There was something wrong with the man's eyes all along. Now the friendly blue eyes were as cold as the steel of his revolver, but he kept smiling.

Chapter Ten

Amanda looked at Moss, her eyes wide with fright, her throat feeling tight. Moss glanced at her for only a moment.

"You just sit real still, Mandy," Moss told her quietly and reassuringly. His eyes quickly moved back to Sollit Weber.

"That's good advice, Mr. Tucker," Weber told Moss with a smile. "This gun blows big holes. So I want you to do everything I say, or I'll blow the little woman's guts clear over to the other side of this car. Understood?"

Moss glowered at the man, already vowing that Sollit Weber would somehow, someday, die by Moss's two hands.

"What the hell do you want?" Moss asked the man. Weber kept grinning.

"Well, now, that's real simple, Mr. Tucker," Weber told him. "All you have to do is remove that gun you're wearing, open the window, and toss it out."

Moss glanced at Amanda again. Her eyes were tearing, and she was rigid with terror. He began unbuckling his belt, infuriated with himself that he'd been so stupid as to not see through Sollit Weber. It only proved how infatuated he'd become with Amanda Boone. She'd kept his mind off the more important issue of watching strangers and seeing her safely to California.

"I'll tell you one thing right now, Weber," Moss growled. The other passengers talked among themselves, oblivious to the fact that Sollit Weber had the barrel of a Colt .45 jammed into Amanda's ribs. "You hurt that woman, and you're a dead man! You might get off a shot at me, but I'd make damned sure you was dead before I went down!"

"Just open the window and toss out that gun, Tucker,"

Weber replied coldly. "You do like I say, and nothing will happen to her. That's all that's necessary."

Moss cautiously opened the window. If it were not for Weber's gun being pushed into Amanda's side, he'd make a dive for Weber. But any wrong move could make the gun fire, and Amanda would be dead. At the moment he had no choice. But his mind raced with possibilities. He would not let this go unavenged. He tossed out the gun.

"Now you're being smart," Weber told him. "You just sit back and relax, Tucker. Have a cigar or something. We have a few minutes yet."

"A few minutes before what?"

"Before the others get here—Rand Barker and his men."

"Rand Barker!" Moss exclaimed, his eyes darkening more.

"You know Rand Barker?" Weber asked with a smile, pushing on his gun and making Amanda gasp with pain. Moss's knuckles whitened as he gripped the arms of his chair in rage.

"You said you wouldn't hurt her!"

"Just a little reminder that she'd best sit still and you'd best not try anything, Tucker," the man replied with a grin. "Now, what's this about Rand Barker?"

Moss glanced at Amanda again. She had not spoken, nor had she removed her eyes from him during the entire incident. He knew she was relying on him to help her, and he felt crazy with desperation. The woman he loved was depending on him, and there was nothing he could do at the moment. The worst part was that he was well aware of the traumatic effect violence could have on a woman as delicate and inexperienced as Amanda Boone. It wasn't right that someone like Amanda should have to see this kind of violence. His only hope now was that whatever was going to happen would be done quickly and that she would not be harmed.

"I know the man," Moss grumbled, looking back at Weber. "Me and him had a little run in once. He didn't like my idea, and I didn't like his. I put a bullet in the man."

Weber's smile faded. "Well, now. I'd say that couldn't happen unless—unless you were an outlaw just like Rand."

Now Moss smiled. "You've got it, kid." Their eyes held. Then Weber chuckled.

"Well, now, that's a good one!" he said casually. "Perhaps you'd like to join us, Mr. Tucker. You see, we've made a little arrangement with Raincloud and the Sioux. They help us stop this train and they get the rifles it's carrying. Rand and the rest of us get the army payroll that's aboard. And everybody is happy."

Moss took a cigar from his pocket. "So, that's it. I figured this train was carryin' somethin' special." He lit the cigar. "I must be gettin' too old. I suspected all along, but I got careless and didn't pay no attention." He puffed on the cigar.

"Well now, that's where this pretty little lady was a help," Weber told him. "You've been so wrapped up in Miss Boone here that you weren't paying much attention to anything else." He jammed the gun again and grinned when she jumped. Then he took his free hand and rested it on her shoulder. "Maybe we'll get more out of this robbery than just money," he added.

Moss's eyes blackened with rage, and he slowly removed the cigar from his mouth.

"Get your hand off her!" he hissed.

Weber turned to look at him, still grinning. "I'd say you're in no position to give me orders, Tucker," he said, his eyes cold as ice. "One little nudge, and her insides see daylight. She's got a small waist, so I'd guess a bullet would rip through her real easy, Tucker." He let his hand fall, gently brushing over her breast and enjoying the fury in Moss Tucker's eyes. Amanda sat frozen and speechless. Moss had been right. There were men who had not an ounce of good in them.

She tried to think clearly, but it was next to impossible. The touch of Sollit Weber's hand on her breast had sickened her, and she felt ready to pass out from fear. But her fear was not just for herself. She knew now that she loved Moss Tucker, and she knew that before this was over the man would try something and perhaps be killed—and it would be because of her. She began to quietly pray and, oddly enough, she prayed for Moss rather than for herself. If God was going to act, He'd have to do it through Moss Tucker.

"So, you know Rand Barker," Weber said to Moss with the ever present grin. "This should be interesting."

The train began to slow down.

"Must be a barrier up ahead," Weber said with a grin.

Amanda's blood chilled at the sound of Indians' war hoops, and people began to panic and look out their windows. Just then a tall, bearded man in buckskins charged through the rear door of the car, brandishing a Spencer carbine. Part of the Barker gang had already ridden up from behind and boarded the train.

"Everybody put their hands on top of their heads!" the man ordered.

Keller, the soldier who had been traveling with Weber, stood up and reached for his side arm. "What the—" he started to say. The Spencer boomed out a shot, and Amanda screamed and covered her ears. As Keller flew backward Moss leaned forward slightly, but Weber quickly jerked Amanda sideways in front of him, his gun now in her back.

"Don't move an inch, Tucker!" he growled. "Check them out, Booner!" he shouted louder. "I've got the only really dangerous one covered down here!"

"Right, Sol!" Booner waved his rifle around, as some of the passengers stared in dismay at the bloodied and dead Private Keller. All the passengers but Amanda were male. None of them put up a fuss when Booner again ordered them to put their hands on their heads.

The train rumbled to a complete stop now, as Indians circled around outside and Rand Barker and the rest of his men approached the train. Seconds later pounding could be heard, as the Indians smashed tomahawks into a boxcar. Two more men entered the passenger car, and Moss recognized Rand Barker. Barker didn't notice him at first.

"Me and Sol have them all covered, Rand," Booner told the man. "Go ahead and have them empty their pockets."

"Move it!" Rand ordered the other man who had entered the car with him. Moss's chest suddenly tightened with dread. He recognized the other man. It was Duke Sage. If Duke saw Amanda…his mind raced. Why on earth couldn't it have been their car that had been broken down and delayed? He had to do something!

Barker and Sage made their way forward, stealing wallets, rings, watches and anything else that appeared valuable.

"Now, wait just a minute!" one man objected. Barker's gun smashed across the side of the man's skull to silence him.

"Empty those pockets without no fuss!" Sage growled to the others. Then he spotted a hat—a woman's hat. He forgot about the wallets and quickly moved forward. His eyes lit up as he stared at Amanda.

"Well, well, well!" Sage said with a grin. "What have we got here, Sol?"

Weber grinned. "A little something extra for you, Sage," he replied, eyeing Tucker. Amanda let out a little whimper as Sage grabbed her from the seat. At the same time Moss lunged for Weber. Weber's gun went off and Amanda screamed as Moss temporarily slumped against Weber. Weber shoved him off and Sage grabbed Amanda tight, her back to him. She was too frozen with fear to even struggle. All she could think of was Moss. Was he dead? She stared at him and began crying, and Sage's hand moved up to grab a breast.

"I got me one!" he called out to Rand Barker. Moss was struggling to his knees, while Rand ordered Weber and Booner to finish frisking the passengers. He stepped up to Amanda and eyed her up and down.

"What's your name?" Rand asked her.

Amanda just stared at him. Rand slapped her hard and she cried out, while Sage laughed.

"I asked you a question, lady!" Rand barked. "You got a name? You married? Got family?"

Amanda could not find her voice. Rand began running his hands over her body, reaching under her dress and feeling her legs.

"I think she's fresh, Rand," Weber called out. "She was traveling to California to be a nun of all things! She's not married, and I don't think she's been had! That man there I shot, I think he had an interest in her. Calls himself Moses Tucker. Told me he knew you."

Rand's attention was immediately drawn away from Amanda. He looked down at Moss, who had now managed to get to his knees. Amanda began weeping as Moss grasped at his side, and blood poured down over his hand, staining the front of his shirt and jacket. He was trying desperately to get to his feet.

"Moss Tucker!" Rand said, smiling. "I'll be damned!"

"It *is* Tucker!" Duke Sage said in surprise. Barker reached down and jerked at Moss, but Moss was too big for Rand to get the man to his feet. Rand let go of him, and when Moss realized who it was, he struggled to his feet by himself, determined to face Rand standing up. Sage was touching Amanda's breasts, and Moss shook with rage.

"You're gonna die for this, Barker!" Moss growled.

Rand laughed. "I'd say you're the one who's dying, Tucker!" he sneered. "I'd put another bullet in you, but I'd just as soon let you die slowly. It would give me more pleasure that way."

"Leave the woman here, Rand!" Moss hissed. "Take me with you! Torture me if you want! But leave her here!"

Rand chuckled. "Come now, Moss. The little lady could be worth something."

Moss looked at the weeping and shamed Amanda Boone. His fury knew no bounds! Men like Rand Barker and Duke Sage should not be allowed to desecrate something as precious as Amanda Boone! How could her God allow this to happen? He had to think! He had to protect her until he was able to help her!

"That woman's never been touched, Rand!" he said in a weakening voice, blood now running down over his boots.

"Moss!" Amanda squealed, trying to reach out to him.

"You...remember that!" Moss went on. "She won't be worth nothing...if you let men like Sage abuse her!"

"And I suppose you intend to rescue her before we get her to Mexico?" Rand said with a chuckle. "That way you'll get her back untouched, right?"

Moss just glared at him. "I'll find you, Barker!"

"You won't live out the day, Tucker!" Barker glowered. "But if you do, I hope you do come after her. I'll enjoy getting hold of you." He turned to look Amanda over again, then lifted her dress and looked at her ruffled pantaloons. Amanda whimpered and began to struggle. Rand turned back to Moss. "All right, Tucker. Tell you what I'll do. I'll give you a few days. If you happen to catch up, then I'll enjoy tying you down and letting each of my men take a turn with her while you watch. That would give me more pleasure than killing you outright. In the meantime, if you should die, you can go out of this world knowing that in a few days your little lady friend here will either be getting broken in by Duke here and the others, or she'll be sold for a tidy profit to a rich rancher in Mexico who's tired of his fat wife."

"You bastard!" Moss growled. He lunged forward, and Barker's gun butt came down hard over Moss's head. Amanda screamed out Moss's name, and Barker laughed. Then he turned to Amanda and jerked her away from Sage.

"You remember what I told you!" he growled to Sage. "I'll decide what we do with her, and she rides with me! Understood?"

Sage looked Amanda up and down hungrily, and she was sure she would be sick any minute. She struggled with Barker, trying to bend down to Moss, but he began pushing her forward to the door.

"Moss! Moss!" she screamed.

Moss could hear her, but he couldn't move. And he

hated himself. Never had he hated himself this much! Of all the scrapes and gunfights and fistfights he'd been in—run-ins with the law, all kinds of tough spots that he'd been able to get himself out of—now the one person he loved and who needed him most could not depend on him. He had failed her! He struggled to rise, but his body would not move. He could hear shouts outside now. Someone was yelling that he had the money. Indians were shouting and cheering and guns were being fired.

Sollit Weber stood over him now.

"Looks like the big, tough man wasn't able to help his little lady, doesn't it?" the boy sneered. "That's what happens when a man gets too carried away with a woman. Takes away his ability to reason." He heard Weber laugh. Then Weber reached over and picked up Amanda's carpetbag, emptying its contents. He'd been curious as to why she'd been so possessive of it. The crucifix fell out.

"Well, look here," he said with a chuckle. "The little lady was carrying something valuable and keeping it a secret. Looks like we're getting a lot more out of this than we expected! Wait till Rand sees this!"

He chuckled again and went out, carrying the crucifix.

Outside the men waited. Weber mounted up and rode over to Barker, who had Amanda astride his horse in front of him, her hands now tied to the pommel.

"Look what I found in the lady's bag, boss," Weber told him.

"No, please!" Amanda wept. "Please put it back! It belongs to the church!"

"Well, then, we'll just borrow it from God for a little while," Barker told her, running a hand over the legs he'd deliberately bared. He had pushed her skirts and pantaloons up so that part of her legs were exposed for the pleasure of his men. Amanda wept, more for the fact that Moss was probably dead or dying than for herself. Barker's men were stuffing money into saddlebags, most of them eyeing Amanda at the same time. Duke Sage sat on his horse nearby, licking his lips.

Just then an Indian rode up to Barker, sitting proud and straight on his mount and holding up a rifle.

"You did not lie!" he said to Rand. "The guns are here! It is good for you that you did not lie!"

"I told you they'd be here, Raincloud," Barker replied. "Thanks for your help."

Raincloud looked at the weeping Amanda.

"Who is the woman? Why do you take her?" he asked, frowning.

"Who or what we take isn't your business, Raincloud," Barker snapped. "You got your rifles. So get moving."

Raincloud stared at Amanda another moment.

"You have no business taking the woman."

"Butt out, Raincloud!" Barker growled.

Raincloud spit on the ground. "You are filth!" the Indian sputtered. "The white man lusts after women and gold! He not only rapes our squaws, but he rapes his own kind! A man who turns on his own kind is worse than a snake! I feel shamed that I have dealt with you. If my people were not starving, I would not have done so. But we need the guns!"

"Then take them and leave!" Rand sneered. He whirled his horse. "Let's go, men!"

The others shouted, cheered, and laughed. The bounty had been good: money, a valuable crucifix, and a woman! They rode off, quickly disappearing in the dust. Raincloud sat there a moment watching.

"Scum!" he spit out again. But Rand Barker had kept his word about the rifles. Therefore, Raincloud would let him go his way. He let out a war cry and signaled his men to leave; they all rode off waving their new rifles.

Moments later the passengers began to cautiously exit the car. The train sat hissing and still, large boulders in front of it.

"Let's get these rocks out of the way and get to Bear River

City!" somebody shouted. "We've got to send a wire to the nearest fort for help. They took a woman!"

Inside the car someone knelt down beside the badly bleeding and now unconscious Moses Tucker.

"They'd better hurry up," the man commented. "This man here needs a doctor real bad."

Chapter Eleven

When Moss opened his eyes, everything was blurry. He moved to rise, and pain shot through his side and the room began to spin. He groaned and rubbed at his eyes, trying to think. Where was he? What had caused the pain? He heard a door close and then footsteps.

"You must lie still, Mr. Tucker," came the soft voice. Was that her? A woman's soft voice. Amanda! But no, it couldn't be. Amanda! Amanda! They had taken her away!

He opened his eyes again to see a young woman standing over him, bending down to put a wet cloth to his head. He grabbed the woman's wrist.

"Where is she!" he whispered. "Where's Mandy?"

"You mean the woman the robbers took, Mr. Tucker?"

His eyes immediately teared, and the young woman applied the cloth to his head.

"I heard about it, Mr. Tucker. How awful! That poor girl. Soldiers are out searching for them now, Mr. Tucker."

"No! No!" he groaned. He grabbed the washcloth, threw it to the floor and started to rise again.

"Mr. Tucker, you're badly hurt! You must lie still!" the young woman protested.

"I've...got to go after her!" he groaned, managing to sit up. "I failed her! I failed her! God in heaven, she's with Rand Barker! And Duke Sage! Jesus Christ, Duke Sage is with them!"

The young woman blushed when Moss threw back the covers, exposing his naked body. Moss was not thinking of anything now but to go after Amanda. The woman fled the room to get help while Moss stumbled around, searching for his underwear. Minutes later a man entered.

"Mr. Tucker, you must get back into bed!" the man ordered.

"I can't," Moss grumbled. "I've got to go after her!"

"But, Mr. Tucker—"

"Where's my goddamned underwear?" Moss shouted.

The man sighed and went to a bureau, opening a drawer and taking out a clean pair of long johns.

"You're making a mistake, Mr. Tucker. I'm Dr. Lumas. You've lost a lot of blood. The wound itself will heal if you're careful, but you're weakened from blood loss and a fractured skull."

"I've been wounded before," Moss grumbled, grabbing the underwear. He stumbled as he struggled to get it on. The doctor grasped Moss's arm.

"Mr. Tucker, you can't do the woman any good if you pass out and die on your way to get her. There are soldiers out searching, Mr. Tucker."

"They don't know where to find men like Rand Barker. I do. I rode with him once. I know where the man hangs out." He pulled on his underwear. "Where's my things?"

The doctor sighed in resignation. He walked to a corner of the room, while Moss's mind whirled with rage, remorse, and terrible dread. Rand Barker had taken Amanda Boone! Would he save her for Mexico? Or would his lust—and that of Duke Sage's—make Barker change his mind and take her himself, only to then turn her over to his men? The men would all want her, that was sure. And they'd do their best to talk Barker into letting them have her. But Barker liked money just a little more than women, and keeping her fresh would make her more valuable. That was Moss's only hope. He felt on fire with vengeance. Amanda Boone belonged to him! Maybe not literally. But if the woman was ever going to give herself to a man, then Moss Tucker wanted to be first. And a woman like Amanda was not to be toyed with. For her to be forced and taken in the filthy way Rand Barker and his men would take her would drive her insane! What a horrible, devastating way for a girl like Amanda to be introduced to men! It tore at his guts and filled him with rage—such rage that he thought he might vomit.

"Mandy!" he whispered to himself, clinging to the bedpost. "Jesus God, Mandy!"

The doctor came over with Moss's bag in one hand, and Amanda's carpetbag in the other.

"The, uh, passengers—they said you'd been a friend of the young lady that was taken," he told Moss, setting the bags on the bed. "They saved her things. Thought you might want them or maybe know where to send them."

Moss stared at the carpetbag, and a tear slipped down his cheek. He hung his head and breathed deeply, wiping at his eyes.

"I'm sorry, Mr. Tucker. Perhaps they'll find her soon."

"Where am I?" he asked in a broken voice.

"Bear River City. If you—if you need money, Mr. Tucker, I'd be glad to lend it to you. I think what those men have done is outrageous. If you intend to go after her, you'll need weapons. The outlaws took everything."

Moss looked at the baggage. Then he walked around the bed and tore through Amanda's carpetbag.

"Damn!" he groaned. "The crucifix! They took that, too!"

"What's that, sir?"

He looked at the doctor. "Never mind." He wiped at his eyes again. "I, uh, I'd be obliged for the loan. I can only give my word that I'll pay it back—whatever good the word of a stranger is."

"Don't worry about it. If you find her in time, it will have been worth it. But I must advise you that another day or two of rest is very important, Mr. Tucker."

"There's no time for that." Moss turned and opened his own bag, taking out some buckskin pants. He sat down on the bed and pulled them on. "I have a knife and sheath with my things here, but I'll need a six-gun and bullets. And I'll need a rifle."

"Three buildings down to the right, Mr. Tucker. There's a blacksmith who sells arms. He can supply you."

"Maybe you could give me some extra bandages so I can change my dressin' a couple of times," Moss told him. He looked down at his gauze-wrapped midsection. "Did they get anything vital?"

"The bullet went through your side, Mr. Tucker. It left quite a hole, and if it had been aimed better, you'd not be here. But apparently the bullet was deflected by a struggle or something. It nicked one rib bone and tore through flesh, but nothing vital was hit."

"How long have I been here?" Moss asked, standing up. He squinted as a pain shot through his head.

"Nearly two days, Mr. Tucker."

"Two days!" Moss exclaimed. "Oh, my God! My God!"

"I can give you some laudanum for the pain, sir. But you must use it carefully. It's a drug, and with a fractured skull, too much could knock you out rather than just dull the pain."

"Fine! Fine!" Moss grumbled, taking out a long sleeved, heavy cotton undershirt and slipping it on. He hurried now, not heeding the pain. His search for Amanda had been delayed much too long already. He slipped on a buckskin shirt over the undershirt and quickly laced up the neck. The doctor watched a moment, as Moses Tucker was slowly transformed into a burly, menacing-looking mountain man. Moss strapped on a wide, leather belt, from which hung a large knife. Even in its sheath, the knife looked deadly. Moss sat down on the bed and began pulling on knee-high, deerskin, moccasinlike boots.

"I'll get the gauze and laudanum," the doctor told him. "I'll also give you a couple extra blankets. If you find her, she'll need them. It's getting quite cold out there now, Mr. Tucker."

"Thanks."

"Oh, and they removed your saddle and other gear from the train. It's downstairs. The train officials said the Union Pacific will give you a free ride the rest of the way to California on the next train, or they'll pay for a horse, if you choose to get one and go on by horseback. Or if, of course, you wish to go out in search of Miss Boone. They suspected you would want to do that. You, uh, should be able to find a good horse at the blacksmith's also."

"Good. Good."

The doctor walked over and took the rest of Moss's clothes from the dresser, and Moss stood up and threw them into his bag.

"Look, doc, I need to travel light. I'd like to leave my bag here—and Miss Boone's. I'll just take out a couple of things she might need and pack them into my own saddlebags."

"That's fine. I'll have my nurse gather together some supplies: coffee and such, maybe some beef jerky and some flour."

Moss turned to the man, perspiring now from pain and weakness.

"I can't thank you enough, doc. You're bein' awful good about all this."

"I don't like what has happened, Mr. Tucker. It's time some civilization came to the West and men like Rand Barker be put out of business." The doctor looked him up and down. "You say you rode with him?"

"Yes, sir, I did. But that was a long time ago. Men can change, Doc."

"I'm sure some men can. But I doubt that a man like Rand Barker ever will."

"I agree with you there." Moss wiped his brow and sat down on the bed for a moment.

"Mr. Tucker, you must ride easy and drink lots and lots of water. Promise me you'll do that."

"I will," Moss said weakly.

"And I insist you eat a good meal before you leave. It's important, Mr. Tucker. You've not had a regular meal in two or three days now."

Moss thought back. He'd not eaten in Salt Wells because he'd been wrapped up in giving the gift to Amanda—the jewelry box. It had not been in her bag. It must have been left behind, perhaps now on its way to California without her. The thought of the little box lying unclaimed under a seat—and its owner now in the hands of outlaws—gripped his insides. She had been delicate and lovely, like the jewelry case. He'd bought it because it seemed a perfect gift for a fragile young woman, its flowers delicate and innocent, like Amanda. Innocent. Innocent and untouched. He remembered how she'd thought the cow being hit by the train was violent. He remembered how she'd cried when the passengers shot at the buffalo. And now she had seen the worst of violence, and would herself probably be the brunt of violence. Rand Barker and his men could be brutal. They were men of cold steel, men without hearts or feelings. How well he knew them. And how close he had come to being just like them! He'd lost his appetite back at Salt Wells because a man had recognized him and blurted out that Moss himself had been an outlaw. He remembered how scared he'd been that she'd detest him for it. But she hadn't. She'd looked at him with forgiving eyes, eyes he was sure were full of love. And she'd kept the little jewelry case.

Now the case was gone. The crucifix was gone. And Amanda was gone. He was glad the doctor had left the room for a while, because Moss Tucker could not hide his tears of anger and frustration and worry. Never had he felt like this about someone, not even the woman he once thought he loved in California. He loved Amanda much more than that. Amanda was extraordinary—full of love and kindness. He had to find her and help her. And once he did, he had to convince her to marry him. But perhaps she would hate him by then. For he had failed her. Never had Moss Tucker let a man get the better of him the way Sollit Weber had. He'd failed the most important person in his life, and Rand Barker would die for it, as would the fresh-faced Sollit Weber and the rest of them. They'd all die!

"God, you gotta help me," he prayed. Moss Tucker had never uttered a prayer in his life. "You gotta help me find her!"

• • •

Moss mounted the reddish-colored gelding. The horse was a big thoroughbred, broad-chested and strong—perfect for a big man like Moses Tucker. He rode the horse around in a circle, getting the feel of him, talking to him gently.

"Okay, Red, you and me have some ridin' to do," Moss said to the animal, stopping the horse and patting its neck. "You've got to go easy so I don't fall off, boy."

The horse snorted and twitched his ears and Moss smiled.

"I think him and me will get along just fine," Moss told the blacksmith.

"He's a good one, Mr. Tucker," the man replied. "You take a stallion and do a little cuttin', and you take all the feistiness out of him. Makes him real obedient. You can count on that animal, Mr. Tucker."

"I'll need to." Moss adjusted his new Winchester in its holder, then rested a hand on the mahogany barrel of his Peacemaker .45. The side arm had a cutaway trigger guard, which eliminated the guard getting in the way of the trigger. Only men well experienced with firearms used such a gun, as a trigger with no guard was extremely dangerous. But it would give Moss an edge when the time came—the split second more he'd need if he had to face Rand Barker. But he'd faced the man before. How he wished now that he'd killed the man then instead of just wounding him. Next to being careless in his judgment of Sollit Weber, not killing Rand Barker had been the greatest mistake Moss Tucker had ever made. Now he'd kill them both and enjoy it. And he'd definitely kill Duke Sage. If Duke Sage raped Amanda, Moss had already decided he'd hang the man by his feet and castrate him while still alive.

"You've got some good weapons there, Mr. Tucker, and plenty of ammunition," the blacksmith told him.

"That's for sure," Moss replied, "thanks to the Union Pacific and the doctor. I'm obliged for your help in picking out the horse and weapons and all."

Moss adjusted his old leather hat and pulled his wolfskin coat closer around his neck. It was cold in this southwestern portion of Wyoming Territory now. He'd be riding south into Utah, but it wouldn't get any warmer. It was mid-October, and the skies over the mountains were gray with snow. It would not be long before snow would also come to the valleys. He thought about poor Amanda, wondering if she was warm enough.

"You sure you don't want some men to ride with you?" the blacksmith asked him.

"I can do this better alone," Moss replied. "I know how Barker thinks. I'll find him. He'll take the woman to Mexico. He's probably at Brown's Park right now, takin' a rest."

"Well, you take it easy, Mr. Tucker. Remember you've been wounded and all."

Moss grunted with pain as he turned his horse.

"It's not likely I'll forget that," he replied. He nodded to the blacksmith. "I'll be comin' back through here with Amanda Boone in a few days," he said confidently.

"I have a feelin' you will, mister," the blacksmith replied with a smile. Moss rode out. The blacksmith watched for a few minutes, as did the doctor and his nurse and wife. Moss Tucker was a big man who seemed to know exactly what he was about. If anyone could find Amanda Boone, Moss Tucker would.

Chapter Twelve

Amanda shivered, numb now from fear and cold and pain. She had spent the last two nights sleeping in a bedroll with the repulsive Rand Barker, who kept her close and often fondled her. She had given up fighting him, for it only brought painful slaps. Her jaw hurt so badly she could barely speak, and her nose had bled several times.

She now had only one hope: that Moss Tucker had not died and that he would come after her. In the meantime, she could only pray that Rand Barker would stick to his idea that she must remain a virgin until they got her to Mexico. That at least gave her a little more time until the inevitable. Perhaps she would be rescued before then. She tried not to think of what it would be like to be forcefully violated by a man.

Amanda never dreamed that there could be men like Rand Barker and his gang. They joked about the crucifix and even discussed poking out the stones to divide them up. But Barker had decided they'd get more money for the cross intact, and said that once they sold it he'd split up the profit.

Amanda was forced to do their cooking and cleaning. And through it all she suffered filthy remarks about what they'd like to do with her, along with pawing hands. She didn't have to wonder any more what men looked like. A few of these men had made sure she knew. She felt the softness leaving her—the love leaving her. If God intended to show her the wicked side of life, He could not have done a better job than through Rand Barker and his men. She tried to understand them, to pray for them. But it was impossible. She hated them. She feared them. And she wished Moss Tucker would come and kill them all. She wanted to be sorry for her feelings, but she could not.

And she'd already decided that if one or more of these men forced her into an act of intercourse with them, she would promptly kill herself. To lie down and be humiliated in such a way would be more than she could bear, and the fear of the pain and ugliness of such an act so overwhelmed her at times that she thought she would faint. She hurt everywhere and had blisters on her thighs and bottom from riding the horse. She had never ridden horseback before, let alone the many miles they had covered.

Amanda knew that her hatred for Barker and the others was not just because of what they were doing with her, but more because they'd left Moss Tucker for dead. Moss had tried to help, and he was probably dead now because of it. She wasn't sure she could go on without him, even if she managed to escape from the Barker gang. She hadn't fully realized until Moss was shot that she loved the man. She tried to analyze the reasons why God had allowed all of this to happen, but she could come up with no answers. She wondered if the sisters in New York had heard about the robbery and her kidnaping, and she wondered what Father Mitchel was thinking. But most of all she wondered about Moss. It was a strange feeling, knowing she loved him. Yet after the way Barker and his men had treated her, she was more certain than ever that she could never willingly give herself to a man. If she should be rescued, and Moss should live, she wondered just what would happen then. She would be in love with a man she could not give herself to. And would Moss be any different than these men if she were his wife and he had the right to take her? Surely he would, but she had no guarantee. Not any more. Men were cruel and brutal. And hadn't Moss Tucker ridden with these very men?

"Hell, little girl, you took up with a man just like us," Barker had told her. "Old Moss used to ride with us. He's been in and out of prison two or three times. His ma was a whore and whores is the only kind of women he's ever been interested in, except for one rich gal out in California once. She gave him the shaft and married her a lawyer and left Moss holdin' the bag." He laughed about it. "That hurt Moss right good. He took to drinkin' and gamblin' and shootin' and robbin' with the rest of us." Barker had looked her over. "What did he see in a straight-laced thing like you, anyway?"

Amanda had looked away and not answered, wondering the same thing to herself.

"My guess is ole Moss was just lookin' for a way to get under them skirts of yours. Once he got a piece of you, he'd have rode off and left you. Moss is a roamer and an outlaw, lady. He wouldn't have done you no good."

She thought about that as Barker now led his horse down an escarpment toward Brown's Park, where he'd told her they'd rest. She shivered again, and Barker put his arms tighter around her. She tried to ignore the now familiar pawing of his hands and concentrate on Moss. She could not believe Moss would behave as Barker said he would. She could not forget the look of pain and love in his eyes when he'd given her the jewelry box and then worried she might not want to keep it. She remembered the sorrow in his voice when he'd told her he was a bastard, and when he'd talked about being jilted in California, and the fear of rejection in his eyes when he talked about having been an outlaw. She remembered his gentle words shortly before the robbery, about how some women are special and a man could only think of them as special. And there was the kiss. The beautiful kiss followed by his apology. But there had been a warm promise in the kiss. Had it all been a lie? Had he been leading her on like Barker said? Perhaps she would never know.

Amanda's biggest fear was that Barker would leave her unprotected around Duke Sage. Sage had said the filthiest things of any of the men. He had pawed her the most. And his eyes were on her night and day. Only the threats from Rand Barker kept the men away from her; Amanda had that much to be thankful for. But she could not be sure how long it would last.

Chapter Thirteen

Barker guided his horse down the side of a flat-topped mesa, rocks scattering in front of him. The ever present scent of sage was in the air, and the grand view of the Green River below would have been spectacular and breath-taking under different circumstances. From this vantage point the river wandered for miles, and the horizon looked days away. But Amanda did not notice. The last days of horror had broken her delicate mind and nature, and now all feeling seemed to be gone from her. She was numb with shame. And she was sick from exposure. She had no clothes left. They had been torn from her amid jokes and laughter, and even though she had not been raped, the humiliation of the ordeal and hands touching places sacred to her had broken her mind and spirit. She had two woolen blankets now to cover her, and Barker had put a buffalo robe over those, but it was too late. She knew the pneumonia would return—and she didn't care. She hoped she would die. And she wondered if God would ever accept her now in Heaven. She felt sinful and dirty.

The nine men made their way down to the river. Amanda saw other men there, camped farther down the river. She was sure it was only more outlaws, and she wondered if Rand Barker intended to barter for her with the other men. Barker dismounted and helped her down. The man seemed to be worried now. Did he regret exposing her to the cold? Now she was sick. If she died, he'd not get his money's worth out of her.

"You don't have to do nothin' this time," he told her. "You lay down. You get any sicker and I'll turn the men loose on you, 'cause you ain't gonna be no good to us no other way."

He unrolled some blankets and Amanda laid down. She

closed her eyes and the others pitched tents and made camp. She tried desperately to pray, but her faith had left her. She simply lay and shivered. A while later, Barker himself came over and offered her some stew. He helped her sit up, then began feeding her.

"There's some other men here," he told her quietly. "If any of them come over here and see you, you act real nice. Don't you go lettin' on you don't like it here, understand? You do, and you'll be feelin' Rand Barker rammin' into you later, you can bet on it. And after that you'll take on eight others. So you do like I say, lady, or suffer the consequences."

She ate part of the stew and said nothing. She wondered why he had said that. If the other men were also outlaws, why should it matter that they thought she was unhappy? Would they actually care that she was being abused? After all, they were men like Rand Barker. Or were they? Perhaps they were more like Moss. It was confusing to think a man could rob and kill, yet be a gentleman around a lady, as Moss had been to her. So then, it was like Moss had told her. There are men who do wrong but who are really not bad at heart. And then there were men like Rand Barker and those who rode with him.

The night darkened, and Amanda lay shaking beneath her blankets, while Barker and his men sat around the campfire counting money and discussing the crucifix. Clyde Monroe found things to laugh about, as usual. Amanda had begun to dread his laugh. She'd heard it the most when the man was allowed to pinch her and bring pain. Pain seemed to please the man greatly. Now every time he laughed her stomach lurched.

The one called Booner just sat quietly, a cold, hard man without feeling. Sollit Weber had constantly reminded her not to trust people who smiled too much, and also told her that Moss Tucker wasn't much of a man since he'd let her slip right out from under his fingers.

Derrick and Higgins sat cleaning their guns, while Dean Taylor stood a few feet away practicing his draw, which seemed to be all he ever did. Amanda couldn't believe a man that young could be a part of such a grotesque gang of men.

She knew all their names now, including the older one, Wade Gillette. At first she'd thought that Gillette might try to help her, as he didn't seem too crazy about bringing her along. But she quickly realized that none of them—no matter how good with a gun or how ruthless he was—dared to go up against Rand Barker. Barker was in full control. And what he said was never questioned.

Amanda opened her eyes with renewed hope when a strange man stepped into the firelight. In an instant, nine guns were aimed at him. The man stood stock-still, his eyes resting on Barker.

"Rand," he said, with a nod. The man was tall and rangy.

"Well. Lonnie Drake. How you doing, Lonnie?"

"Pretty good. Word's been passed down the line you robbed a train up by Bear River City."

"You and your men fixin' do to a little robbin' of your own, Drake?" Barker asked, rising. "Like maybe takin' our loot?"

"Nope. I just come down here to see who it was." The man looked around, his eyes resting on Amanda. Then they shifted back to Barker. "Hear tell you took a woman from that train."

"What's that to you?"

The man looked long and hard at Barker.

"Men like you, they give us honest outlaws a bad name, Barker," the man replied. "Out in these parts a good woman is somethin' to be honored. We might rob and kill, but we don't bring no harm to the ladies. How come you went and disobeyed the code of honor, Barker?"

"That's my business. I don't live by no code but my own, Drake. Get your butt out of my camp."

Drake looked at Amanda again.

"She looks sick."

Rand Barker shifted. "Look, Drake, I took the lady 'cause she was itchin' for some excitement. She wasn't no virgin or nothin' and she's been havin' a good time with us. Hell, you wouldn't turn away a hot one, would you?"

Drake's eyes moved to Amanda's again.

"That ain't the way I heard it. Heard she was a nice lady."

"Well, you heard wrong. Now you get goin' and mind your own business, Drake. You know I can outgun you any day."

Drake looked at Barker. "I'm leaving," he replied, "but you overstepped yourself this time, Barker. Takin' a woman don't set good. You've got the army after you, and I hear tell Moss Tucker's after you."

Amanda's heart almost stopped beating. Moss! Was he really alive then? Her eyes teared at the thought of it.

"Tucker's dead," Barker replied, sounding apprehensive.

"I hear tell he ain't," Drake retorted. "And I wouldn't want to be in your shoes, Barker. Havin' the army after you ain't nearly as bad as havin' Moss Tucker after you."

"I can take Moss Tucker any day."

"Can you?"

"There's nine of us and only one of him."

"That don't mean a whole lot with Moss Tucker. You'd best be watchin' over your shoulder good, Barker, if that there is Tucker's woman. I hear tell he's sweet on her. He ain't gonna be likin' it much, you takin' her like that."

"Shut up, Drake, and get out of my camp before I blow your head off!" Barker snapped. Drake just grinned.

"Just a warning, Barker. You get out of Brown's Park. The men around here might not be no churchgoers, but they don't cotton to hurtin' innocent women. You know the code, Barker. You get out of Brown's Park—and you'd best not stop off at Robber's Roost, neither. It ain't good to get your own kind mad at you, Barker. It so happens there ain't enough of us here to take you right now, but there'll be others waiting, Barker."

Amanda wanted to talk to the man called Drake, but she knew she didn't dare. It was enough to know that Moss Tucker was alive, and he was coming for her. Moss was coming for her!

Barker's obvious anxiousness pleased her greatly. Drake left, and Barker was upset. He began pacing.

"Hey, Rand, we didn't count on this," Weber spoke up.

"Shut up!"

"But he said even our own kind is mad at us! We don't need that, Rand!" Weber argued.

"Look, kid, I'll do the thinking!" Barker shot back. He came over and stood beside Amanda. "You've brought me some bad luck, lady!"

Sweat dampened her hair, even though she was shivering.

"Moss Tucker…will find you," she said weakly.

Barker laughed nervously. "Let him!" he spit out. "I'll tie him down and then we'll all rob you of that precious virginity of yours right in front of him. That'll rile him right good—us takin' what he intends to take for himself."

"I say we get rid of her!" Wade Gillette spoke up. "She's bad luck, Rand."

The older man seemed to be the only one who could speak up to Rand Barker without getting his head bit off. Barker looked over at the man.

"We dump her, and we'll get a lot of people off our backs, Rand," Gillette went on. "It's like Drake said. There's a certain code out here. We can rustle cattle and rob banks. But we don't mess with good women. Everybody knows a woman can ride into any one of these places and not be touched. It's the law of the land, Barker. I say we let her go and get the hell down to Mexico."

Amanda's heart filled with hope. Perhaps there was a God after all, and He had sent Lonnie Drake and Wade Gillette to talk Barker into letting her go.

"I'll think on it," Barker replied. "She rides out of here with us early in the morning. I need another twenty-four hours to think about it."

"You let her go, I want my share of her," Duke Sage spoke up. "I'll not turn that woman loose without gettin' a piece of her."

114

"You'll keep your hands off her!" Barker snapped. "You violate her and it'll just bring our own kind down on us! If I let her go, she stays untouched—understand?"

Sage glowered at the man. "That ain't fair!"

"Those are the orders, Sage!"

"Why don't we leave her right here?" another spoke up.

"Because I'll not have Lonnie Drake know I gave up that easy!" Barker snarled. "If I let her go it'll be someplace where she won't be found right away. I'll not have Drake thinkin' he scared me into givin' up that easy."

"You sayin' you're scared, Rand?" Sage sneered. In a flash, Barker's gun was out, and Sage's eyes widened. Barker stepped up and laid the end of the barrel against Sage's cheek.

"Rand Barker ain't scared of nothing!" the man growled. He backhanded Sage, and as the man went down he kicked him in the privates. "Don't you never say that again, Sage, or I'll blow your brains out!" He looked at the others. "Everybody get some shut-eye. We move out early. Apparently we ain't welcome at Brown's Park this time. Let's get the hell down to Mexico and spend our money."

"I'll keep watch," Wade Gillette spoke up. He walked away to check the horses, and Rand Barker came over and stood next to Amanda.

"So, your lover is still alive," he growled. "You'd better hope he don't find us, lady. 'Cause he won't live through another meetin' with me."

He opened up another blanket and crawled in beside her, pulling her close and cupping a hand over her breast.

"Sleep tight, baby," he told her.

Amanda was so sick and cold that she actually pressed closer to him for more warmth, not caring about anything but to live long enough to see Moss Tucker once more. She smiled to herself. It was obvious Rand Barker was worried about running into Moss Tucker again. He sounded confident, but she knew that on the inside he was feeling quite the opposite. From the way Lonnie Drake had talked, Moss Tucker was a man to be feared. And she knew that now, with Moss after them, Rand Barker would probably not molest her any further.

So even outlaws had a code of ethics. How strange. Everything about this land was strange and wild and crazy. She never dreamed that she would get this kind of view of the West: the West at its worst, its ugliest. It was an untamed land, full of untamed men. But there were those, like Lonnie Drake, with whom she would not have to fear for her person. She closed her eyes. Moss would come; she was sure of it. Moss would come. The night was silent. In the distance a coyote howled, and moments later one further off howled in reply. Soon several were yipping and howling. She wondered if the West would ever become civilized, or if it would remain a wild land full of wild animals and wild men. The sheltered orphanage in New York seemed a lifetime away now—a world that no longer truly existed. She remembered how frightened she'd been of its streets and alleys. Yet this uncivilized West was just as bad or worse. Evil lurked everywhere. The coyotes howled again, and she wondered where Moss Tucker was at that very moment. She fell asleep while trying to piece together the small bits of information she had about Moss's past, trying to decipher how and why he had ended up an outlaw.

Chapter Fourteen

In spite of pain and weakness, Moss trailed Rand Barker and his men relentlessly. He knew the route the men would take through outlaw territory: the long, rocky road to Mexico through canyons, along riverbeds, winding along the vast foothills of the Rockies, and the jigsaw maze of buttes, mesas, and valleys that held hiding places known only to men like Rand Barker and Moss Tucker. It would be a difficult trip for someone like Amanda. It was hard on even the strongest of men, who were accustomed to riding and the outdoors. But for someone like Amanda, if Rand and his men didn't kill her, the elements would.

He turned up his collar against a stinging wind that howled its lonely wail through the cracks and crevices in the vast wasteland of northeastern Utah. This land would probably never be inhabited or used by anyone—except men who wished to hide.

His horse's hooves clattered over ground of pure rock; never had Moss felt more alone. He grasped his side as the pain shot through him again, but he kept going steadily onward. He knew that at first Rand and his men would ride hard and fast—at least to Brown's Park. But eventually they would have to slow up. No animal could take day after day of hard riding. And Moss knew there was one more thing in his favor. Once word got out that Rand Barker had taken an innocent woman, the gang's flight would become even more difficult. Because not only would Moss and the army be searching for them, but also some outlaws. Most men in the West felt it was cowardly and unmanly to abuse a helpless woman. Anyone who did was considered a yellowbelly, and became as unwelcome in outlaw territory as the law itself. What Rand had done would only make his escape more difficult.

Moss slept little and ate little, neither of which helped his recovery. But he was too worked up over finding Amanda to allow his condition to stop him or even slow him down. There would be time enough to rest after he found Amanda. He survived on coffee—which he brewed strong enough to float a rock—and on jerky, and a paste he made with flour and cooked into a flat tasting pancake. He camped in hollows or among trees—places where the smoke from his fire would not be noticed—when they could be found. A man couldn't be sure just who to trust in this country. With his thoughts of Amanda, and what might be happening to her, it was difficult to sleep at night. Usually he kept going well after dark, picking his way carefully on foot to lead his horse away from crevices and boulders.

Moss knew that with a two-day or more lag, his only hope of coming near Rand Barker was to keep a steady pace, with few stops for food or rest. In half the time it should have taken, he reached Brown's Park. He halted Red at the top of a red clay mesa and looked down into the valley. The outlaws often brought stolen horses and cattle here, ranching until they decided what to do with the animals. Rustling was a way of life for these men, just as other men had legitimate jobs. Out here in this wild, savage country, a man could do just about anything he wanted. Yet, in spite of being nothing more than thieves, a lot of these men were not at all bad, and they mixed and mingled in a strange comradeship with a code of ethics understood by all. Still, a man always had to be careful.

Moss squinted with pain and nudged Red down the mesa. It took him over a half hour to get to the bottom. In this country something could appear to be very close, when actually miles away. It was nearly a mile to the valley, and man and horse seemed very small against the vastness of red rock walls that surrounded him. He remembered trying to describe this land to people in Chicago, but he knew a person simply had to see it for himself to truly grasp its endless horizons and immensity.

He headed his horse toward a cabin where smoke curled out of the chimney. He knew that there were probably already guns being leveled at him cautiously from behind rocks and the windows of the cabin. A herd of horses grazed behind the building—most likely stolen horses. He got within about twenty yards of the cabin when the door opened, and a man exited, holding a rifle.

"Speak your peace, mister, and be quick," the man told Moss. "And don't try nothin' fancy. There's about ten more guns on you."

"Moss Tucker. I'm lookin' for Rand Barker," Moss replied.

The man lowered his rifle. "Come on inside."

Moss moved Red forward, then dismounted and tied him. He walked up the steps of the cabin, and the occupant motioned for him to go in. When Moss entered, four men stood inside with guns in their hands, eyeing him carefully.

"Hey, Moss!" one of them finally said, breaking into a smile. "It is you! We'd heard you'd been killed, then that you hadn't. Wasn't sure just which it was."

"Lonnie." Moss shook hands with Lonnie Drake. "Haven't seen you in years."

"You ready to come back and round up more strays and take them to Abilene?"

Moss smiled sadly. "I'm hopin' them days are over, Lonnie, if I find the woman I'm lookin' for all in one piece. If I don't, I reckon I'll join up again, 'cause I'm not gonna care much about anything then."

"If you're talkin' about that Amanda Boone that Rand Barker and them took, I've seen her, Moss. Come on over here and sit down and I'll fetch you some stew."

Moss's heart pounded with a mixture of fear and relief.

"When?" he asked anxiously, not moving.

"Sit down, Moss. Come on now. Sit down. I've seen men

in pain before, and you sure as hell look like you're in pain. Now sit down."

Moss grabbed a chair and sank into it.

"You'll be no help to her in that condition, Moss," Lonnie told him.

"I'm all right. This job's mine, Lonnie. I'm gonna find them and kill them all!"

"I don't blame you there, Moss. I'd have done it for you when they came through here two days ago, but there was only a couple of us here at the time, and you know Barker. We're rustlers, Moss. But we ain't gunmen like Barker and them men he had along. If the rest of the boys had been here, we'd have tried. But with that girl right in the middle—well, I just figured you'd be comin' along soon 'cause I'd heard you had an interest. You know how word travels through these parts. And her bein' kind of special and all—and you havin' the reputation you've got—well, when Barker got here, we knew. I paid him a visit, but he was equipped like a goddamned army, Moss. There was nothin' I could do. Then when the rest of these men showed up yesterday, I figured we'd give you a day or two to get here and see what you intended to do. You're the gunfighter, Moss. You know how to handle Rand Barker. As far as the girl goes, I figured Barker was savin' her for Mexico."

"How'd she look, Lonnie?" Moss asked, his eyes full of pain and sorrow.

"Fact is, she looked sick, Moss. Real sick. The condition she was in, and the way I threatened Barker—about him takin' a woman and all—I've got a feelin' he'll let her go soon, Moss. I really do. He knows a lot of us are pissed about the whole thing. Once he lets her go, it's easy pickings. We'd like to help you find them all, Moss. You should not try to do it alone."

Moss's eyes teared. "She was alive then?"

"Sure she was. Barker knows he don't dare kill her now, or even rape her." Lonnie spooned up some stew. "You in love with her, Moss?"

Moss removed his hat and ran a hand through his hair.

"I reckon so," he said quietly, surprised that he could admit it so freely in front of these men. But these were all men who understood, men who appreciated a good woman and would like one for themselves, if they could find one. "She's pretty damned special," he went on. "Probably too special for the likes of me. I don't know how that part of it will turn out. I only know I've got to get her away from Rand Barker. Duke Sage is with them."

Lonnie sighed. "I saw him. I'm goddamned sorry, Moss. But at the time there wasn't nothin' I could do. I went over there to kind of check on the woman, you know? They was leavin' her alone, lettin' her sleep. But her face was bruised and, like I say, she looked sick. So I warned him. If it's any consolation, I don't think they'll mess with her any more, Moss. And she had lots of blankets around her to keep her warm. But if you hadn't come when you did, we was fixin' on goin' out tomorrow ourselves—now that we've got enough men together—and huntin' them down and takin' the girl. We've already sent a messenger ahead to Robber's Roost to be on the lookout. If Barker rides into that place, he won't ride out, Moss."

"I'm obliged, Lonnie." He took out the small bottle of laudanum and drank some before diving into the stew.

"You stay here someplace warm for the night, Moss, and we'll all leave in the morning."

"I've got to get started right away," Moss replied.

"You do and you'll kill yourself. Now I already told you word's out. Barker ain't gonna do nothin' to that girl now. He's more afraid of us than he is of the law. Between her bein' sick, and men along the trail lying in wait, he ain't gonna get far. You rest here the night and we'll get a clean start in the morning."

"But she's sick, and—"

"Moss, you ain't got a choice. We ain't lettin' you out of here. So you just fill up on that stew and go over there to a bunk and get some sleep. One of the men will take care of your horse. She'll be all right, Moss. I seen her eyes light up when I mentioned you was lookin' for her. She couldn't say nothing, but I seen her eyes. That gal's countin' on you to come, and she's gonna make damned sure she hangs on till you get there."

Moss couldn't hide his joy at the words.

"You think so, Lonnie?"

"I know so. She'll be all right, Moss. She's stronger than you might think."

Moss frowned and rubbed his forehead. "She, uh, she's about as innocent as they come, Lonnie. You know what I mean? She—she don't know nothin' about men." He covered his eyes. "Jesus!" he whispered, making a little choking sound.

The other men in the room turned away, all of them wanting a piece of Rand Barker for themselves now. There was no reason for Moss Tucker to be embarrassed about his feelings, because they all understood how a man felt about his woman. Moss cleared his throat and wearily rose from the chair to walk over to the fireplace. He held his hands out over the flames.

"There's a couple of things I want you to understand," he said to the men quietly. He sniffed and cleared his throat again. "If we find them, Rand and Duke Sage are mine. There's also a pink-cheeked, blue-eyed, blond young man along by the name of Sollit Weber. He's mine, too. He's the one who tricked me on the train and held a gun on Amanda so I couldn't do nothing." He wiped at his eyes and coughed. "He's the first man who's got the better of me like that, and I think I hate him most of all."

"Understood," one of the men spoke up.

"You men help me find them, and you can make your own decision about the money they stole from the train. If you want it, keep it. I don't want none of it. If you want to return it, go ahead. It don't make no difference either way. I just want Amanda. They also took a valuable crucifix that belonged to her. It's got fancy stones in it and it's worth a lot. I don't want nobody takin' that. It belongs to Amanda's mission—the one in California she was travelin' to where she was gonna teach."

"We ain't the kind to steal crosses," Lonnie replied. Moss lit a cigar and turned to look at them.

"None of you have to help at all. It's up to you."

"It's our duty," one of the men replied. "Barker overstepped his bounds."

Moss eyed all of them, and he trusted all of them.

"I'm obliged," he told them.

"Say, Moss, what was you doin' on that train in the first place?" Lonnie asked. "Where have you been?"

Moss puffed the cigar and walked back over to the chair to finish his stew.

"I'd been back to Chicago to look up my ma, only she was dead. Before that I'd been in jail in California. I worked a while in Chicago, till I got a letter my little girl had been orphaned."

"Little girl!" Lonnie said in surprise. Moss grinned a little.

"Yeah. Back in California. Before I was arrested the last time, I was livin' with a prostitute. I don't have no call to believe that during that time she wasn't true to me. She'd given that life up for the time bein' for me. Then I got arrested for somethin' I didn't do, and later she wrote me she was pregnant. It's a long story from there. But I've never seen the kid. While I was in Chicago, one of her ma's friends wrote me that her ma died and the kid was homeless. I figured I'd go out there and make sure she got a good home. Figured it was the least I could do. It wouldn't be no good, me tryin' to raise her myself." His eyes teared a little again. "Then I met Miss Amanda Boone. She was pretty and sweet, everything a man looks for. And I seen some interest in her eyes. And I started to thinkin' about what a good mother she'd make for my little girl."

"Sounds like you fell hard and fast, you ole outlaw, you," Lonnie kidded.

Moss smiled sadly. "I reckon I did," he said in a near whisper. "It wasn't hard."

Everyone was silent for a few minutes, while Moss smoked and blinked back tears.

"She's gonna be okay, Moss," Lonnie finally said. "You get some sleep and we'll head out in the morning. We'll find her, and she'll be okay."

Moss looked at the man and smiled, his eyes looking tired and bloodshot.

"She's gotta be," he replied. "Or I ain't even gonna want to live, Lonnie. Can you believe a man like me could feel that way?"

"Any man can feel that way, Moss."

Outside the day darkened into night, the temperature dropped, and snow began to fall.

Chapter Fifteen

It was a quiet but determined group of men who saddled up the next morning in spite of the bitter cold. Winter would come early. That was evident. The sky on the western horizon was dark and menacing, and the bite of the wind foretold of an early, freak snowstorm for northeastern Utah.

Moss didn't have to tell these men how grateful he was for their aid. They already knew. These were the only kind of men Moss Tucker would have wanted along. He'd turned down other help. To search for outlaws like Rand Barker, the same kind of men were needed: men who knew how a man like Barker thinks and acts, men who had ridden the outlaw trail and knew all its hiding places, men like those with Moss now.

But there was one big difference between these men, and men like Rand Barker and his gang. There was still a little bit of good left in Moss Tucker and the men who would ride with him; there was no good left in Rand Barker and his kind. No good at all. They were all hard meanness: men without feeling, men who lusted for gold, women, and pleasure. Moss thought about how hard it was to draw a line between good and bad when it came to men like those who were helping him now, and when it came to himself. He'd been a mixture of both most of his life. But he knew that if Amanda Boone would marry him, he'd straighten out his life for good. The problem was to find her before she died or was sold off to someone else.

Five men would ride with Moss. There was, of course, Lonnie Drake, a tall, dark and rangy man with a questionable past, but a man of his word nonetheless. Drake was a drifter, in and out of trouble with the law. He was about forty.

The other four were all middle-aged. They were drifters

like Lonnie Drake and Moss Tucker, all outlaws in one respect or another, and most with reasons for their life style. There was Darrell Hicks, Johnny Pence, Cal Story and Pappy Lane. Moss had met Johnny Pence and Pappy Lane in previous years. And, of course, he'd known Lonnie Drake. All these men were rustlers, but Moss knew he could depend on their word to help. But none of them were true gunfighters, not the kind who would stand in the middle of the street and face a man down. Only Moss was what could be called a gunfighter. But Moss knew that all these men were good shots and didn't waste bullets, and they finally cornered Rand Barker and the others, they'd all come in handy.

Pappy Lane was the oldest, in his early fifties. He was a feisty sort, a good aim and well experienced on the trail. Moss was pleased to have Pappy along; as he tightened the cinch on his saddle, it was Pappy who came up to him with further bad news. He stood next to Moss, and the others waited as Moss turned to look at Pappy and noticed the old man held something green in his hands. Moss stared at it a moment, frowning. There was nothing to be said. He reached out and took the article, fingering the green velvet, then putting it to his face and sniffing the lovely, flowery scent. His chest tightened. He lowered the piece of cloth and looked at Pappy with pain-filled eyes.

"I was ridin' into Brown's Park two days ago," Pappy told him. "Come across a place where somebody had camped and found that there woman's cape. 'Course I didn't know then whose it could be, Moss. I kept it and showed it to Lonnie, and that's when he told me about the woman. I, uh, figured I'd show it to you, see if you recognized it. Thought maybe you'd want it if it was hers."

Moss swallowed, then quickly turned away and stuffed it into his saddle bag.

"Thanks, Pappy," he said quietly.

"I—I didn't want to show you last night, you bein' so tired and upset and all, and your wound hurtin' like it was."

"Sure, Pappy." Moss swung himself into the saddle.

"Moss, there's somethin' else," Pappy went on, looking ready to cry himself. Moss's chest hurt with dread.

"What?"

Pappy rested a hand on Red's neck and looked up at Moss Tucker hesitantly.

"Well, you ought to prepare yourself, Moss. I mean, she could be raped or dead—or both. Lonnie already said she looked sick."

Moss's eyes glazed with ice. He jerked at his horse's reins and made the animal snort and move back some. "I know that, Pappy." He looked out over the rocky horizon. "We'd best get riding. If she gets too sick he'll dump her—and God only knows where. She'd die without help. Besides that, if she's no use for takin' to Mexico, they might decide to all get their share."

His rage could be felt by all of them.

"I don't think they'll do that, Moss," Lonnie spoke up. "They know the only way to even consider gettin' the rest of us off their backs is to leave her untouched."

Moss whirled his horse to face the man. "Maybe so, for most of them, but don't forget Duke Sage is with them! And when it comes to women, Sage don't think of nothin' but what's below his belt. Let's move!"

He dug his heels into Red and rocks flew as he quickly moved out ahead of the others. A light snow had already fallen, and the rest of the men took out after Moss, following his tracks. Moss was already cursing the snow. He was a good tracker, but fresh snow on top of a trail would make his job more difficult, and time was of the essence.

• • •

Rand Barker could now barely hang on to Amanda, who seemed to be only half aware of her predicament. She was now too sick to care, and she sat in front of Barker in a state of floating semiconsciousness, as the cold wind penetrated the blankets that were wrapped around her.

"Why don't you dump her, Rand?" Booner spoke up. "She's gettin' to be more bother than she's worth. She ain't never gonna make it to Mexico. She's already dying."

Rand Barker did not like giving up. He was upset with himself for exposing her to the cold the night he'd let the men laughingly remove her clothes. If she died, he'd lose a valuable source of income, and Moss Tucker and others like him would be deeply angered.

The wind blew harder and Amanda groaned and slipped to the side of Barker's horse. He jerked her back up.

"There's a little deserted cabin up ahead," he hollered out, slowing his horse. Snow began falling. "I'm gonna take her there."

"What if she dies?" Weber shouted, the wind picking up now and carrying away their voices.

"They probably won't find her for a while," Barker shouted back. "In the meantime, we can make a lot better time without her along. We'll leave her there and get the hell out of here. If she's dead when they find her, we'll be well on our way south. If not, whoever finds her will want to stay on and take care of her. That will give us even more time."

"Not if they're layin' in wait for us up ahead," Duke Sage put in.

"Could be Drake was puttin' us on when he said they'd be lookin' for us," Barker replied. "At any rate we won't go by way of Robber's Roost. We'll head east of there. They won't find us."

"Seems like kind of a waste, just leavin' her there alone like that," Duke Sage said, rubbing his chin. "Hell, if we can't sell her in Mexico, why not get our piece of her now?"

Barker's face darkened. "You'll go on with us, Sage, and you won't rape her, understand? Our best chance of gettin' Moss Tucker off our backs is to let him find her alive and untouched! We've got enough problems gettin' out of this area. There's no sense gettin' Tucker's dander up any more than it is!"

"You scared of Moss Tucker?" the young Dean Taylor asked sarcastically. Taylor had been practicing and was now cocksure of himself. He couldn't understand why there should be any man Rand Barker was afraid of, unless Barker wasn't as good with a gun as people claimed he was.

Barker whirled his horse and glared at Taylor.

"What was that you said, boy?" he snarled.

"I asked you a question, Rand. How come you're so worried about makin' Moss Tucker mad? You act like you're scared of him," Taylor replied with a grin. "Maybe it's time this outfit was run by somebody with guts who knows how to use his gun and ain't afraid of some half-baked outlaw who's seen his day!"

Barker's eyes lit up like fire. He pranced his horse over to Duke Sage.

"Take the girl for a minute!" he growled. Sage grinned.

"Gladly, boss," the man replied. He pulled Amanda onto his horse, and she groaned with revulsion when his hands immediately began searching under the blanket. She was so sick. So sick! How she wished she would just die. Nothing mattered any more. Nothing mattered but to die. Who was going to find her in this godforsaken land with its labyrinth of canyons, hidden crevices, and pathways to nowhere? Rand Barker was dismounting. She hung her head and closed her eyes, and didn't care what was going to happen.

"Get down off that horse, you smart-mouthed son of a bitch!" Barker snarled to Taylor. "It's too bad your life has to end at such a young age!"

Taylor grinned. "I aim to live a long time, Rand. And I aim to be the leader of an outfit like this one. Only I won't mess things up like you have, 'cause I'm smarter—and I'm faster!"

The boy went for his gun without dismounting, figuring he'd take Rand Barker by surprise. But Barker had been around too long. Every man present was amazed at Barker's speed, even though most had seen him draw before. It was something that never ceased to all but shock these men.

Before Dean Taylor could fire, Barker's gun went off three

times. Two ugly red stains immediately appeared in the middle of Taylor's chest, and a repulsive hole gaped hideously from the middle of his forehead. He just sat on his horse, rigid and staring in shock, in that last split second realizing he had lost the game. Amanda had jumped at the gunshots and turned on impulse to see what had happened. She stared speechless at Dean Taylor, then began screaming when his body leaned backward and then fell off his horse.

This last horrible example of the violence of these men was more than she could bear. Her body screamed with pain and fever, and her voice screamed with devastation at the realization of the kind of evil that existed in some men. Her screams could not be controlled. Duke Sage laughed and clung to her as she struggled. She screamed more, like a crazy woman: struggling, biting, kicking, using up her last, precious bit of strength. Rand Barker walked over and grabbed her down off Sage's horse. Her blankets fell off, and Barker backhanded her hard, knocking her to the ground.

"Quit your screaming, you goddamned bitch!" he growled. His temper was paper thin now. Dean Taylor had infuriated him by questioning his authority and implying he was afraid of Moss Tucker. He'd killed the boy, and suddenly that wasn't enough. This woman had caused it all. He wished he'd never brought her along. If not for her, there wouldn't be nearly so many men out searching for them. He picked her up and hit her again. Amanda tasted blood, but it didn't seem to matter now. All feeling was gone. Another blow, and everything went black.

"You boys get moving!" Barker growled. "Leave the kid here to rot! I'll take the woman to that cabin and dump her there and I'll be along."

Sage rubbed at himself. "You gonna take her, boss?"

Barker looked around at the men. "I'm gonna show Moss Tucker I ain't afraid of nobody. Nobody! I'm gonna take her, and nobody else! She's gonna remember so, if she lives to tell him, she can tell him it was Rand Barker—and nobody else!" His voice had risen to a near scream, he was so filled with rage at Dean Taylor's accusations. He jerked at Amanda, pulling her up as he mounted his horse. "You boys get going! Give me a few minutes with the woman, and I'll be along! I'll show Moss Tucker! I'll break in his little virgin. Let him come after me! Just let him!"

Barker rode off toward a gully where a small, deserted cabin rested, hidden to all but the outlaws who roamed the territory and knew it was there. The others looked at each other and decided they'd best do what he said. They proceeded without Rand Barker. Rand Barker had a job to do.

Duke Sage burned with envy and jealousy. He'd wanted the woman all along and now Barker would get her, and be the only one besides. He decided that first chance he got, after Barker had rejoined them, he'd cut out and hunt up the cabin. By then Barker wouldn't care. He'd want to keep heading south, and Duke Sage could have the woman all to himself—to use however he chose. He grinned to himself and kept riding.

Chapter Sixteen

For two nights and a day, Moss Tucker and his men made their way south, a damp, cold wind penetrating their clothing, and wet snow from a freak storm plastering their faces. But they continued on relentlessly, knowing their only chance of gaining time was to keep going, with little rest and only short breaks for eating. Sometimes they ate while riding, chewing on jerky and longing for a warm kitchen with fresh coffee, steak, and potatoes. But there would be time enough later for that. There was a woman to be found, and vengeance to fulfill. One thing all of them were good at was tracking. Because of their skill at following prints through difficult terrain, combined with a knowledge of the movements of outlaws, they seldom strayed from the right path, and the distance between themselves and Rand Barker narrowed. Rand Barker would have to move much more cautiously because of the many men after him; and he had the woman along, which would slow him up further.

Now that snow covered much of the ground, Moss and his men had to move on instinct rather than actual tracking. There was a route that ran all the way from Canada to Mexico that was considered outlaw territory. They knew Rand Barker would stay within that territory, following the most common trails leading southward and not veering away from that path until he reached Robber's Roost, where he knew men were waiting for him. It was this theory that brought elation to Moss and the others when they found an area where several men had obviously made camp; the spot wasn't more than a day old.

"Let's keep moving!" Moss told them excitedly.

"It's almost dark, Moss," Lonnie told him. All of them were tired.

"We've got a little daylight left! He's still goin' south. You men can come with me or not. But I'm gonna keep goin' till I can't see my hand in front of my face."

He rode off without waiting for their answer. The others looked at each other, and Pappy shrugged.

"You heard the man," he said with a half grin. "Can any of us sit here and worry about our worthless hides, while that girl's still with Barker?"

Cal Story rubbed at his eyes and pulled his hat down farther on his brow. "Reckon not. Let's go," he grumbled. They headed out, following Moss's tracks. Moss was himself already out of sight. A day ahead of them lay the body of Dean Taylor, where Rand Barker had left him for the wolves.

• • •

Amanda lay shivering, wrapped in her two blankets and lying on a bare mattress in the tiny, deserted cabin. Her skin was as hot as fire, yet she was cold. Her body was racked with the pain of her own illness and the beating Rand Barker had given her.

She tried not to think about it. But how could she not think about it? She groaned and began crying again at the memory of the ugliness and the pain of what he had done. Her degradation was beyond description, and she prayed vehemently for death. Her shame was more than she could bear; and the influenza that grabbed her bones and muscles in severe pain only added to her desire to die and be rid of her misery.

For two nights and a day she lay there without food or heat, slowly dying and not caring. She had been only half-conscious when Rand Barker had his way with her—but half-conscious had been enough. He had knocked her so senseless that taking her was a simple matter. She remembered her screams and his laughter. Outside the cold winds howled, and it was as if her very soul were screaming through the canyons.

That death would come to her soon, she did not doubt. But what a strange way for her life to end. Had she ever lived in New York and known the sisters? It was all like a dream now. She would never see Father Mitchel or teach at the mission in California. The precious crucifix was gone. And her own precious virginity was gone. Everything was gone. Moss Tucker would never find her in this hidden, lonely cabin in the middle of nowhere. She would die here, her bones would decay here, and that would be that.

She groaned and tried to move, but her body was paralyzed with pain. Perhaps Rand Barker had broken some of her bones. She cried until there were no more tears, and now she simply floated in and out of consciousness, waiting for her inevitable death. Waiting anxiously.

Sometimes her mind floated back to Moss Tucker. Why had God allowed their quick friendship? She tried to reason it out. Why had He led them together, and then allowed these horrible things to happen to her? Her faith was dashed into near nothingness. And her feelings for Moss Tucker were confused. So much had changed. What would he think of her now? She felt soiled and dirty. And what did it matter? She was dying anyway—and gladly. But even if she didn't, no man would ever touch her again. Of that she was certain. Even if she were to love him, he would not touch her. She hated men. She hated life. And yes, she even hated God for having allowed this to happen. No! She mustn't! She mustn't hate God.

Her tears came again. She begged for forgiveness, begged God to reveal to her the reasons for what had happened; and her heart drifted from hatred to love when she thought of Moses Tucker. One moment she was vowing that neither he nor any other man would ever touch her, and the next moment she was praying that God would protect Moss and keep him alive and help him find her. She thought about the love and tenderness in his eyes, the gentleness of his touch. No. He wasn't like Rand Barker and the others. Yet after what she'd been through, the thought of a man touching her at all brought a sickness to her stomach.

All these things floated through her tormented mind during

the moments when she was conscious, which were becoming fewer. Hunger, sickness, and injuries were taking their toll. Her two thin blankets did little to protect her from the damp coldness of the cabin. Her pain was now compounded by a new pain in her chest and ribs. Pneumonia. She was sure of it. It had not been long since her illness in New York.

As death came ever closer, the faith she had thought was gone began to renew itself. She did not want to die alone. She wanted her God with her. She lay on the cot, small and dying, curled into a tiny ball beneath the blankets, too weak to try to get up and feed herself or make a fire and much too lost in this wilderness to even consider trying to find her way out. So she would die here in the little cabin. But not alone.

"Heavenly Father, please don't desert me," she prayed. It seemed she was speaking aloud, but in reality, only her lips moved—lips turned blue from the cold. *"Please take me to your side. Accept me, oh Lord, for I have committed no sins in my heart. They were forced upon me. Please take me, Lord. Take me to your side. Forgive me for losing my faith."*

Her mind drifted again, until the door suddenly burst open. She opened her eyes, but could not move—not only from her sickness and pain, but because what she saw froze her with fear and black dread. Duke Sage stood in the doorway, smiling.

Chapter Seventeen

"Think it's one of Barker's men?" Pappy asked Moss. Moss kicked the stiff body over on its back again.

"He's just a kid. Must have called Barker out."

"Why do you think it was Barker? Why not one of the others?"

"He's a punk kid," Moss replied, lighting a cigar and looking around. "Probably got to thinkin' he was real good with his gun. Figured the best way to prove it was to go against the best: Barker. But no kid his age is gonna outdo Rand."

"You think you could still take him, Moss?" Lonnie asked.

Moss's eyes were studying the terrain carefully.

"I can take him," he answered quietly.

He walked over to an indentation in the snow, then walked over to another area. Then his eyes lit up as though he had an idea. He puffed the cigar and looked around again, going back to the first indentation.

"What is it, Moss?" Pappy asked.

"They split up," Moss said, throwing down cigar. "For some reason they split up. One went one way, and the rest went another. See the snow here? It's lower. They made tracks through the first snow and then some new snow came to cover them, but it's lower 'cause of the tracks. Look here: a narrow path goin' out to the west, and the rest goin' south."

He began pacing nervously.

"Which way do we go?" Lonnie asked.

Moss studied the single tracks again. "Somethin' smells. Maybe they let her off! Maybe one man took her someplace to hide her."

"If that's the case she must have been dying, Moss," Pappy said cautiously.

Moss studied the pathway. "Could be. If she was, whoever took her to hide her could have—"

He turned and quickly mounted his horse.

"I'm goin' down there. The rest of you go on and follow the other tracks for a ways. Get a good idea which way they're going, then circle 'round back here. If she's there, I might need your help in gettin' her to a safer place." He blinked back tears. "Or I might need your help buryin' her."

"You watch yourself, Moss. Whoever took her down there might still be there with her."

The look in Moss Tucker's eyes sent chills down their backs.

"If he is, he's a dead man!" Moss replied in a growl. He turned his horse and headed down the narrow path that led to a canyon. The others rode on.

• • •

Never had Amanda Boone felt more abandoned by God than when Duke Sage entered the little cabin. To have him touch her would be the final hideous degradation to send her into insanity. She lay still and wide-eyed as Sage closed the door, still grinning, and then walked over to the bed. It was only when he began to bend down that she found the strength to move. She squirmed to the farthest corner of the mattress against the wall, and Duke Sage laughed.

"You look like a little lost fawn," he sneered, "waitin' for her big buck to come along and mate with her."

Her fist came to her mouth like a child in fear, and she felt the great sobs of helplessness enveloping her. Her hair was wet with sweat from her raging fever, yet she shivered from cold and fear. Sage bent over the bed and pushed the blankets up, exposing her from the waist down. All she could do was make little animallike squeals. He moved his hand over her as she struggled to pull the blankets back down. Then he laughed and stood up.

"I've wanted you since that first day I grabbed you up on that train, little girl. That damned Rand Barker broke you in, but you're still bound to be good."

He laughed again, and Amanda wished she would quickly die.

"Well, now," Sage continued, looking around. "Ain't no sense rushin' things. I kind of enjoy watchin' you squirm. So in order to really enjoy our little go-round, I think I'll just warm this place up a mite so I can take off my clothes without freezin' to death."

He rubbed his hands together.

"You stay right here, my little fawn. Before long it'll be nice and warm in here."

He walked over to the bed and grabbed her by the hair, making her groan. "Not so perfect and uppity now, are you?" He slapped her and threw her back down, then went out to get wood. Amanda broke into bitter sobbing, her mind and body screaming to die.

"Please, please help me, God! Please make him go away!" she whispered between great, jolting sobs that brought pain when her body jerked. She wriggled into the corner again, groaning with revulsion and dread, wishing she had a weapon. She had never thought herself capable of killing. But she could kill now. She could kill Duke Sage if she had a weapon. But to fight him without one would be useless. She had no strength of any kind left. She couldn't even get up and walk. If God intended to help her, He would simply have to make her die before Duke Sage returned. She lay in the corner, thinking how much worse it would be to be taken by Duke Sage than to simply die.

By the time Sage returned, her fever and fear had turned her into a moaning, mumbling bundle of flesh that resembled a dying animal more than the young woman she had once been. She lay there, waiting for the inevitable horror. Duke

Sage threw some wood into the stone fireplace, cursing and swearing as he tried to get a fire going. In all, it took him nearly an hour to find the wood, bring it in, and get it to burn.

Finally, it stayed lit. He rubbed his hands together again and chuckled with delight. He removed his hat and coat, then sat down in a chair and removed his boots, looking over at Amanda as he did so.

"Well, now, this here little cabin is right cozy, or will be before long. A warm fire and a woman in my bed. A man can't ask for much more than that, can he?" He chuckled and stood up to remove his shirt. Then he rubbed his arms.

"Still a little too cold," he said. He took a small bottle of whiskey from his coat pocket and drank some. "Ah—that'll help warm the blood. Want some?" He held the bottle out to her and she simply closed her eyes and covered her face. She couldn't bear looking at him. Sage simply chuckled. He came over and sat down on the edge of the bed.

"Please!" she whimpered from beneath the blankets. "I'm…sick! Please leave me alone." The blankets shook with her sobs, but Sage only smiled.

"I wish I'd been the one to be first," he told her. "Ole Rand looked mighty satisfied when he met up with us. Damn him! But then at least this way, we've got lots of time. Rand ain't gonna bother comin' back for me. He'll keep going. In the meantime, you and me, we can have us some fun."

• • •

Moss spotted the cabin from above, smoke curling out of the chimney. One horse stood tied near the door. His heart pounded. Was she in there? Who was with her? Perhaps it wasn't Amanda at all. But if it was, he wouldn't give the man a chance to use her to hide behind. Moss Tucker would not be tricked again. He'd barge in and get the job done and get Amanda away from there, if she was there at all.

He dismounted and tied Red to a scraggly oak tree. Then

he went on down by foot. He was cautious as a cat, bobbing between boulders and trees, quickly descending through the snow. Now he was grateful for the snow, as it softened his steps. He moved ever closer to the cabin, from which no sound came. He pulled the Peacemaker from its holster, smiling to himself at how ironic that it was called "Peacemaker." Moss Tucker had no intentions of making peace with anyone who might be inside the cabin with Amanda.

There was only one window, high up. He'd not bother trying to see inside first. He'd simply move in. He crept around the side, then around the corner to the front. The horse tied there looked at him and twitched its ears, and Moss held his breath. But the animal did not whinny. It bent its head and nibbled at some scrubby grass that poked up through the snow. Moss bent over and walked carefully, quietly, along the porch to the door. And then it was time to move, without hesitation. He stood up straight and kicked in the door.

Duke Sage stood up from the bed, wearing only his long underwear, and holding a bottle of whiskey in his hand. He stood staring in temporary disbelief at the sight of Moss Tucker standing in the doorway. Moss's eyes moved quickly to the bed, feeling a wrench at his chest at the pitiful bit of woman who looked back at him with wide, green eyes. Her lips moved as though to say his name, but no sound came out. The blankets were pushed to her waist.

Moss took in the entire scene in a split second. His gun glared at Duke Sage, its cold steel threatening to send a bullet through the ominous hole at the end of the barrel. Sage stared at it, at first dumbstruck. He met Moss Tucker's eyes, and already felt dead. He backed up, dropping the whiskey bottle.

"I ain't touched her, Moss," he finally choked out.

"It appears to me you either did, or you sure as hell intended to!" Moss hissed.

"I didn't! I swear to God, Moss. I've only been here a little while. It—it was Rand! He brought her here first! It was him! A-ask her! She'll tell you—it was Rand!"

"And Rand will get his turn with me!" Moss growled. "But you get to be first, you snake-belly!"

"Wait, Moss—"

The gun fired, and Amanda's body jumped at the terrible boom. She whimpered and covered her ears. Duke Sage screamed out and crumpled to the floor, as blood poured from one knee.

"Bastard!" Moss roared. Sage looked up at him with pleading eyes.

"God, Moss, let me go!" he groaned. "I'll help you find Rand!"

"I can find Rand all by myself!" Moss growled. He fired again, directly into Duke Sage's privates. Amanda covered her eyes and shook. Duke Sage's screams brought an ugly knot to her stomach. Never had she dreamed men could be so violent. Yet it was Moss! It was him! And the terrible thing he was doing was for her vengeance. Her mind raced with confusion and fear as Duke Sage begged for his life, and then begged for death. Moss walked over and placed his gun directly against Duke Sage's forehead.

"You ain't never gonna hurt another woman again, Sage!" he said quietly, his voice cold steel. He calmly pulled the trigger. The bullet did not exit Duke Sage's skull. Moss backed up and let the body slump to the floor. Then he took the man's wrist and dragged the body outside, kicking it into the snow. He stood there a moment, filled with rage and remorse and wanting to cry at the pitiful condition in which he'd seen Amanda. She would need him now, but he wasn't sure he could even face her. It was his fault she was here. He couldn't be sure if it had been only Rand Barker, or all of them. Either way, they had taken his woman. No. She wasn't really his woman. She belonged to herself. But they had violated her. They had stolen something precious and beautiful. How he wished he could change it all for her! How he wished she'd let him make love to her and show her how lovely it could be. But that could never happen now.

He put his gun in its holster and forced himself to walk back inside. Their eyes met, and she cowered into the corner, making animal-like choking sounds and struggling to keep herself covered. Moss closed the door to keep out the cold air. He walked over to the bed, not speaking.

"Don't be…like them!" she whined.

His eyes teared.

"My God, Mandy, how could you think that?" he said in a choked voice.

"Don't…look at me!" she sobbed.

He took off his wolf-skin coat. "Let me help you, Mandy," he said quietly. "You're sick." He reached out with the coat, cautiously climbing onto the bed. The terror in her eyes tore at his heart. He put the coat over her. "I'm—sorry, Mandy," he said, his voice choking up again. "This is all my fault. I—failed you."

The pain in his eyes and the gentle sorrow in his voice removed some of her fear. This was Moss Tucker, the man who had been so kind to her.

"You couldn't help it," she whispered. "You…tried. And you looked for me." She choked in a sob, grasping the beautifully warm coat tight around her neck. "Moss—they—those men—"

"We won't talk about it now, honey. All we're gonna think about is gettin' you well." He reached out and hesitantly touched her forehead. "My God, you're burnin' up! I'll build up the fire!"

"No!" she whimpered when he got up. He turned to look at her, puzzled.

"What?"

"Take me…out of here!" she said in a tiny voice, beginning to shake more again. "Please! Please, Moss! I…hate this… cabin! Take me…away! Please! Please!"

He sighed. "Mandy, it's blowin' and snowin' out there."

"I don't care!" she choked out. She broke into a fit of coughing, and more tears came from the pain in her chest and ribs. "I don't care…if I die," she groaned. "Take me…away from here!"

He came closer again. He knelt down beside the bed.

"All right. I'll do anything you want, just so you don't cry, Mandy. I can't stand to see you cry." He reached out and touched the bruised face, now so very hot from her sickness. "Let me hold you, Mandy. You need somebody to hold you. And I'm so damned glad I've found you. God, Mandy, don't be afraid of me. This is Moses Tucker, remember? Please let me hold you."

"Rand Barker…said you…were just like him," she moaned, the sobs still coming. His eyes teared more.

"Do you believe that?"

Their eyes held a long time, and then she slowly shook her head. "No," she whispered. "But I'm so scared, Moss. You don't know! You don't know!"

"Yes, I do, honey," he said quietly. "But it don't change you. Nothin' can change the beautiful person inside of you."

She put her face down to the mattress and wept. Moss stood up and gently lifted her into his arms. She felt like a little child to him. She hung limp and weak and unresisting. He carried her close to the fire and sat down, holding her on his lap and keeping the blankets and his coat wrapped tightly around her. The hair that was once combed neatly into a bun at her neck now hung loose and long. She rested her head against his chest, and he caressed her hair as she sat shivering and crying. It took him a few moments to find his voice again.

"There's some men with me," he told her. He felt her immediately tense up again. "It's all right, Mandy. They're good men, all of them. They've ridden with me day and night, wantin' to find you just as much as I did. I reckon they'll be along any minute, and we'll decide what to do with you. We'll sit here by the fire and wait. There's not much I can do till they get here." He sighed and kissed her hair.

How strange it felt to be held so gently by this man who had minutes ago killed a man ruthlessly and without feeling.

And even more strange that it should seem so comforting to rest her head against the broad chest and feel comforted by his arms, when minutes earlier the thought of a man touching her brought on nausea. How could there be such a difference in men? Wasn't Moses Tucker also an outlaw? There was so much about him that she didn't know. Perhaps she never would. As the pain in her chest increased and her breathing became more labored, she didn't doubt that she would die in the next day or two.

She heard horses coming, men's voice. She gripped the front of his buckskin shirt.

"It's all right, Mandy. It's just the men who are helpin' me. Nobody's gonna hurt you again, honey."

His voice sounded distant. Again her mind began to float in a world removed from the present. The door opened, and she shrunk closer to Moses Tucker as men's voices were now nearby.

"Looks like somebody out there run into Moss Tucker," somebody was saying. "You want us to leave him or bury him, Moss?"

"Leave him," came the cold reply.

"You found the woman then," an older man's voice said. It was very close, and someone brushed the hair back from her face. "Looks like they used her for a punching bag."

"Looks like that's not all they used her for," came the reply, a voice strained and cracked. It was Moss.

"Sorry, Moss," someone else spoke up. "What do you want to do with her?"

"She's sick," came the voice of the man who held her. "Bad sick. She begged me to take her out of here, and I promised her I would. Is there anyplace nearby we could take her?"

"Slim Taggart's, about five miles east of here," someone spoke up. "He's settled now. Has a ranch and a good woman—married Willie Tanner. Puts us up sometimes. He'd take her, and Willie would be glad to help. You know Willie, Moss. She's a good-hearted woman. Fact is, I expect the little lady there wouldn't mind seein' another woman anyway. I reckon she's kind of tired of lookin' at men."

"I reckon," Moss replied. "Fix up a travois, and bring me all the blankets you can. We'll wrap her up good, slit open the mattress there, put her right inside it, and strap that to the travois. The feathers around all them blankets ought to keep her good and warm until we get her to Taggart's. I just hope she makes it that far."

"She'll make it, Moss. Didn't I tell you she was a strong one?" Lonnie replied.

Moss's arms tightened around her. "We'd best move quick. She needs help."

"Sure, Moss. What about Barker?"

"Barker won't see many more sunrises," came the cold reply. "And he's still got that cross. Soon as she's out of danger, we're goin' on. I'm gonna blow Barker's guts out, and Sollit Weber's! And I'm gonna get that cross back for her if I die doin' it!"

"We're all with you, Moss. Let's go fix up that travois, boys."

"Sorry, Moss," somebody else said. "At least you found her alive."

"I'm obliged to all of you for comin' along to help like you have. I can't pay you back."

"No need to. Not in a case like this."

Someone went out and the door closed. The older man nearby spoke up.

"She's a pretty lady, Moss. Even with them bruises and all, real pretty. I hope it all works out."

"Thanks, Pappy," came the choked voice. "The main thing now is to keep her alive. She don't sound like she's breathin' good. I don't know what I'll do if she goes and dies on me."

"You keep her warm. I'll go get some water. With that fever she ought to drink a lot of water quick. She'll dehydrate."

"Yeah, Pappy. Go get some water."

More footsteps. The door opened and closed again.

"Don't you go and die on me, Mandy," came the whispered voice near her ear. "Not now. Not now that I've found you."

"I knew you'd come," she wanted to say. But the words wouldn't come. It was too hard just to breathe.

Chapter Eighteen

Amanda opened her eyes to see a fire softly burning in a nearby stone fireplace. The wood made little crackling sounds, and it was warm and comforting. Moss sat nearby, unaware that she was watching him. She made no sound at first, wanting to gather her thoughts. Her memories were vague. She closed her eyes again and felt a black coldness sweep through her at the cloudy recollection of Rand Barker. Perhaps it was good that she had been too sick to remember it all clearly. And then there had been the terrible cold and hunger, and the pain from the rape and beating, and from her own illness. And then Duke Sage! She made a little whimpering sound at the thought of that horrible man standing in the doorway, and Moss immediately turned to look at her.

"Mandy!" he said softly, standing up and coming to her bedside. He sat down cautiously on the bed and reached out to touch her forehead. "You finally back in the real world?" he asked with a gentle smile. "Your fever seems to be gone."

She just stared at him a moment. Moss had come! Yes. Moss had come and killed Duke Sage before…

"You're alive!" she whispered.

He smiled and took her hand. "Takes a hell of a lot to put down an old cuss like me, honey. That bullet went clean through and nicked a rib, but that's all. As far as my head, it's hard as a stone, although I've had some headaches the last few days that made me think maybe I'd be better off dead. But the thought of havin' to find you, that helped keep my mind off myself. The question now is you. How do you feel, Mandy? You had me mighty scared."

"I'm…not sure," she replied in a weak voice. She tried to

147

move and groaned with pain, her body still sore from Rand Barker's beating. She lay still again and realized she was in a large, soft, fourposter bed. She felt clean, and she could smell a lovely, lilac scent that seemed to be coming from her. She took her arms out from under the quilts and touched the long sleeves of a soft, flannel nightgown that did not belong to her. She looked at Moss curiously.

"Oh, that belongs to Willie. Wilena Taggart. Her and Slim Taggart own this place. That's their bed you're in. Me and Willie have been watchin' over you, forcin' food down your throat when you didn't even know what was goin' on."

She began to redden and her eyes filled with tears, and he knew what was going through her mind.

"You were a real sick girl, Mandy. And hurt bad besides. And I care about you. When a man cares about somebody, he don't think about anything but helpin' that person. That's all that matters. Do you think I'd have got out of bed before I was supposed to, and rode night and day—hardly eatin' or sleepin', searchin' like I did—if I didn't care?"

Her body jerked in a sob, and she put a hand over her face.

"God, Mandy, don't do that," he said softly, squeezing her hand. "You remember what I told you once about the different ways a man looks at a woman? Willie needed help with you, so I helped. That's all. I helped her 'cause—'cause I care so much for you, Mandy. And I was so scared you was gonna die on me. And the worst part was it was all my fault. I'll never live down lettin' a man get the better of me like Sollit Weber did. Never. I'm so sorry, Mandy. So damned sorry! I reckon I hate myself more than you ever will."

"No, no," she choked out. "I don't hate you, Moss. I was… so afraid he'd…killed you. You were so…kind to watch after me in the first place. You…hardly know me."

"A man don't need to know a woman like you very long to care about her. I wish you wouldn't cry, Mandy."

"I can't…help it! They were so…ugly! So mean and

ugly!" Her sobbing heightened and he frowned with concern. "They...touched me!"

He stood up and leaned over her.

"You gotta calm down and not think about it, honey. It's over now."

"No! No! Not in my mind! They...took my clothes. I was so...cold! Rand Barker was...angry with me. All of them...so cruel and ugly—"

"Mandy, don't."

Her body was shaking violently now. He reached down and scooped her up in his arms, blankets and all. He pulled her onto his lap and held her tightly; and he was somehow very different from the men who had given her the awful memories. His arms were hard and strong, yet they held her as gently as though she were china. How secure and safe they made her feel!

"Rand Barker...took me to that...cabin—"

"Be still, Mandy," he told her, gently stroking the hair that hung long and thick down her back. His arms tightened around her, and with her head against his chest, she could not see the tears in his eyes, but his voice was choked with compassion.

"He never touched you, Amanda Boone. You understand me? A woman can't be touched unless she's willin' to be touched. And she can't give nothin' away unless she's willin' to give it away. And till that happens, then it still belongs to her. Everything: her body, her soul, her heart. It belongs to just her. And that God of yours, he'd never hold you liable, nor would any man."

"I don't...have a God any more," she whimpered.

"Aw, Mandy, don't you talk like that. Not you."

The door to the room opened a crack.

"I thought I heard voices. Is she all right, Moss?" a woman's voice asked.

"I think her fever's gone," he spoke up. "You think you could fix up some soup or somethin' for her?"

"Sure. I'll be right back."

Amanda's tears subsided somewhat, but Moss continued to hold her.

"Time will heal everything for you, Mandy," he told her. "You're too special, too sweet and lovely and too full of love, to let this change you. Don't let that happen, honey. 'Cause if you do, then Rand Barker will have won. Even when he dies by my hands, he'll have won. 'Cause he'll have beat you down and turned you away from your God and all that love that's inside of you."

She turned her face to look up into his. How gentle his eyes were. How handsome his face was. And how strange to be held in the arms of this man who had killed Duke Sage so savagely. Her mind raced with confusion. How different he was from the others. How could men be so different? And how could this man have killed Duke Sage and then turned around and handled her so gently, his eyes so full of softness and love. Yes, love. It was there, written all over his face. How sad to see that love. For she could never return it, not now.

"What do you mean...when he dies?" she asked in a near whisper.

He reached over to the dresser for a handkerchief that lay on top of it. He gently wiped the tears from her eyes, himself frowning.

"This deal's not over yet," he told her, the eyes suddenly turning colder. "There's vengeance to be had, and they've still got the crucifix. Me and the boys that are along with me, we've all just been waitin' to see if you'd make it. Now that you're better, I'll be leavin' out soon, Mandy. Rand Barker and Sollit Weber have to die by my hands, else I'd go crazy with a need for revenge."

"No!" she whimpered, grasping the front of his shirt. "That's what he wants you to do! That's why he—why he..."

She dropped her eyes, and began to shake again. She put her head against his chest again.

"That boy Dean Taylor...he accused Barker...of being afraid of you," she choked out. "So Barker called him out...

and shot him…and then he—he wanted to prove to the others he wasn't afraid of you or what you'd do if he…hurt me. That's why he—"

"No more, Mandy. Don't you be thinkin' on it no more. He's gonna die, and I'll get the crucifix back, and I'll get you to that mission in California. And by God, nobody will ever hurt you again ever! Not ever!"

"But…he'll kill you! He's so…fast, Moss! So fast!"

"Well, I'm faster. I've already beat him once, only my bullet didn't kill him. That's too bad. This time I aim to make sure he don't ever hurt somebody again like he hurt you. And that pink-faced, smilin' Sollit Weber won't be smilin' when Moss Tucker gets done with him, neither."

His mention of having shot it out with Rand Barker once before reminded her that the man who held her now had once been an outlaw himself. Perhaps he even still was. And Barker had told her Moss was just like the others. But how could that be? Not Moses Tucker. Yet the thought of his mysterious past now frightened her, and he felt her stiffen in his arms. She looked up at him again, and he put a big hand to the side of her face.

"I didn't mean to scare you with my talk, Mandy."

Their eyes held.

"Tell me," she whispered.

"Tell you what?"

"Tell me you—you were never like them."

He frowned and did not reply right away. His eyes filled with remorse, and he suddenly looked like a little boy who had done something wrong and was very sorry.

"No, Mandy," he said quietly. "I was never like that. But I came close. And before I head out after Barker I—I want to tell you somethin' about myself, about why I was goin' to California. Because if I don't come back, there's somethin' I want you to do for me. I don't have anybody else I can ask, and maybe that's why your God led you and me together. Maybe it was supposed to be this way. Now you understand evil and

I have somebody that maybe can help me, and both of us—we've had a crazy kind of friendship, haven't we?"

He smiled softly, but his eyes were full of fear that perhaps she would turn against him. It was much the same look he'd given her back at the restaurant when someone had recognized him.

"I love you, Mandy," he told her, not knowing himself why he had suddenly blurted it out. It was as though someone else had made him say it. But she looked so small and helpless there in his arms. How he wished he could make love to her and show her how sweet and good it could be. She reddened and closed her eyes.

"Don't say that," she whispered. "I can't love you. Not now."

"You're no different than you were a week ago," he told her. "No different. But even without that, I'd not expect you to love me back, 'cause you're one fine lady. Me—I'm nothing, and probably never will be. I only ask one thing in return, Mandy. Just one."

She opened her eyes and looked at him curiously.

"I—I have a little girl in California," he told her quietly. For a brief moment she forgot all her other problems. She was amazed that this man had a child!

"She's—she's got no ma now. I was goin' out there to get her settled someplace. I just want your promise that if I don't come back, you'll go on out there when you're well and see she gets to that mission where you was going. I already wrote a letter givin' my permission, and I have an address where you can find her. Will you do that, Mandy?"

"Of course," she replied without hesitation. "But you've got to explain, Moss."

"I will." He stood up and laid her on the bed, tucking the blankets in around her. She studied him. He wore the buckskins she'd imagined him in when she first met him, and he looked every bit the mountain man, just like the men of the West she'd read about.

"First I want you to get some more rest. Willie will be in here soon. I'll feed you and you can sleep a while again. Then we'll talk and I'll introduce you to the men who are gonna help me find Barker."

"Were they all...there...when you found me?" she asked, turning scarlet and her eyes tearing again. She vaguely remembered her filthy and unclothed condition when Moss had barged in just as Duke Sage was preparing to give her the same horrible, humiliating pain that Rand Barker had given her.

"No. Not right away." He bent closer and stroked the hair back from her face. "They're a damned good bunch, Mandy. I don't know how to explain it to somebody like you. These men, most of them are outlaws, and so was I. But even outlaws have a sort of code among themselves, Mandy. And the first rule out here is a man don't hurt and humiliate a good woman. He don't use his strength against her. That's cowardly, yellow, unmanly. It's damned wrong, and what Rand Barker did— that only got him in deeper, 'cause now he's got his own kind against him. I'm not worried about findin' him, 'cause there'll be more men like the ones with me who'll be waitin' for him down by Robber's Roost. He can't even ride in outlaw territory and be safe now. This kind of news travels fast. They'll all keep Barker trapped and runnin' in all directions till I can come for him. They all know they'd best save him for me."

She thought to herself what a strange mixture of good and bad he was, gentleness and cruelty. How she longed to know more about him. She suddenly wished she could tell him she loved him. On the train she had thought she was falling in love. But how could she love any man the way a wife should love a husband now? How could she let any man touch her that way? It was ugly and painful and humiliating. Could she expect it to be any different with Moses Tucker? Perhaps. But she did not intend to find out, not ever.

The door opened again, and a woman entered. She looked about twenty-five, maybe a little older. Her hair was ash blond and her eyes a gentle blue, and her stomach swelled out in front of her, great with child. She carried a tray, and Moss immediately walked over and took it from her.

"Thanks, Willie."

The woman smiled and leaned over Amanda, feeling the girl's forehead.

"I'm Wilena Taggart," she said in a kindly voice. "You can call me Willie. How are you feeling?"

"Everything hurts," Amanda replied.

"I expect so. You were a pretty battered girl when Moss brought you in. But we're going to see that you get all mended. You're welcome to stay right here in this bed as long as it takes. We've already sent word that you've been found."

"I'm…very grateful, Willie. I…can't thank you enough. I must be putting you out."

"Nonsense! Out here helping people is never any trouble," the woman replied with a smile. "Moss here, and those men out there, they all feel the same way. A pretty girl needed help and she got it." She straightened up and folded her arms, resting them on her stomach. "And if I know Moss, Rand Barker and the rest of them won't be able to run far enough now! They might have a few days' head start, but that won't keep Moss from finding them, will it, Moss?"

"I'd follow them straight into hell," Moss replied, sitting down on the bed with the tray.

Willie Taggart chuckled. "You eat good now, Amanda. I've got six men to prepare a meal for! And I'm eating for two myself!" She smiled and patted her stomach, and Moss looked at her with admiration.

"You're gonna make Slim one happy man, Willie," he told her.

"Well, that's what I'm here for, right?" she replied. She turned and walked to the door. "You call if you need anything else, Moss."

"You take it easy," he replied. "You're workin' too hard."

"Hard work never hurt anybody."

The woman went out, and Moss turned to Amanda.

"She seems very nice," Amanda told him.

"She is. She's just about as good and sweet as you."

Amanda reddened again, and Moss dipped a spoon into a bowl of soup. He held it out to Amanda, and she opened her mouth and swallowed it. It was hot and delicious.

"She's also a good cook," Amanda told him.

"Slim thinks so." He dipped the spoon again. "Slim was a drifter, worthless as hell like the rest of us, till he met up with Wilena. She shook his tail out good, turned him full circle. That man would walk off a cliff, if Wilena told him to do it. Yet she's never raised her voice to him. She just loves him quietly. He's got himself a good woman, set up to ranchin' here, quit his old ways." She watched him as he fed her. "I reckon that's all most men need: a good woman to keep them straight."

Their eyes held a moment.

"I'm...deeply grateful, Moss, for what you've done for me. I wish...I could return your love. But not now, Moss. I can never be a wife." She tried to look away, but his eyes held hers in a strangely magnetic power.

"You shouldn't say never, Mandy." If only she would let him kiss her, touch her. How wonderful it would be if he could marry someone like Amanda and keep his little girl and raise her himself. He would like to live like Slim Taggart did now. And he would like to see Amanda great with child—his child.

A tear slipped down the side of her face.

"I'm...sorry, Moss. All I want now is to go to California... and see Father Mitchel...and try to pick up the pieces."

He swallowed and put on a smile. "Don't be sorry, Mandy. It's good to hear you say even that much." He fed her some more soup. She could see the pain behind his smile of assurance. "You're already thinkin' about goin' on with life, and that's good," he continued. "Heck, I—I already told you I didn't expect nothin' back, me bein' what I am and all. I'll be happy just knowin' all that's happened—well, that it won't change you or make you bitter and sour on life, that it won't take away all that natural love and beauty inside of you. Like I said, that would be lettin' men like Barker win, and that would be a pretty sorry thing to let happen. I just—well, I'd like to bring my little girl to that mission and, like I said, if I don't make it back, I'd like your promise you'll go and get her for me."

"I will, Moss."

She ate some more.

"Moss."

"Hmmm?"

"It's not you. Please believe me, Moss. Please don't say you're not good enough. You are. You're good, Moss. It's just… the others. I don't think I could ever get over it. But it isn't you, Moss. If things were different—"

"It's all right, Mandy. You finish eatin' here and rest some more, and we'll talk before I leave."

Her eyes drooped.

"Will you stay here till I fall asleep?"

"Sure I will."

He managed to get another bite into her mouth, but then her eyes closed. They felt heavy, and she could not make them open.

"Thank you…for being my friend, Moss," she said, her words beginning to slur. He carefully set the tray on the floor. Then he took her hand and held it. How small and light it felt in his large palm.

"Thank you for bein' mine," he replied.

"I hope…you find what you're looking for," she whispered.

He studied her silently for a moment.

"I already have," he replied. "But I can't keep it."

She was already asleep. Their few minutes of conversation had taken their toll on her beaten and exhausted body. Moss leaned down, taking advantage of the moment by kissing her cheek softly.

"Damn it, I love you, Mandy," he whispered. "God help me, I love you so much. I just wish I was good enough for you."

Chapter Nineteen

She was awakened by her own screams, as the nightmare brought leering, oddly proportioned faces into her mind—Duke Sage, Sollit Weber, Rand Barker. She felt the pain—the hated pain deep inside of her—as Rand Barker pushed inside of her, laughing and holding her arms. Someone held her arms now, and she fought and screamed more. It would happen again. She could feel the strength. She would feel the pain again, and she struggled to keep from letting it happen.

Someone was talking to her. Now her arms were brought around to the front of her, crisscrossed and held firmly by the same strong hands that had held her down only a moment earlier. Someone held her tightly now from behind, talking and talking. The voice was not gruff, but gentle. The pain did not come. Yet she was held immobile on a bed—immobile and almost completely engulfed in someone's arms, dwarfed by them. Now she lay gasping for breath, her screams subsiding as reality began to make its appearance and sleep left her.

"Wake up, Mandy!" someone was saying. "It's all right. You was just dreaming. It was just a bad dream, honey."

"Is she all right, Moss?" a woman's voice asked.

"She will be in a minute."

"So...ugly! Ugly! Ugly!" Amanda groaned, her body now shaking with sobs. "So ugly!"

"Hush, Mandy!" he told her. "Don't think on it. Open your eyes now, honey, and get back to reality."

"Don't let them...come back!"

"They won't come back," he promised her. "In a few more days they won't even be alive any more."

"I...feel so...soiled," she wailed.

157

"Don't you say that!" he groaned, keeping a tight hold on her. "Wasn't none of it your fault, Mandy! None of it! You're still beautiful and precious and special. So, so special, Mandy. Don't say things like that. You're much too special. Now you just shake them thoughts out of your head. Willie will get you some coffee, and you and me will talk, Mandy. Okay? Let's talk. Maybe that will help get your mind on somethin' else."

The door closed. Willie had gone out of the room. Amanda's breathing came easier, and she began to relax in Moss's arms.

How soft and sweet she was! And how close her lips were when she turned slightly to look at him—how temptingly close. How he loved her and longed to show her how it could be. How he ached to taste her lips again. He wondered if she even remembered that kiss on the train. Their eyes held. What was going through her mind?

"It's not like that, Mandy. It's nothin' like they made it seem," he found himself saying. She just looked at him. "It's nice, Mandy—beautiful. And you're beautiful," he finished in a whisper.

His lips met hers once more, searching hungrily but gently, parting her own lips without effort, while his hold on her lightened, and one of his big hands moved to the side of her face. He groaned lightly in his terrible need of her, his longing love for her, and she wanted it to be all right. But then the hungry and lonely man within moved too quickly. He whispered her name, caressing her cheek with his lips, and she realized he was still a man—like the others. It was all too new, too soon. Again the ugly memories came. His lips moved to hers again, but she went rigid and pushed at him.

"Go away!" she found herself saying. "You're just like the rest! Go away! Go away!" Her voice broke and the tears came, and she scooted back like a frightened child.

Moss stood up, looking devastated.

"Jesus, I'm sorry, Mandy. I just—I love you. I thought I could show you—"

"Don't you touch me again!" she sobbed, pulling the covers up around her neck. Why was she saying that? The pain in his eyes stabbed at her heart. He looked like a lost child.

"I'm—I'm sorry. I had no right," he replied. "I wouldn't have hurt you, Mandy. Not for the world." Their eyes held, and she said nothing. He reached in his pocket and took out some papers. "This is my letter…and the address where my little girl is. I don't reckon you feel like talkin' to me now. So I guess I'll just be ridin' on, go after Barker. You—you rest, Mandy. I'll be back with the cross."

He laid the papers on the bed and quickly walked out. She tried to call out to him, but the words stuck in her throat.

She heard voices in the outer room. Moss was giving orders. Chairs were scooted around, and then there was the sound of heavy footsteps, voices, and confusion. After several minutes a door opened and closed a few times, and now she could hear voices outside.

"Moss?" she whispered, wiping at tears. "Don't go, Moss. I'm sorry!"

She struggled to get up, and walked on rubbery legs over to the window, pulling aside the curtain. Moss and four other men were walking a distance from the house now, toward a stall. She stared out the window and watched them saddle up. They looked no different from the men who had kidnaped her and abused her, yet they were different. She didn't want them to leave—not yet. She hated herself for being so cruel. He'd been nothing but kind and good to her. And the kiss—she touched her lips. How warm and lovely it had been when, for that brief moment, she had allowed the beauty of it to flow through her. But then came the ugliness, the realization that, in the end, the same humiliating and painful act would occur if she were to marry and give herself to a man. No. She could not bear that. Yet women did it all the time, and they had children all the time. Mrs. Taggart herself was now pregnant. Surely it was not always the way she pictured it. And wasn't that all poor Moss was trying to tell her? Had his intentions been bad after all?

"What on earth did you say to that man?" Willie Taggart's voice came from behind her. Amanda turned to face the woman. She looked Willie over, the stomach large with child. Perhaps this woman could help her sort out her emotions. Amanda had never had a woman to talk to—not a woman who had been through it all and who knew.

Their eyes held a moment.

"I guess I already know," Willie told her. "Did Moss kiss you, Amanda?"

Amanda did not reply. She turned back around and watched out the window. They were mounting up now. Moss moved into the saddle as though he were born to it. He sat there, lighting up a cigar. He glanced back at the house, but he could not see her watching him. He rode out a ways, looking out over the horizon, waiting for everyone to get ready. He rode back, looking magnificent and fearsome on the huge, reddish colored horse. Finally, all of them were ready. They rode out. Her chest felt tight. What if he didn't come back? They'd never even talked like they had planned to do. She turned to look at Willie Taggart again.

"Tell me about Moses Tucker," she said in a small voice.

Willie came over to her side and helped her back into bed.

"You lie down and I'll bring you some hot broth and some bread, and we'll talk," she told Amanda.

Amanda fell wearily back into bed, her heart aching and heavy. What had she done? How she wished he would come back. But she'd made him feel unwanted and unworthy, and perhaps he would die trying to get her cross back for her. She wanted to pray for him, but it was still difficult to pray. She thought about the little ebony jewelry box. What had happened to it? And where were the personal belongings she'd brought along? It seemed everything was gone, including the old Amanda Boone. The past week had drastically affected her life. Had New York and the sisters ever existed? Was there truly a Father Mitchel and a mission school? And who was Amanda Boone now? Was she the same? Surely not, or she would never have been so cruel to someone who had been so kind to her.

Willie left for a few minutes, then returned with a tray and helped Amanda sit up.

"Behind the curtain over there in the corner is a place where you can go to the bathroom without going outside," the woman told Amanda. "Do you need to use it? We keep it very clean, and my husband empties it frequently."

Amanda reddened. "No, I—I'm fine." How primitive everything was out here in this strange land. Life was hard, cruel. No wonder Willie Taggart was married. A woman needed a man in wild, untamed places like this. She needed a man who was strong: a man of courage, sure and quick in his actions. She glanced at Willie Taggart's stomach as the woman got the tray and set it on Amanda's lap. Then Willie pulled a chair over to the bed and sat down, pushing some hair behind her ear and looking very tired.

"Are you...due to deliver soon, Mrs. Taggart?"

"Oh, please, remember to call me Willie," the woman replied with a smile. She sighed and patted her stomach. "It'll be about six weeks yet."

"Aren't you afraid? I mean, you're so far from help."

"I'll have Slim with me. And there are some Arapaho women not far from here who will come and assist me. They'll take care of that part of it, and Slim will give me courage—and something to hang on to!" she added with a light laugh. Their eyes held a moment. Willie Taggart sighed again. "Slim is so excited over this baby," she went on. "I'm proud to give him a child, and glad to make him so happy. He's a good man, Amanda. There's nothing more fulfilling than to be loved and cared for by a good man, and to share everything together. I give him the things he needs, and he gives me the things I need. I know what's going through your mind. But with the right man...it's glorious and wonderful, Amanda. And in my opinion, God led you to Moss Tucker for a reason."

Amanda picked up a biscuit. She stared at it a moment. "Did Moss tell you to say that?"

"No, he did not," the woman replied. "It's my own opinion. He told us all about you—about the mission and all, about your wanting to be a nun. I think that's wonderful. But I also think perhaps God intends for you to do something else with your life. Sometimes we have to go where fate leads us, Amanda."

Amanda took a bite of the biscuit, then drank some hot broth.

"My life…was so different from all of this," she said quietly. She looked at Willie Taggart. "Tell me about Moss. He left so much out. He was going to talk to me, but I…" She reddened. "You were right. He kissed me and I said some cruel words."

Willie smiled. "Moss came out of here looking like a little boy who'd just been punished. He loves you, you know. And when a man like Moss Tucker loves someone, you can bet it's a whole lot, because Moss is his own man—usually quiet and a little mean in temperament. But you could take that big, ex-outlaw and lead him by the nose into quicksand, and he'd go willingly. You've got him lassoed good. I've never seen so much emotion in that man's face. And I caught him wiping away tears more than once when you were so sick we thought you'd die. He's sat here for three days, just waiting to see if you'd make it. And if I were you, I'd give that man some thought. He'd be good to you, Amanda. And he needs someone. He's very, very lonely, and I'm sure down deep inside he'd like to keep his little girl. But he figures a man like him wouldn't be able to raise a child right—not without a woman to help him. If you turn him away—and if he has to give up his little girl because he can't take care of her himself—well, I'm just afraid he'll go off the deep end and turn meaner than ever. Probably get himself in trouble again, go to jail again."

Amanda set her cup down. "He's been in jail before?"

"Oh, yes! And believe me, prison does not help a man! It only makes him meaner and more bitter. And in poor Moss's case, he didn't even do anything to deserve going. His life has been hard luck since the first day he was born."

"He told me…his mother was a prostitute…in Chicago."

A strange look passed over Willie's face, and she reddened slightly. "And what do you think of prostitutes, Amanda?"

Now Amanda reddened, confused as to why the woman would ask her that. "I—I'm not sure. I don't understand why a woman would be that way. But on our trip out here Moss helped me find a place to stay one night—and I'm certain the ladies there were not exactly proper. But they were very kind to me, very kind. I believe that God loves everyone, and therefore I must love everyone…as much as I can. Except people like Rand Barker—I could never love or forgive someone like that. And that's something I have to deal with myself, I guess. I'd not make a very good nun if my heart held the bitterness and hatred it holds right now."

"Time can heal many things," Willie told her. Amanda toyed with a dish of hot vegetables.

"Why did you ask me about prostitutes?" she asked Willie.

The woman looked away and stood up.

"Let's talk about Moses Tucker," she replied. Amanda frowned in curiosity and stabbed at a carrot, then put it in her mouth. She did not know this young woman well enough to pursue the matter.

"I'm sorry," she spoke up. "I'm not very good at making new friends, Willie. I spent most of my life behind the walls of an orphanage with people I grew up with. Please go on—about Moss, I mean. I want to know all about him—and who were those men who rode out with him? And where are my things?"

"Whoa! One question at a time!" She turned to face Amanda again and came back to sit down. "Let's see now. We'll save Moss for last. First off, those four men with Moss were Darrell Hicks, Pappy Lane, Johnny Pence and Cal Story. There was a fifth man, Lonnie Drake. He helped track you down. But he had to go back to Brown's Park. He had business there, and he knows Moss and the others can do a good job of getting Barker's gang."

"Lonnie Drake. He's the one who—who saw me that night in Barker's camp at Brown's Park."

"Yes. But he didn't have enough men with him at the time to do anything about it. So he waited for Moss to come along—which he knew he would—and he helped Moss hunt for you."

"It's so strange—those men caring like that. Are they all outlaws?"

"Most. Oh, a couple of them are temporarily reformed, till the next easy deal comes along." She laughed lightly. "Of course, my Slim is through with it, now that he has a wife, and a child on the way."

Amanda smiled now. This woman seemed extremely proud of her marriage and her pregnancy.

"And where are my things—the things I had on the train?" she asked.

"Oh, they're still in Bear River City, waiting for your return."

Amanda sighed, wondering how she could return now, wondering just how she would start her life over.

"I need to know more about Moss Tucker, Willie. Do you know him well?"

"Yes, I do. And most of us who've known Moss know the story. Slim knows him well. They rode together for a while. And, yes, Moss was born in Chicago to a prostitute, like he told you. There are all kinds of people, Amanda—good and bad—no matter what their station in life. Just like with outlaws. Some are basically good like Moss, Slim, and the others. And some are very, very bad—like Rand Barker. And there are prostitutes who, although their morals are slightly misplaced, are kind and loving people. And there are bad ones. Moss's mother was a bad one. She neglected him terribly, and he ran the streets. That's where he learned to be tough, learned to fight, and got his first lessons in how to steal. He learned that only the strong survive.

"Moss had no family life to speak of. But he knew people had to live better than he did in Chicago. At thirteen he ran away: away from the mother who shamed and abused him, away from the back alleys. He hopped a train to St. Paul, Minnesota. Moss was always big for his age, he tells us. He lied about his age and got a job in a factory. Worked there till he was eighteen—worked about seventy-five hours a week. He saved his money carefully—told us he had decided to go west into country he'd heard some tall tales about. Country where a man could be free, be his own man, breathe fresh air, and start life over. That was his dream. To make good, to make something of himself. So he saved and saved. Then took his money and went west at eighteen to look for gold. He slaved away in the Sierra Nevadas to find his fortune. And that was when he became more mountain man than anything else—learned to fight Indians, and learned to use a gun to protect himself from claim jumpers."

"He told me he once had a claim—struck gold. But he told me he lost it all. He didn't say how or why," Amanda spoke up.

Willie got up and walked over to put some more wood on the fire.

"Yes, he found gold. Staked his claim. Then he spent five years or better working it all by himself. That was near Virginia City. He set up a bank account there, got himself real organized. Moss is good down deep inside—and a hard worker, Amanda. A real hard worker. He'd work his fingers to the bone for the right person. In this case, it was for himself and his dream: to get rich, find a nice woman to marry, and make something of himself. At twenty-four he sold his claim—made a tidy profit, along with what he already had in the bank. He'd made his fortune, and the time had come to find a wife and settle down. So, he cleaned himself up and went to San Francisco."

"The woman," Amanda said, fascinated with the story. "He told me there'd been a woman in California he loved."

"Yes. He met and fell in love with the daughter of a prominent banker. She was wealthy, beautiful and educated. Unfortunately, her interest in Moss—other than his handsomeness and that his big, strong body of his—was the fact that he was rich. In the case of a woman like that, being rich was of the utmost importance. And it was even more important to her father. Yet money alone was not enough. The man had to have background. And while Moses Tucker was following Etta Graceland around like a lost puppy, she was thinking about how much richer she would be if she married him, and her father was having Moss checked out. Well, in a family of money, need I tell you how her father felt about Moses Tucker when he discovered Moss was born a bastard, brought up in a brothel, and ran the streets of Chicago?"

Amanda moved her tray to the side of the bed. She frowned with pity, and Willie nodded.

"Yes. James Graceland, prominent, wealthy banker of San Francisco, could not even consider allowing his lovely and well-bred daughter marry a bastard. He was so angry that Moss had kept it a secret that he set out to ruin Moses Tucker and send Moss back into the cesspool of life where he'd come from—put Moss in his place, so to speak. And James Graceland had power. Without Moss's knowledge of what was going on behind his back, James Graceland made arrangements with the banker in Nevada. The money was funneled out of Moss's account very cleverly. Of course, to this day Moss has never been able to prove that Graceland was behind the deal. He doesn't have the power and the connections Graceland has. But it was pretty obvious Graceland was behind it.

"Then one evening when Moss went to pick Etta up for an evening at the theater, the girl was in tears. She read Moss up one side and down the other—asked him why he lied to her about his past, why he'd led her on. She told him she'd never have let him put his hands on her if she'd known he was a bastard. She kicked him out of the house and told him never to come back. Needless to say, Moss was devastated. He really loved that girl."

"What did he do then? What about his money?"

"He didn't know what to do at first. He was heartbroken over Etta. Even to this day, when he speaks about it, it's obvious it still hurts him. He'd worked so hard to make a better life for himself, to move up a little in life. He returned to Nevada to gather his thoughts, to try and get over Etta. But then when he got there, he was told he had no account with the bank. Moss Tucker was penniless. You can imagine the things that must have gone through his mind then. He'd lost Etta, and now he'd been swindled out of all that hard-earned money. Years, it took. All those years of work and sweat and saving—only to have it all stolen from under his nose, with no way of proving what had happened. Someone had also stolen or destroyed all records of his account. Moss had nothing."

"Dear Lord, what did he do?" Amanda asked, totally lost now in Moss Tucker's plight. She had forgotten the pain and soreness that still grasped at her, and she even forgot the past week and all its horror. Willie was glad to be able to take the girl's mind off herself for a while.

"Well, a man like Moss—he's his own man, Amanda. Moss has a temper. And he'd just been swindled out of all that money. He felt helpless, and the frustration of it—combined with losing Etta—it just got to him. He'd never had a happy life, and after his long struggle to find a little happiness, it had all been thrown in his face. He grabbed the owner of the bank in Nevada and started beating on the man—told him he wanted the truth about what had happened to his money, and wanted a confession that James Graceland had planned it all. But the man wouldn't confess to anything. Moss just went kind of crazy, and he pulled out a small handgun from his vest and shot the banker."

"Oh, no!"

"Oh, yes. Luckily for Moss, the man didn't die. That got Moss five years in prison instead of a noose around his neck.

In prison, his bitterness only got worse. He had five years to sit and brood about James Graceland and the way he had not only cheated Moss out of his money, but also the woman he loved. Not that Etta Graceland would have made much of a wife in the long run. But Moss wasn't thinking about that then. He still loved her. And in all that time he never heard one word from her. He was left alone, broke and without a friend. When he finally got out of prison, the first thing he did was try to find Etta. But she'd married an attorney and moved to Los Angeles, as had her father. So all of it was gone. All of it. And Moses Tucker didn't give a damn about anything, if you'll pardon my use of the word. He figured he was pretty worthless."

"It bothers him very much, doesn't it?" Amanda asked. "His being a—a bastard and all, I mean."

"Oh, yes. It bothers him. I think that's part of the reason he'd like to take his little girl. I'm sure he'll at least make sure she knows who he is. He'll keep in touch, make sure she'll always know who her father is—even though he was never married to her mother."

"Who's the mother?" Amanda asked, feeling jealousy rising again.

"I'll get to that. Moss—he turned very bitter after going back to San Francisco. He just sort of gave up for a while. I guess he figured if people thought him worthless, well, maybe he *was* worthless. And he'd lost his incentive to work and make something of himself. So he went east—oh, not all the way, just to Wyoming—and took up with some men he'd met in prison."

"Rand Barker!" Amanda said in a near whisper.

"Yes. Rand was one. They rode together. And Moss turned to cattle rustling for money. He figured if it couldn't work doing it the right way, he just didn't care any more. And his heart was still shattered over Etta Graceland. Losing the woman he loves can do all kinds of things to a man, Amanda. I've seen men cry, get themselves filthy drunk, even want to kill themselves over a woman. I've seen—"

Willie stopped short and reddened slightly again. Then she quickly continued on talking about Moss.

"At any rate, Moss turned to a life of rustling—even robbed a couple of banks in revenge for what a banker had done to him. And he got much better with his gun. It seemed to be a natural talent for him. His reputation grew, and men called him out. Moss has killed several men, Amanda."

Amanda ran a hand through her hair, trying to get it all straight in her mind. What a complicated man Moses Tucker was, and what a lonely man. She felt sorry for him; yet the fact remained he'd killed men. It confused her feelings.

"They were all worthless and better off dead, Amanda," Willie went on. "And they all called Moss out of their own free will. Moses Tucker does not go looking for fights. They come to him. And he's quite respected among the men who live in this territory. Not one of them in his right mind will give Moses Tucker any trouble—not if he expects to live. That's why Rand Barker is running scared now. He's already gone against Moss once and lost. He's lucky to be alive."

"What was it about?" Amanda asked.

"Well, they picked up Duke Sage along the way."

Amanda made a face and grasped at her stomach.

"He's a horrible man," she whispered.

"I know. But at that time he wasn't quite that bad. Then one night they raided a stockyard. There was a wagon train camped nearby. A woman came out to help her husband try to herd back some of the cattle they'd just sold to the stockyards and that were being stolen by Rand and Moss and the others. Duke Sage grabbed the woman."

"Oh, no!"

"He rode off with her. Moss spotted three small children near the wagon. He knew by the way they were crying and carrying on that the woman must be their mother. He left the cattle behind and rode out after Sage. Rand Barker followed. Duke Sage wasted no time in getting the woman into the bushes, and he was preparing to—well, I don't need to tell you."

Amanda's eyes teared as she tried to keep her mind on Moss and off of her ugly memories.

"Moss rode up and jumped on Duke Sage. He beat the man pretty bad. Rand considered himself the leader of that particular scheme to steal cattle, and consequently he also figured Moss had no business interfering with what the other men did. Rand said it was his place to decide what to do with the woman, and what to do about Duke Sage. Sage was in pretty bad shape by the time Rand got there. Moss went kind of crazy. I guess because of the way his mother had been, Moss—well, he has this very deep respect for a good woman: a woman who lives right, is loyal to one man and all. He just couldn't stand the thought of Duke Sage taking what belonged to another man. At any rate he hollered back at Rand Barker that he had no intention of riding with men who would violate a good woman. Barker got his dander up and said a man had a right to do whatever he wanted. Well, you can imagine how it went after that—two stubborn men who were both good with a gun. Barker drew on Moss—but Moss, he's fast. He's faster than Barker will ever be."

"I—I can hardly believe someone could be faster than that."

"Well, Moss Tucker is. He shot Barker and left him there. Then he took the woman back to her family, and he rode west again. He just lit out and rode back to California. He decided he didn't want to be a part of that kind of thing—not taking women. And he felt stronger inside again, the sores were healing. He decided he'd try once more to do something better with his life. So he got a job in Sacramento working for a blacksmith. He was thirty-four then. He figured with his past, no decent woman would ever marry him. So he took up with a prostitute, Betsy Malone. They lived together, and while they lived together Betsy remained true to Moss. Fact is, I guess she loved him, and Moss loved her. Oh, it probably wasn't the kind of love between a man and wife, but they were good friends and they needed each other. Moss was good to her, and she was good to him. But both knew it wasn't something permanent so they didn't marry."

"I—I don't understand a relationship like that. I mean, I wish I could. But I—I could never live like that."

"Of course not. A girl like you wouldn't understand. She wouldn't be expected to understand."

"And Betsy—she's the mother?"

"Yes. But she's dead now."

"Oh, how sad. Why was Moss in Chicago? Why wasn't he out in California with Betsy and his little girl?"

"Because he'd been sent back to prison."

"My goodness! What for?"

"Well, some money came up missing at the blacksmith's. Moss didn't take it. But since he was fairly new in his job he was suspected. And when the owner found out about Moss's past record—the fact that he'd been in prison before, and that Moss was suspected of partaking in one or two bank robberies—well, Moss's chances of claiming innocence were pretty poor. The money was never found, but they still accused Moss and they sent him to prison in San Francisco when he was thirty-five. It was only after he was sent to jail that Betsy visited him and told him she was pregnant. Moss said he would have married her for the child's sake if not for being in prison. But he didn't want to tie Betsy down in a marriage to a man who couldn't even be with her and take care of her. So they made a pact to marry when he got out. But when Moss was released two years later, he was a changed and bitter man. Again life had dealt him a pretty hard blow. It seems every time he tries to straighten out his life, there's something or someone waiting to bring him back down to hell again. Prison life does little to boost a man's morale or make him turn to the good life. By the time he got out, he'd decided he'd make no decent father. By then Betsy had delivered a little girl. The child's name is Rebecca."

"And Moss never went to see the child?"

"It's not that he didn't want to, Amanda. He loves that little girl with his life's blood—and it was because he loved her that he stayed away. He went to see Betsy, but asked not to see the child, because he knew if he once set eyes on her, he'd want to keep her. But he felt he was no good. Betsy understood. She agreed to care for the child, and Moss promised to send her money to help support little Becky. Betsy said she'd quit the prostitution and raise the little girl properly, and she meant to do that. Betsy was good at heart. So, Moss left. He didn't know quite what to do with himself, so he went back to Chicago to look up the mother he hadn't seen in years. It was only the other night, when he showed up here, that I learned the rest. The mother is dead. He worked in Chicago for a while, till he got a letter from a friend of Betsy's telling him Betsy had died from some kind of fever and his little girl was orphaned. That was when he decided to go back out to California and make sure the child was placed in a proper home. And, well, you know the rest. You ended up on the same train with Moses Tucker. Doesn't it make you wonder why, Amanda?"

Amanda sighed and looked down at her quilt.

"Yes. It does. I was headed for California for my own reasons. Before Moss left, he made me promise to take the child to the mission where I'm headed. I would like to do that. He was a good friend for those few short days we knew each other. It's all very strange. As soon as I met him there was…something there. I don't know what, but it was as though someone were forcing us together."

"God? Fate? Who knows? But personally, I think you belong to Moses Tucker, Amanda. That man worships the ground you walk on. He'd be ever so good to you. And I know that what he'd like more than anything is to marry you and keep his little girl."

Amanda looked away. "No," she said quietly. "I can't…be any man's wife. I can't let a man—"

"It's not the same, Amanda. Not the same at all."

"But I—I wouldn't be just his. I always thought a woman should be touched only by her husband."

"You were forced, Amanda. You've not been touched at

all—not really. Do you think that with a woman as special as you, what Rand Barker did to you would make any difference to Moss Tucker? Besides, a woman can be touched by many men, but she can only be owned by one. And that one is all that counts. The physical aspect means little compared to the emotional, the heart, the soul. Slim Taggart owns my heart and soul—and my body—but others have touched me, Amanda."

Amanda met the woman's eyes. Finally, it came to her. This woman had been a prostitute before marrying Slim Taggart! Why else would she know so much about Moss and men like him? And how else would she obtain this deep understanding of men? Willie blinked back tears, and looked much the same way Moss had looked when he feared Amanda would turn him away and look down on him because he'd been an outlaw.

"I belong to one man now," Willie said, holding up her chin. "And it's wonderful. I'm having my first child: Slim's child. And he doesn't care about the others, because he loves me—just me. And as far as I'm concerned, I've never belonged to anyone else. And on our wedding night, Slim Taggart was my first man—in my mind. Because he was the first man I ever really wanted to give myself to—all of myself—not just physically, but in every way. I didn't have to tell you. But I wanted you to know. Because we all like Moss Tucker very much. It would be very nice to see him happy. And I know that what happened to you—a girl like you—that would hold you back. But you shouldn't let it. You're everything I would have liked to be. You're beautiful and innocent; completely innocent and untouched. To Moss Tucker you're a spotless angel." She smiled nervously and wiped at tears. "In that respect I guess I could never be like you. But I'm loved. And I thought you should know that as far as I'm concerned, to be loved and cared for by a good man—a woman couldn't ask for more than that. And maybe that God of yours means for you to be Moss Tucker's wife and means for you to have children. A woman can serve God in many ways, Amanda. And if you'd not think of yourself for a while, and consider the other side…I mean, perhaps God sent you to help Moss, rather than sending Moss to help you. Did you ever think of that?"

Amanda frowned and pulled at a tuft of yarn on the quilt.

"It is something to think about, isn't it?"

"I think so."

"Oh, but I wasn't very nice to Moss earlier. He might not even come back. And what if—what if he gets killed?" She looked sorrowfully at Willie. "I'll feel so guilty if he gets killed!" she said in a near whisper.

A faint smile passed over Willie's face.

"I wouldn't worry too much about that," she told Amanda. "If you knew Moss better, you wouldn't worry so much."

"But he could get hurt."

"Of course. It's possible. Anything is possible. But I can just about guarantee he'll get that cross back for you. He feels responsible. Right now I think you'd better get some more rest. There's nothing to do but wait. And it's kind of nice for me to have a woman's company. It's been a long time. Slim will be coming home soon. I'll bring him in to meet you. He's a lot like Moss, except he fits his name. He's a tall, gangly ole cowboy whose own big feet get in his way sometimes." She laughed lightly and picked up the tray.

Their eyes held a moment when Willie straightened up with the tray in her hands.

"I'm glad you found him, Willie," Amanda told her. The woman smiled.

"Well, so am I."

"Thank you for telling me about Moss. Do you mind if we talk some more, after I sleep a while? Perhaps you're too busy."

"I don't mind. Slim and the other help do a lot of the work now that I'm so big. What do you want to talk about?"

"Just…things." She reddened. "There's so much I don't know. I've…never had anyone to talk to."

Willie walked around the bed. "Well, there isn't much I don't know about, and not much I haven't done. I'd be glad to talk to you, Amanda. And I'd certainly like to see Moss happy again. I can't tell you how many times he cried in his whiskey over the hard times…" She reddened again. Amanda felt a pang of jealousy, and questions flooded her now. This woman had been with Moss! Of course! She'd been a prostitute before marrying. No wonder she knew so much about Moses Tucker!

"I, uh, tend to open my big mouth a little too much," Willie said, looking embarrassed and flustered.

"Moss never mentioned—"

"Of course not," Willie interrupted. "Moss is a good man. We were…good friends once. And I belong to Slim Taggart now. Moss and the others, they respect that. A married woman is a man's property. They'll steal horses and money, but they won't steal a man's wife." She smiled. "Not that anyone could steal me from Slim!" Their eyes held again. Two women from different paths, yet both good in their own ways, each admiring the other for different reasons.

"Thank you for all your trouble, Willie," Amanda told her.

The woman shrugged. "I don't mind. Like I said, it's nice to have a woman to talk to."

"You're very courageous. You don't give up. I'd like to be like that."

"You are like that. You'll make it okay, Amanda. I'm just sorry you got such a quick and terrible introduction to this lawless land. A woman needs a man out here; men like my Slim, and like Moss, men who know the land and understand it. But those same men need a good woman at their side."

Chapter Twenty

"You'd be Moss Tucker?"

The man who asked the question had bellied up to the bar where Moss stood, in a little tavern in Moab, Utah Territory. Moss and the others had traced Rand Barker to this little town east of Robber's Roost—partly by trail hunting, and partly by word of mouth from other outlaws who had kept a careful eye open. The other four men with Moss were hitting other places in the small, one-street town that consisted mostly of saloons.

"I am," Moss replied, eyeing the man carefully.

"Heard of you," the man replied. He was a medium built man with a two or three-day-old beard and wary eyes that had long ago learned not to trust or believe every man who walked his way. He ordered a beer and gulped some down, then rubbed foam from the grizzly beard with his shirt-sleeve.

"Word's out you're lookin' for Rand Barker."

"I am," Moss replied. "I've traced him this far." Moss took a sip of whiskey.

"And just how do you figure to take Rand Barker?"

Moss leaned against the bar and twirled the shot glass in his fingers.

"Same way I took him before—only the bastard lived then."

He took another sip of whiskey while the stranger watched him. This man had information, and Moss knew the man was making sure of his own hide first. The man pulled his hat down a little and looked around. Then he looked back at Moss.

"Why should I tell you anything? I ain't one to rat on my own kind. And I wouldn't like havin' Rand Barker after me neither."

"He took a woman—a good woman—and raped her. You know how that sets with most of us."

"Your woman?"

"Not exactly. There wasn't nothin' between us, if that's what you mean. She was just a nice girl: young, untouched—headin' out to California to teach at a mission, one step away from bein' a nun." He finished his whiskey and turned to face the stranger. "Now does that sound like the kind of girl that ought to be in the hands of Rand Barker and Duke Sage?"

Their eyes held.

"Barker and the others was here, but they're gone now," the man told Moss. "And they split up."

Moss frowned. This was something he hadn't expected.

"You got any idea who went which way?"

"I do. Ordinarily I'd be expectin' somethin' in return. But since there was a woman involved, I'd just as soon see Barker get his due. You sure he raped her?"

"I'm sure."

"How come he didn't just save her for Mexico? Virgins bring big money in Mexico."

"She got sick, too sick to travel. Then somebody in his bunch accused him of bein' a coward. He figured he'd show me he wasn't afraid of me by doin' the very thing that would bring me after him for sure. When Rand Barker gets mad he does stupid things. Rapin' that woman was the dumbest thing he ever did. 'Cause it's gonna mean his death." The words were cold and matter of fact, with no doubt whatsoever in them. The other man sighed.

"Did she live?"

"She lived."

"Come on outside," the stranger told Moss. He finished his beer and Moss pushed his glass aside and followed the man. Moss Tucker filled the room with his big frame covered with the wolf-skin coat. Others in the tavern all watched out of the corner of their eyes. Most of them knew his reputation, and most of them were outlaws themselves. As Moss walked out, there was hardly a movement he did not notice; for Moss Tucker had long ago learned to be wary of the men in these parts, and to always watch for the one who might want to make a name for himself. But none of them made any strange moves. None of them felt up to facing Moses Tucker. Moss walked through the swinging doors.

"Barker was here to rest up for a couple days," the man told Moss. "Him and his men sort of took over the town while they was here. I'd heard the rumor about what he'd done. Most was waitin' for him over by Robber's Roost, but Barker took a left and come east. He knows, Tucker. He knows a lot of us want him."

"I figured that. So he's tryin' to confuse us by splittin' up, huh?"

"Yes, sir."

Another man ambled up to them, his spurs jingling.

"Got news, Moss?" the older man asked.

"This man says Barker and them split up."

"Split up? That son of a bitch is thinking, ain't he? He figures that'll split you up from the men you've got with you. That makes you a better target for him, Moss."

"No matter. The fact remains we have to do just what he expects us to do. If we want to get them all, we have to split up, too."

"We don't even know for sure who all it was."

"I know," the stranger spoke up. "They was here long enough for me to remember. They bragged about the robbery, spouted off their names to be sure all us less-intelligent outlaws remembered who was the best."

"What's your name, mister?"

"Preston Foster."

"I'm Pappy Lane."

"Oh! I've heard of you, too. You and Moss Tucker both."

"We've been around. Tell us about Barker."

Moss lit a cigar and pushed his hat back, staring down the street at the black outline of mountains. They'd done a good job of tracing Barker, and men along the way had kept tabs, just like Moss knew they would. But Barker had veered just slightly out of outlaw territory. Moss had been able to track him this far. But now things had become more complicated.

"Well, like I say, they split up when they left here. I don't know who took what along. But I watched. Me and a couple others watched, to be sure, 'cause we'd heard Tucker might be comin' a-huntin' for Barker."

"I want them all," Moss said quietly. "Any one of them could have helped her, but none of them did."

The stranger swallowed. "Well, I wish you luck, Tucker. But they're a mean bunch—real mean."

"I can be meaner." Moss turned to look at the man. "Which way did they go?"

"Well, Barker and a real nice-lookin' blond guy called Sollit Weber—they went out that way, straight south."

Moss breathed a sigh of relief. At least the two he wanted most of all were together.

"There was another man went with them—kind of a crazy-actin' guy who laughed a lot. Called himself Clyde Monroe."

"Go on," Moss told him, stepping off the landing and looking up at the stars.

"Two others—Wade Gillette and some big guy called Booner—they lit out east. Probably figure on veerin' south later on and joinin' up with the others. Two young, kind of strange-actin' guys by the names of Henry Derrick and Manley Higgins, they lit out goin' north, believe it or not. I expect they figured nobody would know them or know they rode with Barker. They must have took their share of the bounty before they left." The man removed his hat and scratched his head. "I just can't figure why they'd leave without their share of the cross, though."

"Cross?" Moss asked, coming back and facing the man. "A crucifix?"

"Yeah. Barker waved it all over the place, laughin' about

how he'd borrowed it from God. You know, that whole time he never mentioned the woman."

"That's 'cause he knew better," Moss grumbled. "He took the cross?"

"I don't know for a fact, but I expect he did. After all, he was their leader."

Moss looked at Pappy Lane.

"There's only one thing to do, Pappy. Darrel and Johnny will have to go after the two that went north. You and Cal—you lit out of here east for the other two. One of them is Wade Gillette. He's experienced, so he'll take some work to get down, but I'm bettin' you can do it."

"And you? You're goin' after Rand Barker alone?"

"You bet."

"He'll be wantin' that, Moss. It's risky. Too risky. Let me go with you. Them others won't ever come back. Besides, them two that headed east—Gillette and that one called Booner—they might join up with Barker later, and there you'd be, one against four."

"I can take them. You do like I say, Pappy. And if they do head south, you'll be right behind them and you can help me out if I do get in a fix."

"I don't like the smell of it."

"He's got the cross, Pappy. I want it. I aim to get it back to her." He turned to the stranger. "I'll get my men together, and you go over them names again with them and describe the men to them. Will you do that?"

"Just keep my name out of it."

"Done."

"I'm doin' it for the woman—no other reason."

"Is there a better reason?"

The man suddenly grinned. "I can't think of none."

They all snickered. And it made Moss think of Amanda Boone. He felt an ache deep within himself, a hunger that he knew might never be fulfilled. The taste of her lips lingered in his mind—but he'd frightened her with that kiss. It had been a stupid thing to do, just like the first time he had kissed her, but she'd been there in his arms: so close, so frightened and vulnerable. And he longed to show her the other side of men and love-making. But he'd frightened her right out of his reach. There was nothing to do now but get the cross back for her, even if he had to die doing it. He'd not done one thing right, except maybe the time he'd chased off the two men who had accosted her at Council Bluffs. That seemed like years ago now. He'd get the cross back, get her to California, and then get his little girl settled. Then he would leave. Where and what for, he didn't know. Neither did he know just how he would be able to forget Amanda Boone, nor his little girl once he saw her. But there was no doubt that both of them would be better off without Moses Tucker in their lives.

"We'll stay here one night at the hotel," he spoke aloud. "Mister, you come over there later and give us more details."

"Sure. Say, what about that Duke Sage that you mentioned. There wasn't no Duke Sage with Barker and them. I've heard of that man, heard he's bad—real bad—especially around women."

"Duke Sage is dead," Moss replied, stamping out his cigar. "He won't be givin' no more women no trouble."

"You kill him?"

"I killed him," Moss replied. "Enjoyed every minute of it."

Chapter Twenty-One

Red's hooves splashed and the horse whinnied as Moss urged the animal into the cold waters of the San Juan River. It had been five days now since he had seen another human being, five days of riding ever southward from Moab. He was close to Arizona Territory now, still east of the common outlaw trail and west of the old Spanish trail. He knew that Rand Barker would avoid both routes, where there might be people who would recognize him. He was not wanted in outlaw territory, nor would he be wanted anywhere else where there might be civilization. There would be a danger of soldiers on the old Spanish trail. So Moss smelled out the route the same way he figured Rand Barker would: through uncivilized territory, naked of man and even most animals, mountainous, rocky terrain that few men bothered to enter.

Man and horse forged a narrow part of the river. It was growing late, and now his feet were wet. Moss found a hollow surrounded by a thick growth of yucca bushes. There he unsaddled Red and opened his bedroll, plunking the saddle down to use as a pillow. Then he broke off pieces of the yucca branches for kindling and walked to a spot nearby where he'd seen remnants of a small cart. He yanked out a few pieces of wood for a fire. There were trees on the hills of the mountains around him, but in the spot where he'd made camp there was nothing but sand and rock and a few scrubby bushes and sagebrush. He wondered for a moment how that cart had come to be there. It was very old. Perhaps some Spaniard had left it there, maybe to flee Apache Indians.

He scanned the horizon all around him and studied the upper forests for a sign of life, but there was none. He was well aware that he was not far from the Bavispe—that invisible border line between Apache country and white man's country. But he was too close to Rand Barker now to quit. His fire would have to be small, just enough to heat a little coffee. He'd eat the jerked meat that Willie Taggart had given him.

He thought about Willie as he walked back to his camp. He'd enjoyed his excursions in bed with that woman, and she'd been a good friend. Now she belonged to Slim Taggart, and that was good. She'd be good to him, and loyal. He wondered about the kind of conversations the woman would have with a girl like Amanda. Surely by now they were well acquainted. Perhaps Willie could talk Amanda into giving consideration to marriage—and above all, talk her into giving Moses Tucker a second chance.

He sighed, getting a trace of the fragrant forests on the hillsides around him when he did so. He dropped the wood and knelt down to build a fire. The snow was gone now, and the freak weather had moved on. Today had been more bearable—in the fifties—more common for this time of year. He'd even taken off his wolf-skin coat earlier, but now he put it back on. Night was never warm in these parts, not even in the middle of summer.

He got a fire going and threw some grounds into a small pot with some water and set it over the flames. He knew the coffee would be terrible—thick and black—but that's how it always was for a man traveling alone under the sky. He pulled a piece of beef jerky out of his saddlebag and thought to himself how nice it would be to have a house, to see his daughter playing in front of a hearth while Amanda fixed him a woman-cooked meal with all the trimmings. Then they would all sit down together to eat. Perhaps Amanda would be pregnant. Yes. That would be nice, too. He wouldn't mind having more children. But time was growing short. He was already thirty-eight years old. Perhaps it was too late to start up that kind of life.

He bit off a piece of meat, wondering what made him think he could ever have that kind of life with someone like

Amanda in the first place. He wondered what his daughter looked like, hoping she would be small and blond, like Betsy Malone. He thought about Betsy with a heavy heart. He'd left the woman with a burden. And now the burden was his. But it wouldn't be much of a burden if he could find a mother for the girl and keep his daughter.

The coffee boiled, and Moss removed the pot and poured some into a tin cup. He took a swallow and shuddered. It was worse than he expected; yet it still felt good to drink something hot. He sat there—a lonely man in a lonely land—sipping coffee and chewing on jerked meat while coyotes howled and the stars began to make their appearance. And he thought about Amanda and how much he loved her and how hopeless it was.

* * *

Dawn found him on the trail again. Rand Barker had not only viciously stolen Amanda Boone's virginity, but he had ruined whatever chances Moss Tucker might have had for wooing the woman into marriage. Her experience with men amounted to a few days of savage treatment, which would burn in her mind for the rest of her life and frighten her away from any desire for a sexual relationship with a man. The only thing that would ease the pain of his loss would be to kill Rand Barker and Sollit Weber—and his only chance of winning at least a smile from Amanda would be to present her with the stolen crucifix.

He headed Red down an escarpment, carefully guiding the big animal down the steep embankment as rocks slid and rolled. He'd found a campsite not far from his own that morning—only a day or two old. He'd been right all along. Rand Barker had taken this unused section of land, avoiding both outlaws and civilization. It warmed early enough that Moss could shed his wolf-skin coat for a lighter buckskin jacket. As he neared the bottom of the escarpment, he realized how much he missed Amanda. In those three or four short days of journeying together, he'd become accustomed to her lovely voice, her light laughter, the green eyes so full of questions and excitement. He thought about the feel of her slender body next to his own. Surely he could get his own big hands around her tiny waist without any problem. His groin ached at the thought of her slender thighs and small, flat belly, the memory of holding her beneath him and kissing her. He wondered if perhaps he'd go mad if he could never claim her for his own. He needed to show her how gentle a man could be, and he daydreamed of what it would be like to have Amanda lying naked beneath him, groaning with the pleasure he could give her, whispering his name, her legs open and welcoming him inside. He wondered if anything had occupied his mind as much as Amanda—even Etta Graceland had not been this special. He realized now that even though he'd loved Etta, he'd known down deep inside that she did not truly love him for himself, as Amanda would. She would not have been as kind and forgiving and sweet as Amanda, and their life together would probably not have been a happy one. But he had loved Etta, and it still hurt to think about her sneering words and the revulsion in her eyes when she'd chased him out, screaming "bastard," "no-good," and other choice names. Yet she was right. He was a bastard—literally and probably in other ways—and although he'd tried twice to improve himself, his hopes had been smashed to the ground. So perhaps that was how it would be with Amanda Boone, also. He prepared himself mentally—or at least tried to prepare himself—for the fact that Amanda would never accept him. The most he could hope for was that they could at least be friends. So it didn't much matter to him what happened after he found Rand Barker. The important thing was to get the crucifix for Amanda.

The sun rose higher. Moss was so lost in thought about Amanda that it was midday before it struck him that Rand Barker was leaving him a very easy-to-read trail.

He slowed Red and eyed the jagged rocks around him.

"Whoa. Hold up there, Red," he said quietly. His experienced senses told him something lurked some-where. He'd been following the tracks of three horses all morning: tracks left in the softest parts of the ground rather than the rockier portions, which might throw him off.

A ground squirrel chittered nearby and scurried to its hole; Red snorted and pricked up his ears.

"You smell it too, boy?"

Moss pulled his rifle from its case at the side of the saddle. Holding it on one hand and the reins in the other, he nudged Red forward. He rode several hundred yards more. An eagle flew overhead and screeched. The bird had come from rocks several yards ahead and to the right of Moss.

In this country a man had to use not only his own senses, but the movements and sounds of animals. Red was skittish, and the eagle had flown up suddenly, as though startled. Moss had been eyeing a creek bed to his left for several yards, his experienced mind already looking for cover, if needed. He was close now. Too close. And Rand Barker was smart. At least when it came to plotting schemes he was smart, and he knew the land as well as Moss did.

Moss nudged Red to the left now, first slowly, then at an all-out run. He did not need to see them to know. Someone was up ahead, waiting for him. He headed for the creek bed. The only sounds to penetrate the silence were his own breathing, Red's snorting, and the swishy creak of his saddle as he headed for cover. Red's hooves swooshed into soft sand as he hit the edge of the creek bed. Moss was off the horse before the animal came to a full halt. He hung on to the reins as he hit the dirt with a grunt, and in the next second he wrestled and talked Red to the ground in front of him. The animal snorted and kicked for a moment, then lay still. Moss gently stroked the animal's neck and talked quietly to the horse, while at the same time continuing to scan the horizon. He waited. Just as someone out there also waited. The game of hide and seek would soon come to a conclusion. Moss decided he could wait as long as it took to make Barker—or whoever else was out

LAWLESS LOVE

there—come out from hiding into the open. All this time he'd been the hunter, and that was the way he'd keep it. He did not intend to become the hunted.

He checked his ammunition and cocked his rifle. Red snorted again.

"You just take it easy, boy. I'm not about to let you stand up and make yourself an easy target so they can shoot you and leave me without a horse—not out in this country. We've got a while to wait, so you just lay real still and let 'em come. Just let 'em come for ole Moss Tucker."

187

Chapter Twenty-Two

The afternoon dragged, and Moss spent it smoking and waiting. He contemplated getting up and going on, but his senses told him to stay put. If he continued on at all, it would be after dark. His stomach growled, and he reached carefully into his saddlebag to get a piece of jerky. That was when he saw movement. In a flash his rifle was in his hands and aimed steadily at the rock where something had fluttered.

A moment later there was a bloodcurdling scream, as a painted savage leaped from the rock and began charging. Others followed. The fluttering Moss had seen had been a feather, worn in the hair of an Apache. Although more were coming at him, he drew a bead on the leader and squeezed the trigger. The Indian's chest exploded, and he flew backward. Moss smiled.

"Right in the brisket!" he whispered to himself, quickly cocking the rifle again. "Come on, you bastards! Somebody's payin' you for this, so earn your money!" he hollered, firing again. Another screeching warrior hit the dust, tumbling head over heels.

Two down. About six more came at him. He quickly fired twice more, his aim always sure. Now four were dead, but by then the other four were almost on top of him. Red reared up at the last moment, causing the Indians to dart back quickly for a moment, but in a flash one of them was around the horse and coming at Moss.

Moss swung the rifle hard, slamming it across the man's face. Blood gushed out of the Apache's mouth and nose and he went down. Moss felt a horrible pain in his upper left arm just then, but didn't have the time to worry about what it was.

He swung around, ramming his rifle butt into an Indian's middle, then swiftly pulled his side arm and fired point-blank. The Indian's face disappeared. He fell with a tomahawk in his hand, and Moss still did not realize that the weapon had been used on himself.

By then the remaining two Indians had backed up. This white man was a good warrior—brave and sure in his movements. The Apaches admired bravery and skill above all things in a man. Moss stared at them, and they stared back. Moss did not fire. For the most part he liked Indians, and these two had seemed to change their thinking. There was no sense killing them if it wasn't necessary.

They held out their arms. This white man had killed six of their best warriors, mostly by being fast and sure and not hesitating once in his movements. Now the white man was gravely wounded, though he didn't even realize it. It would be cowardly to now attack this brave fighter, from whose left arm blood ran in an almost steady stream. They turned and walked away.

Moss's head reeled slightly. He watched the Indians walk off, and they became hazy in front of him.

"Barker!" he thought to himself, stumbling over to where Red had wandered. *"Barker paid them off with whiskey or somethin' to lay in wait for me. Figured they'd knock me off and save him the trouble."*

The problem was, he knew the two remaining warriors would go to Rand Barker and tell him the scheme had failed. And Barker would either send more warriors, or come for Moss himself this time. That would be fine. He could handle Barker. He reached up to mount Red, and that was when the pain hit him. He cried out and fell to the ground, grasping his arm. He looked down.

"Jesus Christ!" he whispered. The sleeve of his buckskin coat was soaked with blood. He looked back, and a solid trail of blood led to his horse—his own blood. The dizziness hit him again. And he knew at that moment he was bleeding to death.

He rammed his rifle into its holder and quickly ripped the rawhide strings from his shirt, working desperately against his own fading senses. He placed the rawhide under his arm near the armpit, grabbing one end with his teeth and reaching around with his good arm to tie it. He pulled tightly, groaning with pain as he did so. He tied a knot. Then with his good arm he pulled himself into his saddle. He leaned forward to grab the reins, but he could not reach them. He could not even sit up straight. He lay with his head against Red's neck.

"Take me…someplace, boy. Just…someplace. I need… help. This can't happen. I…gotta get that cross…for…Mandy."

The horse whinnied and bent down to eat some grass, waiting for a heel or a rein to tell him what to do. But Moses Tucker could not give his horse a signal. He simply slid off the horse and landed with a grunt on the ground.

"God, help me," he groaned. "I…gotta get back up."

He wondered if the buzzards would pick at him before he was completely dead. He moved to get up, but nothing would work. Too much blood had flowed from his veins. And there was no feeling in his left arm. He put his head back and closed his eyes.

"So…it'll end…here," he whispered. "Mandy. I sure did… love you."

• • •

It was the cold, combined with pain, that woke him. He opened his eyes slowly, wondering why he was so cold. Two men stood a slight distance away, but they were blurry at first. He could feel gravel against his face, and the moment he tried to move, he realized he could not. He was tied spread-eagled to stakes, lying on his stomach. He had no feeling in his left arm. He struggled to gather his thoughts, when suddenly something horribly sharp stabbed at the bottom of his foot. He screamed out in pain.

"Hey, boss, he's finally awake!" someone shouted. Then

Moss heard laughter. There was a stab to his foot again, and again Moss cried out. Again came the laughter. Clyde Monroe. The man back at Moab had said the one called Monroe laughed a lot. The two figures walked closer.

"Well, well, well," came the familiar voice. Rand Barker. "So, the great Moses Tucker has finally awakened. We've been waiting for this moment, Tucker. You know, without your gun, you're not worth much, are you?"

"You let me...fight you like a man, Barker...and you'll find out how much...I'm worth. You...yellow bastard! How does it feel...to fight...weak women...and men who are...wounded and tied. It don't take much...of a man...to do that!"

Something stabbed his foot again and Moss grunted. Monroe laughed and came around to hold a knife in front of Moss's face.

"This thing is sharp!" he said with a smile. "Hurts, don't it?" The man chuckled.

"Move back, Clyde," Barker told the man.

"When can I whip him, boss?"

"Soon, Clyde. Soon."

Barker knelt down near Moss.

"I, uh, suppose you know I intend to kill you."

"I suppose," Moss muttered, caring only that he would not be able to kill the man who had put his hands on Amanda Boone.

"I thought I'd see if we couldn't bring you around first," Barker went on casually, "just to be sure you knew who was doing the killing. Your, uh, feet are pretty raw on the bottom. Clyde here has been stabbing at them for hours, trying to get you to wake up." He laughed lightly. "Of course, you should want to die, Tucker. After all, this left arm of yours has had it. We wrapped it for you, only because we didn't want you to bleed to death before you came to and knew who was going to put you completely out of your misery. But I'm afraid we didn't do a very good job. If you were to live, that arm would have to come off anyway. Then you wouldn't be much of a man, would you? And that pretty little filly you were trying to impress wouldn't get too excited over a man with only one arm, would she? A woman needs two arms around her, Tucker. And I sure enjoyed putting my arms around Amanda Boone."

Moss jerked at his ropes in rage, but it was hopeless. Barker laughed again and stood up.

"She was good, Tucker," he went on, lighting a cigarette and walking in circles around Moss. "Real good. 'Course any virgin is bound to be good. Her screamin' was music to my ears. That was the most excitin' time I've ever had."

"You're lower than dirt under a snake's belly!" Moss growled.

Barker only laughed again. "She's fresh and pink, Moss. Like tasting fresh fruit, you know?"

They all snickered, and Moss realized the third man must be Sollit Weber, although he could not move his head to see him. He squirmed again, and realized his shirt was off. That was why he felt so cold. He sensed it was early morning. Had he lain there all night this way? Most likely. If only he could get loose! Injured arm or not, his own rage was all he would need to kill Rand Barker with his bare hands! His head swam with the ugly picture of this man with his precious Amanda.

The thought of Amanda made him realize his last hope was that God of hers—the God she'd said loved men like himself and forgave them. Would that God help Moses Tucker now?

"Go ahead, Clyde," Barker was saying. "Have your fun."

Moss heard laughter, and in the next moment a horrible pain gripped his back, and he heard the terrible snap of a whip. He cried out with the sudden and unexpected cut. Seconds later it came again, and Clyde Monroe laughed with glee at Moss's pain. Barker casually stepped away to talk with Sollit Weber, as though nothing at all were happening.

Moss closed his eyes and began praying, not knowing what else to do. Again and again the whip lashed across his back, until numbness set in. Sweat poured from Moss's brow, in spite of the cold. And again, he felt death close at hand and began to welcome it. He tried to concentrate on praying, and on Amanda, wanting her face to be the last thing in his mind.

Then several seconds passed without another lash. What was to come now? He heard the clicking of guns. Would they blow him to pieces then?

"Why do you do this?" he heard a voice ask.

"What the hell do you think you're doing, redskin?" came Barker's voice.

"This man fought my warriors bravely. We left him alive because he deserved to be left alive. Why do you now beat on him this way?"

"Because he's my enemy!" came the angry reply.

"Perhaps he is your enemy, but he is not ours. He fought bravely, and he let two of our warriors go when he could have killed them. Your actions are those of a coward. And a coward is usually also a liar. We will ask the white warrior and hear his side. A man who fights as he fought cannot be the bad man you led us to believe he was. You try to trick us with your lies, and with your firewater. You think we will drink the firewater and then act like fools!"

"Now listen here—"

Moss heard a thud.

"You will not speak more words until we have spoken with the white warrior!" the Indian's voice spoke up.

Now hands were untying the ropes at Moss's wrists and ankles. He groaned as men lifted him. He was placed on something soft. Then something was poured over his back and wounded arm, and he was sure his screams could be heard all the way to Canada.

"The firewater will help keep away evil spirits that make the wounded body sick and sometimes kill it," a man told him. It was an Indian. "We will put bear grease on the lashes. It looks very bad for you, white warrior."

"Why...are you...helpin' me?" Moss groaned.

"You fought us bravely. And you let two of my warriors

go when you could have used your gun on them. You will rest now."

"Don't...kill them," Moss groaned.

"Why should we not kill them?"

"Save them...for me. I need...to do it...myself."

"First we will learn the truth," the Indian replied. "Perhaps it is you who will die after all, no?"

Moss strained to look up at the Indian. The man was smiling.

"Perhaps," Moss groaned before passing out.

Chapter Twenty-Three

Moss was awakened with a splash of cold water on his face. His first reaction was to jump up, but black pain shot through his left arm, intensified by the added pain and burning of his back. He got to his knees and cried out, then just sat there rocking, his left arm hanging limp. His limbs ached from his earlier straining at the ropes, and from the cold that had settled through his skin and muscles. He felt cold clear to the bone, yet feverish.

"It is time to talk!" a voice spoke up. Moss ran a hand through his hair and looked around, everything fuzzy at first. Then it all came back to him. The Indians had come and released him from Rand Barker's torture. Had God sent them?

His vision cleared, as well as his mind, which only made his pain worse. He was now surrounded by Apache Indians, and looked into the face of one who had the marks of a leader. That one was standing, while the others sat in a circle around Moss.

"It is time to hear what you have to say," the leader spoke up. "You are good fighter—brave man. Therefore we helped you, for now. The three white ones over there beat on you when you already seemed to be dying, and tied you so you were helpless instead of allowing you to stand up and fight like a man."

Moss looked over at Barker, Weber, and Monroe, who all sat close together at a distance, surrounded by Apache guards. Barker glared at Moss, and Moss grinned.

"Your plan backfire, Barker?" he asked.

"That man's no good!" Barker shouted back to the Indian leader. "I told you that before! He's raped squaws and will kill any Apache in sight. He hates Indians! And he killed my wife! That's why I wanted to kill him—why I asked you to help me!"

Moss turned to face the leader.

"Is this true?" the Indian asked, his dark eyes flashing and his black, straight hair hanging to his waist in a tangle. The Indian's arms flexed in anger. Moss knew the Apache to be vicious killers, especially of men they thought cowardly or men who killed without just cause.

"None of it's true," Moss replied, holding the Indian's eyes steadily. "For one thing, if I was an Indian killer, why would I have let them two warriors go back there? I could have shot them without no trouble at all. But I could see they was through with me, so I was through with them. I've never killed an Indian that didn't attack me first."

He grimaced in pain and looked down at his arm. It was difficult to tell how deeply it had been severed, as it was wrapped in mounds of bloody, dirty gauze. The thought that he might lose the arm passed through his mind, but now was not the time to fret about it. Now would be his only chance to get the cross back for Amanda.

"And have you raped squaws?"

"I've never raped any woman!" Moss shot back. "It's Rand Barker over there who's the rapist! He robbed a train I was on up in Wyoming Territory. I had a lady friend with me—a nice girl that didn't belong to no man, never been touched by a man. But Barker there dragged her off with him. And he raped her. You yourself know it's bad enough for a white man to rape a squaw. But to rape his own kind makes him doubly guilty. There's nothin' lower than a man who'll turn on his own kind. And that's not the only way he turned on his own. He got a bunch of Sioux Indians to help him rob the train—promised them the guns that was on the train, even though he knew them Indians would probably use the guns against whites eventually. Now I'm sure you'd be all for them Sioux gettin' the guns, but the fact remains that Rand Barker helped them Indians get the rifles—which is the same as a man turnin' against his own brother. Can a man like that be trusted?"

The Indian turned to stare at Barker.

"Don't believe him!" Barker protested, but his eyes betrayed the fear that was inside the man, and the Indian sensed it right away. There was only one reason for Barker to be afraid, and that would be because this man was telling the truth.

"The woman. She was yours?" the Indian asked.

"Not really. It's kind of like when one of your own young girls glances sideways at you, and you get this kind of ache inside to make her your wife, you know?"

Their eyes held and then the Indian smiled. "I know."

Moss smiled back. "I sure could use a cigar. I had some in my buckskin jacket."

The Indian motioned to one of the other Apache, and the man retrieved the jacket for Moss.

Moss put the cigar in his mouth with his good hand, then struck a match on a nearby rock and lit it. He puffed it a moment, and it seemed to help the pain somewhat. He wondered what his back looked like, and rage built inside of him at Clyde Monroe, who had so gleefully whipped him. He glanced at Monroe, and the man smiled. Moss wondered if perhaps Monroe was insane.

"How do I know all of this is true?" the Indian asked.

"You check out Barker's saddlebags," Moss replied, with the cigar still at the corner of his mouth. "You'll find the money he stole from the train—money that was part of a payroll for some soldiers. And you'll find a Christian cross, with pretty stones in it. It's quite valuable, and it belonged to the woman. She was real religious. The cross was a gift from her church in the east to a church in California, where she was headed. Stealin' that cross is like somebody stealin' one of your most precious objects of worship—like takin' somethin' from a sacred burial ground, or takin' an instrument that belongs to one of your medicine men. It's the same thing. The cross is strong medicine. He had no right takin' it. You check his things and you'll find it. I don't doubt you might even find some of the woman's clothes. It would be like him to keep them as a sort of souvenir to brag about to somebody later on."

"He said you killed his wife."

"Men like Rand Barker don't take wives. They take other men's wives. Or better yet, they take fresh ones—sometimes rape them, sometimes take them to Mexico to sell, where in the end they'll still be raped."

The Indian put his hands on his hips and walked a circle around Moss.

"Ask yourself why I was followin' them," Moss went on. "I was out for revenge. Rand Barker took an innocent young woman that I was interested in maybe marrying. And he took the cross, which was very precious to her. I come down here for vengeance, and to take the cross back. That young girl is feelin' shamed and soiled. The only thing I can think of to help her feel better is to get that cross back to her."

The Indian paced some more. Then he motioned to two of his men. "See what is in their bags!" he announced.

"Now wait just a minute—" Barker started to protest. One of the Apache guarding him placed the end of a rifle against Barker's neck.

"You will not speak!" he ordered.

The Indians ripped through the three men's saddlebags, spilling out food and supplies, then shouting with excitement when they found several bundles of money, just as Moss said they would. Then one of them pulled out the crucifix and held it up in one hand. In the other hand he held up a pair of pantaloons. They were white and lacy, and Moss's chest tightened at the sight of them. He wanted to cry and kill at the same time.

The leader walked over to inspect the items. He brought them back to Moss and laid them in front of the man. Moss picked up the cross and studied it closely. He'd never even seen it up close before now. It was dazzling: deeply carved and golden, filled with precious stones. He felt unworthy to even touch it. He laid it down and lightly touched the lace of the pantaloons. The Indians retrieved all the money they could find and laid it in front of Moss. Moss looked up at their leader.

"It is as you say," the man told him. "The man called Barker tricked us into thinking you were the one who should die. But he is the one who will die!"

"Wait!" Moss spoke up as the Indian started to walk toward Barker with his knife pulled. "Killin' is my job...my privilege!" He squinted with pain even as he spoke. He'd been trying to ignore the throbbing in his arm, but he knew that if he didn't get some whiskey in his belly soon the pain would be unbearable. The Indian walked back to Moss.

"You are gravely wounded. And you are weak. How would you propose to take them?"

"You help me up...put my gun on me...and give them their guns," Moss replied. "I can...take all three of them."

The Indian frowned, and Sollit Weber chuckled. Weber's fears were alleviated now, as well as those of the other two men. At the hands of the Apache, they would have no chance. But Moss Tucker planned to kill them himself, and he was badly wounded. None of them figured there was any real danger.

"It is a foolish thing you ask!" the Indian told Moss.

"You've never seen me use my gun in a one-on-one gunfight," Moss told him. "And when I'm mad I just get faster. Now I'm too weak to take them on bodily. And I'm not a man to tie another man down and murder him without him havin' no defense...no matter how bad the man is. So that leaves... only one alternative. Them three are mine...and I aim to have the pleasure of gunnin' them down while they're standin' on their own feet lookin' me in the eye."

"One at a time then," the Indian told him.

"No. All three at once."

This time Rand Barker laughed, and Clyde Monroe cackled, rubbing his hands together.

"And if you lose?" the Indian asked.

Moss looked from the Indian to Barker, then back to the Indian.

"I lose...they go free."

Their eyes held, and then the Indian glanced slyly over at Barker.

"For a time," he replied. "Whoever remains will get a head start. But it would be wise for him to quickly get out of Apache country. News travels fast among us when there is a coward in our midst. Especially when the coward is white!"

Moss smiled to himself. If he lost this gunfight, any man who remained would probably not get far before running into more Apache.

"And the cross?" he asked the Indian.

The dark man knelt down, picked up the crucifix and studied it closely, holding it in hands gnarled and creased by time, wind, and weather.

"Some of my warriors will take it to the soldiers if you die. Would the soldiers see that the woman gets the cross?"

"I expect they would. They all know the story."

The Indian laid the cross down.

"What about the money?" Moss asked.

The Indian stared at the bundles of greenbacks a moment. Then he spit at it.

"The Apache has no use for the white man's money! It is his lust for money that makes the white man evil! I will have nothing to do with the evil this money brings! And where would I spend it even if I kept it? The white man will not let us go into his fancy stores. And if we keep it, the white man will hunt us for it. No. It will be given to the soldiers with the cross."

Moss threw down his cigar.

"Help me up...and get my gun," he told the Indian.

Two warriors helped him to his feet, and Moss cried out when one of them touched his wounded arm. For a moment everything spun around him and the black pain swept through him like a giant wave from hell itself. He clung to one of the Indian bucks until the dizziness went away. He longed for some whiskey, but that would have to wait until the killing was done. His senses were already dulled from the pain and loss of blood. He broke out in a cold sweat, and the terrible burning in his back seemed to get worse. But he concentrated on Amanda and what Rand Barker had done to her; it helped ease the pain and get his mind on vengeance. He thought about the crucifix, and wondered if he should pray for help in this thing he was about to do. But he decided that was something a man didn't ask God for—help to murder someone. He suddenly wondered if there was any hope of him getting to heaven.

"Slim chance," he mumbled, his breath coming in short gasps now while an Apache buckled his gun belt for him.

Moss took out the Peacemaker with his right hand to make sure it was loaded, spinning the cartridge with his thumb while holding it in the same hand. He tried not to think about the fact that he could not move his left arm or hand at all.

Now he forced himself to breathe deeply and concentrated on only one thing: the gunfight. Rand Barker was fast. And he was rested and unharmed. He had no idea if the other two were any good with a gun, but it was unlikely they came anywhere near Rand Barker in speed. So his first concern would have to be Barker. Once Barker was hit, the other two would be easy. Moss counted on having time—time between drawing and shooting Barker, and the time it would take for the other two to draw and react. They were not professionals. They would hesitate. Barker would not.

Now guns were being given back to the three prisoners. Barker eyed Moss steadily, realizing the match he was up against. Moss Tucker could not be taken for granted, even though he was wounded. Moss Tucker had a temper—and a vengeance to satisfy. Barker was certain his two companions would never survive the gunfight, but that mattered little. In fact, it would be nice if they did get killed. If Barker were the only survivor, perhaps he could talk the Indians into giving the money back to him. At the least, he could go on down to Mexico and spend the money the others had kept; they were all to meet in Mexico eventually. Rand Barker did not know that Moss had sent men after the rest of his gang. Barker also had money hidden inside his shirt and pants, and under his saddle. Things wouldn't work out half bad if he could just kill off Moss Tucker.

Moss studied Sollit Weber for a moment, enjoying the flush of nervousness on the young man's boyish face.

"What's it feel like to know death is only minutes away, kid?" he asked the young man.

"Shut up, Tucker!" Weber snarled.

"You'll pay for the trick you pulled on me, you bastard!" Moss growled back. Dizziness swept over him again, but he held his ground and forced himself not to show it.

Clyde Monroe just stood staring and smiling. The three men spread out slightly, all eyeing Moss closely now, and Moss backed up slightly.

"I'm ready any time you are, Barker!" Moss grumbled.

"You mean I get to go first?" Barker asked with a sneer.

"You bet!" Moss replied. The thought of Amanda struggling and screaming while this man beat and raped her burned in his gut now. He flexed the fingers of his right hand. There had to be no hesitation—not even for the slightest fraction of a second. *"Alert! Alert! Stay alert and ignore the pain,"* he told himself. Perhaps he would die of his wounds. But dying would have to wait until later. First he must do this. First he must kill Rand Barker.

There! Barker went for his gun. Their timing was almost simultaneous. But Moss Tucker did not hesitate. There was such little difference in the time they fired their guns that the onlookers were certain they went off at the same time. But Moss Tucker's went off first, and Rand Barker's bullet whizzed across the top of Moss's shoulder, led astray by the jolt to Barker's body when Moss's bullet hit him square in the center of his chest. The rest was easy for Moss. A surprised Sollit Weber stared in disbelief after a quick second shot from Tucker's gun hit him. The young man staggered backward and fell dead, his boyish face now turned to stone, the blue eyes staring up emptily.

Clyde Monroe had not even drawn his gun. He'd been so certain that Barker would take Moss Tucker, that he'd figured it wouldn't even be necessary to draw. When Moss's bullet found its mark in Monroe's chest, the man just stared, and then actually laughed. Moss fired again at the crazy man. A large hole appeared in the man's forehead, and the laughter stopped. His body slumped to the ground.

For at least a full minute the only sound was the wind. Sweat trickled down the side of Moss's face, even though a chilly wind caused him to shiver. He stood there shirtless and rigid. It was over. He'd killed Amanda Boone's rapist and saved the precious crucifix. Now the problem was to get it back to her. He'd rather hand it to her personally and see the look on her face. But now that he'd done his killing, he had time to remember—remember the pain, and the fact that his arm was severed deeply, perhaps through the bone itself. Now all of his other senses returned. The pain hit him, and he reeled from the still-fresh wounds, the savage whipping, and his too cold body. He was suddenly spent and sick. He slumped to the ground while the Apache just stood and stared, overwhelmed at Moss Tucker's performance with a gun.

Chapter Twenty-Four

Amanda set the coffee down in front of Darrell Hicks.

"I thank you, ma'am," he told her.

Amanda looked at Willie with worried eyes. Moss had been gone too long. He, Pappy Lane, and Cal Story had still not returned. She had so much she wanted to say to Moss. Perhaps she would never get the chance now. Perhaps he had died trying to get the crucifix for her. She felt guilty, lonely, and cruel. With all the time she'd had to heal and to think, she'd slowly come to know the real truth. She was in love with Moses Tucker. How she would deal with all the ramifications that love would bring was another matter. The important thing was to have the chance to tell him.

"Why aren't they back yet?" she asked in a shaky voice, walking over and setting the pot on the stove.

"I wouldn't fret too soon, Miss Boone," Johnny replied, "Sometimes these things take time."

Amanda walked over to the fireplace. "I don't know what I'll do if—if something terrible has happened to him," she said quietly, reddening at the admission. Johnny Pence, Darrell Hicks, Slim and Willie Taggart all sat at the nearby table. They looked at each other. Amanda Boone's love for Moss was becoming obvious, which made all of them happy. But the fact remained that Moss had still not returned, and they were all more worried than they let on. Amanda had done enough suffering—physically and mentally—in the five weeks since she was first abducted. There was no sense in adding to her woes.

Amanda seemed almost fully recovered physically. But it was difficult to tell just how deeply ran the scars in her mind from being a victim of Rand Barker and his men. Willie suspected the best cure would be Moss Tucker's arms.

"Well," Darrell spoke up, "I reckon maybe me and Johnny ought to go out huntin' for him if he don't show up by tomorrow. Our orders was to find Derrick and Higgins and come on back here. We found 'em, and we buried 'em—and here we are."

The statement was made matter-of-factly, as though killing the two men meant nothing to the man. Yet Amanda was beginning to understand these men better. Out in this land men made their own laws. Even outlaws had their own code. These men had helped find her—and they had helped Moss hunt her abductors at a risk to their own lives. But they'd gone anyway, and now two more horrible men from Rand Barker's gang were dead. The money Derrick and Higgins had been carrying lay in a trunk in the bedroom, waiting for the others to return with the rest of it—if they returned at all.

Johnny got up and paced. "Maybe they ended up all the way down in Mexico," he commented, rubbing his chin. "That would take some time."

"Yeah, but that also means ridin' through Apache country," Slim Taggart spoke up. Willie looked at him with worried eyes. Slim stood up and put a hand on her shoulder. "Don't you be fretting, honey. I don't want you gettin' all upset. We don't want that baby to come too soon."

Willie reached up and took his hand. Amanda turned to look at all of them. What a strange group this was: outlaws—some reformed and some not—and a former prostitute. Yet they were all concerned. They all loved Moss Tucker—and they'd all been kind and helpful to her. Where did God draw the line with people like this? She could not help but care for all of them herself. And she'd had a lot of talks with Willie Taggart, who knew everything there was to know about men.

"Do you think if Mr. Story and Mr. Lane—if they got the two men they were after, would they go south to help Moss?" she asked, now looking at Darrell Hicks.

The man's eyes quickly scanned her slender body, mostly out of curiosity about the woman Moss loved, and out of admiration. She was all lady. Moss would do well to lay his claim on Amanda Boone—if the man was still alive.

"I think they would," he replied. He pulled out a cigar and lit it. Then he puffed it for a moment. "My guess is them two Cal and Pappy was after veered south. They was a lot closer to Moss in distance than we was. We ended up goin' way north. But Cal and Pappy—goin' east-southeast like they did—they'd be likely to keep goin' once they caught up with them two. You shouldn't fret too much, Miss Boone. Even without their help, ole Moss will come through all right. He'll show up. You'll see."

Amanda swallowed back her tears and rubbed her hands nervously down the sides of her dress. She looked at Willie, who gave her a smile of assurance. But Amanda read through the smile.

"I—I'll start supper if you like, Willie," she said quietly. "I need something to do."

Willie sighed and put her hands on her stomach. "Lord knows I'd just as soon stay in this chair, Amanda," she replied with a light chuckle. The others grinned. Amanda suddenly wondered if Darrell Hicks and Johnny Pence had both done business with Willie before she married Slim Taggart. Moss had, and they'd all been friends over the years. Yet it didn't seem to matter. It had little effect on her opinion of Willie. Perhaps the woman had reasons why she had done what she did, and they were none of Amanda's business. The important thing was that Willie had changed her ways, had married Slim Taggart and was apparently true to the man. Sometimes love worked in strange ways, but everyone had a right to it. Even former prostitutes—and former outlaws like Moss Tucker. Amanda Boone was ready to love him, but perhaps now it was too late. If there was to be a man in her life, it had to be Moss or no one. She'd already decided that if he didn't return, she'd go to the mission and take her final vows. The only nagging question remaining was whether God intended for her to marry or to be a nun.

She was still not positive which God expected of her, and she hoped she would not be forced to choose between God and man. Yet that was what it seemed to be narrowing down to.

Amanda turned to walk to the pantry, taking out some potatoes. The house was quiet, everyone quietly worrying and contemplating what might have happened. Darrell puffed his cigar thoughtfully.

"Riders coming!" one of the help hollered from outside. Amanda's heart pounded. She threw down a potato and the knife she held and ran to the door, reaching it before anyone else and throwing it open. The others followed her out, Slim keeping a supportive arm around Willie and grabbing a jacket first to put over her shoulders.

It was a chilly, crisp day, the sky a deep blue. Two horses had appeared on the horizon, riding slowly. Amanda's heart fell. Perhaps it was Cal Story and Pappy Lane, returning without Moss. She walked out a little farther, oblivious to the cold.

Now they came closer. Moss! It was Moss! He had a beard again, and wore the wolf-skin coat. But something was wrong. He sat slightly slumped in the saddle, and he rode slowly. She was sure the other rider was Pappy Lane. She'd never been formally introduced to the men before Moss rode out with them when she'd been so sick. But she knew by the description the others had given her that it had to be Pappy who rode with Moss now. Where was Cal Story?

As Moss came closer, his eyes met hers. It was difficult to read them. He looked pale. Was he perspiring? How could he be in this weather? Something was very wrong! He pulled his horse to a halt.

Pappy quickly dismounted and came over to Moss's side, reaching up for him.

"I can get down by myself!" Moss snapped in a strained voice.

"You're hurt!" Amanda cried out, tears coming to her eyes.

"It's...nothing," he replied, trying to smile for her. He dismounted, but he clung to the pommel with his right hand

and half slid out of the saddle, supporting himself only with his right arm.

He grimaced with pain and clung to the pommel for a moment even after he got down, seeming to need the horse for support. Amanda watched helplessly; their eyes remained glued on each other.

"They're...dead, Mandy," he told her in a weak voice. "Barker...Weber..." He swallowed. "And Monroe. I got... all three of them...at once. They're dead...and no man's ever gonna...hurt you again."

"Moss, you've got to get inside!" Pappy spoke up with concern. "You've got to have that arm looked at."

"Not yet," Moss told him, his eyes still watching Amanda.

"Moss, what happened!" she asked, stepping closer. "If you need help—"

"Wait," he told her. He let go of the pommel and stood on his own two feet. He moved his hand back and reached into his saddlebag, pulling out the crucifix. Amanda's heart overflowed with love when she saw the precious cross. Moss held it out to her.

"I believe this...belongs to you," he said quietly. She looked up at him, tears running down her cheeks. Then she reached out and grasped the crucifix.

"Moss, I—you didn't need to—can you ever forgive me, Moss?"

"For what? I'd say...I'm the one...who needs forgivin', I failed you...bad...real bad. And I...stole a kiss before I left... that didn't belong to me. That was the second time I stole...a kiss. Maybe the cross...will make up for all your...sufferin'... at least a little. And for...me steppin' out of line like that."

She just shook her head, swallowing to find her voice, loving him with all her heart.

"It's all my fault!" she choked out. "I allowed myself to look to you for help. No one would have expected you to help me on that trip like you did. You—you didn't even know me!

How can you say you failed me, when you didn't need to be concerned for me in the first place!"

"I was concerned...because you were so much more... special...than anybody else on that train," he replied. "And the only reason...I messed up so bad...was 'cause...'cause I was so wrapped up in that...pretty face and them...green eyes...that I wasn't payin' no attention to things at hand, Mandy...like that Sollit Weber."

She reddened and hugged the crucifix to her bosom.

"Thank you, Moss Tucker," she said in a near whisper.

"All I want...is to see you smile again," he told her, his voice sounding even weaker now. She struggled to find a smile, but her tears only flowed harder. It was more than obvious this man was gravely wounded.

"Please, Mandy," he continued. "I'm...dying, Mandy. I gotta see you...smile...before I do."

Her eyes widened and she looked at Pappy, who seemed ready to cry himself.

"We gotta get him inside, Miss Boone," the older man told her.

She turned her eyes back to Moss. And she finally managed to put on a smile for him.

"You won't die, Moses Tucker," she said assuringly. "Who's going to take care of me if you die? I happen to be in love with you. If you go and die on me, you'll have failed me worse than ever! I'd never forgive you for it!"

He grabbed the pommel again and groaned.

"You're...just...sayin' that...for now," he gasped.

"No!" she cried out. "It's true, Moss! I swear it!" she said, coming closer. She reached up and touched his right hand as it rested on the pommel. "I love you, Moss. I loved you before— before any of this! It's just so hard for someone like me to admit to something like that!"

He looked at her as though she were a saint to be revered. Then he slowly shook his head.

"I'm...no good for you," he said in a near whisper. "I..."

His eyes suddenly looked desperate. "Mandy?" He swayed and she reached out for him, but his big frame was far beyond her ability to support, and he fell to the ground before Pappy Lane could grab hold.

"Moss?" she cried out.

"I told him he was pushin' himself too hard," Pappy grumbled. "We gotta get him inside, Slim!" he spoke up louder, as Amanda knelt over him. "Apache got to him down near Arizona Territory, sliced into his left arm with a tomahawk!"

Amanda gasped and stood up as Slim, Darrell, Johnny, and one of the hands picked Moss up to carry him into the house. Another hand hurried to help as the four men struggled with Moss's big frame.

"I wanted him to go to the nearest fort and see a doctor," Pappy fretted as he and Amanda and Willie followed. "But he insisted on comin' straight here, babblin' on about givin' that cross to you, Miss Boone. Said nothin' else mattered."

Amanda clung to the cross and sobbed. All this had happened because Moss Tucker had felt sorry for a young woman who was traveling alone. He'd taken on the responsibility of watching out for her without being asked.

They all hurried into the house and hustled Moss to the bed. Amanda followed, clinging to the cross and feeling helpless. Moss groaned and shook as the men began peeling off his clothes. The coat was not so difficult, but the buckskin shirt and jacket beneath it were partially stuck to him from dried blood. Amanda felt nauseous as an ugly odor began to fill the room from old blood and rotted flesh.

"Willie, you get out of here!" Slim demanded. "This ain't nothin' for you to see in your condition."

"But I want to help."

"You can help relieve my mind by leaving—please, Willie!"

Willie wiped at tears and turned to leave the room.

"One of you boys go with her," Slim ordered. "Have her get her coat and get out of here for a while. You'd best leave, too, Miss Boone."

Amanda looked lovingly at Moss, her heart filled with pity and sorrow, mixed with horror at the ugly wounds on Moss's back as the men cut off his shirt.

"I'm staying here," she said quietly. "I have to stay. Please let me stay!"

"He ain't a pretty sight, missy."

"It's all right. It's time I—I learned to be stronger. And he might need me."

She walked around to the foot of the bed, while Slim ordered lots of whiskey and asked someone to boil some water. They cut the sleeve off Moss's arm. Amanda gasped, and even a couple of men gasped. It was greenish yellow, and nearly black around the horrid wound. The smell was very bad. At first they were all speechless.

"I didn't know it was this bad!" Pappy finally spoke up in a choked voice. "He wouldn't let me look at it—just kept sayin' we had to get back up here first."

"Oh, dear God!" Amanda whimpered, putting her hand to her mouth. "Moss!" she whispered.

Pappy turned and walked to the window.

"It's got to come off, or he's gonna be dead in a matter of hours," he said quietly.

"No!" Amanda wailed.

"There's no choice, ma'am—unless you want him dead," another one of them told her.

"Losin' an arm would be worse than death to a man like Moss," Darrell put in. "I don't know, Pappy."

"You aimin' to just let him lay there and die?" Pappy growled, whirling to look at all of them. "I say it's got to come off! Look at it! The damned thing is dead! And Moss will be dead if we don't get that stinkin' flesh off him!"

"And what's he gonna think when he realizes what we've done?" Johnny asked. "What's he gonna have left to live for—a man like Moss?"

They all looked at each other, and then Pappy's eyes met Amanda's.

"Could be he'd have plenty to live for, if the right person made him want to live."

Amanda still held the crucifix close to her breast.

"I love him," she said, looking steadily into the man's eyes.

"Well, I reckon maybe that love could pull him through, ma'am, 'cause it's surely a fact that man loves you. Our biggest problem will be to keep him alive after it's done, and then convincin' him he's still a man, even without one arm."

"You do what you have to do," she told the man. "I'll take care of the rest." She looked down at the crucifix. "God will take care of seeing that he lives, and I'll take care of seeing he knows he's still a man," she added, looking back at Pappy confidently. A faint smile passed over Pappy's lips.

"I reckon you could do a right good job of that, ma'am," he told her. Amanda reddened slightly, but she smiled.

"You'd better hurry, Mr. Lane."

Pappy sighed and looked at Johnny.

"Go get a saw from outside, son," he said, his voice choking slightly. Then he looked at Amanda. "You staying?"

"I am." She walked to the window. "I—I can't watch, but I'll stay here…and pray."

She felt a hand on her shoulder.

"I'm awful sorry, ma'am. You've been through hell these last few weeks."

"And so has Moss," she said quietly, looking out at a cloud.

Pappy turned away and began giving more orders. "Tie his legs down. Tie his free arm down. Somebody sit on him—he's unconscious, but he won't be when we start cuttin'. Get some whiskey down his throat—as much as you can. Throw some on his arm. Be ready to tie it off good near the armpit. We'll cut it about five or six inches above the elbow." There was the sound of shuffling feet after that, and little talk. Someone else came inside. It must be Johnny with the saw. Pappy ordered him to hold it in boiling water first.

She wondered where the awful, ugly stripes on his back

had come from. The Apache? Rand Barker? No matter now. There would be time later for explanations.

"Pappy, where's Cal?" somebody asked.

"He's dead," came the reply. "The one called Booner got him. But then I got Booner and the other one. I buried Cal down on the Green River, near the Colorado—a real pretty place."

"Damn!" somebody whispered.

Amanda wanted to scream. These man had made sacrifices for her revenge. And none of them had been forced. They had all volunteered. Cal Story had lost his life. And now perhaps Moss would lose his. There was a terrible grating sound, and then a moaning that began to build. She hung her head and wept and prayed, clinging to the crucifix. The more Moss screamed, the harder she prayed. It seemed hours before it was over—hours of horrible screams and the sound of men cursing and swearing. Someone even seemed to be crying, and she could hear them scuffling, most likely trying to hold down Moss Tucker. She knelt to her knees by the window and continued to pray and weep.

Then things quieted. There were footsteps, and someone went out. More orders. "Tie it off. Get some clean sheets under him. Douse it in whiskey and wrap it up." There was a terrible moaning, as though from the depths of someone's soul.

"Mandy!" someone sobbed. She trembled and could not get up. Now someone was helping her to her feet.

"You all right, ma'am?" Pappy was asking her.

She clung to the crucifix, her arms bent stiffly. She was not able to unbend them.

"Ma'am? You want to go out?"

She swallowed. "No," she whispered. She managed to turn on rubbery legs and look at him. He was drenched in sweat; his body shook and his head tossed. It was difficult to tell just how conscious he was, but he groaned and said her name again. She stared at the stump, its end wrapped in gauze which was already stained with blood.

"Keep him covered well," she said, wondering where the voice had come from. "He's in shock. Keep him warm, Pappy."

"We know that, ma'am."

"Get me a chair. I want to sit beside him."

"Ma'am, maybe you ought to leave for a while."

"No. I'll stay right here until he comes around fully. I should be the first one he sees."

Slim got her a rocker and set it beside the bed. The men seemed to be stumbling over each other to help her. Someone helped her sit down, and someone else brought a quilt to put over her knees while another stoked up the fire. She could not remove her eyes from Moss's ashen face, nor had she yet let go of the crucifix.

"I guess—I guess all we can do is wait now, ma'am," Pappy was telling her.

"Yes, Pappy," she replied. "That's all we can do, other than to pray."

"Well, ma'am, I expect that's one thing you're real good at—better than any of us scoundrels."

She looked around the room at them, as they stood there rather awkwardly, some splattered with blood.

"I wouldn't say that," she replied. "And I'm deeply grateful."

Johnny shrugged. "You're a nice lady, and Moss is our good friend, so we helped. That's all. Don't lay no praise on our worthless hides, ma'am."

"I'll be forever indebted to all of you," she replied.

They looked at each other rather sheepishly and nodded to her.

"We'll, uh, be right outside, ma'am," Johnny told her. He and the others left the room—all but Pappy, who hesitated at the doorway.

"Moss—he's, uh, he's a good man, Miss Boone. I mean, ain't no woman gotta be afraid of him, you know? Oh, he's—he's an ornery bear when he wants to be, and he ain't wearin' no halo, that's for sure. But he's had a hard life. A woman like you—she could change it all for him. He'd straighten out right good for a woman like you. And I just know he'd like to keep that little girl of his."

"I know, Pappy," she said softly. Their eyes held a moment. Then he sighed.

"I expect I'll go wash up now. You gonna be okay alone for a while?"

"Yes. In fact I'd like to be alone."

"Oh. Sure. I'll be back in a while to check on things."

"Thank you, Pappy."

He nodded and went out. The room was suddenly silent, except for Moss's uneven breathing, frequently accompanied by the deep, bitter groaning.

"Mandy," he muttered again. She could not be sure how conscious he was, but she leaned forward and took hold of his right hand.

"I'm here, Moss," she whispered. "I'll always be here."

Chapter Twenty-Five

"What happened, Pappy?" Amanda asked quietly, as she wrung out a soapy wash cloth. She began to gently wash Moss's neck.

Pappy watched her. She looked tired, and had deep circles under her eyes. It had been a hellish night of intermittent moans and screams, semiconsciousness and unconsciousness. The arm had been rewrapped twice, and more whiskey poured down Moss's throat. Amanda had been up with him all night. The others had at least been able to take catnaps. Now the normally shy and inhibited girl, who still hardly knew Moses Tucker, was washing him gently, ignoring her own shyness and her own weariness to help the man she loved.

"How did he get those awful cuts on his back? Did the Apache do that, too?" she was asking. She sponged off Moss's chest and arm as she spoke.

"Barker did it—leastways, one of his men did it," Pappy replied. He saw her face turn ashen at the mention of Rand Barker. Would she ever get over the rape? Perhaps Moss could help her there.

"After I got done buryin' Cal, and since I was already down by the Colorado—so far south and all—I figured maybe I'd better keep goin' south and see if I could find Moss. I figured my best bet at findin' him would be to hit the Indian camps. Indians have a damned good communications system. You want word spread fast, you ask an Indian to spread it for you. They don't need no telegraph lines."

He grinned, and Amanda looked at him and smiled softly. She put the rag into the bucket of soapy water, took a towel, and began drying off Moss.

"And they helped you find him?"

"Well, I have one pretty good friend among the Arapaho—Eagle Beak. He agreed to take me down into Apache country. Most white men ain't too eager to go into that territory alone, and I'm one of them. So Eagle Beak went with me, kind of actin' as a go-between, you know? The first Apache camp we come to, the people told us they'd heard six Apache was killed by a white man farther south. The Apache love combat, and they get ecstatic over bravery and fighting skill. So it was a big story to them. Some white men had paid eight Apache with whiskey and trinkets to attack and kill one white man. They'd told the Apache the white man was real bad, raped squaws and all. So the Indians attacked the man, but the man fought back damned good. Killed six of them, some of them after he'd already been gravely wounded with a hatchet. Well, I figured that could be Moss, 'cause I've seen him fight, and even a grizzly bear would be best to stay away from Moss Tucker when he's mad."

"Help me roll him up on his right side, Pappy. I want to wash his back and sprinkle some cornstarch on it and on the sheets. That will help soothe his back and keep him dry."

Pappy got up and walked over to her side. He carefully pulled Moss up onto his right side, cautiously avoiding touching the man near his severed arm. Moss groaned but did not speak, and Amanda quickly began bathing his back.

"You still haven't explained his back, Pappy."

"Well, when the Apache told me what happened, I knew it had to be Moss—and that the white men who'd asked the Apache to kill him had to be Rand Barker and them other two. They said the remaining two Apache in the bunch that went to kill the lone white man backed off and left him, 'cause he was already wounded and had fought bravely. And they admired him 'cause he could have killed them, but he didn't. Moss likes Indians in general. He knew they figured he deserved to live after the way he fought them. Moss respected that decision, and he'd know the Apache would look in favor on a white man who'd not kill one of their own unnecessarily. They told me they left the white man to go his own way, but then the men who'd set the Indians on the white man come along and grabbed the wounded one while he lay unconscious. They tied him and tortured him, and when he was fully awake, one of them commenced to lashin' into him with a bullwhip—while he lay there tied and wounded and helpless."

"Dear God!" Amanda whispered, her eyes brimming with tears. She began sprinkling cornstarch over Moss's back. "All for that crucifix! Oh, Pappy, he didn't have to go after it!"

"Well, ma'am, you don't know Moss too good. I've known him a long time. And I know he feels kind of worthless, 'cause of his background and all. I expect he figured maybe that was one good thing he could do—go after that crucifix. And I don't reckon he'll ever forgive himself for lettin' that one man get the better of him on that train."

He gently rolled Moss onto his back again. Without hesitation Amanda pulled the blankets farther down and removed the towels between Moss's legs that had been put there to absorb urine. She quickly washed him, and Pappy could see she was not really looking at anything. Perhaps she was blocking from her mind the realization of what she was looking at, for she acted as though it were nothing more than washing his arm or his neck. But she did redden, and he knew it had to be very difficult for her to do these things. She powdered him and put fresh towels over him, throwing the used ones into a separate tub of hot water, where she would wash them later. She covered him now, and Pappy wondered what things were going through her mind. Her memory of taking a man had to be ugly and repulsive, yet she'd admitted to loving Moses Tucker. Perhaps these two could help each other, once Moss recovered. Moss would wonder if he was still a man, and Amanda would need her thinking changed about men.

"Oh, Pappy, there he goes again!" she fretted, as Moss's entire body began to shake violently. "Grab his legs, Pappy." She sat on the bed and leaned over him, half lying on him and putting her arms around his neck, holding his head to her breast, while Pappy sat next to his legs and held them down. "It's all right, Moss," she said quietly, keeping the blankets tucked around his neck and hugging him tightly. "Mandy's here. It's all right."

The only reply was the deep, shuddering groan that tore at her heart. She closed her eyes and quietly prayed, keeping his head against her breast and holding him for over five minutes, until the shaking stopped. Then she straightened slightly and caressed his face—a face lined from the hard knocks of life, but still handsome.

"How did Moss get away from them?" she asked Pappy. The old man got up and lit a pipe. He walked to the window.

"Well, the Apache, they ain't much for jumpin' on a man who's fought bravely and has already been wounded. And they wasn't too fond of Barker and them doin' it, neither. They stopped the whippin' and waited for Moss to come around so they could hear his side. When he got through talking, and when the Indians found the stolen money and the crucifix—well, then it was Barker who was in trouble for lyin' to them and trickin' them. The Apache don't like bein' made fools of. They said they'd kill them for Moss, but Moss asked to be allowed that privilege. Standin' up and facin' him like a man, and lettin' them have their own weapons so it would be fair and square. That's where the Apache get all excited tellin' the story. I guess none of them figured, with the condition Moss was in, he'd ever be able to take them three, but if I'd been there I'd have told them he could do it. And he did do it." He chuckled and shook his head. "Them Apache got excited as little kids tellin' about it. Old Moss got all three of them, even as badly wounded as he was. Then I guess he passed out for a while and the Indians loaded up his horse with the stolen money—even found some more money on Barker's person and under his saddle. They stuck the crucifix in Moss's saddlebags and took Moss, his horse, and Barker's three horses to their camp. They was gonna keep Moss there till he healed, but soon as he came around, he insisted on headin' out of there. Said he had to get the cross back to a woman farther north."

"Perhaps if he'd waited there, maybe the arm would have healed."

"It's possible. But I doubt it, ma'am. It was already cut almost clean through. Them villagers told me he insisted on leavin' the camp where he'd been kept, so the Apache packed him up and helped him get on his way. But they watched him without his knowin' it. Word spread fast that a very brave and skilled white man was passin' through goin' north—badly wounded by an Apache tomahawk. They felt it their duty to keep an eye on him, but they knew the man in him didn't want no help. So they sort of helped from a distance, sendin' word along the way to watch out for him in case he should pass out again or maybe die. That's how I found him so easy. Them villagers knew exactly what direction to point me in so I'd find him. I caught up with him near Fort Wingate. We rode in there to deliver what money we'd recovered, and they actually gave us a little reward." He chuckled. "Can you imagine that? Givin' us outlaws a reward 'cause we'd recovered stolen money and returned it!" He laughed harder. "That's a switch! You've had quite an effect on ole Moss, ma'am. On all of us for that matter. There just ain't no way we could have kept that money."

He turned to look at her and she smiled at him. Then he walked over to look down at Moss.

"I wanted him to stay at Fort Wingate and have that arm looked at. But he refused. He was like a crazy man, wantin' to keep ridin' and get that crucifix up here to you. Well, you know the rest."

She sighed and stroked Moss's thick, dark hair.

"Yes. I feel so guilty about it. He didn't even know me."

"He admired you, ma'am. Somethin' as special as you don't often come into the life of a man like Moss."

"Well, I think he's very special, too, Pappy. And I made a pact with God. I told Him if Moss died, I'd know the Lord meant for me to go on to that mission and take my final vows.

But if Moss Tucker lived I'd have to marry him. Because I'd know I could never go out of his life, Pappy—or let him out of mine. It frightens me, yet I know I have no choice. We'll go get Moss's little girl, and I guess Father Mitchel will just have to find another teacher at the mission. I'd like the Father to marry us, and then I'd like to come back here. Moss likes it out here, and I know with men like you around, we'd have friends we could depend on. The biggest problem will be convincing Moss he's no different now that he has only one arm. Do you think that will be difficult, Pappy?"

Pappy sighed. "Ma'am, I'm afraid it's gonna be just about impossible. A man like Moss—that ain't gonna be an easy thing to take. Not an easy thing at all."

Chapter Twenty-Six

Pappy's prediction had been more than right. It was the third morning after the amputation when Moss became fully conscious. Amanda had her back to him, as she stood looking out the window, watching Darrell Hicks break a horse.

"Mandy?" came the raspy voice. She turned to face him.

"Moss! Are you—are you really awake now?" she asked, hurrying to his side.

He put a hand to his head. "What—what's been goin' on? I—I remember comin' back…givin' you the cross…and you…" His eyes met hers. "You said you loved me."

She took his hand. "And I meant it. I've had time, Moss. Time to heal and to think, and to talk with Willie." She reddened. "I'm not—I'm not ready for everything, Moss, but I do love you. And Willie told me all about you. And she—she knows so much, she's been a wonderful help."

"Mandy, I wouldn't want you lovin' me out of pity…over my past and all. I'm not worth much, Mandy, and you—you're too special to be givin' yourself to somethin' like me."

"Moss, it has nothing to do with pity," she replied quickly. "I loved you before I knew anything about you. Don't you remember me telling you that? I loved you from almost the first moment. But love is so—so new and different for me, Moss. At least that kind of love is. I just—I didn't know how to tell you, but I knew inside that I was falling in love."

Their eyes held another moment. She trembled on the inside, but she bent over him and brought her lips close to his. She closed her eyes, and their lips met gently. He reached up with his right hand and grasped her hair at the back of

222

her neck, pressing her harder against his lips. Then he tried to reach around her with his left arm.

She felt him go rigid. He moved his lips away from hers and held her hair so tightly it hurt.

"What the hell…" he whispered hoarsely.

"It's all right, Moss," she whispered, caressing his hair.

He let go of her hair and pushed her back, reaching over to feel for his left arm.

"It's gone! Jesus God, it's gone!" he cried out.

"Moss, it was dead—rotted!" she told him firmly. "It had to be done, Moss, to save your life!"

"For what!" he groaned, looking at her with frightened and horror-filled eyes. "So I could live out my life bein' half a man? So people could laugh at the cripple? So you could take pity on the man who lost his arm for you and marry him 'cause you feel obligated? I'd be better off dead!"

He threw back the covers, oblivious to his nakedness, and started to get up.

"Get me my gun, 'cause I intend to use it on myself!" he shouted. She grasped his shoulders.

"Moss, you can't get up!" she shouted, tears flowing.

"You stay away from me, woman!" he yelled back, shoving her violently with his right arm. "I don't want you lookin' at me! Don't you look at me!"

She fell against a dresser.

"Slim! Pappy!" she screamed, now sobbing. She immediately went back to him and threw herself against him before he could get all the way up. Three men came charging into the room: Slim Taggart, Pappy Lane, and Darrell Hicks. Willie followed, putting a hand to her mouth and immediately beginning to cry at the sight of the struggling and desolate Moss Tucker. He shoved Amanda again, then fought with the three men who wrestled him back down to the bed.

"You stay in this bed or we'll tie you down, damn it!" Pappy yelled.

"You goddamn sons of bitches!" Moss screamed at them.

"You cut off my arm! What kind of friends are you! You should have let me die!"

He landed his right fist into Slim's middle and sent the man flying, and none of them doubted at that moment that Moss Tucker would be any less ferocious and dangerous with only one arm. Amanda stood back, crying and confused.

"A man isn't a man when he's only got one arm!" Moss shouted. Willie hurried out to get more help. Moss Tucker was a big man, and he was mad and frightened. Now he punched Darrell Hicks in rage and tried to get up again, shaking violently and half crying. Then came a punch to Pappy.

"Bastards!" he roared. "Why'd you go and cut it off! Why'd you do it!"

Pappy wiped at the blood on his mouth, while Moss pushed his way out of the bed and stood up, holding a blanket in front of himself. He backed himself up to a wall, glaring at all of them.

"How does it look!" he shouted. "Real ugly ain't it?"

"Oh, Moss, please don't," Amanda whimpered, her arms crossed in front of her as though in pain, and tears streaming down her cheeks. "We all love you. We didn't want you to die! And I—I don't want to live without you, Moss!"

"Bullshit! You're just sayin' that 'cause of my arm!"

"No! No! It's got nothing to do with your arm!"

His eyes softened slightly. But he shook his head.

"I still love you, Mandy," he told her in a choked voice. "But a man—he's no good to a woman when he's only got one arm. He's no good to nobody!"

"That's stupid talk!" Pappy sputtered. "You big, stupid son of a bitch! I never thought I'd see the day when you was afraid of something! You ain't never been a coward, Moss Tucker! You gonna be one now, in front of your woman?"

Moss stayed huddled against the wall, his breath coming in short gasps, his whole body shaking. He stared at Pappy, tears running down his face, his eyes a mixture of hatred and fear and confusion. How she wanted to hold him! How she wished she knew the right things to say!

"You've still got your shootin' arm!" Pappy hollered at him. "Hell, with your skill with a gun, that's all you need, Moss! You can make it as good as any man!"

Moss put his head back against the wall and closed his eyes.

"I'm not a man!" he groaned through gritted teeth. "I'm half a man!"

"You stupid son of a bitch!" Slim spoke up, standing up now and holding his stomach. "It wasn't no half a man that just punched me in the gut! Felt more like three men!"

"Get out!" Moss groaned. "Just leave—all of you!"

Willie returned with more men, who now entered the room. Moss looked down at the stump, wrapped in bloody gauze. He made a strange grunting sound and lifted his head again.

"God help me!" he muttered.

"Moss!" Mandy whimpered, reaching out to him.

"Go away! Don't touch me!" he groaned.

"Moss Tucker, that woman's been with you night and day since we got back!" Pappy shouted at him. "She ain't eaten and ain't hardly slept. She's done nothin' but pray, and it's her that's been washin' you and cleanin' up after you! And she loves you, Moss! It ain't got nothin' to do with the damned arm! It ain't even got nothin' to do with you gettin' that crucifix back! It's just you! She loves you! Jesus Christ, man, the best thing that's ever happened to you is standin' right in front of you! Don't go and throw it away! You've had enough bad luck in your life. Now some good luck is starin' you in the face. You mess this one up, and it'll be your own fault!"

"Get out!" Moss retorted. "I promise to get back in the bed. Just get out—all of you. I gotta think!"

"Moss," Amanda started to speak. He whacked his right arm across the dresser, sending objects flying to the floor and startling everyone. The blanket fell and he quickly knelt and grabbed it up in front of him again.

"Get out!" he screamed. "Get out and don't look at me! Leave me alone!"

Amanda crumpled in devastated sobbing; Willie hurried over and put an arm around the girl.

"Hasn't she been through enough, Moss?" Willie snapped. "I've talked and talked to her to get her thinking straightened out! She's talked about nothing but how much she loves you all this time—long before she knew you'd lose an arm! Are you going to make things worse for her by making her feel even more guilty than she already does for what's happened? Is that how you show your love? I guess maybe you are just half a man—but not because of your arm, Moss! You're half a man for the way you're treating the woman you love, and the way you're treating all these men here! Do you think it was easy for them? To cut off the arm of one of their best friends, to go through the horror of an amputation and watch you suffer? They did it because they love you, Moss Tucker! And because they couldn't let you die!"

She led Amanda out of the room. Some of the other men left. Pappy stared at the broken Moses Tucker.

"So you've lost an arm, Moss. So what? Men have lost limbs before. The important thing is are you gonna let yourself lose somethin' a lot more important than that damned arm? You lose Amanda, and you'll suffer a lot more than you're sufferin' now."

"I'm no use to her this way."

"That's a fool talking! You're still able to love—and you've still got all the parts a man needs to love a woman physically. And you've still got your shootin' arm. You're still…" He waved Moss off disgustedly. "The hell with it," he went on. "You get back in that bed, and you do some thinking." He walked to the door.

"Pappy," Moss groaned.

"Yeah?" the old man asked.

"I—I didn't mean to push her. Tell her I'm sorry, Pappy. I didn't mean to do that."

"You tell her yourself!" the old man replied. He went out and closed the door.

Moss looked down at the stump again. He grimaced in pain and disgust. Then he sat down on the bed, suddenly feeling dizzy. He lay back and tried to gather his thoughts. How could he be of any use to Amanda now? And what about his little girl? How could he be responsible for a child and a woman with only one arm?

He rolled onto his stomach and wept.

Chapter Twenty-Seven

The next four days were a living hell for all of them. Now that he was fully conscious, the pain in Moss's arm seemed unbearable at times, its dull throb worsened only by the awful realization that he was missing a limb. And it was hell for the rest of them because they felt so helpless, not knowing just how to help Moss. It was worst of all for Amanda. Moss refused to allow her into the room. He refused anyone's help. It was like living with a wild bear in the next room.

Amanda, Willie, and Slim slept on cots in the main room while the other men slept in the bunkhouse, ready to come if needed. A deep depression was setting into Moss, which had been heightened by his learning of Cal Story's death. Cal had been a good friend; he had volunteered to help Moss and had died for it.

On the fourth day after he'd become fully conscious, Amanda insisted on being the one to take Moss's tray to him. She wondered if she'd get all the way inside without dropping it, her hands trembled so. But Willie had given her a wink of assurance and a little nudge, and a moment later she found herself standing next to Moss's bed. He lay turned away from her.

"I brought your lunch," she said quietly.

He turned to look at her, then pushed himself up with his good arm into a sitting position.

"Leave the tray and go out, Mandy," he said, reaching for some cigars on the dresser. She watched him put one in his mouth. He struck a match and lit it. She set the tray on his lap, then sat down in the rocker next to the bed.

"I'm not going anywhere," she replied. "I need to know that you understand how grateful I am to have the crucifix, and how sorry I am for…" She looked down at her lap, unable to go on. She could not stop her tears.

"Fate is fate, Mandy. That's just how things worked out, that's all. None of it is your fault. People make their decisions. I made mine. You just—you have one of the boys take you up to catch another train. You get yourself out to California and out of my life, and I'll stay out of yours. I would like it, though, if you'd go get my kid. That's the only thing I'd ask of you."

"Moss, stop it!" she choked out. Her body shook in short little gasps as she wept quietly. "Don't you…love me…like you said?" she sobbed.

He put his head back and sighed deeply, then puffed the cigar.

"Of course I love you, Mandy. But all this—it just shows me even more how wrong I am for you. A man can't take care of a family when he's not even all there. It's all different now. I was worthless enough to begin with—"

"But it's not different!" she cried. "You're still Moss Tucker, and I'm still me—and I love you! Before you left I said some cruel things, but I was just afraid, Moss. And I—I couldn't forget your kiss. I've never been kissed like that. And I knew down deep inside I wanted you, needed you. I still need you. Don't make me go on to California alone, Moss. I couldn't be happy alone now. I'm—I'm scared, Moss. I want to be with you. And I—I want children, and you're the only man I could…" She covered her face and wept harder. "Please don't make me go away, Moss!"

For several seconds there was just silence. Finally he spoke up again.

"Mandy, I've been around. Believe me, it's best in the long run. I love you too much to see you stuck with a no-good like me. I've got no right claimin' somethin' like you. You were made for better things."

"Moss, I love you. I don't want you to be alone any more. And I don't want to be alone. Don't you see? You've never really had anyone and, even though we grew up differently, I've never really had anyone either. I need you as much as you need me. I've never had anyone in my life."

His eyes met hers and held them for a moment.

"Remember how it was on the train, Moss? It was so…nice between us. Surely you knew then I was falling in love with you. Surely you knew that, Moss. It's got nothing to do with your past or your arm. How can you think I'd be that shallow?"

He studied the tear-stained, tired face. She seemed smaller than ever, she'd lost so much weight. Again it burned at his insides to imagine Rand Barker taking her. It could all have been so different. And he'd dreamed about taking her himself, showing her how it could be, and perhaps now she would be willing—but now the ugly stump was there. He could not put two arms around her. He could not pick up a child in two arms. The arm changed everything.

"You go on to California, Mandy," he told her quietly, his own eyes brimming with tears. "I'm sorry I ever told you I loved you. I shouldn't have done that. I didn't have no right lovin' you, and no right kissin' you like I did. I'm sorry, Mandy, for offendin' you, and I'm sorry for the other day—pushin' you away like I did. I just felt…crazy, you know? I've never hurt no woman before, and I hope I didn't hurt you then."

She pressed her quivering lips tight together, trying to suppress more tears.

"Just get yourself to California like I said, Mandy. In a while you'll forget about lovin' me—you'll be doin' what you was cut out to do. And I promise to stay out of your life."

"But I don't want you to stay out of it," she whimpered.

"Mandy, everything I touch turns sour. I'm not about to let it happen with you. Look what's already happened. I failed you miserably, Mandy. I'm feelin' pretty good now. So in a day or two, I'll be on my way and get myself out of poor Willie's hair. I expect her and Slim would like to have this bed back. I'll see one of the boys gets you to California, and—"

"I'm not going to California without you!" she retorted, rising from the chair.

"Mandy, startin' out life as a young married woman, well, it's not right startin' out married to a man sixteen years your senior, who's spent time in prison, who's a border line outlaw, and who's a cripple besides! I'm a bastard, Mandy! A bastard and a cripple and a loser! So find yourself some other man, 'cause I'm not the one! You hear? I'm not the one!"

She burst into renewed tears and fled the room. Moss punched a pillow and sent it flying across the room. Amanda closed the door behind her and looked at Willie, who came up and put her arms around the girl.

"Just give him a little time, Amanda," the woman told her. "Men like Moss—something like this is awfully hard on them."

"He said he's leaving in a couple more days, and he means it, Willie! He means it! I can't let him ride out of my life! I can't! Oh, Willie, I don't know what to do."

Willie led her over to the table, and Slim sighed and got up from his chair.

"I'm goin' out to feed the horses, honey," he told his wife. "And don't you be overdoin' yourself in here."

"I'm fine, Slim," Willie replied. Slim walked over and leaned down to kiss her cheek. Then he patted Amanda's shoulder and went out. Willie took Amanda's hand and held it between her own.

"Amanda, I have an idea."

Amanda looked at her, wiping at tears.

"What is it?"

Willie studied her a moment. "How brave are you, Amanda?"

"I—I'm not sure what you mean."

"Well, I just think Moss Tucker needs to be shown how much you love him, and reminded how much he loves and needs you. There's one way you could help each other out."

"But how?" Amanda asked innocently.

Willie smiled and leaned back. A naughty, wicked look came into her eyes.

"I know how I'd handle it," she said with raised eyebrows.

Amanda stared at her for a moment. Then her eyes widened.

"Oh, no, Willie! I—I couldn't do that! I'm not even ready for that myself! And—and we're not married!"

"All I know is Moses Tucker thinks he's not a man any more. You could change that for him. And you have a certain problem of your own that he could help you with. You do love him, don't you?"

"Of course I do, but—"

"Do you think God really would condemn both of you for helping each other out through and because of your love?"

Amanda swallowed and looked at the table. The thought was terrifying, yet a strange warmth ran through her veins. She felt the same pleasant urging inside that she had experienced on the train when she talked with Moss, the desire she had not fully understood.

"Listen, Slim's taking me to visit late this afternoon," Willie told her. "We have new neighbors to the west of us. They're from Salt Lake City. I'm thrilled to death to have a woman neighbor, even though they are five miles away. I want to go and meet her. The house would be empty, Amanda, for several hours, except for the men outside. They never come in unless someone asks them to. So you'd be alone with Moss." She squeezed Amanda's hand. "Alone, Amanda. Take it from an old pro. Moss Tucker is saying one thing, but he means another. That man doesn't want to ride out of your life any more than you want him to. He's screaming out for you, Amanda."

"Do you really think so, Willie?"

"I know so."

"But…what if he gets angry or—or hates me, or loses his respect for me."

"Amanda, you've got to trust me on this one. None of those things will happen. I guarantee it."

Amanda looked at the table again, reddening deeply.

"I don't know, Willie. I don't think I could."

"Amanda, haven't you been listening to me all the times we've talked? Sure, it might hurt a little. Moss is a big man. But I know he'd be ever so gentle, and you'll find out that pain can be lovely and welcome. It wouldn't be anything like what you're thinking, Amanda. And in the long run you'd be helping him."

Amanda smiled nervously.

"I—I wouldn't even know what to do."

"With Moss you don't have to know. He'll take care of that, once you get him into a helpless situation."

Amanda raised her eyes to Willie's, and the woman smiled slyly.

"You think about it, Amanda. If you're going to straighten out Moss Tucker, you'd best do it soon, or he'll stick to his stubbornness and ride right out of here—and out of your life. I know Moss. He'll do it. He's too stupid to accept happiness when it's handed to him on a silver platter, I guess because he figures he doesn't deserve it. You've got to serve the happiness, Amanda. Not just present it to him on that platter. You've got to go one step further."

Amanda got up from the table and walked over to pick up the coat Willie had loaned to her.

"Where are you going, honey?" Willie asked.

"Just out for a walk. I have to think, Willie, and pray."

Amanda put on the coat and turned to face the woman.

"I'll think about what you've said, Willie."

"Good," she answered with a smile. "You're quite a girl, Amanda Boone. I've enjoyed knowing you."

"And I've enjoyed knowing you," the girl replied.

She quietly went out into the cold, November air. A few light snowflakes were falling. She walked a short distance from the house and studied the colorful Utah horizon. How beautiful yet dangerous this country was. The things that had happened to her out here seemed incredible. And the girl who had been raised in an orphanage by nuns seemed like someone else now—not Amanda Boone. She'd learned more in these past three or four weeks than she'd learned in her whole lifetime.

She was unaware that Moss Tucker stood at the window watching her. How he loved her! And how he hated hurting her!

"Mandy!" he whispered. "God, I love you, girl."

Chapter Twenty-Eight

Amanda swallowed back her nervousness and opened the bedroom door with a trembling hand. Was she crazy? Would she burn forever in hell? So much of her thinking about what was truly right and wrong had been altered. Surely God did not want her to let Moss Tucker ride out of her life, to live out his life forever alone and lonely—away from his child, away from the woman he loved, with no one to love him and teach him that his past and the missing arm did not matter. Surely God had led her to this moment of decision.

She quietly entered the bedroom on shaking legs, closing the door softly and sliding down the latch from the inside so that no one could enter. Moss lay on his right side, his back to her, breathing steadily and deeply. He was asleep. The curtains were closed, and the house was empty and quiet.

She walked around the bed, her eyes filling with tears because of her nervous indecision. She was terrified to be taken by a man again, yet fascinated by Willie's description of how it could be with the right man. If any man was the right one, it was Moses Tucker. And if any man needed a woman at the moment, Moss did. They both had a need that the other could fulfill: she to know the lovely side of sex, and he to know he was still a man.

She stood before him and began undressing—quickly now, deliberately—before she could change her mind and run out of the room. She felt foolish. She knew nothing about how to trap a man or lead a man on. Willie knew all the right moves, the right looks, the right words. Amanda knew nothing—nothing except fear of pain, fear of the memories it could bring her, and fear of failure.

Her clothes dropped to the floor, and she stood there shivering slightly in the cool room. She bent down to pick up the clothes, and when she straightened he was looking at her. She froze, holding her dress in front of her, but one thigh and hip, and part of a breast were still bared. She turned crimson and stood there speechless as Moss slowly sat up, looking at her with surprise at first, then concern.

It was strange, how they just stared at each other. Yet both knew then. They knew.

"You don't have to do that, Mandy," he said softly.

"I can't let you leave," she said in a near whisper. "It's the only way I can think of…"

He reached out with his good arm, looking at her lovingly, as though she were a precious jewel.

"Come and lie beside me, Mandy."

She obeyed, not even sure why. She clung to the dress and sat down hesitantly on the bed. He was still sitting also. He reached out and softly caressed the hair that was undone and hung to her waist. Then she felt his lips on her shoulder, her neck.

"Moss, I…don't know what to do." She felt stupid and childish.

"You don't need to know," he replied. His hand caressed her shoulder and back now. She closed her eyes and turned her head, and his lips met hers. What a gentle, lovely kiss it was! She was hardly aware of being gently urged down to her back, or that he pulled the dress away from her. He still slept nude. And now he casually moved on top of her, his lips still searching her own. She whimpered at the feel of his chest against her breasts, and the frightening hardness against her flat belly. His lips moved to her cheek.

"It won't be like you think, Mandy," he said softly, his lips now relishing the soft neck and shoulder. "You and I have a couple of things to find out, don't we?" He moved back to her lips, then raised up just slightly.

"Open your eyes, Mandy," he told her. She had closed

them tightly as though anticipating a beating. She looked at him now.

"It's gotta be, don't it? You and me. It just scares me, Mandy. 'Cause you're the most precious thing I ever ran across, and I'm not worth one hell of a lot."

"You're worth everything, Moss Tucker," she whispered. "You're worth giving my life to." Her blood ran with fire, and she felt the pleasing ache in her groin that she now understood.

"I love you, Moss," she went on, a tear slipping down the side of her face. "And I need you. I can't go to California without you. I just can't! I never thought I'd ever say something like that to a man, but with you it's so different. And I need you to show me. I can't live with the ugly memory. I just can't!"

Her voice choked, and his heart felt pierced. His lips met hers again, a hungry groaning kiss, filled with a desire to make it beautiful for this innocent—the way it should have been for her. She felt small and soft beneath him. So small and soft. And even with the missing arm, he felt large and masculine above this woman-child he loved so much. It was a very nice feeling. Yes. He would make sure he was still a man, and he would make her feel like a woman. He would show her how nice it could be. She wanted to know and he would show her.

His lips searched her lips, her neck, her shoulder—down to the tender young nipples. She whimpered and grasped his hair then, partially out of ecstasy and partially from fear. He moved back to her cheek, reaching under her neck with his arm and working his own legs between hers. She ran a hand along the hard muscles of his right arm, and it made her feel secure. She suddenly knew that if she asked him to stop right now, he would. She did not have to test him to find out. She didn't want him to stop—now or ever.

"Don't be afraid, Mandy. If you want to quit, you tell me, honey," he was telling her, as though he were reading her mind.

She trembled and cried softly.

"No," she whispered in reply. How enchanting she looked, lying naked beneath him, the long hair spread out on the pillow, just as he had pictured her so many times. It was like living a dream.

"I love you, Mandy. That's the only thing I can promise you."

"It's all I want except—except to have children," she replied, her green eyes glistening with love and anticipation and still a trace a fright.

"Hang on to me real tight, Mandy, and remember it's me—nobody else, nobody that wants to hurt you—just a lonely man who loves you enough to die for you."

"Oh, Moss!" she whispered. She encircled her arms about his neck. And in the next moment came the pain—at first terrifying. She cried out, but the cry was stifled by his own lips, as he grasped her hair with his hand and pushed deep inside of her. From there it was automatic—natural and necessary. As soon as he entered her and heard her cries of pain, and then ecstasy, he knew he was still a man. The slender body beneath him only brought out his masculinity. And his missing arm did nothing to deter from the beautiful moment.

And Amanda finally knew the beautiful side. She was giving herself willingly to a man—at one with the man she loved, in union, lost in a glorious swelling of desire and the sudden knowledge of how it was supposed to be. She arched up automatically. It was something no one had to tell her. He groaned her name, his breathing hard, and she knew she was pleasing him. This was all something she had never imagined she would ever do. But now she knew. Here was where she belonged: here, beneath this man of courage and gentle love.

He was all man, even with one arm. The shoulders broad, the arm rock hard. He'd just learn to do everything with one arm instead of two. And she knew his heart was full of courage—and of love. Surely God had led her to him. Surely God meant for it to be this way. She would be Moses Tucker's wife, and she couldn't think of any more wonderful goal than that, except to have lots of babies.

Then it was over. They lay there for several minutes in one

another's arms, neither of them speaking. Finally he raised up on his elbow and looked down at her—her hair a tangle, her eyes glowing softly with love.

"You're beautiful," he told her softly, kissing her lips lightly.

"So are you."

"You're also deceitful, little girl. Who put you up to this—Willie?"

Amanda grinned. "Sort of."

"Mmm-hmm. Willie knows men pretty good."

Amanda ran her hand over the hairs of his broad chest. "She knows you pretty good—too good, I might add. I don't intend for any woman to ever know you like that again, except me. You belong to me now."

He smiled. How good it was to see his handsome smile. It had been so long since she'd seen him last smile. He bent down and kissed each breast, and again the fire was building deep in her loins. She could hardly believe it had been so wonderful.

"Is that so?" he asked. "And do you belong to me, Mandy?"

Their eyes held, and she saw a sudden, boyish fear in his.

"Yes," she whispered, reaching up and touching his hair. "Willie told me once that a woman can be touched by many men but only one man can own her, possess her. She can give her heart and soul to only one, and that one man then becomes the only man who's ever truly touched her. I believe that now. I've given everything to you, Moss Tucker. And you erased the ugliness." Her eyes filled with tears. "You can't chase me away now because I belong to you, whether you want me or not."

"Oh, I want you, all right. I didn't really mean all them things I said, Mandy."

"I know that."

"I swear to God I'll be good to you, Mandy. I'll figure out a way to provide for you and my Becky."

"And our own children," she added.

"Yeah. And our own."

"We'll go get Becky and come back here to live. You'd like to live in Utah, wouldn't you?"

"Wouldn't you be afraid to live in these parts?"

She smiled. "Not with you at my side, Moss. Did you know the Apache think you're one of the bravest and most skillful men they've run into?"

"That so?"

"Yes." She sobered slightly. "You can be just as good with one arm as you were with two, Moss. You'll see. I'll help you. And at the same time you can help me. I have so much to learn about men, about living out here. I don't have to live fancy, Moss. I don't expect a gold mine and riches. I just want a roof over my head—and babies."

He looked down at the tender, young breasts.

"Well, now, I expect I can provide them things."

"Maybe I could start a school out here, Moss. They must need one. I could still serve God—only right here. I think that's what He wants, Moss."

"Sure you can. You can do whatever you want, Mandy. Just so I've got you beside me in the night."

Their lips met again in a long, hungry kiss. Then he held her tight against him with his strong right arm.

"God, I love you, Mandy! I'll never let you regret marryin' me—never."

"I know you won't. And I'll be a good wife. When we go to get Becky, I'd like to go to the mission and have Father Mitchel marry us. Is that all right with you?"

"You know it is. Won't he be upset—you marryin' me instead of stayin' there to teach?"

"He'll understand. I have to do what's right in my heart, Moss. I'll give him the crucifix and…"

Their eyes met again. How ironic life was! She remembered how afraid she'd been to even let this man fix the handle of her bag because the crucifix was inside. She remembered his kindness: the way he'd watched out for her, stepped in when the two men bothered her in Council Bluffs.

"It all seems like such a long time ago," she said with tears in her eyes.

"Yeah, it does," he replied softly.

"You'd better hurry and get well enough to travel, Moss. We have your little girl to get, and a cross to deliver."

"And a train to catch?" he asked with a smile. She smiled back, but tears slid down the sides of her face.

"And a train to catch."

"Well, plenty of trains go by everyday, Miss Boone. Right now I've got my woman beside me, and she feels mighty good. We'll catch that train later."

"That's fine with me, Mr. Tucker."

His lips met hers again, and their love-making began all over. He wondered suddenly what had ever happened to the little jewelry box he'd bought her. No matter. He'd buy her another one. There would be plenty of time.

• • •

A lonely coyote howled in the distance, a part of the untamed land that had introduced itself so cruelly to Amanda Boone. Now she would become a part of that land. Far to the north a whistle wailed its long, solitary cry over the rocks and canyons and deserts of the American West; the Union Pacific continued to rumble its way into the new frontier.

In that year of 1869, and the immediate years to follow, more railroads invaded once quiet, untamed places. There was an ominous moan in the Chinook winds that scooped down from the Rocky Mountains across the plains and prairies, the cry of wild things dying—the buffalo, the Indian. It was a painful time, those growing years. Painful not just for those things becoming extinct, but for the settlers who came to replace them. It was that "middle period"—when there was only the law of survival, when men set their own rules, and those with money and power could own whole towns and the people in them—in which Amanda and Moses Tucker found themselves struggling to cut their own niche in the land of sand and rock and harsh, cruel reality.

Only the devoted love they shared kept them going. Fate had led them together and Amanda found a life far different from anything she had known before. Yet she knew this was her true calling: to bring happiness to a lonely, struggling man, to give love and a gentle upbringing to his child, to minister— in her own quiet way—to the rough and rugged men in this land who knew little of love and gentleness, and to do what she could to help the Indians she came to know, whose pride and freedom had been destroyed.

It was Utah they chose in which to settle, in the midst of Indians, outlaws, and settlers alike, all sharing the same western sun, all struggling to survive, all caught in the wedge between lawlessness and civilization.

PART II

PART II

Chapter Twenty-Nine

1874

Amanda Tucker pulled the biscuits from the oven of her wood stove, breathing deeply the wonderful scent of freshly baked pastry, and smiling in anticipation of how pleased her husband would be when he came in. She set the biscuits on the table, then turned when she heard a shout outside. Someone had called out, as though hailing an approaching stranger. In this untamed land called Utah, strangers were always suspect at first; all who rode onto Tucker property were stopped and questioned.

Amanda hurried to the window, her eyes widening at the sight of a very beautiful woman, who presented a picture of wealth by her exquisite clothing and the grand palomino she rode sidesaddle. Two men rode with the woman, and one of them helped her down while a ranch hand questioned all three of them.

Amanda turned from the window and hastily patted back the sides of her hair, suddenly aware of her appearance. It would be fun to have a visitor, especially someone as mysterious as the woman outside; but she had been baking all morning, and she was sure her dark hair must have flour in it. She quickly untied and removed her apron, just as footsteps could be heard on the porch and someone knocked at the door.

Amanda hurriedly pushed some strands of hair back into hairpins and walked to the door. Today she wore her long, thick hair in a plain bun to keep it out of her face. If only she'd had time to fix it differently, in a prettier do. Had Moss seen the woman yet? Then she felt disgusted with herself for her vanity and she quickly opened the door, smiling kindly at the somewhat older and very striking redhead who stood there.

"Good day," the woman said, giving Amanda the once-over. "And you must be Moss Tucker's wife?" The woman's voice purred like a kitten, and her English was exact. But in that respect, Amanda felt on an even course with the beautiful intruder. For Amanda herself was well educated, and even ran her own little school for local children—Indian and white alike—three days a week in a separate building on the ranch.

"I'm Amanda Tucker," she replied in her own smooth voice. "What can we do for you, ma'am?"

"She says she's here to talk to Moss," a ranch hand spoke up. Amanda forced back a small pang of jealousy.

"Oh? Why would you need to talk to Moss?"

"I'd rather wait and tell him that, Mrs. Tucker, if you don't mind. My name is Landers. Etta Landers. It was Etta Graceland when Moss knew me. But, of course, that was some years ago."

Etta Landers enjoyed the rather fallen and jealous look on Amanda Tucker's face at the mention of her name. So, Moss Tucker had told her about the love he once had for Etta Graceland.

"You're Etta Graceland?" the ranch hand spoke up with a scowl. The redheaded beauty turned to look him over, frowning at the old man's work-worn clothes.

"You say that as though you don't approve," she said haughtily.

"You bet I don't!" the old man growled. "What are you doin' here, botherin' Moss now for? You walked out of his life a long time ago, and caused him considerable trouble besides! He's married and settled now, and—"

"Pappy, don't be so rude!" Amanda interrupted. "If Miss Graceland, or rather, Mrs. Landers, wants to talk to Moss, then she can talk to him."

"Why, thank you," Etta said in her purring voice. "Then may I come in and sit down? I'm very tired. It's been a long ride, and this hot, Utah country has me drained! My goodness, I must say, the weather up in Wyoming is certainly better than this!"

"One gets used to it," Amanda replied, stepping back and allowing Etta to enter. "Please come in and have a seat. Pappy will go and get Moss for you." She turned to the old ranch hand and winked. "Go find Moss and Becky, Pappy. Lunch is nearly ready anyway. And see that the two gentlemen who rode in with Mrs. Landers are comfortable, and water their horses."

"You're bein' awful gracious to that no-account woman, Amanda," the old man grumbled. "Appears to me you shouldn't be too anxious for Moss to be seein' her."

Amanda folded her arms in front of her. "Pappy Lane! If I felt that way I wouldn't be married to him! Now just go and get him, will you?" She smiled lightly and patted his arm, and the old man grudgingly stepped off the porch.

Amanda watched him a moment. Pappy Lane was probably Moss's best friend. And in spite of what she'd told him, it did upset her somewhat to have Etta Landers make a sudden appearance out of nowhere, looking for Moss. She turned and reentered the house, studying the lovely form of Etta Landers as the woman removed pins from her hat.

"Have a seat, Mrs. Landers, in the rocker there. It's the most comfortable chair." The jealousy rose to Amanda's throat again, seeming to choke her. She felt plain and ordinary, and had never felt more self-conscious. She knew it was foolish; if only Moss hadn't once loved this woman, it would not seem so bad.

"Please, call me Etta," the woman replied with a smile. She quickly glanced around the simple log cabin. The Tuckers' home consisted of one main room and two bedrooms, one for themselves and one for the little girl Moses Tucker had fathered by another woman before he met Amanda. The girl, Rebecca,

247

was seven now, a lovely little blond girl with dancing blue eyes and a close, loving relationship with her father.

"All right—Etta," Amanda replied, walking up to shake the woman's hand. It struck her that Etta's hand was cold, in spite of the very hot, July weather. "It's nice to meet you. Moss has told me about you."

The woman's eyes turned rather icy. "I'll just bet he has. I don't suppose he had anything good to say?"

"I'm afraid not," Amanda replied coolly. Then she remembered her Christian faith and squeezed Etta's hand. "But what's past is past. You're welcome here. I don't know what your business is, but I know you're tired. So just have a seat and I'll make you some tea. When Moss gets here, you can tell us both why you've come."

"Oh, I would like some tea. Thank you so much." The woman's eyes and manner did not seem to warm to Amanda's sincere attempt at making her welcome. Amanda released her hand and walked over to fix the tea.

"Will Moss be back soon?" Etta asked.

"I sent Pappy for him. He's out south of the ranch, looking for strays and riding with our little girl."

"You mean *his* little girl, don't you?" the woman said, rather sarcastically. "I heard about Moss and that tramp he lived with after he got out of prison. I must say, he could have done better than that."

Amanda's jealousy turned to anger, and she turned to glare at Etta Landers.

"He tried to do better than that once," she said quietly, her eyes boring into Etta's. "But I believe the woman considered herself too good for him." The two women stared at each other a moment, then Etta flashed a lovely smile.

"Oh, don't mind me, Mrs. Tucker, I mean Amanda. I've just—I've been through so much the last couple of years that it's made me rather bitter and not a very nice person, I'm afraid. It wasn't very kind of me to mention that woman. Besides, now Moss has you. Why, I hear you're just a dear." Her eyes ran over Amanda's supple, young body quickly, noting the natural beauty of the young woman and feeling her own jealousy. "They even say you once intended to be a nun. Is that true?"

Amanda could not be sure if the woman was serious or laughing beneath the cold, blue eyes.

"Yes," she replied quickly. "I was raised and educated by nuns in an orphanage in New York. But then I met Moss on my way to California to teach." Her eyes softened at the memory of the kindness Moss had shown her on the train trip west, and the feelings she had had for the man—feelings new and strange for a young virgin who knew nothing of life and men.

"Yes, I've heard the story. I must say, when I set out to trace down Moses Tucker, I set myself up for some wild tales! Were you actually captured by notorious outlaws and stolen away, and then rescued by Moss Tucker?"

Amanda's eyes filled with pain and remembered fear and horror.

"I'd rather not talk about it. It's over now," she replied, turning to remove the biscuits from the baking sheet and place them in a basket.

"Oh, but of course," Etta replied coolly, studying the young woman again, and wondering if she truly had been raped. "And, uh, you look so much younger than Moss. I mean, Moss must be…let's see—"

"Moss is forty-three, and I'm twenty-seven," Amanda told her curtly, placing a cloth napkin over the top of the biscuits and setting the basket on the table. "Little Rebecca is seven, in case you're wondering about that, too. And how old are you, if I may ask?"

Etta's eyes iced over. "I'm thirty-six now."

"Well," Amanda replied with a feigned smile. "You don't look your age at all." She turned and walked into the bedroom to quickly check her face and hair and make sure all the flour was gone. She was glad that she was younger than Etta Landers, although it didn't seem to matter—not when considering the woman's looks and stylish clothing. Amanda looked down at her plain, gray cotton dress. Then she raised her eyes to the small crucifix sitting on her dresser. She walked up and touched the cross.

"Holy Mary, Mother of God, forgive my vanity and my jealousy," she whispered. "Moss is a good, good man, and a good husband. I have no reason to feel this way. Help me to treat Mrs. Landers with respect and love."

Just then she heard horses, and she heard Moss's voice, and little Becky laughing. She hurried out into the main room and opened the door to see Moss talking to Pappy. Another ranch hand was helping Becky down from her horse, while Moss dismounted and glanced at the house. He caught Amanda's eyes. He smiled briefly, then said something more to Pappy and walked toward the house. He removed his hat on the way and banged it against his pants to pound the dust out of both. Sweat streaked the handsome, dark face, and Amanda watched him lovingly as he approached. He didn't look or act his age, and every part of him—every movement and every muscle of the large, sturdy frame that stood over six feet in height—bespoke the man that he was, even though he had only one arm. With a man like Moss, a person quickly forgot the missing limb. His manliness and strength shone through so readily that it seemed inconsequential. She suddenly realized that Etta Landers did not know—or if she did, had not seen Moses Tucker since he lost his arm.

"Hi, Mandy," Moss greeted her when he came up the steps. He grabbed her up in his strong, right arm and kissed her lightly. Then their eyes held for a moment, and she knew all she needed to know. "It's all right," he said quietly, now kissing her forehead. She just nodded, suddenly wanting to cry, as Becky rushed past them into the house.

"Daddy! Daddy! There's a pretty lady in here to see you!" the little girl shouted moments later, coming back to the door.

Moss frowned slightly and gave Amanda one more squeeze.

"I know. Let's go meet her," he replied rather reluctantly. They stepped inside together.

Etta rose, now flushed and not quite so sure of herself.

"Moss!" she said softly. "I—it's so good to see you!" She glanced briefly at the left shirt-sleeve that was rolled up and pinned beneath what was left of his left arm. "I heard about your arm. I'm so sorry."

Amanda moved away from him, gently pulling Becky away from Etta. The little girl was staring at the puffy scallops of Etta's soft blue riding habit, and was touching them with her pudgy fingers.

"Why don't you go to the bunkhouse and eat lunch with Pappy today," Amanda said quietly to the child, as Moss and Etta simply stared at each other. "Wanda came and cooked for them today."

"She did? I can eat with Pappy?"

"Yes, dear, go ahead."

"Wanda said she'd show me how the Navaho ladies make their baskets! She said she could show me how to make one good enough to hold water!"

"Good, Becky," Amanda replied softly. "Run along then."

The child flew out the door, and Amanda began to blush with slight embarrassment, as Moss had not yet said a word of greeting to Etta Landers. Etta herself was reddening with indignation.

"Well, I thought you'd be a little bit happy to see me, Moss," she finally said, turning away slightly.

"Why should I be?" he replied. "What the hell did you expect, Etta? That I should greet you with smiles and kisses?" His eyes moved to Amanda. "I'm goin' into the bedroom to wash up." Then his eyes returned to Etta. "I imagine I don't look too good to Mrs. Landers here," he added with a slight sneer. "She prefers suits and silk vests."

"Moss, please!" Etta said in a near whisper. "Even—even your wife told me what's past is past."

"My wife's a good person," he replied tartly. "The kind of goodness you'd never understand."

He turned and left the room, and Amanda quickly prepared more tea.

"I'm sorry, Etta. But the things that happened with you and your father out in California left Moss very bitter. Prison didn't help."

"No, I—I guess not. Perhaps I shouldn't have come. But I didn't know who else to ask. And everyone says Moss is so good with a gun—"

"A gun!" Amanda exclaimed. Her heart pounded with fear. She had nearly lost him once. She did not like the feeling. "What are you talking about?"

"Oh, I—I'll explain when he returns, if he'll talk to me at all."

"I don't want Moss put in danger, Etta," Amanda said flatly. "He's through with that kind of life—violence and guns. He's through with it." She turned away to dish out some stew, and Etta watched her, smiling lightly.

Moss reentered the room, his thick, dark hair now neatly combed, and the streaks of sweat washed from his darkly tanned face. His huge frame seemed to fill the room, and Etta felt a deep stirring. She suddenly regretted turning him away and demanding he get out of her life so many years earlier. It would surely be very pleasant to share a bed with Moses Tucker, certainly more enjoyable than it had been with her own husband or any of her lovers.

Etta sat down at the table, where Amanda was placing bowls of stew. Moss sat down wearily in a chair at the head of the table.

"Becky's not gonna have one feminine habit left if you keep lettin' her go and eat at the bunkhouse," he commented to Amanda with a wink.

"She loves it. And out here she might as well learn to be as tough as any man," Amanda replied. She set his stew in front of him and bent down to kiss his hair. "Perhaps you'd like me to go out there with them, so you and Etta can talk about whatever she wants to discuss alone."

"You sit right down to the table with me, Mandy," he replied. "Anything we've got to say can be said in front of you." He looked at Etta at last, his eyes taking a quick scan of her voluptuous form. Old emotions gnawed at his heart, painfully and rudely awakened by someone from the past. "Start talking, Etta."

He put a spoonful of stew in his mouth, and Etta swallowed with nervousness. What had she expected? That he would be overjoyed at seeing her and instantly in love with her again? It was a foolish hope. The man obviously had himself a lovely, young wife who was very good to him. Why had she even come?

"Moss, I—I want to tell you first that I didn't have anything to do with—with what happened—with the banker in Nevada, I mean. Well, I mean, daddy didn't tell me—not till years later, Moss, after it was too late—"

"Don't lie to me, Etta!" he grumbled. "Your pa found out I was a bastard, my ma a prostitute. So I wasn't good enough for you, even though I'd made my own little fortune with my gold mine—a gold mine I sweat and toiled at for five long years. Five long years!"

His voice rose now and he stood up, suddenly no longer hungry. Amanda stood near the stove, her heart aching for him.

"I worked hard to make somethin' of myself, Etta! And I loved you, wanted to marry you! And you turned and threw it all in my face like my feelings didn't mean a thing! Bastard, you called me! A worthless bastard! Told me you wanted to puke at the thought of me puttin' my hands on you! And as if that wasn't bad enough, after you jilted me I went back to Nevada and was told my money was gone—all of it! Every last penny! Cheated—that's what I was! Cheated! By your pa and that goddamned banker, Miles Randall!"

"Moss, please don't cuss," Amanda said quietly.

The man sighed and ran a hand through his hair, as Etta sat at the table looking ready to cry. She stared at the biscuits as Moss rambled on.

"Even if you did find out your pa planned it all, even if you did find that out after I got out of prison for half-killin' that banker, you still could have come forward and cleared my name. But you just let it lie. Why didn't you come forward and help me, Etta? Why?"

"I—I couldn't get daddy in trouble, Moss."

He laughed sarcastically. "No, of course not. Daddy always came first, didn't he?"

"Why did you turn to outlaw life?" Etta asked in a choked voice.

"I tried to find you, Etta, after I got out of prison. But you were gone—run off and married that fancy lawyer, gone on down to Los Angeles. What could I do then? You'd turned me away, helped hide facts that could have kept me from prison, and you never even wrote me or tried to find out what it was like for me in that stinkin' prison!"

"Moss, I was younger then. I—I only listened to what daddy told me. I was spoiled and terrible. I know that."

"And don't try to tell me you're different now," he growled. "I'm not the same dumb bastard I was then, Etta! And I'm not stupid enough to think you came here just for a friendly visit, to renew old friendships!"

"Moss, don't be so cruel," Amanda said softly. He turned to face his wife, and their eyes held for a moment. He pulled a prerolled cigarette from his shirt and lit it.

"You ask Etta about cruelty. She can tell you all about it, Mandy," he replied coldly. He sat back down in his chair, and Etta raised her eyes to meet his. Her eyes were full of tears, and he wondered if they were genuine or part of an act. Etta Landers was a magnificent actress, depending on the occasion.

"You haven't answered my question," she told him. "Why did you start riding with outlaws?"

He took a deep drag on his cigarette.

"Etta, when a man gives all he's got to make somethin' of himself, and gives his heart and soul to a woman, then has both things grabbed right out from under his nose, he don't much care about anything for a while. And I'd been in prison for five years. Prison don't help a man, Etta. It only makes him worse. I didn't have nothin'; all that money I'd worked for and the woman I thought I loved was gone. I didn't give a damn. So I took up with some men I'd met in prison. I rustled horses and cattle, even robbed a few banks. I still hate banks—and bankers. Then I finally straightened out some, went back to California, and got a job."

"Is that where you met the child's mother?" Etta asked rather disdainfully. She saw the remark surprised him. "I've done my homework, Moss. In my attempt to find you, I've learned a lot about you. The little girl's mother was a prostitute, was she not?"

"Betsy Malone was a nice girl," he said flatly, glaring at her. "She was a mixed-up kid, but she was good to me and true to me."

"And why didn't you marry her?"

"Because I got accused of somethin' I didn't do and went back to prison," he replied coldly. "By the time I got out I figured I wasn't much use as a father to a little girl, so I went back to Chicago to look up my ma. Then Betsy died, and I was on my way out to California to see to her when I met up with Amanda here."

He leaned back and actually smiled. "That's when my life finally started goin' right. I married Mandy and we went and got my little girl. That was five years ago."

"You seem to be very happy."

"A man couldn't ask for better," he replied proudly.

Etta wanted to ask more about Amanda, about the story of how she and Moses Tucker met. But she decided against it. This was not the time. Perhaps Moss wouldn't want to talk about it in front of his young wife.

"I'm…glad that you're happy now, Moss. I truly am." Etta seemed to be struggling for the words, and if she was acting, it was very difficult to tell. To Amanda her words sounded sincere, and now a tear slipped down her cheek. "I can't…

apologize enough, Moss, for the cruel words I spoke…that last day I saw you. But, my God, Moss, I was only eighteen then! I didn't know anything about life—what was real, what had true value and what didn't. And I swear to God I had nothing to do with that bank swindle. I didn't know about that till later. Truly, Moss!" Her eyes met his pleadingly. "Can't we just… forget all that…and be friends? I—I need help, Moss. I don't know who else to ask."

"You need help?" he asked sarcastically. Amanda walked over and put her hands on his shoulders.

"Calm down, Moss," she said softly. "Can't you see how upset she is? Let her tell us why she came here. Surely the fact that she's even here—knowing how you probably felt about her and all—surely that means something, Moss."

He reached up and took her hand.

"I'm sayin' you don't know her, Mandy," he said softly. Etta dabbed at her tears with a lace hanky.

"Perhaps not. But I do remember a time when I was in trouble and had no one to depend on except you," Amanda replied. He looked up at her and she blinked back tears. "Give her the benefit of the doubt, Moss."

He put Amanda's hand to his lips and kissed the palm. Then Amanda walked over and put a hand on Etta's shoulder.

"I want you to eat, Etta. You and Moss both. Eat now, and then you can tell us all about it. There will be no more harsh words." She looked chidingly at her husband. "No more harsh words in my house."

Moss returned a look of love, half grinning at her words, which he knew were final. Amanda Tucker was not a woman to say cruel words or hold grudges. To him she was nothing short of a saint. She was everything he'd ever wanted in a woman. His love for Etta had been more an infatuation with someone from a world of wealth he never dreamed he could have. But he'd been much younger then, more foolish. Now he'd found what real quality was. And it was all wrapped up in Amanda: all the softness, loyalty, and love a man could ask for.

For the next few minutes nothing more was said. Moss put out his cigarette and began to eat. Etta sniffed and blew her nose, and began eating, surprised and pleased at the deliciousness of the stew.

"I see your lovely wife can even cook well," she finally spoke up.

"Amanda does everything good," Moss returned, breaking open a biscuit to butter it. Amanda blushed deeply and continued eating. She glanced sideways at Moss and he grinned at her; Etta felt a sharp stab of jealousy watching them.

"You go and have a seat in the rocker," Amanda told Etta when they finished. "Moss and I will pull up some chairs, and you can tell us why you're here."

Amanda's voice was cool and collected. All jealousy was gone now. For whatever Etta Landers was, she was still a woman—and apparently she was a woman in trouble. Amanda could not find it in her heart to be angry with the woman. What had happened had been long ago, and now Moss Tucker belonged to Amanda. It was unchristian to feel hatred or jealousy for Etta, or to turn the woman away without giving her a chance to explain herself.

"I'll get us all some coffee," she told them.

Etta rose and walked to the rocker, a graceful package of woman who looked far younger than her thirty-six years. Moss remained suspicious, but he knew Amanda hated arguments and raised voices, and above all, cursing. So he would try to hold his temper. He pulled a kitchen chair over in front of the hearth where Etta now reclined in the rocker, and lit another cigarette. Again there was silence. Etta's eyes met Moss Tucker's eyes, and they held for a moment. Both thought of things that could have been. But only for a moment. Amanda carried over a tray with three cups of coffee. She set it on a stool and handed a cup to Etta. Moss picked up his own, and Amanda took hers and sat down.

"I need guns, Moss," Etta spoke up suddenly, unable to keep from spilling her problems any longer. "You're good with a gun and you know other men who are good with guns. I need those guns. I don't know who else to ask."

Amanda looked at Moss with frightened eyes.

"I...told you...Moss is through with guns and violence, Etta," Amanda said in a shaky voice, moving her eyes to the woman.

Moss leaned back and took a deep drag on his cigarette. "Let her finish, Mandy," he said quietly. Amanda looked down at her lap, swallowing fear and dread.

"I'm sorry to interrupt your life like this," Etta told Amanda. Then her eyes moved to Moss. "But if you can't go yourself, perhaps you can at least give me names, round up some good men for me. Surely you still know some men from your outlaw days who were good with guns—guns I could hire to protect me and my ranch."

Moss frowned. "What ranch? You got a ranch in California? Where's that lawyer husband of yours?"

"Ralph and I are...divorced," Etta replied quietly, looking at the floor. "We divorced two years ago, and—and daddy died five years ago. Ralph..." She blinked back tears. "Oh, Moss, he cheated me out of everything! Everything! He took it all, everything daddy planned to give to me! Ralph planned and connived and handled daddy's papers so that when we divorced I had nothing! Nothing!"

Amanda felt like crying herself, but Moss watched, untouched by Etta's plight. He quietly puffed the cigarette.

"Why did you get divorced?" he asked coldly.

Etta covered her face and looked away. "I—I'd rather not go into it—not here, not now. The point is we are divorced. And daddy is dead and can't help me. And Ralph—he took everything from me, everything but some land in Wyoming that he didn't know anything about." She wiped her eyes and faced Moss again. "It's my land, Moss. And it's all I have left. Ralph didn't know about it. All the papers are legal and he can't touch it! But he's—he's vicious and selfish and—and he wants it all. Everything I have. He's bought off everybody in town, even the law! He harasses me, kills my cattle, burns my crops, threatens me. He's even had some of my help killed. Others have left, afraid for their lives." She stood up and paced. "He can't get the place legally, so he's trying to scare me off of it, badger me into giving up and leaving!" She whirled to face them both. "But I won't leave, Moss! I won't. It's mine, and it's all I have."

She burst into loud sobbing and leaned on the mantle, her shoulders shaking in what appeared to be genuine tears. Amanda turned to look at Moss, whose eyes were studying the lovely form of Etta Landers, the woman he had once loved and for whom he now held nothing but contempt. This woman who once had everything now had nothing: nothing but loneliness and threatened poverty. And Moss, who once had nothing, now had the most important wealth of all: a woman who loved him, a home, and a child. Their small ranch did not bring them wealth, but they lived comfortably.

Moss turned his eyes to meet Amanda's.

"Moss, it sounds dangerous," Amanda whispered, searching his eyes. "You haven't even worn a gun for the past two years!"

He reached over and patted her hand. "It's not somethin' you forget, Mandy. It's kind of like learnin' to walk. Once you learn it, it always stays with you. But don't go gettin' all lathered up yet." He leaned over and kissed her cheek, then stood up and paced a few minutes while Etta struggled to regain her composure. Finally she breathed deeply and turned to face him with red-rimmed eyes, but Moss was not touched.

"Where's your ranch?" he asked.

"It's about three hundred miles north of here," she replied, her eyes lighting up with hope. "On the Green River in Wyoming, north of Rock Springs."

"Prime grazin' country," Moss told her, putting out his cigarette.

"Oh, it's beautiful, Moss! I just can't let go of it. Daddy gave it to me, and it's good, rich land."

Moss frowned, and a trace of a grin passed over his lips.

"Since when did things like that matter to you? You're city-bred, remember?"

Etta stepped closer. "It's important because it's all I have left. I've learned to love it. And I intend to keep it. Please help me, Moss."

He felt an old stirring as the soft blue eyes penetrated his own. And the jealousy Amanda had managed to bury struggled to let loose inside of her again. She quickly and silently prayed for forgiveness—and for the strength and courage to understand and cooperate with whatever decision her husband made. Moss sighed again and walked to a window.

"You're askin' a lot, Etta. I haven't even had to use my gun in a while. And I'm settled now. I have a wife and a kid, and I own this place. It's not much, but it's home. I'm needed here."

"I know that. But surely you—you know some men who I could pay—"

"Oh, I expect so. This here ranch is smack in the middle of outlaw country. But most of them know me, and they respect Mandy. So they don't bother us. Sometimes one or two will even stop over here; Mandy feeds them and we put them up for the night. We don't ask questions long as nobody causes us no trouble."

"Then perhaps you could round some up for me."

He turned to face her, rubbing his chin thoughtfully.

"I could. But I'd feel responsible. And I'm the one they'd kind of look to for leadership. I'm the, uh, top gun, so to speak." He grinned a little, looking embarrassed.

"I heard that when I asked around about you," Etta replied, looking him over admiringly. "They say losing that arm didn't change a thing."

"Yeah, but gettin' married did change things. I can't just go runnin' off right into a gunfight."

"Perhaps if I told you who helped my husband swindle me out of everything, and who has set up a bank in Rock Springs, just waiting for Ralph Landers to add my land and earnings to the account he already has at that bank, perhaps then you would help me."

Moss studied her, his eyes turning colder.

"Yes," she said with a sly grin. "Miles Randall. The same Miles Randall who helped daddy cheat you out of all your money. The same Miles Randall who obliterated your account in Nevada and swore you never had one there. The same Miles Randall you nearly killed and went to prison for shooting."

Moss's eyes lit up with hatred, and Amanda got up from her chair.

"Moss, I don't like it," she said in a shaking voice. "You could get hurt or get in trouble again!"

But she could already see the wheels turning, and her heart pounded with fear.

"Miles Randall?" he asked, still staring at Etta. He had the look of an eager little boy.

"Yes, Moss!" she said, smiling now. "This is your chance to show him you're still around! He'd die of fright if Moss Tucker came riding into town! They'd all be afraid! Moss, you can chase my husband and his men out. I know you can! Maybe you can even show Miles Randall up for what he is and get rid of him, too. Oh, Moss, please, please, help me!"

Moss grinned almost wickedly. "Do I hear you begging, Etta?"

She stiffened, her cheeks flushing. "I suppose you do. And I'm sure you're enjoying it. I...don't blame you, Moss."

His eyes made her feel uncomfortable. "There was a time I needed you, Etta, and you failed me. Now you need me. Why shouldn't I ditch you just like you did me?"

She held up her chin and faced him defiantly. "Because you hate Miles Randall more than you hate me," she replied defiantly. "Because through me you can enjoy a sweet revenge!"

The room hung in silence for a moment, as Moss and Etta glared at each other. "Moss!" Amanda spoke up then, her voice seeming to break some kind of spell. Moss turned as though startled. "I have never told you what to do, Moss," Amanda went on sternly but quietly, "and I won't stop you from this thing if you feel you must do it. But let it be for the right reasons. Let it because there is an evil that needs to be set right, not for your own vengeance. If you let it be for vengeance, then the evil lies within yourself. You've already learned the loneliness and emptiness vengeance can bring."

Etta watched, seeing a love she envied deeply, a loyalty that could endure many things. Amanda Tucker did not want her husband to go away, especially to walk into a dangerous situation. But he was her man, and she would not stop him from something he thought he had to do. Etta's heart fell. She had thought that perhaps she could just walk right back into Moss Tucker's life, and prove that he still loved her and desired her. But she had met a challenge bigger than herself.

Moss sighed, his mind in turmoil. He had to get out of the cabin. It suddenly felt stuffy and close. "Come and walk with me, Mandy," he told his wife. He walked over and put an arm around her. Amanda did not reply; her throat felt constricted, and tears ran unwillingly down her cheeks. They walked outside together.

Etta sat down in the rocker to wait. A clock on the mantle ticked away quietly. She wondered if her husband's men had already taken over the ranch. It had taken eight days to get down to Moss's ranch in Utah. What a desolate area this was! Perhaps after having Moses Tucker to herself for several days—even weeks—and once he enjoyed the luxuries of her vast ranch in the cool grasslands along the Sweetwater, perhaps she could make him forget the plain little wife he'd left behind in the hot wastelands of Utah. She pulled at a red curl at her cheek and smiled prettily to herself. "He *is* just a man, after all," she thought. "And all men are the same."

Chapter Thirty

They walked quietly, the only sound being their footsteps, a grating sound against the red, dry earth of their small Utah ranch. Amanda put a hand to her cheek, wondering if the hot, dry air would age her before her time, wondering how she looked to him now, compared to Etta Landers. Yet all the time she knew it was a foolish thought. She was younger, and her skin was still soft and supple, and yet...

"Come on over here and sit down, Mandy," he was telling her gently, leading her to the large, flat boulder under the sparse shade of a poplar tree. It was the only tree for miles around, and he knew this spot was her favorite. They sat down, and she leaned her head against his shoulder. He put his arm around her and kissed the dark hair that he loved. A fox squirrel ran in front of them and scurried up the tree.

"You want to go," she finally said.

"I'm not sure, Mandy."

"Yes, you are." She sighed. "We haven't been apart since we got married, Moss. Since before we got married."

"I don't like the thought of bein' apart any better than you do, honey. But the men around here—they'd take care of you, as far as that part of it goes. And you've got Becky and the school. And I'd try to get back soon as I could."

"And then again, maybe you wouldn't come back at all," she said quietly, watching the squirrel.

"Come on, Mandy. You know I can handle myself. There's not a man can outgun me, and even that Apache's hatchet couldn't put me down. And I get along just fine with one arm."

"And perhaps you'd never come back even if you didn't get

yourself killed," she said in a near whisper. "She's very beautiful, and you did love her once, you know."

He sighed and hugged her closer. "Don't do that, Mandy. That's not how my woman talks. You know better than to say a thing like that."

She turned and flung her arms around his neck, bursting into tears. He grasped her tightly around the waist and stood up, holding her so that her feet didn't even touch the ground. To him she felt small as a child, and in many ways she was still as innocent as one. He kissed her hair over and over and let her cry. He knew she had worked hard all morning and was tired. And having Etta Landers appear out of a clear blue sky, catching her unprepared and suddenly seeming to challenge her had not helped. But he knew the kind of woman Amanda Tucker was, and he knew she just needed a little time to think about it, to remember the kind of love they shared.

"Moss, you're doing this for vengeance," she wept. "It's wrong, Moss!"

He pulled away and took her hand. "No I'm not, Mandy. There's just apparently some very wrong things goin' on up there, and I don't like seein' a woman abused like Etta is bein' abused."

Their eyes held. "Moses Tucker, don't lie to me. You might feel sorry for Etta, but there is too much hurt there for you to go running off risking your life for her. I warned you it shouldn't be for vengeance. But I saw the look in your eyes when she mentioned that Miles Randall."

His eyes hardened again and she nodded, wiping at her tears.

"It's just as I thought." She frowned. "Moss, that's the worst reason."

He turned away, running his hand through his hair. "It's the best reason, Mandy. I'm damned sorry, but that man has to be stopped. And I can't help but enjoy the fact that Etta Graceland Landers is begging me to help her. I know all them feelings are wrong, but I can't ignore them. A man has his pride, and that whole affair with Etta and that banker and all—all of it has eaten at me all these years, kept me from feelin' like a real man. Now I have a chance to make up for it all, and to earn us some money besides. Etta's got money. She'll pay me good and maybe I can buy us some more land, build you a nicer house."

"Moss, I don't care about those things."

"Well, I do!" he said in almost a biting voice. She flinched, surprised and hurt; his eyes were instantly apologetic as he reached out and touched her face. "Mandy, you deserve the best I can give you. This is my chance to get back some of the pride Etta destroyed, to enjoy revenge, and to make us some good money besides. Don't hold me back, Mandy. I'll never feel right if I don't do this."

Her face fell in resignation. "A man must do what he must do," she answered quietly then. "Lord knows part of what I love about you is your pride and manliness. I just don't believe that anything good can come of vengeance, Moss. Try to use your common sense. Don't let hatred be your guide and cause you to do something foolish."

He pulled her close again. "I'll try to remember those words, Mandy. And you know I can sure as hell take care of myself. It's just that—God, Mandy, how can I pass up this chance? All of a sudden all that ugly past has come back to hit me right in the face. Maybe if I go do this thing, I can finally lay them memories to rest."

She clung to his shirt. "Moss, I'll be so afraid while you're gone."

"You've got protection here, honey, all kinds of it." He knew she was remembering her abduction and rape five years ago, an event that still haunted her and often made her wake up screaming in the middle of the night. But he'd always been there to hold her and help her forget again. Perhaps it was wrong to leave her now. He gently urged her back to sit down again, and he sat beside her with his arm around her shoulders. She wiped at her eyes again, and he noticed the pins coming out of her hair. He grinned and began pulling them out so that her hair fell to her waist. The thick, dark waves had a reddish tint in the sun.

"Maybe it would be good for me to be away a while, Mandy," he told her softly, running a hand through her hair. "You shouldn't still be so afraid. And out here in this wild country, there's no guarantee I'll always be around. It could help you learn not to be so afraid all the time, and you could spend even more time at the school without me to be lookin' after and cookin' for and all. You've always said you'd like to teach more than three days a week, and you wanted to teach Wanda and a couple of them other Navaho women more—the ones you told me are so anxious to learn to read and write better. This would give you a good opportunity."

"That's true," she replied, dabbing at her eyes. She turned to face him. "Tell me you love me, Moss."

He flashed a handsome grin. "You crazy kid. Do I really need to do that?" He pulled some of the long hair in front of her shoulder and ran his hand through it, letting the back of his hand rest lightly against her breast.

"I guess I keep forgettin' you still don't know everything about men," he told her, studying her with eyes that shone with love. "My God, Mandy, all the wealth, all the beauty in the world—they don't mean anything compared to havin' a woman like you. You fill needs in me that a woman like Etta could never satisfy. The kind of life I've led—hell, I never dreamed I could end up with somethin' like you."

She reddened slightly and looked down at her lap; he moved his hand to the back of her neck. "And you're ten times prettier than Etta Landers, woman. You know it just as well as I do. And I don't mean just in looks. But if you want to talk about looks, hell, you've got the prettiest hair I've ever seen on a woman, and big, pretty eyes, and that skin—it's soft and pretty all by itself. You don't need all that stuff on your face—painted eyelids and painted lips and black junk on your lashes. A girl like you don't need any of that stuff. But all looks aside, you've got a beauty inside you that radiates right out and snags just about every man that looks at you. So I don't want to hear any more talk about how pretty Etta Landers is. 'Cause her kind of prettiness don't go too awful deep. And I know that woman, Mandy. I'm not the stupid kid I was eighteen years ago. It's all different now. There's not a woman alive can take me from you. And because I'd be lonely as hell and wantin' to get back to you, I'd hurry and get the job done and be extra careful, so I could get back here soon as I could and all in one piece."

She still looked at her lap. He took her chin and forced her face up, and in the next moment his lips met hers while his hand moved to the back of her head and pressed her mouth tightly to his own. It was a gentle, lingering kiss, and she could taste his loneliness and his hunger; and even after five years she never ceased to be surprised at her own ability to return a kiss just as hungrily. But Moss Tucker had taught her everything about the art of making love, and had changed her from a frightened girl into a willing woman.

"Nothin' and nobody can keep me from comin' back to my pretty, young wife," he was telling her, his lips moving to her neck. He kissed her throat where the neck of her dress lay open, then moved down to nestle his face between her breasts. He made a growling sound and she laughed lightly and put her hands to his thick hair, stroking it and thinking quietly for a moment. Moss closed his eyes and enjoyed the warm, comforting feeling of a woman's breasts—the woman he loved.

"I wish I could give you a son, Moss," she said, suddenly sobering. "I'd be so happy and contented, if I could have my own child—a child that was just yours and mine. You'd think after all, I mean, as good as things are in bed…"

He sighed and sat straighter, stroking her hair again.

"Don't dwell on it, Mandy. I've told you that before. If you never give me a child, it don't matter. Havin' you is all that matters. But I hope it happens, for your sake. I know how much you want a baby." He grinned a little. "And God knows I'm trying." She blushed and he kissed her forehead. "But God also knows what's best, and when it's the right time, if ever. You've done a lot of healin' these past years, and not just mentally. Maybe—maybe what happened with them outlaws—maybe somethin' got damaged, you know?"

Her eyes filled with the remembered horror, and he kept stroking her hair reassuringly.

"Mandy, I don't mean to bring back old memories. I'm only tryin' to make you understand some of the possible reasons. Now maybe God knows when it's the right time for you to have a child, when your mind and your body are ready. You understand what I'm saying?"

"I…pray and pray and pray," she gasped, a tear slipping down her cheek.

"Come on, Mandy, don't do that. Maybe you should quit tryin' so hard. I've heard talk that sometimes a woman can just try too damned hard and it never happens, you know? I don't know much about them things, but maybe that's so. Maybe that's another reason why I should go away for a while. It'll make you quit tryin' so hard, get your mind on more teachin' and such. And when I get back, who knows? Hell, I'll be so glad to see you I'll have you in bed twenty-four hours a day. You're bound to get pregnant then, right?" He flashed a grin, and she couldn't help but smile, at the same time reddening. How he loved her blush! His advances toward her and his remarks about making love always made her blush like a little girl, and it only made him want her even more.

"I reckon we'll have to move the men out of the bunkhouse and let Etta stay there the next couple nights till I get some men rounded up."

"Oh, Moss, you can't make her stay out there!"

"Oh, yes I can. If I'm gonna be leavin' you, I intend to have you all to myself the next few nights, woman. I don't want to have to worry about somebody hearin' us."

Their eyes held, and she felt a warmth rush through her and actually blushed. Why was this man still able to make her blush? She couldn't help but feel quietly victorious at his suggestion. Yes, Etta Landers should not stay in the house. The house belonged to Amanda and Moses Tucker. Moss was her man, shared her bed, touched only his Mandy in the night. She felt a sudden terrible possessiveness as he bent to kiss her, and she returned the kiss with great passion, fire swelling through secret places that only Moses Tucker had touched with her consent.

He rose then and took her arm; she hesitated before walking back. "Tell me the truth, then, Moss," she told him, meeting his eyes. "You've decided too suddenly to leave me, this place, everything that is important to you. Such a sudden decision can only be made that quickly because you are still so full of hate for Etta, for this man called Miles Randall. You're going just to get back at both of them, aren't you? It's strictly hatred and vengeance."

Their eyes held, and his took on a defensive look. "I suppose it is, Mandy. I know it's hard for a woman like you to understand that. But if I do this, maybe I can at least be at peace with myself once and for all."

"And maybe you can finally get Etta Landers out of your heart?"

He could see the uncertainty in her eyes. "She's been out of my heart for years, Mandy. Ain't no woman in my heart but my Mandy. No woman. What I feel for Etta is a long, long way from love, and to have her beggin' me for help feels mighty good."

She swallowed back an urge to scream and yell and order him not to go. But no one ordered Moses Tucker to do anything, especially not his woman. She usually got her way just by being herself, by loving gently and talking quietly. But she sensed that even those things would not work this time. Her man had already made up his mind. Perhaps it was necessary after all. She loved him. She trusted him. Moss Tucker would not betray her.

"Come back to me, Moss—unhurt and still mine."

He flashed a handsome grin. "You can count on both, Mandy. I'd die before I'd leave you or hurt you. I couldn't live without you, and you know it." He bent low and kissed her lightly, then turned and began to walk, his arm about her waist.

As they neared the house, they could see Etta pacing outside, one of her men walking with her. The two of them appeared to be arguing, but both quieted when Moss and Amanda came closer. Etta gazed hopefully at Moss, while the man beside her glared disgustedly. For a moment, no one said anything. Etta looked from Moss to Amanda, who had apparently been crying. Then she met Moss's eyes again.

"You're going to help me?"

"I'll help," he replied, taking his arm from around Amanda and pulling a prerolled cigarette from his shirt pocket. "But not because of any feelings I might have for you, Etta. It's to get a chance at Miles Randall and to earn me some money. And I'd help any woman in your state, so don't go thinkin' it's got anything to do with you in particular."

His gaze moved to the man beside Etta. Moss struck a match, lit his cigarette, and studied the man's eyes. Moses Tucker knew how to read eyes, and this man didn't like him. The stranger was slightly shorter than Moss, but built just as broadly. He looked like the type who could hold his own in a fight. Moss guessed him to be about the same age as Etta, perhaps even younger, and he was a handsome man, with sandy hair and a firm jawline. But the contempt he held in his eyes at that moment detracted from his looks.

Etta's eyes darkened at Moss's remark, but she held her tongue in check. After all, he was going to help her. She looked from Moss to the man beside her, then back at Moss, noticing nervously how the two eyed each other.

"Moss, this is Lloyd Duncan. Lloyd is my top man. Lloyd, this is Moses Tucker. I've told you enough about him—"

"You're hirin' a cripple for this job?" the man interrupted, studying Moss contemptuously. Amanda's heart ached for Moss at the remark, and Etta gasped in embarrassment. Moss seemed undaunted, as he took a deep drag on the cigarette.

"Mister, I aim to help Etta, and the only way I'm gonna

be able to do that is if everybody cooperates," he said calmly. "That goes for you, too. Till this job is done, I'm the boss. And if you don't like it, we can have at it right now. I'm ready any time you are—my one arm against both of yours, or we can use guns. Don't make no difference to me."

"You'll do no such thing!" Etta spoke up disgustedly. She whirled to face Lloyd Duncan. "You apologize for that remark, or you're fired!" she barked at the man.

Duncan glared at her a moment, clenching his fists. Then he moved hostile eyes to Moss.

"Sorry," he grumbled.

Etta put her hands to her waist and glowered at Duncan.

"It will be just as Moss says," she said sternly. "Whatever Moss says, you do. Understood? I need Moses Tucker's help."

"You're a fool!" Duncan snapped. "I could have handled this!"

"Then why haven't you?" she hissed through clenched teeth. "You and Danny are the only good men I have left! The others have either been killed or ran away with their tails between their legs, and some of them were probably bought off! You're a good man, Lloyd, but Moss is better and he knows what he's doing! So it's his way, or you're out!"

Duncan stood there a moment longer, then turned and stormed away, kicking at dirt and stones as he walked. Etta turned to Moss, instantly softening again and putting on a sweet smile, determined to soften the man's hatred of her, and afraid he would change his mind about helping her.

"Oh, Moss, I'm so sorry. But I can handle him, really. He won't give you any more trouble." She reached out and touched his arm. "Thank you, Moss! I'll pay you well. I'll pay all of them well. You go and get however many men you think you'll need."

"Couldn't be Duncan's a little jealous, could it?" Moss asked matter-of-factly. "He one of your lovers?"

Etta reddened, and her smile faded. Amanda looked away, embarrassed for the woman.

"I'm not holdin' you guilty of nothing, Etta. You've got your reasons for whatever you do. But I've got me the feelin' you buy men with more than money. That's just fine, if it's what you want. But playin' around with men's feelings cause one hell of a lot of trouble when it comes to gettin' cooperation from everybody," Moss went on sternly. "And I'll need cooperation. So you get it straight with your men that this is strictly business between you and me and nothin' more. And I'd best not catch you tryin' to entice any of my own men into your bed, 'cause they're gonna need to concentrate on gettin' this job done. I'm not gonna have them quarrelin' among themselves over which one is your favorite! Understood?"

Etta blinked back tears, and again he wondered if they were feigned.

"Moss, I—"

"I told you I don't blame you for nothing. I don't know the circumstances surroundin' your divorce and I don't know what your needs are and I don't care. I'm just tellin' you I don't want no playin' around with my men. And I need to know where things stand with your own men if I'm to know how to handle them. Is Duncan your lover?"

"Moss!" She choked the word out, putting a hand to her throat.

"I'll go get Becky," Amanda spoke up, eager for an excuse to leave to lighten Etta's embarrassment. She walked away.

"He...was a lover," Etta replied, looking at the ground. "The other young man with me, Danny Green—we've never— there's nothing between us, and he's a good man. Lloyd and I—it was just a passing thing..."

"Well, maybe not to him, Etta. You still don't think much of a man's feelings, do you?"

She raised her eyes to his. "Moss, you don't understand why I've had lovers. It's not—not what you think, Moss. You don't understand what it was like with Ralph..."

"You can explain later," he replied, his eyes roving her body with a mixture of sorrow and disgust. "I've got things to do."

• • •

Amanda folded a shirt and put it into one of her husband's saddlebags that lay on a chair in the bedroom. He watched her, lying in bed and smoking quietly.

"Why don't you stop that and come to bed?" he told her, more of a command than a question.

She smiled, feeling the desire awakening in her blood. The thought of their impending separation heightened their need for one another, but her own fears for his safety made her want to ignore the fact that he would leave.

"You'll have some riding to do the next few days just to round up some men. I thought I'd pack some of your things tonight. You said you wanted to get an early start."

"Not that early. If it means losin' some time with you tonight, then the hell with it."

She blushed and laid another shirt near the saddlebags. "Moss…"

"Get them clothes off, woman, and get over here. I intend to stamp you real good into my memory before I leave."

She laughed lightly and moved toward the bed, bending to blow out the lamp.

"Leave it," he ordered.

She looked at him in surprise. "Why?"

"So I can see you good. I want to remember every inch of you."

She blushed more. "Moss, I can't—"

He grabbed her wrist and pulled her onto the bed, smothering her sweet laughter with hungry kisses until she lay unresisting, returning the kisses as she helped him remove her clothes and throw them to the floor. He felt a wonderful excitement when she responded to him as she was now, whimpering when his fingers touched the silky moistness in that hidden crevice that belonged only to him. This was a far cry from the shy, inhibited girl she had been when he met her, a girl who knew nothing about men and passion. And it was also a far cry from the frightened, tortured girl she had been after her abduction and rape.

Moss Tucker had transformed her into a whole woman, bringing out her beautiful ability to respond to a man in the way only a pure, giving woman like Amanda Tucker could respond. She was such a warm, giving, generous wife, even in bed. He only wished he could put both arms around her; but it didn't seem to matter to her that he could only support himself with what was left of his left arm, so that he could gently work his magic with his right hand. She had never seemed to be bothered by the missing arm, but then a woman like Amanda would not be disturbed by such things. He had found a treasure, and he would never give it up.

She whispered his name as his lips caressed the swollen nipples of her full, tender breasts and his fingers explored the private property of Moses Tucker. He could sense her building passion and he quickly moved on top of her, wanting to be inside of her when the final explosion of heated desire took place deep in her belly, wanting to feel her pulling him inside her with sweet abandon. He entered her with a gentle thrust, always afraid of hurting her, always finding it difficult not to push himself wildly because of his great need of her and his very deep love for her. But this was his sweet, still almost innocent Mandy. He treasured her, he adored her, he all but worshiped her, and above all he respected her and could not bring himself to use her like some kind of animal.

He felt the lovely pulling sensation then as she cried out his name and did her best to give him pleasure while enjoying her own. They were wrapped together then, two beings becoming one, each telling the other that everything was all right: that he would come back, that she would wait, that he would be true to her, just as she would be true to him. There was no doubt about any of those things. He was her man, and she was his woman, and nothing was going to change or destroy that. He released his passion and his life flowed into her womb, and both secretly prayed that perhaps this time the seed would take hold and sprout into the child she so desperately wanted.

• • •

It took four days—of sending telegrams from Hanksville, the nearest town but still some fifty miles away; and a visit to Robber's Roost by Moss and some of his men, a thirty-mile jaunt—to gather up enough good men: men who were good with guns, men of action, with no homes or wives to hold them back. They were drifters, outlaws, some simply men always looking for adventure. Most of them had been in prison more than once; some were still wanted by the law, a few had never been in trouble. All of them respected a good woman and secretly yearned for a home and a woman of their own. But for a variety of reasons, most known only to themselves, such things had never been and would probably never be theirs. Moses Tucker had simply been one of the lucky ones.

Slim Taggart agreed to go along. He and Willie had two children now, both sons. The man's wife, an ex-prostitute, had turned into one of the best women a man could ask for. All she had needed was the honest love of a good man, and she had found that in Slim. Willie and Amanda Tucker, although from vastly different backgrounds, had become fast friends. Now Slim, a longtime friend to Moss, agreed to join Moss's growing band of men; for the man had secretly longed to ride the trail with old friends again, wanting—as most men do—a chance to ride free and wild once more, in spite of how much he loved his wife and family.

Pappy Lane, now sixty-five, insisted on going, even though Moss was totally against it. But Pappy wanted to prove he still had a good fight in him, and Moss knew that the man was not only reliable and a good shot, but also his best friend. If all the others failed him, Pappy would not. So Pappy would go. It was difficult for Moss to say no to the man; there were still times when Moss could see the sorrow in Pappy's eyes—sorrow the man still carried for having been the one who decided to cut off Moss's arm. But the decision was made, and removing the infected arm had saved Moss's life. Moss still regretted the violent, cruel words he had screamed at Pappy those first awful days after he lost the arm. He'd long since forgiven Pappy for taking the arm, which had obviously been the right decision. But he often wondered if the old man would ever forgive himself.

In the days that the men gathered at the Tucker ranch, memories returned to Amanda that she would rather have left forgotten.

"Hey, pretty lady, you're lookin' right good! Right good!" Johnny Pence called out to her on the third morning. Amanda blushed as he rode up on his horse and leaned over to shake her hand. "I hear tell you're takin' real good care of Moss."

"I try," she replied bashfully. Johnny squeezed her hand. He was in his late thirties now, his face leathered by years of living under the stars.

"Try, hell. You're the most talked-about woman west of the Mississippi! And I'm right proud to have had a hand in helpin' Moss find you a few years back. It's damned good to see you again, Amanda."

"It's good to see you, Johnny. You shouldn't have stayed away so long."

"Oh, well, us drifters figure it's best we stay away from settled men like Moss. Might rub off, you know?" He winked and chuckled and headed his horse for the corral. Amanda watched him. It was good to see them all again, but it brought back the memory of the circumstances under which she had met these men. Johnny, fifty-year-old Darrell Hicks, and Lonnie Drake, now about thirty—they'd all helped Moss search for her after a different breed of outlaw had captured her. But the filthy deed had been done by the time Moss and the others reached her. She was dying then. If they hadn't come when they did…She shuddered and shook the thought from her mind. So some of the old bunch—Pappy, Darrell, Lonnie, and Johnny—would go along. She was relieved for that much. She knew Moss could depend on all of them.

There were others, four whom she had met before: men who had stopped by on their trail to nowhere to get a good woman-cooked meal and a real bed for the night, men whose pasts were known only to themselves, men whom neither Amanda nor Moss questioned as to where they had come from or where they were going. But all men that Amanda had learned to trust. Moss was right. If something did happen to him, Amanda could ask any one of these men to help her, and she'd get the help, without having to worry about her person. They all knew Moss Tucker, and none of them cared to be a victim of his vengeance. But there was more to it than that. Most of them just simply had a deep respect for a good woman. Women were scarce in this land, good ones even more rare. Most of the men considered it unmanly and cowardly to insult or harm a woman. Of course there were exceptions like Rand Barker, the man who had kidnaped and raped her, but they were few. And in spite of being a mixture of rustlers, robbers, gamblers, drinkers, and murderers, the men Moss was gathering together were not molesters of women. They got what they needed from the prostitutes who inhabited "The Line" in the numerous cowtowns of the West. There had been a time when Moses Tucker was just like them. But those days were over now. He had Amanda. It relieved her somewhat to see the men Moss would be taking along to back him up.

There was Les Trainer, Tom Sorrells, Max Cornell, Dwight Brady, Hank Stemm and Brad Doolittle. Then there was the silent blond man simply called Bullit, and a half-breed Navaho called Sooner. Moss always said when there was trouble, Sooner was there before anybody else—hence the nickname. Besides, they all had trouble pronouncing his Indian name.

Most fell into the mid-thirties age bracket; a couple of them were in their late twenties, a few in their forties and fifties. They were an interesting mixture of sizes; and wore a wide array of clothing, from pointed-toe leather boots, leather chaps, and calico shirts to buckskins and moccasins. All rode sturdy mounts, and Moss intended to take five extra of his own horses, just in case there should be a problem along the way. Sooner would be in charge of the extra mounts. The trip would be a combination of horseback and train.

Amanda guessed that most were going not for the money, but for the adventure and to help out a woman in distress. Not many things brought them together any faster than that. And once each man got a look at Etta Landers, none regretted taking on the job. Amanda had a feeling that keeping the men's eyes off of Etta would be a tougher job for Moss than helping Etta fight Ralph Landers.

Six other men, who normally stayed around the ranch, would remain to keep up the chores and watch over Amanda. And Wanda, the widowed Navaho woman who cooked for the ranch hands, would stay full time and keep Amanda company inside the house. She would sleep in Becky's room, and Becky would sleep with Amanda.

Amanda watched the little girl now, ecstatic with excitement over all the strangers and all the movement that was now taking place. Moss kept his daughter with him almost constantly, wanting to see as much of her as possible before he left. Amanda had fallen in love with little Rebecca instantly when she and Moss had gone to get the girl in California. Becky was only two then, a fat little bundle topped off with a cascade of blond curls. Now she was seven, a bright, pleasant child, a willing help-mate and a good friend to Amanda, who was "mother" to Becky.

The day of departure came all too soon. Amanda awakened to the screech of a hawk somewhere outside—and Moss Tucker's lips moving over her neck.

"I see you left that gown off like I asked," he whispered, moving his lips to her breasts.

"I do everything you ask," she replied with a soft smile. She closed her eyes and breathed deeply, the excitement building within her again as he gently tasted the taught nipples. He groaned, and she ran her fingers through his hair and over the brown, muscular shoulders. Everything about him was hard muscle and masculinity, and he knew all the moves to make. His lips moved down to kiss her flat belly, and it didn't matter that they had already done this once before in the past eight hours. He was leaving, and he would not leave without being one with his wife once more.

Her breath quickened as his lips moved down even farther, relishing private places that belonged only to him, then worked their way back up while his fingers touched the soft warmth between her legs and made her whisper his name. Then his lips were covering hers, forcing hers apart, while his fingers explored until she felt on fire with desire. The basics were always the same, yet each time was so different, wonderful in a new and different way. This time the act was more urgent than it had ever been. He was leaving today. He was riding into danger, and the thought of his doing so with Etta Landers at his side made Amanda respond with a clinging possessiveness.

He moved on top of her with ease, and she opened herself up to him to take in that part of him that revealed his manliness more than anything else. Everything about Moss Tucker was big, and there had been times when he wondered how he managed to fit into the small woman who lay beneath him. Her cries were a mixture of pain and pleasure and glorious ecstasy.

His desire for her had not dwindled even the slightest in their five years together, for there was so much about her to love. And when he felt her reach the height of her climax, arching up to him in pulsating desire, he groaned out her name and thrust himself deep inside of her, stretching out the ecstasy for as long as he could bear it before releasing his passion.

They lay there together until their fever began to subside. It was already warm outside; Moss rolled off her and pushed her damp hair from her brow.

"Good morning, Mrs. Tucker."

"I'm not even completely awake yet," she whispered.

He grinned and kissed her breasts.

"Perhaps I should try again to wake you up."

"You'll get a late start, and everyone will know and I'll be embarrassed!" she replied with a smile.

He nuzzled her neck and growled. "They'd all just be jealous," he whispered. He raised up and saw the tears in her eyes.

"Be careful, Moss," she whispered. "And come back to me."

"I'll do both."

"And be true to me."

"Oh, Mandy!" he said softly, shaking his head. "You know you don't have to tell me that."

She blinked back more tears and traced her fingers over the dark hairs of his chest.

"You belong to me, Moss. You're my whole world."

He kissed her forehead. "And you're my whole world—you and Becky. A man who's been through what I've been through don't throw away somethin' like that."

"You'll send word—let me know how things are going, won't you? Don't leave me in the dark, Moss."

"I'll send word."

"She'll try to seduce you."

He chuckled lightly. "What's left to tempt me with after bein' in bed with you, hmmm?" He kissed her again, and she returned the kiss hungrily, desperately, wrapping her arms around his neck and wanting to hold him forever.

"Look me straight in the eyes, Mandy," he told her softly, releasing the kiss. "Tell me you trust me. 'Cause if you don't, this marriage don't amount to much. I can't do or say much more to convince you you've got nothin' to worry about. So tell me you trust me, Mandy, so I can ride out of here in peace and not worry about things goin' through your mind, things you shouldn't be thinkin' at all."

Their eyes held for several quiet seconds, and she thought about how lonely this man had been when she first met him. He'd been good to her, settled down, worked hard to keep her comfortable. She remembered that he had risked his life for her—more than once—and she remembered his suffering when he lost his arm.

"I trust you," she said softly. "It's her I don't trust!" she added with raised eyebrows.

Moss laughed and began tickling her. She screamed automatically, then rolled away from him.

"Everyone will hear us!" she whispered, wiggling out of his way. He grabbed her back and began kissing her again, over and over until he felt her go limp. His lips moved over her mouth, her neck, her breasts, and he knew she was still warm and excited from her recent climax. He moved on top of her and nibbled at her ear.

"Once more," he groaned.

"Moss Tucker, are you crazy?" she squealed. "It's impossible!"

"Why?" he asked, kissing her eyes.

"Well, it just is! You just got through—"

"Yeah, but this is different. I don't want to leave you."

He kissed her lips, and to her surprise she felt his hardness against her stomach. His lips moved across her cheek.

"Moss, I don't think…"

He worked himself between her legs, then pushed his knees up, forcing her legs apart.

"Moss, you'll be late…"

"Be quiet," he moaned. He pushed himself inside of her, and she had no more objections.

Chapter Thirty-One

Amanda, Wanda, and even Etta, spent the morning serving a home-cooked breakfast to Moss's small army of men before they made ready to ride. To Moss's pleasure, he could see a difference in the ways the men looked at Etta and at Amanda. Etta they eyed hungrily, as though she might make a tasty dessert after a hearty meal. But when they looked at Amanda, it was different: there was a deep respect there, as if she were something to be revered. Amanda was the hearty meal, a woman who left a man satisfied in more ways than one. The kind of pleasure a woman like Etta brought was only temporary. The pleasure Amanda could give was permanent and lasting, and they all knew it—and they all envied Moses Tucker.

Amanda fought tears at the sight of Moss coming out of the house that morning wearing his gun, hung low on his right hip. It had been a long time. Their eyes held for a moment, and nothing was said. Then the business of breakfast took over their time and thoughts.

Breakfast was finished all too soon for Amanda and Moss, for everyone's gear was packed and there was little else to do but to leave. Moss gathered the men together in front of the house for final instructions. Most knew why they were there, and most didn't care. It was simply an adventure for them, and a way to earn some good money. Such men had nothing better to do, and many had been earning their money illegally, and they didn't mind. Besides, Moses Tucker was a good friend and a natural leader, a man still good with a gun in spite of his missing arm.

The men gathered around, some lighting cigarettes, a couple sitting down with their backs against fence posts and their hats pulled down over their eyes, listening without watching. One man took out his six-gun and toyed with the chamber, whirling it anxiously. Moss lit his own cigarette and walked among the group of men.

"You've all met Etta Landers," he told them. There were some grins and sidelong glances at Etta, who stood aside with Amanda and Wanda. She reddened slightly and looked at the ground. "I want to get a few facts straight before we leave," Moss went on. "A lot of you know Mrs. Landers and I almost got married once." He scanned them with warning eyes. "But that was a long time ago, and it's over. Any of you wants to suggest I'm goin' up to Wyoming to help her for reasons other than money and revenge against one of the men who's botherin' her, you can leave now. You all know my wife, and you also know that with somebody like Amanda a man don't have eyes for no other woman."

This time Amanda reddened and smiled bashfully.

"That's easy to understand," one of the men drawled. The rest of them smiled good-naturedly, and Moss had to grin himself. He took a drag on his cigarette before continuing.

"What am I aimin' at," he continued, "is to make sure you all understand what we're doin' and why we're doin' it. Mrs. Landers is divorced, and her husband stole everything from her: all her land and possessions, except for a spread up in Wyoming he didn't know anything about. He's followed her there and is tryin' to scare and harass her off the property. It's all she has left and she wants to hang on to it. She don't know nobody in those parts, so she came to me for help. She knew I was good with a gun and figured I could round up some men skilled enough and brave enough to go up to Wyoming and help her fight for her land. You'll each get two hundred bucks a month plus an extra hundred each once this thing is settled. That's damned good pay and you all know it, so I expect you to do your best for Mrs. Landers. Once we get where we're goin' we'll decide just how to go about fightin' Landers and his men. In the meantime, I want no talk about me and Etta—not even a suggestion, unless one of you wants to take me on. In addition to that, Mrs. Landers here bein' single don't make her a lump of sugar for you bunch of no-good bucks. You'll treat her with respect. Things will get dangerous where we're going, so keep your minds on the business at hand. And if any of you figures on makin' any advances toward Mrs. Landers that she ain't wanting, you'll feel lead pushin' your belt buckle into your gut. Are we straight so far?"

The men nodded, a few clearing their throats. When Moses Tucker meant business, he meant business. Etta watched Moss with admiration. What a fool she had been to turn him away so many years ago! In the short time she had been at the Tucker ranch, she had learned to envy Amanda Tucker, to whom Moss was very obviously totally devoted. There had been few words between Moss and Etta, and those few out of mere necessity. The woman knew he still held her in contempt, and that Moss Tucker was enjoying the fact that Etta had literally begged for his help.

"Now Ralph Landers is a very powerful man," Moss went on. "He pretty much owns the closest town and the local law, and this thing could get messy. Some of you could even get killed. So if you don't like the odds, get out now."

"The odds are what made me want to go," one spoke up. He looked at Moss with a half grin, as he chewed on a weed. Some of the others chuckled.

"The woman's got herself fixed between a rock and a hard place," another spoke up. "We was figurin' on wedgin' her out of there."

Moss grinned and puffed his cigarette.

"Well, that's about it, I guess. The main thing I want is to get this over with and get back home."

"Can't imagine why," Darrell Hicks spoke up. They all laughed lightly and Moss grinned even more. Amanda reddened deeply and fussed at picking a weed out of Becky's hair, trying to avoid their looks.

"I'd be in a hurry, too," Hank Stemm added.

Most of them got up from their seated positions on the ground and made ready to go to their horses.

"Wait a minute!" Lloyd Duncan spoke up, stepping forward. Etta's heart pounded with fear at what he would say, and anger for his interruption. "There's one thing to be settled here!"

Everybody turned to look at the man, who had sulked around the last few days, talking to no one.

"Lloyd, just get your horse and let's get going!" Etta spoke up.

"Why? You afraid I'll show Moss Tucker up for what he is—a cripple?" the man sneered. "I say he ain't fit to run this outfit. It should be my job. At least I've got two arms!"

Everyone quieted, and Amanda stepped back, pulling Becky with her. Moss moved closer to Duncan, pushing his hat back a little.

"Well, well," he said in a steely voice. "You're actin' like a stud stallion, wantin' to show the herd who's boss." He threw down his cigarette. "Is that what you're wanting, boy?"

"I don't take orders from no cripple!" Duncan growled.

"You don't know what you're saying, mister," Johnny Pence spoke up. "If you knew Moss better, you'd be lickin' them words up out of the dirt. That man deserves respect, and you'd best give it to him."

"Respect?" Duncan snickered. "He's a crippled, middle-aged man who's doin' this for one reason only: to prove he can still be Etta Landers's man!"

Amanda covered her mouth and Etta gasped; Duncan had barely spoken the last word when Moss's huge fist landed into his belly. Duncan grunted and bent over, and Moss's knee came up in the man's face, knocking his head backward before his feet could go in the same direction. He bent at the knees and went down. No one made a move. Moss stood his ground while Duncan rolled over to his hands and knees, gasping for breath from the unexpectedly powerful blow. After losing his arm,

Moses Tucker had concentrated on building up the strength in his remaining arm to a surprising power.

Duncan struggled to his feet and turned to face Moss. He dove into the man, knocking Moss to the ground, but Moss quickly pushed up with a knee and shoved the man over his head, then got up quickly and whirled, kicking Duncan in the ribs. Duncan wriggled away, got up again and came at Moss, Moss waited until the right moment and backhanded the man with a snapping blow that made everyone wince. Duncan whirled and went down, blood pouring from his nose. Moss bent down and jerked the man up.

"Mister, I consider that remark an insult to my wife, and you'd best go and apologize to her right now!" Moss growled. He began dragging Duncan toward Amanda, and even with two hands free, Duncan could not pull himself away from Moss's powerful grip. He coughed and sputtered, blood running over his lips and down his chin, as Moss jerked him over in front of Amanda.

"Tell her!" Moss snarled.

"Moss, it's all right," Amanda said quietly, looking down at the ground.

"It's not all right!" Moss snapped.

He jolted Duncan again. "Tell her!" he growled.

Duncan swallowed and reached up to wipe some of the blood from his lips. He looked sullenly at Moss, then shifted his eyes to Amanda.

"Sorry, ma'am," he mumbled.

"And now you can apologize to Etta!" Moss snarled, shoving the man over to the other woman. Etta looked contemptuously at Duncan, enjoying the show and secretly stirred by Moss's power and sureness.

"Sorry!" Duncan spit out at her, hating her and loving her both at the same time.

Moss gave the man a violent shove to the ground.

"You got any more doubts about my authority, mister?" he snarled.

"Just one," Duncan sneered. He slowly stood up, panting for breath, then dusted himself off some. "Back in Wyoming, I was top man at Etta's place." He pushed some of his hair back and spit out some blood, then backed up a little, planting his feet slightly apart. "It was mostly because I could use a gun. You and this motley bunch here have been talkin' about how well you handle your gun. So let's see you use it, boss man!"

Etta's eyes widened and Amanda gasped as Duncan went for his gun. But it wasn't even half way out of its holster before Moss's was drawn. The movement was so quick that it took a second for them to realize Moss had his gun out. Amanda closed her eyes and held her stomach, and Duncan froze at the sound of the click of the hammer of Moss's gun. He stood motionless and staring wide-eyed at the barrel that was pointed directly at him.

"Mister," Moss growled, "I'm figurin' all you wanted was to see how fast I was. This is the first time I've ever drawn this gun without firin' it. But my little girl is standin' there watching, and I don't aim to let her see a man die—or see how big a hole this thing can make in your brisket! So you consider yourself real lucky! You ever go for your gun against me again, and they'll be carvin' out a tombstone for you. Now you get on over to a waterin' trough, cool yourself off, and wash that blood from your face. That is, unless you've got any more questions about my authority!"

Duncan swallowed and slowly let his own gun fall back into its holster. He was visibly shaken now, and although he still hated Moses Tucker—and considered him competition for Etta Landers—the surprise and new respect was evident in his eyes. He straightened and turned to walk off.

"Duncan!" Moss called out. Duncan stopped in his tracks, his back to Moss. "You tell all of us who's runnin' this outfit!"

Duncan sighed and clenched his fists. "You are," he mumbled.

"I didn't hear you, Duncan!"

"You are!" the man yelled out. He stalked off. Moss gently

released the hammer of his gun and slipped it back into its holster. Several of the men grinned, finding humor in the sullen Lloyd Duncan. All had eagerly watched the challenge, fully aware of how it would turn out, and enjoying the opportunity to see Moses Tucker in action again. It had been a long time.

"We leave in ten minutes," Moss told them.

"Whatever you say, boss," Tom Sorrells replied with a smile. "It's gonna be kind of nice, ridin' with Moses Tucker again."

Moss turned to Amanda and saw the terror in her eyes.

"I'm sorry, Mandy. He pushed it."

"It's bad enough you'll be riding into a camp of enemies, without one of her own men being one!" she answered, blinking back tears.

"I'll, uh, go get my things ready," Etta said quietly, hurrying away. Inside she was jubilant. Moss Tucker was more man than she had figured on.

"Mandy, he won't give me no more trouble," Moss was telling his wife. "He knows better. It's okay, Mandy."

She hugged him around the middle and he held her tightly.

"Come on, Mandy. There's nothin' to worry about. I'll be back in no time at all." He kissed her hair and squeezed her, then turned her to face the corral, where men were saddling and bridling their horses, joking together, laughing with the excitement of the impending adventure. "Look at all them men: every one of them is dependable, Mandy. It's gonna be okay. You know how they are. Oh, I don't expect there's many sins they haven't committed, but at the same time they'd turn right around and die for each other. One of their kind died helpin' me find Rand Barker. Remember?"

"Oh, Moss, I'll miss you so much! Couldn't you wait one more day?"

Their eyes held, and she knew he was determined to go, no matter what. "Puttin' it off another day just means another day before I get back again," he told her. "Come on, now. You're gettin' me all lathered up again. Wouldn't you be embarrassed if I told all them men to wait while I take my woman back in the house for a while? Hmmm?"

She smiled through her tears and pulled away to blow her nose. "Moss Tucker, don't you dare!"

He smiled and pulled her close.

"One good kiss before they all gather around too close again," he told her, relishing the feel of her breasts against his chest and wanting to remember it. He bent down and met her lips, and for the next few seconds they both forgot anyone else around. They hungrily grasped at the last sweet kiss, both realizing there was no telling how long it would be before they could do this again. He finally left her lips and moved his mouth over her cheek to her neck.

"You stick close to the house and the school and take one or two of the men with you wherever you go, understand?" he said softly.

"I will."

"And keep the bed warm."

"You know I will. It will be hard to sleep at night, Moss."

"Hard for both of us." He kissed her again. "I love you, Mandy. God, I love you. Don't you ever, ever forget that for a minute. Don't be makin' up crazy things in your head, understand? I'm goin' up there to straighten things out fast as I can, and then I'm comin' back here to my woman. You know how much I love you, how much you mean to me. You're the best thing that ever happened to me."

"You watch yourself, Moss. Please be careful. Oh, Moss, I love you! Come back soon!"

They kissed again, hungrily, desperately trying to make time stand still just a little longer. Then they heard someone clear his throat. Moss released the kiss and kept a tight hold on Amanda as he looked up at Johnny Pence, who sat astride his horse near them.

"Keep that up and we'll never get started!" Johnny said with a grin. Moss chuckled and released Amanda, who turned crimson. "'Course," Johnny added, pushing his hat back and eyeing Amanda up and down, "I reckon I'd have a little difficulty leavin' somethin' that looks like her myself, Moss."

"You bet you would," Moss replied, walking over to pick up his hat, which had been knocked off in his fight with Lloyd Duncan. Becky ran up to him for a last hug, and Moss picked his daughter up and whirled her around, nuzzling her neck and kissing her cheek. "You take good care of mommy, and you get your learnin' done, you hear? I don't want you growin' up talkin' like your uneducated pa."

"I'll study hard, daddy," the tiny voice replied. She hugged him around the neck. "When you come back, we'll see who can spell the best."

"I already know who can spell the best!" Moss told her with a hearty laugh. "You can out-spell me already!"

"Daddy, take me with you!" the child asked, looking him in the eyes. "I wanna go. I'm big now!"

Moss studied the blue eyes, so full of love and happiness. She reminded him very much of her mother, the mother she could hardly remember now. To her, Amanda was the only real mother she had ever had. And it was likely best that way, although the child's mother had not been bad—just lonely. And she had been very pretty. It was obvious Becky would look just like her, and Moss already was planning how he would handle the men in his daughter's life. If they hurt or insulted or abused her, Moses Tucker would simply shoot them and ask questions later. Nothing but the best would lay a hand on Becky Tucker. And even then he'd best be gentle.

"Now, Becky, you know you can't go. Ridin' the trail isn't somethin' for a delicate, pretty little thing like you to be doin'."

"But that pretty lady is going," the girl replied with puckered lips. "She's delicate, and all dressed up, and—"

"Yeah, but that pretty lady is only goin' 'cause it's her home she's goin' to. She has to go."

Amanda looked over at Etta, who now sat sidesaddle on her splendid palomino. Today the woman wore a deep purple riding outfit, with a wide-brimmed hat to shade the still young-looking skin of her face. Amanda wondered how Etta Landers had remained so perfectly coiffed and cool looking on this already hot Utah morning. Yes, she trusted Moss. But still, Etta was so beautiful, and he would be with the woman night and day for weeks now, and Amanda Tucker was not foolish enough to believe that Etta would not try to prove to herself that Moss Tucker still loved her. Amanda's only consolation was the knowledge of how much Moss loved her. Of that love she was sure. And she felt a warm flush inside herself at the memory of their love-making just that morning. And, after all, Moses Tucker was a grown man who knew how to handle himself. She didn't want to be a nagging wife, or stand in the way of Moss's decisions, and she knew full well how destitute Moss Tucker would be if he lost her. He was not likely to do something to risk that. Amanda had given him the love he'd never had before he met her; and she'd given him a home, and given her soul and body to Moses Tucker. Now if only she could give him a child.

Moss put Becky down and stepped up to Amanda again, and she was struck by tears in his eyes.

"Take care of yourself," he said in a strained voice.

Her lips were pressed tightly together to keep from crying. She nodded. They studied each other as Pappy Lane rode up, leading Moss's horse behind him.

"She's all saddled up, Moss. We'd best get riding."

Moss continued to look at his wife. "You remember what I told you this mornin'…what you promised me about not worryin' about things you don't need to worry about."

"I'll remember," she said in a near whisper.

Moss reached out and put his big hand to the side of her face, blinking rapidly and clearing his throat.

"You're all right here, Mandy. You're safe."

"I know," she replied, giving him a reassuring smile.

He bent down and kissed her forehead. "I love you," he whispered. She grasped the wide, solid wrist.

"I love you, too."

He slowly and reluctantly let go of her and walked over to mount his horse. He looked down at Mandy and Becky.

"Good-bye, ladies," he said with a sad grin.

"Bye, daddy," Becky replied, waving a fat hand.

"Good-bye," Amanda whispered, an unwanted tear slipping down her cheek. "God be with you. I'll…pray for you, Moss."

"Well, then, I reckon I don't have anything to worry about, not with the likes of you prayin' for me," he answered with a wink. He started to turn his horse.

"Moss!" she called out, quickly removing a crucifix she wore around her neck. She reached up and handed it to him. Moss enclosed her small hands in his own large one for a moment, then took the cross. "Wear it, darling," she told him. "Keep it close to your heart."

"Yes, ma'am," he replied. "I'll do just that. And thank you, Mandy, for understandin' why I have to do this."

"I love you," she told him again.

He nodded, then forced himself to turn away, digging his heels into the large, buckskin-colored quarter horse he rode, heading it out in front of the others.

"Bye, Amanda. You take care," Pappy told her.

"Watch out for him, Pappy," she said pleadingly.

"Don't I always?" he replied with a wink. He reached down, patted her cheek, and rode out after Moss.

Next came Etta, who slowed her horse and nodded to Amanda. "Good-bye, Mrs. Tucker," she said sweetly. "I won't keep him too long. I promise."

The two women looked challengingly at one another.

"See that you don't," Amanda replied. "He's my husband. I love him. And he has needs no one else can fill for him. He's doing you a great favor, Etta. I hope you appreciate it."

Etta scowled slightly and rode off after Pappy and Moss. She was followed by her two men, the moody Lloyd Duncan and young Danny Green.

The others all followed, each nodding their farewell to Amanda, some removing their hats first in a gesture of respect.

"We'll take real good care of him, ma'am," Lonnie Drake promised her. "Don't you worry one little bit."

"Thank you, Lonnie. You're a good man—you're all good men. God bless you."

"Ain't no God gonna bless the likes of me," Max Cornell spoke up with a chuckle.

"He will, Mr. Cornell," Amanda replied. "I'll be praying for all of you."

Cornell shook his head. He held a great admiration for Amanda Tucker.

The rest rode by: Darrell, Johnny, Slim, Brad, Les, Tom, Bullit, Dwight, Hank, and Sooner. Counting Moss and Etta's two men, there were sixteen all together. A tiny army headed north to Wyoming to set things right for a woman. Hopefully, the woman was worth it.

Amanda watched as the string of horses became smaller, difficult to see through the cloud of dust they stirred up and left behind them. Then one rider appeared through the haze, one who had turned back for a moment. He waved. It was Moss.

She waved back. He seemed to hesitate there a moment. Then he turned and rode off again.

"How long will daddy be gone, mommy?" Becky asked.

"I'm not sure, darling," Amanda replied. Her heart felt like a piece of lead. "But he will come back. You can be sure of that. He'll come for us both, just like he searched for us and found us five years ago. He'll always come back to us that way."

"But what if he gets hurt?"

"He won't," Amanda said quickly. "Remember the Holy Mother and pray to Her, Becky. We'll pray together. And I gave daddy my crucifix. A crucifix saved him once. It will save him again. Come inside now and we'll pray for him at the little altar in our bedroom."

Becky ran into the house to get her rosary beads and

Amanda turned to look at Wanda, the Navaho woman who would stay and help her.

"He is good man," Wanda told her. "He will be fine."

Amanda nodded, then burst into tears and hugged the robust Indian woman. Wanda patted her shoulder.

"Not to worry," she told Amanda. "Moss Tucker good man. Many times I wait for my warrior husband to come home from battle. I know how it feels. But Moss Tucker is good warrior. He will come."

Chapter Thirty-Two

The rather quiet procession moved from Moss's ranch, which was nearly on the Utah-Arizona border, northward across the San Juan River, then along the Colorado River to where it branched into the Green River. The small troop of rugged, hard-muscled men would follow the Green River through the famous outlaw hangout of Robber's Roost and catch the Denver and Rio Grande Railroad, which would take them into northern Utah and to its junction with the Union Pacific, which they would ride east to Rock Springs; there they would disembark and ride to Etta's ranch.

Etta and her two men kept slightly apart from the others, but Etta listened with interest to some of the stories they swapped along the way, amused at the efforts the men made at avoiding foul words in a lady's presence. She wondered what kind of tales they would tell if she were not present.

Moss watched all of them carefully, fully aware of eyes that rested longingly on Etta Landers' lovely form as they rode. Riding the trail could bring out a hungry need in a man; appetites that only grew more painful with time and the loneliness of riding outlaw country, where jackrabbits were a more common sight than humans, and beautiful women were in very short supply.

But all of them kept their distance and obeyed the strict rule Moses Tucker had given them to keep their minds on business. However, Etta Landers did not lack for servants. Pappy did the cooking, and there was always a scuffle over who would take a dish of food to Etta. Not a physical scuffle, but teasing words and daring looks and near threats. Her canteen was always full, shady spots were always picked for resting, the softest places were always offered to her for sleeping, and no one complained when he was appointed the one to keep guard over Etta Landers for the night. And when the woman did her bathing and changing behind blanket screens, the tension among the men would have been humorous if not for the ache that gripped their insides as their imaginations wandered; each man fantasized in his own way over what he would do with the woman if she were willing.

But Moss knew that as long as Etta kept her distance and conducted herself properly, not one man in the bunch would make an advance of any kind. He often smiled to himself as he watched them out of the corner of his eye: burly, rugged men, outlaws and killers, yet all of them a little nervous and even somewhat uncomfortable around a beautiful and proper lady. It made him think of the time some of these men had helped him search for Amanda. They respected Moss's feelings for her, and they were all just as angry over her abduction as Moss had been.

Moss sighed and leaned against a scrubby oak tree that was half dead. He lifted a tin cup of coffee to his lips and listened to the crickets. It was their fourth night on the trail, a black night, with seemingly zillions of stars overhead. Tomorrow they would ride through Robber's Roost and catch the Denver and Rio Grande. Somewhere in the background someone played a mournful tune on his harmonica, and Moss closed his eyes. How he missed her! He wasn't even at his destination yet, and he was ready to go back. What was she doing now? Asleep, most likely. And a restless sleep it would be, just as his own would be.

"Miss her bad, hmmm?" Hank Stemm spoke up. He sat nearby rubbing his toes.

"You bet," Moss replied, lighting a cigarette.

"I gotta get me some new boots," Stemm told him, now wiggling his toes. "These things hurt my feet." He sighed. "You're a lucky man, Moss. That woman of yours, she's beef-steak and potatoes, know what I mean?"

Moss shifted, longing to be in his own bed beside Amanda.

"I know exactly what you mean." He took a deep drag on his cigarette, and a welcome cool breeze ruffled his thick hair. "How come you never settled down, Hank?" he asked.

The man removed his socks. "Well, I'll tell you, Moss. A man has somethin' good once—well, nothin' seems to compare after that. I, uh, had me a girl once, about fifteen years ago… pretty little thing. That was back in Kentucky." He lit a pipe.

"What happened?" Moss asked.

"I married her. And I had one week with her. Then one day she went walkin' in the woods, lookin' for flowers to pretty up our table. And she seen this real cute baby bear. And the damned fool kid walked up and tried to pet it."

His voice died off and he cleared his throat and swallowed.

"Its ma was nearby?" Moss asked.

"Yeah," Hank replied in a choked voice.

Again there was silence, except for the harmonica in the background.

"I'm damned sorry, Hank. I shouldn't have asked. Didn't mean to dredge up bad memories."

"You didn't know." The man cleared his throat again. "At any rate, after that—hell, a man don't care much no more, you know?"

"I know."

"You'd feel the same way if somethin' happened to that nice gal of yours. You'd never marry again, would you?"

"I expect not," Moss told him. "I expect not."

"Same here. I guess that's why I ain't worth much now. I mean, it don't matter now, you know? It just…don't matter." He stretched out on his bedroll and closed his eyes. "It just don't matter."

Moss smoked quietly and looked around at all of them—hard, lonely men. If not for Amanda, he would be just as hard and lonely, going nowhere. They had no one to care when they met their maker, no one to care how often they gambled or got drunk, or if they were sick or well. Men joked a lot about being tied down by a woman and losing their freedom, but women like Amanda didn't tie a man down. And to be without her would not be freedom at all: it would be hell.

He heard footsteps crunching behind him and turned to see Les Trainer standing there.

"I'm in charge of the lady tonight," the man told Moss. "She, uh, has some, uh, personal business to tend to. I'm walkin' her out a ways. Just wanted you to know so you don't get alarmed when you see she ain't in her bedroll."

"Go ahead. Just be sure to turn your back," Moss replied with a grin.

"Jesus, Moss, what kind of man do you think I am?"

"A normal one," Moss replied.

Les chuckled and walked off. Moss watched him scuffle his feet nervously and fidget with his hat as he waited for Etta. Then they walked off into the darkness. Moss leaned back again and closed his eyes.

• • •

Les Trainer led Etta to a large boulder, instructing her to go behind it to tend to her personal needs. He turned around, but heard no footsteps.

"Les," she whispered. He frowned and turned back around.

"Somethin' wrong?"

He felt her fingers toying with the buttons of his shirt.

"I don't really have to go, Les. I just…Les, a woman has needs…same as a man. And riding with men like you, day and night—I've been watching you, Les."

She stood on her tiptoes and kissed the hairs of his chest that were exposed where she had opened his shirt.

Les Trainer swallowed and began to perspire.

"Ma'am, you shouldn't…do that. You know we ain't supposed to touch you, ma'am."

"Oh, Moss only means you shouldn't force yourselves on me. But if a woman is willing, Les—"

"Ma'am," Les swallowed again. "I don't think Moss meant just that. We'd best get back, ma'am."

"And I thought you were a man of decision," she whispered, her face close to his. She ran her hands down the sides of his legs, then gently probed the hardness between them. "I need a man, Les. No one will know. Even Moss won't suspect."

Her full lips were close to his, and her light perfume was tantalizing. It was an offer few men such as Les Trainer would turn down. After all, the woman was practically begging for it. What was the harm, as long as they were quiet about it?

He pressed his lips to hers, pulling her into his arms and groaning at the feel of her large bosom against his chest. She returned his kiss hungrily, thrilled at how quickly she had been able to seduce him, excited at another victory. If she couldn't have Moss Tucker, she would have one of these men, who were just like him. Les pushed her to the ground, moving a leg on top of her and fumbling at the buttons on the front of her dress.

"Let me help you, darling," she whispered, her heart pounding at the exciting hardness he pressed against her thigh. She unbuttoned her dress and the man eagerly pulled one side off her shoulder, exposing the large, soft, milky-white breast, with its inviting pink nipple barely visible in the frail light of the moon.

"Ma'am," he whispered. "I don't know why you'd let a worthless bum like me enjoy this beautiful body, but if you're willin' I ain't gonna argue about it."

She smiled and grasped his hair as his mouth moved down to her breast. His hand reached down and pulled up on her dress, then pushed down her pantaloons, shoving them to her ankles and then caressing the soft patch of hair exposed willingly.

"Oh, Les! Les!" she whispered. "I knew I could count on you. It's…been so long since I've been with a man…especially a real man like you."

It took only seconds for him to move on top of her and find his way between her legs—legs that opened willingly for him in her own desperate need. He smothered off her moans of delight by covering her mouth with his own as he rammed himself inside of her. Rules or no rules, a man couldn't turn down this kind of offer. She raised up to meet him and he reached under her hips to feel of the firm, round bottom; moments later he released himself in near pain at the excitement of it. Never had a woman like Etta Landers offered herself to him. He let out a long, shuddering sigh of pleasure, and they both lay limp and satisfied.

But then a gun clicked; Les whirled and found himself looking up at Moss Tucker. Etta gasped and wriggled back, struggling to pull up her pantaloons and push her dress down.

"Get up and get out, Les," Moss said quietly.

"Moss, I—my God, Moss, she begged me!"

"That's not true!" Etta whimpered. "He—he forced me!"

"I've been watching, Etta," Moss hissed. "I didn't see no strugglin' and I didn't hear no screaming." He stepped a little closer. "Get them pants buttoned and get going, Les. You're out."

"Moss, I promise I won't—"

"I don't blame you for any of it, Les. But if you stay on, you're gonna be rememberin' tonight, and you're gonna be wantin' it again. Only maybe next time she'll take on some other man. And maybe you'll get jealous and do somethin' stupid like kill somebody, or maybe you'll want to impress your beautiful lover and do somethin' stupid to look brave in front of her and get yourself killed by disobeyin' some order I give you. It's best you leave now, Les. Go now and I'll forget it, and the next time we run into each other we won't mention it."

Etta broke into tears of shame.

"I—I'm sorry, Moss," Les spoke up, quickly buttoning his pants. "Why in hell didn't you speak up sooner?"

"'Cause I'm a man. There ain't nothin' much more painful than tryin' to stop yourself right in the middle. She was askin' for it. I figured it's been a long time for you. So I let you finish. The damage was already done anyway."

Les could sense the smoldering anger beneath the quiet voice. He swallowed and looked at the gun.

"I really am sorry, Moss. I didn't want to go against what you asked, but she—goddamn, Moss, she offered herself up like a damned piece of pie!"

Moss sighed. "Just leave, Les. If anybody asks, you just tell them you changed your mind. Make somethin' up. But don't you breathe a word of this to any other man, or every one of them will be pantin' after her like she was a bitch in heat, understand? Right now they all consider her...respectable." He sneered the word, looking at a cowering, crying Etta as he did so. "You understand what I'm tellin' you, Les? It's important they all think she's a proper lady."

"Sure, Moss. I—I won't say nothing." He bent down and picked up his hat. "See you around, Moss."

"Yeah."

Les walked off, and Moss put his gun back in its holster. He walked closer to Etta and glared down at her. "I thought I'd seen everything," he told her with disgust in his voice. "When I knew you, I was lucky to get to kiss your cheek. You was uppity and spoiled, I'll admit. But you was a virgin, and I respected that. What the hell happened to you, Etta? Just bein' divorced wouldn't make the Etta I knew spread her legs for any man that came along."

"Stop it!" she groaned, hanging her head. "It's none of your business how I conduct my private life!"

"If I'm gonna go all the way to Wyoming and help you save your property—and risk my life and the lives of all these other men here—then I say it is my business, Etta."

"You hate me now, don't you?" she whined.

He sighed and turned away, as she rose and smoothed her dress.

"The hatred I held for you has suddenly turned to just plan disgust, Etta, and right now I'm wonderin' why in hell I'm goin' through all this. I enjoyed seein' you beg, and I hated you. But somewhere down deep inside I still respected your virtue. You might have been a liar and a spoiled kid, but I respected your person."

Her heart ached at the revulsion in his voice. "I…I need… to be touched," she whimpered. "I need to know that men desire me."

Moss frowned. "That's the craziest thing I ever heard. My God, Etta, there isn't a man alive who'd look at you and not desire you. What the hell is the matter with you, woman?"

She choked in a sob and Moss fought an urge to feel sorry for her. He wondered what could possibly have happened between her and Ralph Landers to turn her into such a woman. This was not the Etta Graceland he had left behind eighteen years ago, the haughty, prim young lady who had considered him unworthy of touching her because he was a bastard and did not have the proper "bloodlines."

He turned to see her standing there with her hands over her face. He grasped her wrists almost angrily and jerked her hands away. "Why, Etta? Why did you lower yourself like that?" he hissed, trying to keep his voice down.

She met his eyes defiantly, tears on her cheeks that he could see glowing lightly in the moonlight.

"Because Les was a man," she hissed through gritted teeth. "Just like you're a real man, and the others! Eighteen years ago I threw away my chance at being a real woman! I got married. Yes. A lovely wedding it was: a fine young gentleman marrying the proper young lady!" She stepped back. "Picture yourself a woman, Moss! How would you feel, if two weeks after your wedding you found your husband in the arms of another man!"

She burst into renewed tears and ran off before he could catch her or reply. He stood there in the dark, speechless. What kind of horror had she lived with? No wonder she needed reassurance she was desirable. Her own husband had not wanted her, preferring men to his own beautiful wife. What a stinging blow to a young, budding woman.

"My God!" he whispered to himself. The news helped his decision. Few things were more appalling than a man who would lie with another man. Ralph Landers was a pervert; it suddenly occurred to Moss that perhaps Miles Randall was one of his lovers. It all made sense. Moses Tucker would thoroughly enjoy murdering such filth. It angered him to realize the kind of woman Ralph Landers had made out of Etta. Now his hatred for Miles Randall was multiplied. He had all the more reason to go through with his promise of helping Etta. Ralph Landers and Miles Randall would both pay—and pay dearly!

Moss heard a horse galloping away. That would be Les Trainer. He regretted losing the man. Les was one of the better ones. But to stay around would be too much temptation for the man. And none of the others must know about Etta Landers's strange needs and desires. If they did, pure havoc would let loose, and Moss would lose all control over the men. He walked back to camp.

"Boss, that crazy Les just rode off," Tom Sorrells spoke up. "Said there was a gal over in Colorado he'd been thinkin' about and tryin' to stay away from. And now all of a sudden he decides he's got to go to her. Can you beat that?"

Moss laughed lightly and lit another cigarette. "Well, when I think about my wife, I can understand it," he replied casually.

"What a man wouldn't do for the woman he loves," Sorrells said, shaking his head. He turned over and snuggled down into his bedroll. Moss walked over to Pappy, who stood away from the others and was watching the extra horses for the night. Pappy never was one to sleep a lot, and Moss knew the old man would be awake.

"I'll be watchin' Etta myself from now on, Pappy," he told the old man. "Somethin' happened tonight. It's best I watch her myself."

Pappy lit a cigar. "That somethin' wouldn't have anything to do with Les Trainer, would it?" the old man asked.

"It would." Moss took a deep drag on his cigarette.

"Gonna tell me about it?"

"No. Maybe some day. But not till this is over."

"No matter." The old man puffed his cigar. "Just so you

ain't forgettin' you've got a pretty little waif waitin' for you down south of here."

Moss turned to face him. "A herd of buffalo stampedin' over my skull couldn't make me forget that, Pappy. And I don't want to hear you suggest such a thing again. 'Cause if you do, I'll knock your teeth out, old man or not."

"Just checking. You and me have been friends a long time, Moss. But if I had to make a choice, I'd choose Amanda, and you know it."

"I wouldn't blame you. She's a hundred times the person I'll ever be. You really think I'd be crazy enough to break her heart by cheatin' on her?"

"I hope not. But a woman like Etta can turn a man's head pretty far, and you did love her once."

"That was a long time ago." Moss sighed. "And things are different now—real different, especially Etta." He rubbed at the stump of his left arm.

"That thing hurtin' you tonight?"

Moss shrugged. "Just the cold night air, I guess."

Pappy puffed on his cigar. "I'm obliged for the home you've given me, Moss, the job, lettin' me come along and all—"

"Goddamn it, Pappy, will you quit blamin' yourself for my arm? It's been five years!"

"But I'm the one who made the decision, and I'm the one who cut it off!"

"And you saved my life, Pappy!" Moss said flatly.

"True. But who's to say—"

"My God, Pappy, there was no way to save it! I know that now. The arm is gone, and it's nobody's fault but mine. It's not even the Apaches' fault! I had lots of chances to save it; we could have stopped in any town or fort and seen a doctor. I was the stubborn one. Blame it on me bein' crazy from the infection, my crazy quest to get that crucifix up to Mandy, whatever. But it was my decision not to get help—mine alone. You had no choice by the time we got there. So I don't want to hear any more about how it's your fault."

Pappy blinked and puffed his cigar.

"I know how I talked right afterward, Pappy. But I was just scared, sickened. But Mandy, she changed all that. When I'm with Mandy I know I'm still a man. There's no doubt in my mind. And I'm probably stronger now than I was before. So it doesn't matter any more, Pappy. You know that."

Pappy looked away. "I love you like a son, Moss. I couldn't let you die."

Moss put a hand on his shoulder. "'Course you couldn't. I'd have done the same thing with you, or Mandy, or even Becky. It's livin' that counts, Pappy—especially when you've got somebody to live for."

Pappy turned to face him. "Has Etta Landers got somebody to live for, Moss? She looks like a pretty empty lady to me."

"She is, Pappy. She's got nothin' to live for right now except that ranch. And I'm gonna see she keeps it." He turned to look out at the main camp. "For more reasons than one, Pappy." He could not help but think that Etta Graceland Landers had probably got what she deserved for marrying a man strictly for his wealth and good standing. That fact quelled his own appetite for revenge against her. But the kind of man Landers had turned out to be was worse than even Etta deserved, and amid Moss's contempt for the woman, he could not help but feel some pity; the sweet revenge he had tasted when she begged him to help her was souring. Amanda was right. Revenge wasn't always satisfying; at least in Etta's case it didn't feel as good as he had hoped.

He looked at Pappy again. "I guess everybody makes mistakes, don't they, Pappy? Etta made hers, and she's payin' for it. I guess after all these years I've got no call to make life even more miserable for her than it already is. That's what Amanda would say, anyway. And God knows if Amanda wasn't willin' to forgive me for my own mistakes, she never would have married me. I enjoyed seein' Etta beg me to help her back when she first came to me. But now I guess I'll just help her because, as

Mandy would put it, it's the right thing to do. Know what I mean, Pappy?"

"I reckon I do, Moss. You, uh, go on and get some rest now. We have a train to meet tomorrow."

Moss stepped out his cigarette. "Yeah."

"Les gone for good?"

"Yeah. He won't be back."

"Just make sure her problem—whatever it is—don't cost any of these men their lives, Moss. They're good men."

"I realize that. That's why I sent Les packin'. See you in the morning, Pappy."

Moss walked over and picked up his bedroll and moved it closer to Etta. She appeared to be asleep, but he didn't believe she was. Her humiliation and shame had to be too fresh in her mind to make her able to relax enough to sleep. Moss opened his bedroll beside hers and sat down. She lay on her side, facing him, her eyes closed. He knew even in the darkness that they were red and swollen. He reached over and grasped one of her hands and felt her trembling. He heard a sniffle, and he squeezed her hand.

Chapter Thirty-Three

Etta spoke to no one the next morning, especially not Moss. Her degradation at the thought of Moss watching her grovel in the dirt with a cowhand sickened her, and she hated herself. Now he knew the whole dirty truth. She wondered why he hadn't just knocked her to the ground and left her. How must she look to him now, compared to his pure and perfect wife? It brought tears to her eyes and shame to her heart. Surely she had ruined any chance of gaining his respect and of winning his heart away from Amanda Tucker. Her land was all she had now. Her need to keep it grew more desperate. If she had nothing and no one else, at least she had her ranch. But she knew that would not be enough now. She hungered for Moses Tucker, and she would likely remain hungry.

They rode through Robber's Roost, calling out hello's to the surly, untrustworthy men who hung out on the streets eyeing Etta. She knew most of them had to be outlaws. This was the outlaw trail; Robber's Roost was one of their favorite hangouts. She'd heard that as she'd traced down Moses Tucker. Moss rode close beside her, watching the men in the streets carefully.

"What are you guarding?" she asked coldly. "Surely not my honor."

He turned to look at her, but she looked straight ahead. "Maybe you think there's nothin' to guard, but believe me, Etta, there's a difference between Les Trainer and some of the men who are watchin' you now. Wrestlin' with one of them in bed would be like gettin' beat up by a grizzly. It wouldn't be no picnic. And it wouldn't be no pleasure."

She wondered to herself how gentle Moses Tucker would be in bed. Surely it would be lovely. Otherwise a delicate young woman like Amanda Tucker wouldn't appear to be so happy. She thought how nice it must have been for Amanda to have a man like Moss help her get over her cruel rape.

Two buxom beauties hung over the railings of a whore-house farther up the street, squealing and waving to the small troup of men who rode through. Dwight Brady and Hank Stemm gave out a holler and galloped past the others, standing up on their horses' saddles and grabbing the railing. The girls screamed as the two of them hoisted themselves up, climbed over the railing, and disappeared inside with the women.

"My goodness, such chivalry," Etta mocked, putting a hand to her throat as though shocked. "You've just lost two men, Moss."

Moss chuckled. "They'll catch up." The others behind them laughed and joked, but Moss knew the emptiness inside their souls that was covered up by the laughter. Lonely men, all of them.

They made it out of the sprawling, awesome valley wherein lay Robber's Roost, and headed toward a huge mesa. As much as Etta liked men, she couldn't help be glad to be out of Robber's Roost. Moss had stuck to the basic outlaw trail because some of the men with him were wanted in Utah for various reasons. Once they got to Wyoming, they would be safe. Several of them would ride in the baggage car, or with their own horses, once they got on the train so that not too many people would see them. The law and the general public would have to be avoided until they were out of Utah.

They headed up a steep escarpment, and Etta's horse stumbled. She screamed as the animal slid backward and literally sat down on its rear. Etta fell off and the horse barely missed landing on top of her. The palomino struggled to its feet again, and Sooner hurriedly dismounted and helped Etta up. Moss turned his own horse and carefully led it back down the embankment.

"You okay?" he asked her.

"Just embarrassed!" she said, beating dirt from her clothes

in frustration. She looked up at him. "I seem to have a way of making a fool of myself in front of you."

Moss grinned. "Adds spice to life. Mount up with Sooner and ride with him till we get to the top. Pappy will lead your horse for you."

"Now that's a job I don't mind," the half-breed said with a smile.

"You tend to business and get the lady up there safely," Moss said sternly.

"Yes, sir," the man replied. Moss held Etta's eyes as Sooner lifted her to his horse.

"It's all right, Moss," she said, assuring him she would not do something foolish.

They headed back up the steep bank with no more problems, and Etta looked back at the place they had just left. What big country this was! Robber's Roost was a small dot below, and she could barely make out the two riders—probably Dwight Brady and Hank Stemm—hurrying to catch up. She turned to see Moss gazing back also, but his eyes looked beyond Robber's Roost southward into the miles of land they had already covered, straining to see through the haze in the distance. She realized how much he must miss his wife and the little ranch he had left behind. She knew that was what he was thinking of, and her heart burned with jealousy.

Sooner helped her down and she mounted her own horse again. They headed for Green River City, and the Rio Grande Railroad.

* * *

Etta took her seat, relaxing into the welcome softness of a real chair rather than a saddle. She put her head back and breathed a sigh of relief, as Moss showed the porter their tickets and sat down in a seat facing her. They both sat next to a window, and the seats beside them were empty. Moss lit a cigarette and stared out the window; Etta was struck by the fact that there seemed to be tears in his eyes as he stared out at the mountains beyond.

"What are you thinking of, Moss?" she asked softly. "Your wife?"

His eyes shifted to hers. "I met her on a train…sittin' near her like this." He sighed. "Sometimes it seems like yesterday, her sittin' on that train all alone…a scared young girl not knowin' who to trust. I reckon maybe I fell in love with her the first time I ever saw her."

"I'd love to get my mind on something besides myself and my ranch," she told him. "I heard bits and pieces when I was looking for you. Maybe you wouldn't be so lonely if you talked about her a little. Tell me all about her, fill in the details. I'm willing to listen."

He studied her eyes, surprised that she seemed sincere. After her shameful deed with Les Trainer, she seemed subdued and less haughty; now that he knew the lurid fact that her husband had been homosexual, he found it hard to hate her or accuse her. Things were much different now than they were eighteen years ago, different than even a few days ago. He took out a cigarette.

"She was on her way to California to teach at a mission. She was the next thing to bein' a nun herself," he told her. "I was on my way from Chicago to see what I could do about Becky 'cause her ma had died. I ended up on the same train with Amanda. I could see how scared and inexperienced she was. She wouldn't even look at me or talk to me at first, but I sort of kept an eye on her, felt sorry for her, helped her out of a couple of tight situations and slowly won her confidence. And I guess I knew in the back of my mind I was fallin' in love with her. But she was untouchable, and what she knew about men you could put in a thimble."

He lit the cigarette and took a drag. His eyes moved over Etta, and she reddened, still feeling ashamed and embarrassed. "We all start out not knowing much," she said rather sadly, looking at her lap then.

He smoked quietly for a moment, trying to sort out his feelings. "Etta, about your husband—"

"I don't want to talk about it," she interrupted. "Or about last night, except to apologize. Maybe when we get to the ranch, where I can relax…" She sighed. "I just can't talk about it yet, Moss."

"All right. But I'd like to know if Miles Randall is that way, too."

She swallowed and nodded, unable to meet his eyes. "Miles is the one I…found my husband with."

The train rattled along rhythmically, and Moss turned his eyes to look out the window at the swiftly passing terrain. "Well, Etta, I may not feel like goin' through with this just for you. I've half a mind to turn around and go back to Amanda. But I've brought the men this far, and they're lookin' forward to a little action, some good pay, and a chance to help you out. I'll not let on about some of your personal escapades, because the more they respect you, the harder they'll fight for you. Just don't give me reason to regret my decision by pullin' somethin' like that again."

"I won't, Moss. I promise."

He studied her lovely form and beautiful clothes. Yes, there was a time, but many things had changed since then. And there was Amanda—sweet Amanda. "At any rate," he continued, "I'm goin' through with this mainly to get my hands on Miles Randall again. There's nothing I want more than that. That man ruined me, stole everything I had ever worked for. And now that I know this other thing about the man, it just gives me more incentive."

He smoked quietly for several seconds, as Etta took out a handkerchief and dabbed at her eyes. "You didn't finish telling me about Amanda," she told him, still wanting to change the subject. "I was told she was kidnaped from the train."

Moss sighed deeply and put out his cigarette. "That's so," he answered quietly. "I was wounded tryin' to stop them, and when I come to I was in Bear River City and four days had gone by. I felt like the dumbest bastard who ever walked. All that time I'd been watchin' over her, but I couldn't do anything for her, and it tore my guts out."

He went on to tell her the whole story, how he had found Amanda and got her to safety, and about the Apache and how he had lost his arm to an Apache warrior's hatchet in his long search and struggle for revenge against the men who had harmed Amanda.

"Ole Pappy removed the arm, it got so badly infected," he told her. "He still feels guilty about it, but he shouldn't. I could have got help, but I refused. I just wanted to get back to Amanda, to take her that crucifix I had got back from those men who stole it from her. If Pappy hadn't taken the arm, I'd be dead. And I'm used to it now. I don't think about it much any more. At first I thought it would make me less of a man." He gazed out the window longingly again. "But Mandy—she changed that for me."

"You helped her get over her fear of men, and at the same time, she helped teach you that you were still a man yourself."

"Somethin' like that. When I make love to her I feel ten feet tall."

"Aren't you?" she asked with raised eyebrows. Moss met her eyes and laughed lightly.

"Close to it, I reckon. I never was small."

"And in her eyes you probably are ten feet tall. You look at her with near devotion in your eyes; perhaps you don't realize she looks at you the same way. I envy her. I envy both of you."

Moss just smiled and roved her body with his eyes again.

"You could have any man you wanted, Etta. A woman like you shouldn't envy anyone."

"Oh, but I do. I envy Amanda's ability to love, and especially to love one man, to be true to one man. I tried once, and what I got back was worse than a beating or a rape!" Her voice was bitter now, and she watched the scenery out the window. "Now I'm afraid to love. I have no love left in me. And I'm deathly afraid to ever get married again. It's better this way."

"What way? You bein' no better than a…loose woman?"

"A prostitute?" she added for him. "I detest prostitutes. They're filth! And then I look in the mirror, and I…" She swallowed and looked at her lap. "I wonder where the difference is, and I realize there is none, except that I don't accept money for my favors." She looked up at him with hard, cold eyes. "From now on the only person I care about is me, worthless as I might be. And the only love I have is for my land. Nothing else matters, Moss."

"You can't live like that forever, Etta. No woman can live like that forever."

Their eyes held a moment.

"I think I could be true to one man, be happy with one man, Moss—if the man were you."

He frowned and leaned back into his seat.

"There's plenty of men out there, Etta."

"It's too bad that there isn't one more like you, Moses Tucker. I guess that leaves me out in the cold, doesn't it?"

Their eyes held for a very long time, and the only sound was the rickety-rack of the train as it rolled northward through desolate Utah country.

"I reckon it does," he finally said. "Least ways for what you're talkin' about. Don't go thinkin' things that aren't so, Etta. I'm in this for the money and to get Miles Randall. And maybe somewhere along the way we can at least be friends. In the meantime, I gave you my word to help you, and I will. I won't let you down."

"I know you won't," she said, a tear slipping down her cheek. "I appreciate your help." She sighed deeply. "Isn't it strange, Moss?"

"What is that?"

"Out of all the men I've gone to bed with, none of them are really my friends. And the one man I spurned and cursed years ago—the one man who should hate me, the man I do love and have never been to bed with—now he's the only friend I have. Isn't life ironic?"

313

He sighed. "Get some rest now, Etta. I learned a long time ago it's impossible to figure out life. Fate takes a lot of turns."

"Yes, it does. Doesn't it?" She sniffed and put her head back and closed her eyes. But all she could picture was lying in bed with Moss Tucker.

• • •

"Whoa! Easy boy!" Sooner shouted to his skittish horse. The animal's hooves clattered as he led it down the plank from the train car. There were shouts and whistles as the other men led their animals out. Etta watched, and several of the horses snorted and reared when the Union Pacific train engine hissed steam, belched and jolted.

"This is a good idea, Moss," she told him as they watched. "Stopping the train like this before we get to Rock Springs."

"No sense goin' all the way into town and announcin' our arrival—not if your ex-husband has everybody paid off like you say. I figure we might as well make a surprise entrance to the ranch. You think we'll get a reception there?"

"I'm sure of it," she replied, pacing now. "I had hardly any men left. Ralph will have taken it over by now. The buildings and animals are probably all right. He wouldn't want to destroy what he considers his own now. He's probably hoping I won't return at all. But once I'm back and begin showing some force of my own, everything I own will be in danger."

Moss grasped her shoulder and turned her to face him.

"What about you? Would he hurt you?"

"Only as a last resort. He'd rather have it the easy way, just scare me off. But hurting a woman isn't beyond him. When we were married…" She looked away. "Never mind. Let's get started. The ranch is a day's ride from here."

"You know something? You never even told me the name of the place or how big it is."

"And I also never told you what I'm paying you personally for this."

He shrugged. "I never thought of it. I figured I'm bein' paid the same as my men."

He started to turn to get his horse, and she touched his arm. "Two thousand, Moss."

He turned back around, his eyebrows arched in surprise. "Dollars?"

"Of course!"

He shook his head. "That's too much."

"Why? You're the leader of this bunch. If we succeed, it will be because of you. Besides, you deserve it, after what I did to you eighteen years ago. Maybe this way I can make it up a little."

His eyes hardened and he jerked away. "You can't make up for somethin' like that with money, Etta. Apparently that's somethin' you still haven't learned."

"Moss, I didn't mean—"

"Leave it be, Etta! All the money and all the sweet talk in the world isn't going to make me feel any different about you. I'll take your money because, by God, you do owe it to me! I'll take it for Mandy's sake, to give her a decent house to live in. And I'll take it because I'm doin' a job for you, not as some kind of handout to poor Moss Tucker because you hurt his feelings years ago! And I'll do this job because I aim to get Miles Randall!" He turned again and she grabbed his shirt.

"Moss, I didn't mean to make you angry. I...I thought you'd be happy about the money. I just wanted to do something nice for you."

Her eyes teared, but he was not touched. "You lost your chance to do that a long time ago, Etta. It's a little late. If you want to pay me that much, fine. I'll take it and enjoy the fact that I earned it after you begged me to help you. I thought maybe you had changed some, but you still judge everything by money, don't you?"

Her own eyes hardened then. Winning him back looked more and more impossible. She seemed to keep doing and saying all the wrong things. "Think what you want," she replied curtly. "At any rate the name of the ranch is the E.G., for Etta Graceland. I'm in the process of having my name changed. I want everything about Ralph out of my life, including his name. When I was Etta Graceland, I was…respectable and honored."

Moss laughed bitterly. "Oh, yes. You were all of that, weren't you?" He walked to his horse, as the other men were now mounting up. Brad Doolittle brought Etta's horse to her and gave her a hand into the saddle.

Moss looked around the surrounding scenery. This was magnificent country, so much cooler than Utah this time of year, so much greener. He studied the surrounding Rocky Mountains, their jagged peaks capped with snow and reaching for the heavens. This would be good country for Amanda. Perhaps he should consider moving north.

Etta watched him. She was sure he loved the country already. If only she could convince him to stay with her. She clung to the slim hope that his natural manliness and the love he once had for her would slowly but surely lure him into her bed—and into her life to stay, in spite of his stubborn pride. Here in Wyoming, perhaps he would begin to detest the thought of going back to his small, hot, dusty ranch in southern Utah. And if she were to offer him enough bait…

Moss mounted his horse now. How it stirred her to see him astride a horse. He was as natural on one as a leaf on a tree. He was a big man, and seemed even bigger and more masculine when he sat on the broad-chested buckskin thoroughbred he'd brought with him. He slipped his rifle from its leather holder. The mahogany butt of the well-oiled Winchester glinted in the sunlight. She watched in fascination as he opened the chamber and checked to be sure it was loaded, then closed it and slung it back into its holder, all with speed and ease—and with only one hand. He reached around his left side and whipped out another rifle: a wicked-looking, sawed off shotgun. All the men were checking their arms now—a virtual small army. Etta's heart pounded with excitement. She had help now. Real men who knew their business! Moss shoved his shotgun back into its berth and slid his revolver from its holster on his hip, whirling the chamber of the Colt .45 double action gun. She noticed the trigger guard was cut away.

"Do you always carry around broken guns?" she asked.

"Hmmm?" He looked over at her, then at his gun. "Oh, that." He held it up. "A quarter of a second can sometimes mean a man's life. Sometimes a trigger guard gets in the way. If you don't know your business, it's pretty risky usin' a gun without one. But I prefer mine this way. Gives me that much more speed in a pinch."

"I see," she replied, her eyes roving his body. Moss just scowled at her deliberately provocative look and turned his horse, ignoring the old feelings she sometimes managed to stir, and angry at her and at himself for feeling anything at all. "I want to say something to all the men before we head out, Moss," she was telling him.

The train belched and grunted; its wheels created sparks as the big engine groaned to get under way. The men talked gently to skittish horses. Moss waited until the train chugged past them heading on into Rock Springs, then ordered the men to stay put while Etta had her say. Some of the men lit up cigarettes and cigars, and all leaned forward to listen to Etta, none of them minding the opportunity to study her voluptuous figure more closely.

"The ranch is about a day's ride from here," she told them. "I have five thousand acres." Moss had not expected quite that much. The others looked at each other.

"Ma'am, uh, that's a lot of territory to cover, if you don't mind me sayin' so," Bullit spoke up.

"I know that. But we'll round up most of the cattle and bring them in closer to the house and buildings so you won't be scattered all over the place. The first thing I want you to know is that I appreciate what you're doing. I should pay you more, but my funds are dwindling, thanks to my ex-husband." Her eyes hardened. "But you'll have a good bunkhouse to sleep in, and there will always be plenty of food. I also have water—

plenty of it. The name of the ranch is the E.G. And besides the money I'm paying you to help me protect it until this thing is straightened out, I'll pay you regular ranch-hand wages to help me catch up on the regular work. I have fences that need mending, cattle that need branding, things I haven't been able to keep up with because I've lost so many men. Those I have left have been so busy just guarding the place that the work has fallen far behind. Will you help me?"

"For a few extra bucks and good food, why not?" Hank Stemm replied. "That's more than we've got most of the time."

They all chuckled, and Etta smiled.

"When it comes to protection and going after my husband and his hired killers, Moss is in full command. As far as work around the ranch goes, my own man, Lloyd Duncan, will be in charge." She turned to Moss. "Is that all right?"

"Good idea. I won't have time for both. And Lloyd knows the place, knows what's needed." He looked over at Duncan, who had not spoken to him since the day of their fight, before the group left. "Agreed?" he asked the man.

"Sure," the man grumbled. "Anything you say, boss."

Moss turned his horse and walked it over closer to Duncan.

"I'm not tryin' to take over the ranch, Duncan. That's your territory, and I have no intentions of movin' in on it. Why don't you just relax and let bygones be bygones?"

Duncan looked from Moss to Etta. His own manliness had been challenged in front of her, and he'd lost—to a one-armed man. He could not forgive that. Nor could he help but see the way Etta Landers looked at Moses Tucker. Lloyd Duncan was out of her life now, and he didn't like it one bit. He loved her, even though he felt like beating her to death. She was no more than a whore as far as he was concerned, but he loved her, nonetheless. And he could hardly believe Moss Tucker hadn't already been under her skirts. If not, it wouldn't be long before he was. He looked at Moss again.

"I'll do my job and you do yours," he grumbled. "And we'll

just try to stay out of each other's way." He reined his horse and trotted it to the back of the group. Moss turned to Etta.

"You through?"

"I guess so," she replied.

"All right, men, pay attention," Moss told them. "It's likely the ranch is already overrun with Ralph Landers's men. We're gonna go in from the back side and make our way real slow: spread out and keep your eyes and ears open. We'll work our way in real careful. Sooner, you stay back and keep Etta with you. As we move in we'll signal you to bring her on up. I want her out of the line of fire till we know it's safe. When we get close to the main house and buildings, we'll have to be extra careful, 'cause that's where most of them will be waitin' for us. Far as I know, they don't know we're comin'. But we can't be sure of that." He took a drag on a cigarette. "Everybody ready to ride?"

They all nodded.

"Let's get the hell going," Max Cornell growled. "I don't like the name Ralph Landers, and I don't like a man tryin' to destroy a woman who's helpless against him. If she was my wife, I'd sure not be fightin' against her."

They all laughed, itching now for some action. Etta grinned, aroused by the look Cornell gave her.

"Thank you—thank you all," she told them. "Let's go home! I'm tired and want a bath."

A round of whoops and whistles came from the group, and heels dug into horses and they were off, moving at a slow gallop and pulling the extra horses, packed with extra supplies, along behind. Moses Tucker and his men were headed for the E.G., and woe to any man who was there and would try to stop them from coming in.

Chapter Thirty-Four

They spread out—a line of hard men—rifles drawn, and resting on thighs, their barrels pointing upward and glinting in the sun. Five thousand acres was a lot of land, and Moss was not concerned about any men who might be lurking in the outer perimeter. They could be cleaned out later. For now they would ride straight through the middle in pairs, spaced about fifty yards apart.

The E.G. lay in a vast, green valley, surrounded by towering, icy summits. The sturdy mounts the men rode crushed daisies and buttercups as they made their way steadily across Etta Landers's land toward her home, which was not yet even in sight. No one spoke. The only sound was a soft breeze that smelled of fragrant flowers and the song of the bluebirds that flitted among pine trees in the surrounding hills.

All eyes and ears were alert for any sound, any movement that was out of the ordinary. Etta and Sooner hung back a few hundred yards, and Etta's heart pounded with fear. Then several men made themselves seen, men just as rugged looking and threatening as Moss and those with him. They suddenly appeared from behind rocks and trees like ghosts, moving together and riding toward Moss and the others. Sooner stopped his horse and reached over and grasped Etta's bridle.

"Come on," he said quietly. He led her horse across the valley to a grouping of large boulders. "Get down," he told her, keeping his own eyes on the confrontation about to take place ahead of them. He crawled up to the top of the rocks and lay down flat, cocking his rifle. Etta slid off her horse and crouched behind the rocks, now afraid for Moss. She strained to hear the voices in the distance.

"Hold it right there!" the apparent leader of Ralph Landers's men spoke up. There were about fifteen, and they formed a solid line across Moss's pathway. "You're trespassing, mister."

Moss sat straight and unflinching, not even holding the reins of his horse, as his good arm held his rifle.

"We work for the owner," he replied calmly.

"The owner left. This place has been claimed by Ralph Landers."

Moss scanned the group with his eyes.

"Is Landers here now?" he asked.

"He don't stay here. He lives in town and conducts his business from there. We watch the place for him."

"Well, Ralph Landers don't own this place, and you know it same as me," Moss replied. "The owner just took a little trip. She's back now; you can tell Landers that. And she's back to stay."

The other man's eyes narrowed.

"What's your name, cripple?" he asked.

Moss just grinned. "Name's Moses Tucker. You tell Ralph Landers that Moses Tucker is here—and be sure Miles Randall knows it, too. Fact is, I expect I'll be ridin' into town soon to pay them both a friendly visit."

"You won't be ridin' no place. Except back where you came from."

"Mister, I'll tell you just once. These here men are a pretty rowdy bunch. Most of them have killed men, and they're just itchin' to do it again. Now we've been hired by Etta Landers to keep her goddamned ex-husband off this property, and that's what we're gonna do! So you just take your men and you ride off this property, 'cause as of now you're officially trespassers. We shoot trespassers. That's the rules of the E.G. You've had your warning."

The man swallowed, not sure how to handle the unexpected situation. When dealing with strangers, it was difficult to tell when a man was bluffing. But Moses Tucker struck him as being totally serious and not easily backed down.

"Ralph Landers ain't gonna like this one bit, mister!" the man snarled.

Moss grinned. "Good. Anything he wants to do about it is fine with me. I'll be waitin'."

The other man reddened with anger and frustration. "Mister, there's guns on you—not just these men here, but more in the hills," he told Moss. "If you don't ride out right now, you're a dead man!"

Moss slowly lowered his rifle so that it pointed at the man's belly.

"That could be," he replied. "But you just remember this: if you give the signal for men to commence shooting, the first thing I'll do is pull this trigger, and the only thing left in your saddle will be your own guts. Could be your men will get every one of us. But the fact will still remain that you will be a dead man. And when you consider that, it makes you wonder if it's worth it, don't it?"

Beads of sweat broke out on the man's forehead. He fingered his reins nervously.

"Make up your mind, mister," Moss told him. "Back off now or confess your sins."

The man swallowed and moved his horse sideways. Moss kept the rifle barrel aimed straight at his middle.

"Let them through, men!" the leader growled.

"First off we'll take them rifles and guns you're toting," Moss told the man. "Could be you've got some back shooters among you."

The man hesitated, and Moss pulled back the hammer of his Winchester.

"Hand them your weapons, men!" the leader spoke up.

"But, boss—"

"Do like I say!" the man barked.

The others grudgingly unbuckled, handing over side arms and rifles to Moss's men, who received them with grins and nods.

"Now, I doubt there's more men in them hills," Moss told

the leader of Landers's men. "It strikes me you just said that to try to get the better of us. If they'd been there, they'd have shot at us by now. And you'd not have given up them guns so easily. I want to know where the rest are."

"They're all at the house—about twenty more," the man replied.

"You yellow bastard!" one of his men shouted. He reached into his jacket, and Hank Stemm fired his rifle without hesitation. A large red hole instantly appeared in the middle of the man's chest. He sat rigid on his horse for a moment, then slid off with a thud, a .45 revolver spilling from his jacket.

"Sooner! Sooner, what happened?" Etta asked from their hiding place several yards back.

"It's okay, ma'am. Hank just shot one that put up a fuss. Ole Moss already had the rest of them talked into givin' up their arms."

Etta breathed a sigh of relief, then smiled.

"I knew he could do it."

"Well, we ain't all the way to the house yet, ma'am. One step at a time."

"The rest of you pick up your friend and get the hell off this land," Moss said calmly. "At the moment I don't have anything in particular against you—not unless you come back. Consider this your lucky day."

Two of Landers's men got down and picked up the dead body of their comrade, slinging it over the man's saddle and securing it with rope. No one spoke. But the glare in the men's eyes told Moss they would be back in full force.

"Move it," Moss said coolly.

"You haven't heard the last of Ralph Landers!" the leader spoke up.

"I'm countin' on that," Moss told him. The Landers men rode out around Moss's men and headed out.

"Spread out a little more, boys, and keep a watch behind," Moss told his men. They obeyed without speaking. "Sooner!" Moss yelled out.

"Yes, sir!"

"Wait till they're out of sight. Then bring her forward real careful!"

"Right!" Sooner looked down at Etta. "Stay down there, ma'am. Landers's men are ridin' by us. Soon as they're gone we'll head farther in."

She nodded, now trembling. She breathed deeply and put a hand to her throat.

"I'm so scared," she whispered.

Sooner grinned. "You've got nothin' to be scared of, ma'am. It's gonna be okay."

"I can't thank all of you enough. If you hadn't come I'd never have been able to come back here."

Sooner remained on top of the rock, now looking out at Moss and the others again. He watched the Landers men ride by, remaining still until they were out of sight.

"Let's go, ma'am," he spoke up, sliding down off the rock.

• • •

They rode forward, fourteen hard-bellied men with cold, steel guns, the fifteenth coming from behind with the woman. Again there was near silence. Moss noticed with envy some fat, sleek, black beef cattle grazing calmly in the distance. He wondered just how many head of cattle Etta owned. This was a grand place, the kind of place men like Moss dreamed about owning. He could have owned a place like this, if Miles Randall hadn't cheated him out of the fortune he'd made from the little gold mine he sold so many years ago.

It was a cool, crisp day, and colors burst around them: an array of wild flowers mixed with the deep green of the pasture, framed by purple mountains, with white caps that in turn were set against a vivid blue sky. He thought about how much Amanda would like a place like this. And he wondered at how ironic it was that a place of such beauty could actually be almost a battleground.

It had taken all day to reach the ranch, and by the time they reached the rise that looked down on the house and buildings at the center of the property, the sun had nearly set. Moss motioned for all of them to stop and dismount. He waved his hat, telling Sooner to catch up with Etta.

"Get the horses down into that clump of trees and out of sight," he told the men quietly. "We've got some plannin' to do. It's gettin' dark, and I don't intend to spend the whole, cold night out here. We're gonna root out the rest of them men and sleep in real beds tonight. How about it?"

"Sounds good to me, boss," Max replied with a grin. "Besides, we sort of promised Mrs. Landers she'd be able to take a bath tonight and sleep under a roof."

"That's just what she'll do," Moss told him. "No campfires, men, and don't light no cigarettes till you're down in them trees."

They moved quickly and quietly, talking softly to their animals to keep them from whinnying. Sooner caught up and led Etta into the circle of men.

"What's up, boss?"

"It's gettin' dark, but we're gonna move in anyway, Sooner. There's no sense in lettin' Landers's men have all the comforts of home. They've had their turn. I brought Etta home, and she's goin' in there tonight."

Sooner helped Etta down from her horse.

"I need to know the layout," Moss told her quickly.

"Directly below this rise is a long storage shed, usually full of cattle feed. I doubt any men would be in there," she replied in a near whisper. "To the right of that is a huge barn, and in front of that two more sheds for tool and supply storage. Over on the left side of the feed shed are two long bunkhouses, and in the center is the main house. It's big, Moss. I have six bedrooms upstairs and downstairs is a kitchen, parlor, sewing room, dining room and living room, with a large veranda across the front. You can walk out onto the roof of the veranda from the upstairs bedrooms, so it's possible men could be up there, too."

"How particular is Ralph Landers about his belongings?"

"What do you mean?"

"Would he let men stay at the house, or would he most likely not want it messed up?"

She frowned and put a hand to her lips. Then she looked up at him, trying to ignore how handsome he looked in the dusky moonlight.

"I think he'd try to keep the house decent. It's possible he'd have one or two men in there, maybe a cleaning lady. Once he's sure the place is his, he'll move in. He's a coward, Moss. My guess is the only reason he isn't out here now is because he was afraid something like this might happen. In the meantime, my guess is he'd have most of the men stay inside the bunkhouses."

"I'm figurin' the same." Moss turned to Sooner. "We're gonna spread out. Me and you, Hank, Max, Tom, Brad…"

"Yeah, boss?"

"All of us will hit the bunkhouses, hard and fast—no hesitation. Duncan, I want you to come with us. You know the layout."

"I'll come," the man replied dryly.

"Danny?"

"Yes, sir?"

"You're also familiar with the grounds. You take Dwight, Darrell, Bullit, and Slim to the house. Hit it front and back. Search every room and watch out for that balcony."

"Glad to do it," Danny replied, loading his pistol.

"Pappy—you and Johnny go east and west. Hide out in the shadows and shoot anybody that runs past you. Lonnie, you stay here with Etta."

"You mean I don't get to join the fun?"

"Don't worry. There'll be more good times to come," Moss answered sarcastically. They all snickered.

"Everybody straight?" Moss asked. Various affirmative replies came back at him. "The important thing is that you don't hesitate," Moss told them. "When a man knows the other man means business, that's half the battle. Tell them they either leave or die. If they put up a fuss, shoot 'em. If they even look like they're goin' for a gun, shoot 'em. I don't want to lose none of you. Talk fast and hard and show them some steel. Let's get this over with quick. I'm tired."

"You ain't the only one," Pappy whispered.

"Let's go," Moss whispered hoarsely. They left their horses tied and disappeared into the darkness like silent Indians, and Etta grasped her stomach, feeling ill.

"You okay?" Lonnie asked her.

"I just feel so badly, that I have to ask men to risk their lives just so I can sleep in my own house," she whispered. "It's all so unfair."

"That's why they're doin' it. After we're here a while, I expect that ex of yours will give up or die, whichever."

Etta listened for the inevitable gunshots and prayed.

• • •

Moss and his men moved stealthily among yucca plants and sagebrush, Moss pondering how quiet the mountain nights were. It was an almost deafening silence at times, broken only by the occasional howl of a coyote. They moved up on the two bunkhouses. Both had men inside, men who had begun to carelessly take it for granted that Etta Landers would not dare return, and so had not kept a good watch. He signaled to Sooner, Hank, and Duncan to stay with him, and Tom Sorrells went on to the other bunkhouse with Brad and Max. At the same time Bullit, Dwight, Darrell, and Slim headed for the house.

Moss moved to the front door of the first bunkhouse, amused at how easy it had been to sneak up on Landers's men. He looked over at Tom, who was at the next bunkhouse, then nodded. Simultaneously, the two men shoved their feet into the front doors, slamming them open and startling

327

everyone inside. Moss moved inside quickly, brandishing his Winchester; Sooner, Hank, and Duncan moved in beside him. Four men looked up from a table where they had been playing cards, and seven more jumped up out of bunks. They all momentarily froze.

"Grab your things and get out!" Moss growled.

"Who the hell are you?" one of them asked.

"Name's Moss Tucker. We work for Etta Landers, and you're trespassin'. Get your asses out of here before I plant your belt buckle against that back wall over there!"

The men all looked at each other a moment.

"Just the four of you?"

As soon as he said it, there were gunshots from the next bunkhouse. Shouts could be heard from farther away, probably the house. More gunshots.

"More than four," Moss said with a grin. "Leave your guns and pick up your gear and leave."

There was a movement from one of the bunks. Moss caught it and whirled, firing the Winchester. A little flame shot out from the barrel and one of Landers's men screamed out, blood pouring from his belly. Then he slumped to the floor. One of the men sitting at the table dove for his gun, which was hanging from a bedpost nearby; in a split second Moss cocked his rifle in midair and shot again. The second man screamed and grabbed his wrist; blood began flowing from his hand where Moss's bullet had gone through it. There was another movement from one of the bunks, and Sooner whirled and raised his rifle.

"I wouldn't, mister," he said calmly, as the man hesitated in reaching for a rifle in the corner. "All the pay in the world you might get from Ralph Landers wouldn't be worth it."

The man swallowed and eased his hand away from the rifle. There were two more gunshots from somewhere outside, and then momentary quiet. Then someone could be heard running, and Tom Sorrells appeared at the doorway.

"Everything okay here?" he asked.

"These men was just leavin'," Moss replied, backing up some.

"There was eight at the other bunkhouse," Tom told him. "Three are dead and the rest are saddlin' up right now. I'm not sure yet what happened at the house."

Moss stepped up and lay his rifle barrel against the throat of one of the men.

"How many were there all together?" he asked.

The man swallowed. "Twenty-two," he replied. "F-four were in the house, three out keepin' watch north of here."

Moss backed up again. "You pack up and get out, and tell them three north of here that they'd do well to leave also, 'cause come mornin', we'll be out huntin' for more Landers men. Move it!"

Those who had guns on their hips removed them, and they exited one by one, most giving Moss a sullen look on the way through the door. The last one to leave turned to face Moss.

"You'll regret this, mister. Ralph Landers is gonna be damned mad. He owns the town—and the law!"

"And how does he pay everybody off, besides with money?" Moss asked.

"What are you talkin' about?"

"I mean whose bed is he sleepin' in, mister? Yours?"

The man turned gray. "Are you crazy?"

"No. But maybe you're ignorant! You'd best wonder what kind of man you're workin' for, mister, if he can be called a man at all!"

The man swallowed. "I—I don't believe you."

"Believe what you want. You ever seen Etta Landers?"

"Sure, I—"

"Kind of pretty, wouldn't you say?"

"Sure, but—"

"How many men would turn away a wife that looked like that?"

The man frowned.

"Think about it. And think about the fact that he's already

rich, but he's bent on pickin' on a helpless woman to satisfy his own lust for more land and power. He's ruthless and a tyrant—owns the law and the town. He'll own you before long! Any time you want to join up on our side, you come on back here and talk to me."

The man eyed them all for a moment, then quietly left. Moss gripped his gun, again inflamed with anger over what Ralph Landers was and what he had done to Etta. He kicked the bunkhouse door hard, making it slam against the wall.

"That true, Moss? What you said about Landers?" Hank asked.

"It's true," Moss snarled. He turned to look at them. "Don't let on to Etta that you know. It embarrasses her too much. Don't even tell the other men. They don't need to know. I just figured if I could plant a seed in one man, maybe it would grow. If I can win a few men away from Landers, more power to us. In the meantime, there's always them that will do anything for money and don't give a damn who they're workin' for. So our work is still cut out for us." He looked over at the dead man still lying on his bunk. "Sooner, get outside and make sure one or two of them men get back in here and pick up this man. Let them bury their own."

"Sure, Moss."

"The rest of you come with me. We'll check out the house." They stepped inside. "Everybody okay out here?" Moss hollered out.

"Got the house cleaned out for you, Moss!" Dwight yelled from an upstairs window.

"Get on down here then. You fellas make yourselves at home in the bunkhouses. We're gonna sleep in real beds tonight!"

There were cheers and laughter.

"Max, you and Brad keep watch for a while, then roust somebody out later to take over."

Pappy Lane rode in just then. "You okay, Moss?"

"Sure, Pappy. Any trouble out there?"

"I winged one earlier, but he kept ridin' and ought to be a good ways from here by now."

"Good. You okay?"

"Can't get the best of an old dog like me."

"Ride on up and tell Lonnie and Etta to come on down. I'm goin' to the house."

"Sure." Pappy started to leave, then hesitated. "Moss?"

"Yeah?"

"You sleepin' in the house tonight?"

Moss sighed and put his rifle on his shoulder.

"Yes, I am. Somebody's got to stay at the house with Etta. I reckon I'll sleep downstairs, and I'll set up a guard or two outside."

"It's been a long trip, Moss. You're tired and that house looks pretty fancy. I expect it has fancy beds, too. A mite temptin' to a lonely man."

Moss grinned a little and shook his head.

"It's not the bed that counts, Pappy. It's the woman in it. There won't be no woman in my bed tonight, so it don't matter if it has satin sheets, or if it's made of straw. Quit worryin', damn it."

Pappy smiled. "Just checkin'."

"You're worse than a naggin' old woman." Moss chuckled and walked toward the house.

• • •

Moss's boots echoed in the high-ceilinged hallway as he casually walked over gleaming, hardwood floors. The house was cool and clean, beautifully decorated with painted vases, plants, oriental rugs, and expensive looking paintings. He was more than impressed. It brought back memories of the days when he courted Etta Graceland, the young, spoiled, but beautiful daughter of a wealthy California banker. A house like the one he walked in now was unusual in the West, which only made it seem even more elegant and wondrous. But it was the only kind of house a woman like Etta Graceland Landers would live in.

"I'll bet she even has indoor plumbing," he thought to himself.

Then his thoughts turned to Amanda. How wonderful it would be to give her a house like this one. She would fit perfectly. She had all the education and elegance of an Etta Landers, yet she was so much more a woman, a woman who deserved a house like this one. He knew Amanda could have done much better than to marry him, but now she lived in a small log cabin in the hot canyons of southeast Utah. His chest felt tight with the desire to make a good life for Amanda. And he already knew what he would do with the two thousand dollars Etta would pay him. He would build Amanda a house. It wouldn't be quite as grand as the house he was standing in now, but it would be large and cool, and maybe they would even have indoor plumbing.

He roamed the rooms, each one large and airy with lovely curtains at the windows, heavy oak doors, delicate and expensive knickknacks sitting here and there. Every table had a lacy cloth on it. He wandered up the stairs, picturing Amanda standing at the head of the stairway in a soft gown, waiting for him to come to bed. He ached all over in his need of her.

The stairway was circular. He walked along the balcony, peeking into each bedroom, each one with its own fourposter bed. Then he came to the room he knew had to be Etta's. Everything was pale green, and the bed had a ruffled canopy over it. He wondered how many men she had entertained in this bed. He shook the thought from his mind and quickly left the room. He headed back down the stairs, to see Etta standing below. She was pale and shaking.

"Are you all right?" she asked quietly.

"Sure am," he replied with a smile.

"Oh, Moss, thank you!" she told him sincerely, beginning to cry. "I'd never have been able to come back here...if not for you."

His smile faded and he came down the stairs. "Well, you're here now," he told her quietly. "And you're tired. Go on up and take that bath you wanted and get to bed."

Their eyes held for a moment. "You could come up with me, Moss. You don't have to make any promises. Just come up and sleep with me tonight. Who's to know?"

He studied the blue eyes, shaking his head with wonder at her inability to understand he no longer wanted her, and angry that she dared to tempt him this way, making his job more miserable. Moses Tucker was not a man to go for long without a woman, and there was only one woman he truly loved and wanted. But to have this object of beauty offer herself was cruel, especially when she knew he once loved her. The thought passed his mind of taking her simply to know the feeling of finally conquering Etta Landers. But the fact that she was degrading herself by standing there and offering herself for free was satisfaction enough.

"I'd know, Etta. And Mandy would know," he answered. "She'd die a little on the inside. And so would I. Somethin' special we share together would be lost forever. We have somethin' you'd never understand. Now get on upstairs and have your bath and go to sleep. I'll be down here on the couch if there's trouble." He removed his gunbelt. "Tomorrow I'll go visitin'."

She reddened with indignation, wanting him even more, hating him, loving him. "Visiting where?" she asked coldly, wiping at the tears and walking to the steps, moving on up past him.

"Into Rock Springs. Where else? I figure it's about time I met Ralph Landers, and I'd like to look up my old friend, Miles Randall."

"Oh, Moss, you can't go into town! You can't!" she told him, coming back down a couple of steps. "They'd kill you!"

"In broad daylight? In front of all them fine citizens?" He threw his gun over the back of a chair. "No way. If Ralph Landers intends to do me in, it'll be in the dark—most likely a shot in the back. You hired me to get rid of him, Etta. And

I intend to. My first step is to make him sweat and worry. I'll badger him till he's gonna wonder if this place is worth it. If that don't work, I reckon I'll have to shoot him eventually."

She watched him longingly as he sat down to pull off his boots. "You're probably right about Ralph doing nothing in the light of day," she answered. "I wish I could be there to see his face when you go into town."

"That would be too dangerous." He pulled off his boots and looked up at her, his eyes running over her. If he were not attached, he would gladly use her to his heart's content, then leave her. How he would enjoy hurting her that way! But she had been hurt plenty by Ralph Landers already. That thought always brought a little feeling back into his heart for her. "You got any paper and pens around?" he asked. "I want to write to Mandy, tell her things are okay so far. Long as I'll be goin' into town, I might as well use the opportunity to get word to her. It might be a long time before I'm allowed back into Rock Springs."

She fought her jealousy of Amanda Tucker.

"In the parlor—there's a roll top desk in there. You'll find your paper and pencils there."

"Thank you, ma'am," he told her mockingly, rising from the chair.

"Do you know how to spell, Mr. Tucker?" she asked sarcastically. "Or do you need my help for that? I apparently can't do anything else for you!"

"Mandy's used to my poor education," he replied with a grin. "She'll forgive the misspelled words."

"Yes. There are things more important than knowing how to spell, aren't there?" she replied.

"I expect so, ma'am."

"If you need anything, Moss, I'll be…bathing for a while…and then I'll be in bed. Just knock."

"Your hospitality is appreciated. I'll just stretch out on the couch, like I told you."

"But there's a bed in every room up there!"

"I know that. I've already seen them. And they're all too close to you. A man can only stand so much, and I am a man after all, as you damned well know. I'd appreciate it if you'd respect what I'm doin' for you, Etta, and respect my marriage. You ruined my life once, and I'll not let that happen again. I'd like to think there's at least a little bit of decency left in your heart, so quit throwin' yourself at me like a whore."

He walked into the parlor, and she stared after him. If she didn't need him so badly, she'd have gladly shot him in the back; yet never had she wanted him more than at that moment.

Chapter Thirty-Five

"Everything okay. Give Becky kiss for me. Could be here at least a month. I love you. Miss your cooking. Most of all miss you. I'm a lonely man. Write care of Rock Springs, Wyo. Will come home as soon as I can, Love, Moss."

"You got all that?" Moss asked the telegraph man.

"Yes, sir."

"Get it out right away to Hanksville, Utah. It's for Amanda Tucker, at the Red 'C' Ranch down on the San Juan River."

"The Red 'C'? That's an unusual name, sir."

"My wife named it. It's not really the letter 'C', but it's easier to brand the cattle that way. It's really Red Sea—you know, like in the Bible?"

"The Bible?"

Moss grinned. "Yeah. My first name is Moses. Get it?"

The man stared at Moss a moment, then broke into a smile, then light laughter.

"Oh! Moses! Red Sea!" He laughed again. "Of course. What a clever idea."

Moss grinned and shook his head, reaching into his shirt pocket and taking out a prerolled cigarette.

"My wife knows a lot about the Bible. It was her idea. Kind of crazy, huh?"

The man laughed again. "Well, considering your reputation, Mr. Tucker..." The man suddenly lost his smile. "I—I mean—well, you're sort of the talk of the town. Some here had already heard of you, and they say you're..." The man glanced at Moss's gun, hung low on his hip. "You're, uh, an outlaw and good with that side arm you're wearing."

Moss shrugged. "You know how them stories get exaggerated."

The man swallowed. "They're waiting for you, Mr. Tucker."

"I figured as much. That's why I rode in the back way, so I could get this letter off first. Figured maybe I wouldn't be around later to send it." He leaned over the counter, the cigarette dangling from his mouth. "I don't suppose you'd fill me in on what I'm ridin' into, would you?"

The man looked around first to be sure no one else was looking.

"Well, Mr. Tucker, frankly, some of us here in town are a little tired of Ralph Landers running everything, including the law. And his friend, the banker—he's robbing the citizens blind with his interest rates, and forecloses in a second if a person can't pay his mortgage. Some have even been physically threatened by the sheriff."

"Where is everybody now?"

"Most of them are at the Golden Spur Saloon. It's a fancy joint up the street. That's where Landers hangs out most of the time. I'll tell you, Mr. Tucker, I've seen that man's ex-wife, and if I were him, I'd be going over there to make up and forget about fighting!" The man chuckled, and Moss smiled.

"So, everybody knows I'm comin' in, huh?"

"Oh, yesterday and last night Landers's men kept straggling into town—one of them with a wounded hand, some dead and slung over their horses. Everybody knows what Ralph Landers has been up to. Now that Mrs. Landers has some help, we're all kind of sitting back to watch the show, you know? I'm glad she found some good men. Landers's men didn't keep it any secret what happened. I don't think any of them expected Etta Landers to even return, let alone come back with a virtual army. What will you do now, Mr. Tucker?"

Moss straightened and put his cigarette out.

"Well, I reckon I'll go get me a drink—at the Golden Spur."

The man's eyes widened. "Good luck, Mr. Tucker."

"Obliged," Moss replied with a nod. He walked through the door, stepping outside cautiously. Darrell, Pappy, Johnny, Bullit, and Sooner all waited outside on their horses.

"Got the letter sent," Moss told them. "The man in there tells me most of them are at the Golden Spur Saloon. So I figured that might be a good place to go get us a drink. What do you say, boys?"

Pappy grinned. "I'm mighty thirsty myself."

"Figured you was," Moss replied, sliding up into his saddle. The six of them headed up the street.

* * *

"They're comin', Mr. Landers!" one of the local barflies shouted excitedly, leaning out the swinging doors and staring down the street at Moss and his men.

"What do you want us to do, boss?" one of Landers's men asked.

"Let him come," Landers replied, looking cool on the outside but shaking on the inside. "The man wants to talk, so we'll talk. Besides, this Moses Tucker was an old lover of Etta's. I'd like to see what he looks like before he dies."

"I'm leaving!" Miles Randall told him, rising from his chair.

"You're staying right here! You turn tail and run and it will be all he needs!" Landers snapped.

"Moses Tucker almost killed me a few years back!" Randall hissed, leaning toward Landers. "Half the reason he's here is because your ex-wife told him I'm in town! I know it! I know it in my bones! You've got no right to make me stay here!"

Their eyes held a moment, Landers's steely cold. Miles Randall knew if he didn't obey, Landers might be angry with him, and Randall couldn't bear the thought of it. Randall slumped back into his chair as though physically defeated. Landers looked around the room.

"You men keep an eye on them. I don't feel like dying this

morning. But there will be no rough stuff today. We'll see what Moses Tucker wants, and we'll tell him the way it will be, and that's that. I don't want any out and out killings in front of the fine citizens of Rock Springs."

Horses could be heard outside now, and Ralph Landers's heart pounded. Miles Randall felt short of breath, and beads of sweat broke out on his forehead. A large, shadowy figure appeared at the swinging doors, difficult to see because the sun was at his back. The figure loomed inside, and Miles Randall gripped the edge of the table tightly, his knuckles turning white. His face was the first one Moss saw. Moss stood still a moment, struggling to keep his temper. The man he was looking at had stolen from under his nose every last cent Moss had earned by the sweat of his brow, after five years of patiently mining his own gold and then selling his little claim. It was this same man Moss had nearly killed in rage. Moss had gone to prison for it: five more long years behind concrete and steel walls, suffering starvation, beatings, sickness, and filth. But as he stared at Miles Randall, he knew his vengeance was already being fulfilled. The man looked green, and Moss thought Randall would puke any moment.

Moss pushed his hat back. "Long time, Randall. You look like you got your health back."

Randall opened his mouth, but no sound came out. Moss shifted his eyes to the very well-dressed man who sat across the table from Miles Randall. He knew who it had to be. So this was Etta's husband. It did not surprise him that the man was extremely handsome. Etta would not marry an ugly man. But it did surprise him that such a well-built, dark and handsome man could be what Etta claimed he was.

"Mr. Landers I presume?" Moss asked, as five of his men came through the door behind him. Pappy and the others spread out slowly, eyeing everyone in the room cautiously and getting some cold stares in return. The tension was almost painful.

"I'm Ralph Landers," the man replied, standing up. "You, uh, already know Mr. Randall here."

Moss reached into his shirt pocket for another cigarette. He looked at Miles Randall again, who in turn was staring at Moss's missing arm.

"Apache," Moss told the man, lighting his cigarette. Randall looked up at Moss's eyes.

"Indians?" he choked out.

"You know anything else that's called Apache?"

Randall just swallowed.

"Men like me don't die, Randall," Moss added. "They've got ways of comin' back. Too bad, isn't it?" He took a deep drag on his cigarette.

"Mr. Tucker, let's get down to business," Landers spoke up.

"First things first," Moss replied. "I'm thirsty." He looked over at the bartender. "Me and my men want some whiskey. Pour it."

The bartender started to get out some shot glasses.

"Don't you give them a drop!" Landers ordered.

Moss shifted his eyes to Ralph Landers, his hatred building.

"You own this place?"

"I do. I own half this town."

"Yeah. That's what I heard. That's not all I heard about you, Landers."

Landers turned white, then red. He swallowed and took a deep breath. "What the hell are you talking about, Tucker?" he hissed.

"You know what I'm talkin' about," Moss replied in a low and threatening voice. "You've all but destroyed Etta Landers. Mister, what you do with your life is your private affair. But pickin' on a helpless woman irritates me like a burr between my ass and my saddle! She's suffered enough, and you're rich enough. So back off, 'cause if you don't, you'll be one hell of a sorry man!"

"And who's going to make me sorry? You?" Landers sneered. "A one-armed man and a few paltry cowhands?"

"Me and these few paltry cowhands sent every last one of your men on their merry way last night. And anybody that comes back to bother Etta Landers is gonna die. And I'm here to warn you personally to back off and go on back to California, or there's certain things I'm gonna expose. I'll bring in a U.S. marshal if I have to, and as a last resort I'll kill you myself!"

Landers' eyebrows went up. "It's dangerous to threaten a man in front of witnesses, Mr. Tucker. Especially when you're an ex-convict."

"If I worried about dangers, I'd curl up in a closet and never come out. I've told you how it's gonna be, Landers."

Landers grinned. "Tell me, Mr. Tucker. How long did it take for my lovely ex-wife to get you into her bed? Is that part of your payment?"

His last word was barely spoken before he felt a stinging blow across his lips. Moss backhanded him hard, knocking Landers sideways across the table. At the same time several of Landers's men went for their guns, but Moss's was out and waving before any of them could fully draw, and Moss's men now had their own guns and rifles aimed at specific targets.

"Everybody stand real still and nobody will get hurt," Pappy warned. Ralph Landers clung to the table, still lying on it and spitting blood from his mouth. Miles Randall had jumped up and was now cowering behind one of Landers's men. Moss looked over at the bartender.

"We'll have that whiskey now," he said calmly.

The bartender hesitated, while Ralph Landers scooted off the table, choking and wiping at his bloody lips with his expensive suit. Blood was now spattered down the front of his white, ruffled shirt.

"Now!" Moss barked at the bartender, making the man jump. "Bring it to us on trays! We don't intend to turn our backs on the scum in here!"

The bartender hurriedly put glasses on a tray and began pouring whiskey into them.

"I'll see you die for this," Landers sputtered, on the verge of tears.

"Could be one of us will die, Landers. You think about

that," Moss replied. "I'm not ready to yet. Death just has a way of side-steppin' my doorway."

The bartender came over with the whiskey.

"Hand my glass to Mr. Landers here," Moss told him. "He's gonna put it to my lips and tip it so I can swallow it without lettin' go of my gun."

Landers' eyes widened and the man turned purple with rage.

"I'll do no such thing!" he growled.

"You will. Or I'll swing this gun and break that nose, Mr. Landers. You're a handsome man. But a broken nose could change all that, couldn't it?" His eyes moved to Miles Randall. "Certain people might get upset by that." His eyes moved back to Landers. "Especially the…ladies," he added with a knowing grin. Landers was so red, Moss wondered if the man's head would explode. He grudgingly took a shot glass from the tray, and the bartender hurried to the other men to give them their drinks. All of Moss's men still held guns on the Landers men.

Ralph Landers held the glass up to Moss's lips and tipped it; Moss quickly swallowed the whiskey while his gun barrel rested against Landers's ribs. As soon as he was through, Landers threw the glass across the room, and it crashed against the wall.

"Thanks. You're right sociable," Moss told him.

Just then a man came barging through the doors, brandishing a rifle. Pappy grasped the rifle barrel before the man realized what was happening, ripping it from the man's hands and throwing it behind him to the floor. The man stood still in surprise, then frowned. He wore a star on his vest.

"What the hell is going on here?" he growled.

"Where in hell have you been!" Landers snapped back. "These men have been holding us at bay, and this one hit me! They barged in here and began bullying everyone in the place. What kind of a sheriff are you, Tillis?"

Moss backed up so that he could get a better view of the

sheriff. Tillis glanced around the room, surveying the situation. Then he looked back at Landers.

"Ralph, I—I just got back from Green River. Somebody said there was trouble over here—"

"You bet your ass there's trouble over here!" Landers roared back at him. "Look at my mouth! Arrest these men!"

Tillis stared at him dumbfounded, then smiled nervously.

"Just how do you propose I do that?" he asked.

Landers bristled. "You worthless—at least tell them if they ever come into town again they'll go to jail!"

Sheriff Tillis looked up at Moss. "I have to agree there, mister. What the hell do you think you're doing, coming in here on a peaceful Saturday morning and creating this disturbance?"

"You know good and well why I'm here, mister." Moss replied calmly. "And I don't take no orders from a weak-kneed sheriff who takes bribes to look the other way when laws are bein' broken, or who thinks money is more important than goin' to the aid of a helpless woman. You take that tin star of yours and cram it up your ass, mister! And I'll ride into this town anytime I feel like it. You'd best do your duty right, or I'll be havin' a talk with the local citizens. Maybe it's time they got themselves a new sheriff."

Tillis stood there in near shock, as Moss moved toward the doors now.

"You remember my warnin'," Moss told Landers. "I've come here to deliver it, fair and square. What happens after this is up to you. But if you expect to live to a ripe old age, you'll be headin' back to California and out of Etta Landers's life, or there'll be law here that's bigger than that hick sheriff of yours—and more likely than that, you'll be spittin' lead out of that mouth instead of blood!"

Moss and his men backed through the door, quickly turning to scan what was behind them as they did so. No one outside made a move. Several local residents stood around gawking as Moss and the others mounted their horses. Moments later they disappeared, and the citizens immediately began gossiping among themselves.

Inside the tavern Ralph Landers paced, wiping at his mouth and kicking at chairs in his rage.

"What a bunch of ninnies!" he fumed at his men. "Etta comes back with a few men and in one day you're all shaking in your boots!"

"They don't look like no easy bunch to deal with, boss," one man spoke up.

"Well, we will deal with them!" Landers barked. "I have more men than he does, if you can call yourselves men! You'd better start doing your job or there will be no more good pay and free whiskey!"

The man then grabbed one of the saloon girls and walked toward the stairs. "I'm going upstairs with Rachel, and then I'm going to decide what our next move is. Maybe you're all afraid of a one-armed, aging outlaw, but I'm not! I'm going upstairs to have a good time with a woman and let her nurse my sore mouth. Then I'm going to decide how to get rid of Moses Tucker, and all of you had better decide whether or not you've got the guts to carry out my plans!"

He stormed up the stairs, half dragging the girl with him, and one man watched him suspiciously, remembering the mortified look in Ralph Landers's eyes when Moses Tucker had said he'd heard things about the man. The man who watched Landers was Damian Kuntz, the same man Moss had talked to the night they raided Etta Landers's ranch, when Moss suggested Ralph Landers was some kind of pervert. Now Kuntz wondered if it might be true. Why had Landers suddenly grabbed the saloon girl and made a big show of bedding her in the middle of the day? It seemed almost a defensive move.

The rest of the men mumbled among themselves, but Damian Kuntz sat down quietly to watch the shaking Miles Randall, who kept looking up the stairs with an almost jealous gaze. Then Randall also went upstairs, going into the same doorway Landers had taken the girl. Kuntz frowned, then rose, and went out the door and around back to a stairway leading to a balcony beneath the upstairs rooms.

• • •

Two quiet weeks went by; a total of three long weeks away from Amanda. Moss dealt with his painful need for her by keeping himself so busy that he fell asleep quickly at night from pure exhaustion. There was a lot of work to be done around the E.G. An elderly neighbor woman who had once been Etta's housekeeper, but had been scared away by the feuding, was finally persuaded to return. Etta convinced the woman that the ranch was safe, now that Moss Tucker and his men were there. She helped Etta clean the house from top to bottom, while Moss and several of his men rode the perimeter of the ranch night and day, watching for intruders. Lloyd Duncan, in the meantime, led the other men in the general chores that had long been neglected.

Feed was cut and stored, fences were mended, and buildings repaired. Cattle were herded in closer to the house and buildings, where they could be watched without scattering the men dangerously thin. Almost one full week was spent branding calves, and at the end of that week Etta held a huge cookout for all the men. She flitted around in a yellow dress with a daring neckline, an agonizingly tempting employer who made the men's mouths water. It was just as hard on Moss as the rest of them, since his own manly needs were only heightened by his constant longing for Amanda.

The men ate heartily, thinking in the back of their minds how soft and full Etta's breasts looked, wondering how the red hair would look unpinned and falling over bare shoulders. But still they kept their distance, remembering Moss's warning and realizing the sense of it. If they gave in to their desires, they could be at each other's throats in no time at all, and divided they would be of no use to Etta Landers or Moses Tucker. The important thing was to finish the job they had come to do. For they were all men of their word.

The day of festivity was spent eating, drinking, and relaxing for the first time in three weeks. The men relieved their tensions by making a contest out of taming the wild mustangs they had gathered up along with the cattle. Etta enjoyed the show herself, as the men whooped and cheered each man who decided to mount a bucking bronc to see how long he could stay on.

Moss was pondering what his next move should be when someone shouted that a rider was approaching. Everyone quieted and turned to see one of Landers's men slowly advancing his gun slung over his horse's neck, his hand holding a stick with a white handkerchief tied to it, signifying he came in peace. The man came close to Moss before he halted his horse. Moss recognized him as the same man he'd spoken to the night he and his men took over the E.G.

"Somethin' I can do for you, mister?" he asked.

"My name is Damian Kuntz, and I want to talk to you, Tucker—in private."

"Landers send you?"

"No, sir. I came on my own. I want to join up."

Moss's eyebrows went up and the other men looked at each other in surprise.

"What changed your mind?" Moss asked.

"I'd rather discuss it alone," Kuntz replied, glancing at Etta Landers.

Moss pushed his hat back. "All right. Get on down off your horse and we'll take a walk."

The man dismounted.

"Could be a trap, Moss," Pappy spoke up. "Better check him for a knife. Maybe Landers sent him to do you in."

Moss studied Damian Kuntz closely. "I know a good man when I see one," he replied. "Let's go, mister." They walked off together, and all of them, including Etta, watched in curiosity.

The party had quieted, and Hank Stemm ran to the bunk-house, returning with a banjo.

"Where in hell did you get that thing?" Sooner asked him.

"Hell, I can play it!" Hank replied.

The men all chuckled and Hank began strumming a lively tune, to everyone's surprise. As Moss and Damian Kuntz walked off in the distance, Slim Taggart stepped up to Etta.

"Ma'am, I'm missin' my wife 'bout as much as Moss is missin' his. I sure wouldn't mind steppin' around a mite with somethin' soft and pretty, if you'd oblige."

Etta smiled and put out her hands.

"After all you men have done for me?" she replied. "I owe each of you one dance."

Slim grinned, took her hands, and they sidestepped back and forth to the banjo music. Soon the men were all clapping their hands, laughing, and taking their turn at a dance with the lovely Etta Landers. Lloyd Duncan watched, his heart burning with jealousy. Since Moses Tucker and his men had entered Etta's life, she'd not given him the time of day; Lloyd Duncan ached to get back into Etta's bed.

• • •

"How do I know you aren't a spy?" Moss asked Kuntz, when they got away from the others. The two men looked straight at each other.

"You said you could tell a good man when you saw one," Kuntz replied. "Landers told us a bunch of bull about his wife—how she slept around and all, said she just married him for his money. But it didn't all quite fit. I mean, maybe she's a little loose now, but anybody can tell she's an educated, refined lady. So I kept wondering how a lady like her—why would she lower herself like that?"

Moss's eyes turned cold, thinking of the horror a young married girl would feel discovering her husband was a homosexual.

"So, you finally figured it out?"

"Mister, I'm like you. I can read people pretty good. And I figure you for a good man, one that wouldn't lie. So I did some investigating of my own. I won't go into details except to say that you were right. I can't stomach working for a man like that, so here I am."

Moss studied him closely, then nodded. "Fine. You're hired. I gotta say I thought maybe Etta made it all up to get me to help her, but she seemed awful serious about it. I feel a little better havin' somebody else confirm it."

Kuntz took out a pipe and began packing it. "Well, I won't say just how I found out. It almost embarrasses me to talk about something like that. So I'll let it rest. I'm here to help however I can."

Moss waited while the man lit his pipe and puffed it for a moment. "Well, Kuntz, you got any ideas as to how to get Landers out of Etta's hair for once and for all?" he asked. "I can't stay here forever. I've got a woman of my own to get back to. I'm thinkin' about bringin' in a marshal, but that would be a legal mess, and some of my men are wanted. A marshal would make them uneasy, and the waitin' would make them more uneasy. They're anxious men, like me—anxious to get the job done. Seems it's easier just to talk up and pump lead into the man than do things by the system. Simpler that way."

Kuntz nodded. "Sometimes it is. There is one way, though, that could at least get things rolling if you want to do this on the up and up. Landers, he's been sitting around waiting for you to make a move, not sure himself what to do about all this. You and your men are more than he expected. He owns the town and its people, Tucker. But that doesn't mean they all like him. And I think they'd be glad to be rid of Miles Randall. What you need is more people on your side. Like the ranchers around here who owe Randall money. Some of them have had a hard time and he threatens them. They'd like to see him gone and a more honest man handling their banking affairs."

"Then why shouldn't they help Etta? I've been too busy

around here to go and see any of them, but I haven't noticed anybody comin' around, neither. I know everybody's busy, just like us, but down in Utah—well, I see my neighbors pretty often, even though we're far apart."

"It's the water, Tucker. If she'd share the water, she'd get some help."

Moss frowned and stamped out his cigarette.

"What are you talkin' about?"

"Didn't she tell you? The only good water supply around is on Etta Landers' property, and she won't let nobody touch it. That's why she's got that damned barbed wire fence running around the place. It's not to keep out enemies. It's to keep out the other ranchers. And it's been a dry summer, Mr. Tucker. Them ranchers need that water, and she won't let them at it. Landers—he's promised them that if they stay out of it, as this place belongs to him they can have all the water they want. That's a pretty strong argument, Tucker, to a rancher—even strong enough to keep them from coming to the aid of a helpless woman."

Moss's eyes had darkened with anger as Kuntz spoke, and he turned to leave.

"Uh, Mr. Tucker?"

"What?"

"Where are you headed?"

"I've got a bone to pick with your new boss," Moss grumbled. He walked straight up to the laughing, dancing crowd and grasped Etta's arm. "You and me have somethin' to discuss," he told her, gripping her arm firmly. "You've been holdin' out on me, lady."

"What? What are you talking about?" she asked, swallowing and looking surprised.

Moss looked at the others. "You men have yourselves a good time. Mrs. Landers will be back soon." He nodded toward Damian Kuntz, who had hurried to catch up. "He's one of us now."

Without further explanation, Moss walked off with Etta.

Chapter Thirty-Six

"But I can't give them that water!" Etta insisted, pacing and wringing her hands together.

"Are you crazy? If you give them the water, they'll come over to your side! They'd help you guard this place, Etta, help you keep Landers off it. What are you afraid of?"

She turned to face him, tears in her eyes. "I'm afraid—afraid to trust anybody, Moss. And—and if I share my water, well, I don't know. Maybe I'd run out of water, or what if I share it and then need their help some other way, and they don't help me? I just—Moss, this place is all I have! Don't you see? And that water is part of it!"

Moss grasped her arms. "Damn it, if you want to keep this place, then share the water and make friends with your neighbors. You say this is all you've got, but it's never gonna work this way, Etta. And if you want me to help you, then you have to help me!"

She burst into pitiful sobbing; he pulled her head to his chest and let her cry: choking, wrenching sobs raked up from her soul after years of torment, turmoil, and terrible disappointment.

"I don't...have anything!" she wailed, clinging to him tightly.

"Yes, you do," he replied with a sigh. His talk with Damian Kuntz had again brought out his pity for her. "You've got this place, and you'd have damned good neighbors if you'd share that water. And a lot of the men here—hell, I reckon when this is over they'll stay on and keep helpin' you out. And some day you'll find a man you want to settle with—a man who can be a real man to you, and you can be the kind of woman you was meant to be, Etta."

"I only want you," she cried.

"Don't say that, Etta," he replied quietly. Her body felt good against his, and her light perfume aggravated his baser needs. He gently pushed her away.

"Why don't you tell me about Ralph Landers, Etta?"

She dropped her eyes. "Must I?"

"I wish you would. Maybe it would be good for you to talk about it instead of keepin' it inside like you do."

She sighed and turned away, walking over to the buffet and opening a bottle of brandy.

"Would you like some?"

"Never turn it down," he replied.

"You mean your...wife lets you drink?"

"She knows I can handle it."

Etta turned and handed him the drink.

"After you left—or rather, after I threw you out—daddy moved down to Los Angeles and I, of course, went with him." She walked over and sat down on a love seat, patting the cushion next to her in a signal for him to join her there. Moss sat down, looking out of place on the velvet seat in his cotton pants, calico shirt, and slightly worn cowboy boots.

"I had lots of male escorts to various parties and so forth," she went on, looking at her drink and swirling it. "Oh, I was quite the fashionable, young, beautiful virgin." She smiled rather sarcastically. "And I saved myself for the right man. Then Mr. Ralph Landers came to one of daddy's parties. I looked at him and he was so dashing, so handsome, older, already established in his own law practice. He was a prize catch, and daddy thought so, too. He commented that the man never dated much, but we attributed that to the fact that he was so busy with his career."

She sipped her drink and kept staring at it.

"I had stars in my eyes. And I thought he loved me. It wasn't until after we were married that I discovered what a greedy man he was. All he wanted was to win me, and win my father's confidence, to be in charge of our financial affairs, from what I can figure. My father introduced me to Miles Randall. Later on Ralph and Miles became…close…and they cooked up a scheme to rob me and my father of everything we had. Sometimes I think—sometimes I think they had something to do with daddy's death. But I can't prove it. They say he died of a heart attack. But he was in good health."

She raised her eyes to meet his, and Moss was listening intently. She wondered what went on behind his dark eyes, and where the secret lay to seducing him.

"I was excited on my wedding day, like any young girl. And I was scared." She looked at her drink again. "But I was confident that whatever a man expected of a woman in bed— Ralph Landers, with all his worldly experience, would know what to do. We sailed through the wedding and the reception, and I was the envy of all the other young girls there. And then we rode away in a grand carriage, headed for a honeymoon in San Francisco. We stopped at this real fancy hotel, and got a room, and I…wanted to please him. He still acted just fine. We had dinner and some wine, and I went into the powder room to put on a fancy negligee. When I came out he was lying in bed already, and he said he felt sick."

She stood up and walked over to refill her glass.

"Isn't that a laugh?" she said, her back to him. "I'm the scared young virgin, and he's the one who claims he's sick! I always thought it was supposed to be the girl who sometimes messed up the wedding night. There I was, scared to death I'd have to ask him to slow down but instead there I stood, gaping at a sick man. But I was young and in love, and I accepted the fact that he really was sick. I laid down beside him, and I'll never forget the look in his eyes: like a scared little boy. In a sense I have to feel sorry for him. Something happened to him in his early years. I don't know what it was, but it made him like he is. I guess I don't hate him for that. I hate him for marrying me, lying to me about it, shocking me and denying me the chance for a normal married life—and his attempt to cheat me out of everything I had coming to me."

She sighed and swallowed her drink, her back still to him.

"On the second night he—he managed to do something about my virginity. I guess it was his feeble attempt at pretending he was a man. But he was clumsy and quick. And afterward, I just felt sick. It wasn't the way I'd pictured it at all. I guess even then the idea was growing in my mind that some day I'd have to lie with another man, just to find out if there was something better. A wall started building between us. I was young and inexperienced, and I didn't know what to say to him, didn't understand why he seemed to have no interest in his new, young bride. I blamed myself and thought something was wrong with me, thought maybe he'd been so disappointed that first time that he didn't want me anymore. We smiled a lot, partied a lot, went on to San Francisco and put on a great newlywed show. But something was horribly wrong; I didn't know what it was, and he wouldn't discuss it. And then he started asking me to do things I thought were horrible and ugly. I refused. A couple of times he got angry and hit me, but I didn't care. His strange needs frightened me more than a beating."

She quietly poured herself more brandy, and Moss was so full of pity and rage that his head began to ache.

"I'm sorry, Etta," he said quietly.

"I have no one to blame but myself." She turned to look at him with tear-filled eyes. "Look at the man I could have had." She feigned a smile and walked toward him.

"I was so stupid. I still hadn't caught on. Then after we were married one month I…caught him with Miles Randall. Afterward I threw up for two days and was in bed for a week. And I told him if he ever touched me again I'd kill him. And by God, I meant it!"

"Why didn't you just leave him right then?" Moss asked her quietly.

"I was…too ashamed, even to tell daddy. I was afraid if our

marriage failed so soon everyone would think it was my fault rather than his. I was...proud...and deeply hurt, and stubborn...determined to show the world that everything was all right. And soon I was just too damned scared. Because I could see that if I ever left him, he'd take me for everything. And it didn't take long for me to figure out that he'd do the same to my father, who had entrusted all his money and belongings to Ralph, who was supposed to put it all in trust, and wills, and so on. If I left Ralph and daddy ended up broke, I'd have felt guilty and responsible. I loved my father too much to make him suffer for my own error. Then when daddy died, it gave me the courage to leave Ralph and risk the consequences. By then we'd been living our own separate lies—me with my lovers, and he with his. The only difference was that my affairs were with someone of the opposite sex. His weren't."

She turned and walked back toward him, stumbling slightly from too much brandy drunk too fast. She reached up and took the pins from her hair, letting it fall over her shoulders. Then she unbuttoned the front of her dress, revealing a lacy undergarment and the full breasts that protruded from it. She sat down close to him and leaned forward, putting a hand on Moss's thigh.

"Make me feel like a woman, Moss," she whispered. "Please."

Their eyes held for several long seconds. Then he shook his head, feeling only pity.

"It has to end somewhere, Etta. You can't go on like this, from man to man. I can get Ralph Landers out of your life, but only you can get all them bad memories out of your mind. And only you can make up your mind to stop lettin' what he is make you into somethin' bad, too. You've got to be you, Etta, and this is not you."

"Moss, please..." she whispered.

"Stop letting that man destroy you, Etta." He rose quickly, afraid someone would come in and see her throwing herself at him. "You're letting Ralph Landers win when you act like that." He walked over and poured himself another drink. "There's not much I can do about this part of your problem," he added. "And I'm damned sorry about it. But all I can do is help you keep the ranch. What you do about the rest is up to you. Tomorrow I'll go and see the neighboring ranchers and try to get things straightened out."

She nodded without looking up from where she sat, surprised at his ability to resist her. It was frustrating. She was accustomed to men falling at her feet, and more disappointing was the fact that she could have had this man at one time.

"I'm going upstairs," she told him. "I suddenly don't feel like partying any more." Her words were slurred from alcohol, and when she stood up she stumbled. Moss grabbed her and helped her toward the stairway.

"Come on. I'll help you to your room so you can sleep this off." Nearly all his hatred and disgust for her were gone now, leaving simply pity. She slumped to the floor, unable to even climb the steps. He stooped down and worked his way under her, then stood up, slinging her over his shoulder and grasping her around the thighs with his arm to carry her up the stairs. He would have called for help, but he didn't want the men to see her drunk.

He quietly mounted the stairs, unaware that Lloyd Duncan had entered the back way looking for her. Duncan had come into the house stealthily, sure he would catch Moss Tucker and Etta Landers in each other's arms. But what he saw was just as frustrating. Moss was hauling her up to her room. Duncan held little doubt as to what Moss intended to do with the obviously drunk woman once he put her on her bed. Duncan watched quietly with clenched fists, afraid to confront Moses Tucker and get into a fight with the man, and hating Moss for stealing Etta Landers from his own arms. He quietly left to get drunk himself, and never knew that only moments later Moss Tucker exited Etta's room without ever having touched her.

• • •

Mrs. Webster, the small and aging widow who had come to help Etta keep up her large house, now set a cup of strong coffee in front of Moss, who sat at the kitchen table.

"It's going to be a hot one, Mr. Tucker."

"Appears that way. Thanks for the coffee."

"How many eggs this time?"

"Four ought to do it."

The old woman smiled and shook her head. "It's a good thing this place has its own beef and chickens, else the food wouldn't last a day with all your men around. I hear tell that old Pappy Lane does a fair job of cooking for the men."

"Yeah, Pappy used to do a lot of cookin' a few years back on the trail, when we herded cattle to Abilene and Dodge City."

"Stolen cattle?" she asked chidingly.

Moss grinned and lit a cigarette. "Sometimes," he replied.

"Well, whatever you and your men are, or were, it doesn't much matter to me. It's a sorry state Mrs. Landers was in, down to her last man. She wasn't even sure she'd get away alive to go for help. I'm glad you menfolk came up here to help her, and I don't mind cooking your meals for you."

"Well, I don't mind eatin' them, neither," Moss replied with a chuckle. "You're a good cook, Mrs. Webster. And I'm glad you're willin' to risk comin' back here to help out Etta. This is a lot of house for one woman."

"Hmmph," she sniffed, breaking eggs into a pan. "It needs a man—a permanent one—and kids."

"I agree."

Mrs. Webster remained silent, and Moss wasn't sure just how much she knew about Etta, or just exactly what her opinion was. Etta came straggling in just then, wrapped in a pink velvet robe, her hair hanging in tangles about her shoulders.

"You find me a man as good as Moss Tucker, and I'll settle with him," she told Mrs. Webster in a tired voice. She yawned and looked at Moss, who gave her a chiding look. Mrs. Webster turned to look at her and smiled, a little embarrassed at Etta having heard her last remark.

"I'm sorry, Mrs. Landers. I—"

"It's all right. Besides, you're right," Etta replied, walking to the table and sitting down near Moss. She blushed slightly under his eyes, recalling she had drunk too much the night before, and vaguely remembering him having to carry her up the stairs. "I guess I made kind of a fool of myself last night," she said, resting her head in her hand. "I seem to do that a lot around you."

"I've made a fool of myself that way lots of times," he replied. He took a deep drag on his cigarette. "Besides, you needed to let go a little. You're carryin' a lot of burdens."

She looked over at him, her eyes slightly bloodshot. "You're some man, you know that? Where do you get all that patience, and understanding, and, uh, willpower?"

"My wife has taught me most of it. She's a patient and understandin' woman. And she has an inner strength I admire." He held her eyes. "You do, too. You're hangin' on to this place for dear life. And I'm gonna help you by goin' out to do a little visitin' this mornin'." Mrs. Webster set the eggs in front of him and he dove into them, continuing to talk between bites. "I'm gonna go offer your neighbors water rights, Etta. And you're gonna hold to what I tell them." He swallowed some coffee.

"Do you want me to go with you?"

"No. Besides, you probably don't feel much like goin' out and ridin' a horse this mornin'. I can handle it."

"You'll take someone with you, I hope."

"I'm takin' Hank Stemm. We'll stick to the trees till we get to the first ranch. I figure on ridin' north to the Simpson place first. At least that way we'd be headin' even farther away from town. But I don't expect no trouble. According to Damian Kuntz, Landers hasn't quite made up his mind yet what to do, so I'm gonna muster up some help in makin' his decision for him. I sent Kuntz back to town with a letter to Mandy. Nobody knows yet that he's gonna work for me, so I figure he can safely get a letter off for me. He brung me one yesterday from Mandy. It had been layin' and waitin' for me, only nobody brought it out to me—and I couldn't send nobody in for it. It's a little old, but it sure was nice to get it."

"What did it say?" she asked slyly. Moss grinned.

"Personal," he replied.

"I thought so. Is she all right?"

"Yup. Just lonely, like me."

"I'd be lonely, too, if I were used to having someone like you around."

Moss finished his food without a reply, then rose to leave.

"You take it easy today. Most of the boys are out doin' your chores. I'm headin' out."

"Moss, be careful."

"No need to tell me that. See you later today."

"Moss, thank you."

He grabbed his hat from a hook near the door.

"Anytime."

• • •

Moss stepped outside and pulled the letter from his pocket again. After he had put Etta to bed the night before and rejoined the men, Damian Kuntz had given it to him. The man had forgotten all about it when he first arrived, more concerned with talking to Moss about Ralph Landers. Moss appreciated the man's thoughtfulness in checking to see if there was mail before he came to Etta's ranch. And the blessedly welcome letter had been there. He unfolded it.

> My darling Moss,
>
> Things at the Red "C" are going fine. Except for myself. I miss you so much that sometimes my heart actually hurts. I'm teaching every day, and you should see all the new words Wanda can read and write. And your daughter learns so quickly, Moss. She's so bright and quick. She misses you, too, darling, and both of us pray for you every morning, at lunchtime,

and every night. The nights are the worst. And I can imagine they're no easier for you. I hope that whatever you have to do, it won't be too much longer. How is Etta? She must be very happy to be home.

I don't worry about you and Etta, because since you left, I've had so much time to think. And the one and only thing I am sure of—besides God's love—is your love, Moss. And we mustn't ever allow anything—or anyone—to interfere. What we have is from God, a precious love that must be guarded and treasured. And I felt folded into your arms when I read your wire to me, for though it is hard for you to come up with written words, I could hear your voice saying those words. And I know you are lonely, as I am lonely. You must remember that I am always with you, through prayer. And I am with you in the night, in my dreams. My body aches for you, Moss.

I love you. What more can I say than that? And although I am protected here, it's you I need, Moss. So do not take too long. I send you kisses from Becky. The table seems so empty without you. And the bed is the loneliest place of all. I love you. May God be with you and bring you home soon—unharmed. In the meantime, you can be sure that you are loved, and guarded through prayer.

Take care, my darling.

Amanda

He sighed and folded the letter again, feeling empty and painfully lonely. He could hear her voice in the letter, and pictured her whispering words of love beside him in bed, and could hear her grateful sighs, his name whispered as he became one with her and poured his life into her. His chest hurt with love, and his body ached with need. He adjusted his hat and stepped off the porch to go and saddle his horse.

• • •

Etta went to her room and locked the door. She sat down in front of the mirror and pouted, irritated that Moses Tucker was so difficult to get into her bed, and angry that she should have to give up her water rights. She picked up a brush and began raking it through her hair briskly, wondering how much longer her beauty could last, wondering if she was already too old to have children. She put the brush down and studied herself a moment, proud that she was still so beautiful at thirty-six. She tried to understand why Moss could keep turning her down. It hurt her, bringing back the ugly memories of wondering why her own husband had not wanted her.

She pulled her robe from her shoulders, then untied it and let it slip down over the chair. She sat there naked in front of the mirror, studying the full breasts and the milky white skin. Perhaps if she were to go to his bed in the middle of the night, crawl in naked beside him...

A figure loomed behind her in the mirror. She gasped and jumped up, grabbing for her robe, but a hand clamped over her mouth.

"It's just me, Lloyd," came the hoarse voice.

He jerked her around and clamped his mouth over hers, kissing her so hard it hurt her lips. Then he threw her onto the bed. Etta gasped for breath and wiped at her lips, wiggling up toward the headboard and grasping at the covers.

"Why hide it?" Lloyd sneered. "You flaunt it in front of everybody else! And you flaunted it for me once!"

"Get out of here!" she shrieked. "How did you get in here!"

"I walked in while you was sittin' down in the kitchen with your lover! You look tired, baby. Did you and him have a heavy go-round last night?"

"Moss Tucker has never touched me!" she spit at him. "And don't think you're going to!"

He sneered at her, stepping closer to the bed and unbuttoning his pants.

"I seen him carryin' you up the stairs to your room last night, you all drunk and hangin' all over him. Your dress was hangin' open. And don't try to tell me you don't love him, 'cause I know better! And don't tell me a man like him turned away a tasty item like you! He's not that loyal to that wife of his!"

"He is that loyal!" she hissed. "And last night he made me realize that I want to be different. I'm not going to sleep around any more, Lloyd. Not with you or anybody else who just wants to use my body."

He chuckled. "You amuse me. I'd laugh out loud…" He suddenly sobered. "If I didn't love you myself. And I'll be damned if I'm going to be pushed out of your bed by a man fifteen years older!" He lurched forward and grasped her arms, pushing her backward and landing on top of her, kissing her painfully again.

She struggled against him, suddenly repulsed, even though she had entertained him in the very same bed more than once. Now it all seemed wrong. He moved his lips to her neck.

"Get out now or I'll scream, and every one of Moss's men will be in here!" she gasped. "They'll kill you! Or they'll save you for Moss and he'll kill you!"

He jerked her arms up over her head. "You won't scream. 'Cause if you do, I'll say as how I seen Moss Tucker carry you to your room. And I'll testify that I went to the door and I heard noises, and that because I loved you, I pushed the door open a crack and saw you and Tucker goin' at it. Now maybe I didn't see it, but I know it happened!"

"They wouldn't believe you," she whimpered, struggling.

"Some wouldn't. But they're all men, Etta. And they'd begin to wonderin' how Moss Tucker could sleep in this house every night without beddin' you. And they all know that when you and him came to this house to talk last night, you never came back out! Maybe he did later. I don't know. I was too drunk and I didn't rejoin the party. All I know is I saw him carryin' you up to your bed. And there's bound to be some of his men gonna believe it happened. And then that's gonna divide them—not just against each other, but against their boss! He told them you was a forbidden fruit but he don't mind pickin' it himself, does he!"

He pressed his lips to her mouth again, and she knew what he said was true. If he accused Moss of having an affair with her, it would divide the men. Some wouldn't want to believe it, but they would, nonetheless. And if they lost faith in Moses Tucker, he'd lose his power to control them and some would leave, and she would lose the E.G. To fight Lloyd Duncan now would be foolish.

The brutal beginning to their love-making turned to a queer and violent passion, as Lloyd Duncan devoured the body he had missed, and Etta Landers pretended that it was Moses Tucker who was touching her. Duncan's cruel words turned to a gushy display of the love he had for this older woman, who had charmed him to her bed a year earlier and had invited him there often after that. But Etta began to hope he would finish soon. Duncan was overjoyed that she had relaxed and seemed to have given in to him, sure that it was because down deep inside she loved him and wanted him. But when he raised up on his elbows, he caught her frowning as though repulsed.

"Hurry up and get it over with!" she hissed through gritted teeth.

He moved off of her, jerking her up by the hair of her head, then slapping her hard. Etta cried out and fell to the bed.

"It's him, isn't it! You were wantin' him!"

She fought her tears, rising slowly and rubbing the side of her face. She sat up on the bed and faced him. Lloyd now stood at the edge of the bed half naked, and she looked him up and down scathingly.

"Yes!" she sneered. "I love him! And even with one arm he's more man than you'll ever be!"

Duncan swung, backhanding her hard across the mouth.

"All right, slut!" he growled. "I'm through with you! I'm goin' over to Ralph Landers's side!"

"Then go!" she screamed.

"I will. And after Landers gets through burnin' and runnin' you out, you'll be left with nothin'! He'll kill Moss Tucker, and you'll have nothing! Nothing! And then I'll be back, baby. And you'll be beggin' me to take you in. You won't be so high and mighty then!"

"Ralph and his men will never be able to take Moss!" she hissed, wiping at blood on her lip.

"Maybe not. But there's other ways. Landers is probably thinkin' up a way right now, and if one thing don't work, there's always another!"

"Like what?" she sneered.

"Like ways to get Moss Tucker to leave this place without firin' a shot!"

She quieted and wiped at her lip again as their eyes held.

"What are you talking about?" she asked.

He tucked himself back into his pants.

"I'm sayin' maybe there's an easier way to take down a man like Tucker than with a gun. Sometimes the woman a man loves is a greater weapon than a cannon."

Etta frowned, still unsure of what he meant.

"Havin' trouble puttin' two and two together, baby?" he asked with a grin. "I'll add it up for you. You were just his fling in bed, to tide him over till he got back to that precious wife of his. Maybe you like his body, but she owns it! And she owns him! And if she was ever in trouble, Moss Tucker would come running."

Her eyes widened. "You wouldn't dare!"

"Oh, yes I would," he growled. "If Landers don't think of a way to get rid of Moses Tucker soon, I have an idea of my own. Could be Ralph Landers just might pay me to carry it out."

"You stay away from Amanda Tucker! She's a good person!"

He snickered. "You stickin' up for the only woman who stands in your way?"

"If she gets hurt over this, Moss would hate me!"

He grinned more, and she realized she'd said the wrong thing.

"All the more reason for me to pay her a visit, wouldn't you say? Ralph Landers moves in here when Moss leaves, Moss finds his wife dead and never comes back here 'cause he don't give a damn any more, and Etta Landers is wanderin' around with no money and no home, just needin' a man to take real good care of her."

"And that man would have Moses Tucker after him!" she spit at him. "He'd best remember that! And Moses Tucker bent on revenge would be like a mother grizzly after someone who bothered her cubs! You'd never be able to sleep at night for fear of getting your throat slit, Lloyd Duncan!"

"I'd find places to go." He winked and reached for his hat. "You'd best clean up now, Mrs. Landers. You want to present a pretty picture for all them men out there. I'm leavin' now— goin' into town. You won't see me again, at least not till you come beggin' to me."

"I wouldn't come to you if you were the last man on earth!" she replied in a raised voice. "Get out! Just get out!"

He put out his hands as though in defense.

"Yes, ma'am. Thanks for the good time."

She threw a pillow at him. "Get out!"

He ducked through a window and walked along the upper veranda to the stairs that led to the ground. Etta sat on the bed, rubbing at her lip and pondering what he had told her. She could hardly believe he would be jealous enough to try to hurt Moses through Amanda. Should she tell Moss?

She got up from the bed and walked to her dresser to study the puffy lip.

"No," she thought to herself as she poked at the lip. "I'll not tell Moss. If he suspected for one second that his wife was in danger, he'd leave to go to her. And then I'd lose my chances of getting him into my bed and winning him away from her. I'll not say a thing. And if something happens to her, and he's angry with me, I'll just fling myself at him and cry. Moss hates crying. And *there he'd be—a lonely man needing a woman—and there I'd be. Maybe Lloyd would be doing me a favor in the long run."*

She began brushing her hair again, inwardly satisfied at the realization that a man as young as Lloyd Duncan hungered for her as he did. Surely Moss could not resist forever. And the little spark of decency Moss had managed to draw from Etta the night before suddenly died out. The years had buried the once-proper and proud Etta Graceland, leaving a hard and scheming woman in her place.

365

Chapter Thirty-Seven

Moss and Hank Stemm cautiously approached the Crooked "S", walking their horses through a gate entrance with the ranch's name burned into wood across the top. The ground was dusty and hard, and trees were scarce. This was not the lower, greener land that Etta owned, but higher, rocky, waterless land—land on which only the fittest of cattle could survive. Moss noticed a few scrawny-looking heads of beef to his left, but his eyes were fixed on four riders who approached from a distance.

"Keep your guns in place," Moss said quietly to Hank. "We're comin' here as friends."

"I don't like it, Moss. You don't know how they're gonna react. And you don't know what Ralph Landers has told these people. Could be the battle is lost before it's begun. This has been a dry year, and these men are probably pretty bitter."

"If I'd come ridin' in here with a whole troup of men, it would only make them angry before I could say a word," Moss replied.

The four men came close now, two of them pointing rifles at Moss and Hank.

"State your business, mister. This is Simpson property," one of them spoke up.

"Are you Simpson?" Moss asked.

"He's back at the house. I'm his foreman. What is it you want?"

"I'm Moses Tucker."

The man's eyes darkened and he looked almost as though someone had hit him.

"If that's the case, then you ain't goin' no further till you

366

unload your weapons!" the man told Moss. "That goes for your friend, too."

"I've come here in peace," Moss replied.

"I've heard about your kind of peace, mister. And on top of that, you're workin' for that Landers bitch! Get them guns off or you'll get a piece of lead in the brisket! I expect there's a few ranchers around here who wouldn't mind that one bit!"

Moss looked at Hank. "You heard the man," he said, taking his gun from its holster. "Do like he says. Maybe then Simpson will believe I've come here as a friend."

"Friends share their water!" another man growled, cocking his rifle.

"That's exactly why I'm here," Moss replied calmly, as he handed his gun and then his rifle to the apparent leader.

"That's a hard one to believe, mister. But we'll take you to Simpson and you can talk." The two with rifles nudged their horses around behind Moss and Hank, and the other two led the way.

More men gathered as they approached the ranch house where Paul Simpson lived. Moss had mistakenly picked a man who was already bitter about losing a wife the winter before to fever. Now some of his cattle were dying. The ranch house itself was a sprawling, wooden structure that needed painting. Weeds and rose bushes grew wild around a sagging porch. A grizzly-looking man stepped out of the door, scratching a three-day-old beard that had a considerable amount of gray in it. His red but faded undershirt showed perspiration under the arms and hung open at the neck where buttons were missing. The man glared at the two intruders and stuffed his hands into his pockets.

"What have we got here, Lance?" he asked his foreman.

"One Mr. Moses Tucker."

The man straightened and stared at Moss a moment, then looked at one of his men.

"Ride to town and get Ralph Landers!" he ordered right away.

"Wait!" Moss spoke up. "Don't you even want to know why I'm here?"

"I don't care why you're here, mister!" the man snapped. "You brought that Landers woman back, and you mended them fences! Only thing I know is my cattle are dyin'! I lost a wife last winter and I ain't got nothin' left I care about except this place, and now I'm losin' that!"

"I'm here to tell you Etta Landers is ready to share her water, Simpson! You are Paul Simpson, aren't you?"

"It's me, all right." He looked at his foreman. "Get him down off that horse and bring him in the house! And keep an eye on his friend." He looked at the man he had told to go and get Landers. "Get moving! I gave you an order!"

"Yes, sir!" The man mounted up and galloped away.

Lance poked a rifle barrel into Moss's side, and Moss dismounted. He walked toward the house and suddenly felt a painful jab in his back. His temper flared and he whirled, swinging a stiff arm and a big fist as he did so and whacking Lance across the side of the face in a wicked blow that sent the man reeling. The rifle went off and took a chunk of wood off one of the support posts to the porch roof. Immediately there were several more guns aimed at Moss Tucker.

"I came here in peace!" Moss roared. "Is this the way you greet everybody?"

"Only our enemies," Simpson sneered.

"I'm not your enemy!" Moss yelled.

Lance slowly got to his feet, coughing and choking, stunned by the sudden and unexpected blow. Moss planted his feet apart and glared at him.

"Nobody shoves a goddamned gun in my back!" Moss told the man through gritted teeth. Lance clenched his fists and started for him.

"Lance!" Simpson shouted. The man froze. "That's enough! We'll let Ralph Landers decide how to handle this!"

The man picked up his rifle and stalked away, and Moss turned and followed Paul Simpson into the house. When they got inside, Moss could tell the place had once been well taken care of. There were still curtains at the windows, and a vase sat on the table holding flowers that had long since withered. Apparently nothing had been touched since the woman of the house died. He thought of Amanda, and he suddenly understood. Simpson ordered him to sit down in a chair at the table, and the man sat down across from him. Moss started to move the vase, which was between them.

"Don't touch that!" Simpson snapped.

Moss pulled his hand back and leaned back in his chair, reaching in his pocket for a cigarette.

"I'm sorry about your woman," he said quietly to Simpson. Four other men stood inside now, all with guns held on Moss.

"Bein' sorry don't bring her back," the man replied bitterly. "She was good. The night her fever got so high I knew she was dying, I sent one of my men after the doc in town. It was a bitter cold night and there was lots of deep snow. And that man's horse got tangled in Etta Landers's goddamned barbed wire fence! My man got off and started on foot. He never made it. He froze to death, the doc never came, and my wife died."

The awful realization that he had chosen the wrong rancher to visit weighed heavily on Moss. He wondered how Etta could be so cold as to keep these people from water. Perhaps she didn't even understand. And most likely, she didn't even know what had happened to Mrs. Paul Simpson, or why. If she had, she surely would have advised Moss not to go to Simpson's place.

"Some things just happen, Mr. Simpson," Moss told him quietly. "Fate…God…puttin' somethin' off too long…lots of things—"

"You sayin' it was my fault? You sayin' I should have gone for the doc sooner?" the man shouted, rising and pacing now.

"I'm sayin' Mrs. Landers would never have wanted that to happen. I'm sayin' maybe you don't understand her side. That place is all she's got, and her husband is tryin' to steal it from her."

"I can't feel sorry for a ruthless woman who's a goddamned

whore besides! How many times have you shoved yourself between them pretty thighs, mister!"

Moss stood up quickly, knocking his chair backward, and immediately four guns were cocked.

"Mister, I've got a good woman of my own." Moss hissed. "And she's waitin' for me down in Utah. Etta Landers is nothin' to me, except an old friend who needs help. Now I'm damned anxious to get back down to my wife, and when I found out about the water situation, I knew that was the real problem here! I'm tellin' you Etta is willin' to share that water now! She'll put it in writin' if you want. So help her keep her place and you can have all the water you want."

Simpson stepped closer to Moss.

"Ain't no way I'm gonna help a bitch like that. Every night I go to bed and I think of my Amie, and my guts burn and my arms ache to hold her. And I hate Etta Landers just a little bit more. It ain't fair that a high and mighty bitch like that should be livin' in all that comfort, on all that rich land, sleepin' around, no better than a goddamned prostitute while my Amie lies in her grave!"

"Jesus Christ, Simpson, use your head! Ralph Landers is a hard, ruthless, selfish man! He wants that land for himself, to increase his fortune. He's the kind of man who never gets enough. Do you really believe he'll share that water with you? You're a fool! As soon as that place is all his he'll starve you out and burn you out and threaten you until he gets this place— and then the next neighbor's, and the next! That's the kind of man he is! He already owns half the town and the people in it!"

The man laughed sarcastically and paced again.

"She's got you fooled good, Tucker! That woman gets her nails in a man and he believes everything she tells him! All she has to do is wear a low-cut dress, bat them big blue eyes, and she can talk a man into anything. Well, I don't like havin' no scheming woman ownin' that much land right next to me! A man ought to be runnin' a place like that! It ain't right havin' a woman there."

"She'll hire good men to run it. Don't you see, Simpson? Ralph Landers is tellin' you things that aren't true just to keep you against her."

"Same as she's sayin' things about him."

"And how long does it go on?" Moss asked impatiently. "I'm tellin' you a woman can do you a lot less harm than a man like Ralph Landers. The man is powerful, a lawyer. And his best friend is the banker, Miles Randall. I know that man! He cheated me out of hundreds of thousands of dollars once. I went to prison 'cause I tried to kill that man for what he done to me. And ten to one you owe Randall money. Jesus, Simpson, the man is just waitin' for you to go broke so he can move in and take this place—him and Ralph Landers! If you side with Etta and accept the water rights, you can get back on your feet again—and keep Landers and Randall both off your back!"

Simpson paced and pondered. Moss plunked back down into his chair and smoked quietly for a moment. Then Simpson turned and stared at him.

"The woman's a selfish bitch," he snarled. "Ain't no other way for me to look at it. I got no use for her—no respect for her. Landers has told us how she lies, how she cheated on him all the time, and how that land belongs to him. I believe him!"

"The land is legally hers, Simpson. Why do you think Landers is resorting to force and threats to try to get her off it? If it was legally his, he could bring a U.S. marshal here to make her get off. Use your head!"

Simpson came closer. "I've already done that!" he snarled. "And I've got a good enough head on my shoulders to know the kind of woman Etta Landers is! And anybody that helps her is the same kind of scum!" He motioned to one of his men, and before Moss realized what the signal meant, he felt a grueling pain in his lower back as one of Simpson's men slammed a rifle butt into his kidneys. Moss cried out and went to his knees, and another man kicked his ribs. He doubled over, grabbing a chair for support and tried to struggle to his feet again as he heard shouts outside and then a gunshot.

371

"Hank?" he shouted. Then there came a thunderous blow to the back of his head, and everything went black.

• • •

Moss awakened slowly, groaning and rubbing his eyes. When he opened them, it was dark and the room he was in smelled damp. Moss started to rise, and a black pain enveloped his head. He groaned again and stayed prone, struggling to think. He looked around the room as his eyes adjusted to the dim light that came from a large crack beneath a heavy door not far away. He heard voices in the outer room. As his vision cleared, he saw them—bars! Memories of his times in prison swept over him, and he felt a heaviness in his chest. Bars—how he hated bars! Where was he? How could he get back to the E.G. or to Amanda? He struggled again to get up, and managed to sit up on the edge of the small cot. His back ached fiercely.

Moss sat there a moment, breathing deeply, straining to hear the voices beyond the door. Then he rose, but dizziness consumed him and he stumbled, grabbing at a small table and knocking over a tin cup. Seconds later the outer door opened, and light filled the miserable cell where Moss crouched on his knees, clinging to the edge of the cot. He turned his head and looked up to see Ralph Landers and Miles Randall standing outside the cell and smiling.

"You made a very big mistake this time, Moss Tucker," Landers said cheerfully. "You picked the wrong neighbor to visit. Now here you are in jail."

"For what?" Moss demanded. "Simpson attacked me. I didn't do anything to him!"

Landers grinned more. "Well, Mr. Tucker, everybody knows you're after me—and therefore, after the law in this town also. You tried to come into town last night, didn't you?"

Moss frowned. "What are you talkin' about?" he said in a near whisper, struggling back to the edge of the cot and running a hand through his hair.

"I'm talking about the fact that someone shot our fine sheriff last night—in the back."

Moss's eyes widened in shock.

"Who?"

Landers chuckled. "You, of course. I even have a witness."

Now Moss managed to stand up, clenching his fist in rage.

"A paid witness! You're framin' me, Landers!"

"What better way to get rid of you than to have you hanged? After all, everyone in town knows you've been in prison twice, that you once tried to kill Miles Randall here, and that you're an outlaw."

"All they know is what you tell them!" Moss growled.

"Precisely," the man replied with a handsome smile. He looked Moss up and down. "Have a good rest, Mr. Tucker. I want you nice and healthy and alert when they put the noose around your neck."

Landers started to leave.

"Where's Hank Stemm?" Moss asked him quickly.

Landers turned back. "The man who was with you at the Simpson place?"

"That's him."

"He's dead, Tucker. Seems he heard the fight inside the house and tried to come in and help you."

Moss blinked, a deep sorrow engulfing him.

"It's just as well," Landers told him. "One more Tucker man out of our way." He paused. "No! Two more out of our way. Lloyd Duncan has joined us, or did you already know that?"

Moss glared at him, eager now for the chance to murder Ralph Landers. But at the moment he was helpless.

"How'd you win him over, Landers?" he sneered. "Did you pay him, or take him to bed?"

Landers paled; Miles Randall gasped and quickly exited, afraid to even be in the same room with Moss Tucker, even though Tucker was behind bars.

"I'll let that one go," Landers said quietly, nervously twisting a pair of black gloves in his hand. "It doesn't matter anyway.

You'll be dead in a few days, your men will be murdered one by one, and my lovely Etta will simply have to go away. Or maybe I'll just turn her over to my men to do with as they please, or perhaps I'll kill her. I haven't decided yet."

Landers walked out, closing the heavy door behind him and throwing the cell into darkness again. Moss laid back down, rolling onto his stomach and wanting to vomit.

"Hank!" he groaned. Hank Stemm was a good man. Moss felt responsible for the man's death. He'd asked all of them to come, and the pay they were getting wasn't really worth the risk they were taking. They all knew it, but they'd come anyway—for Moss Tucker and no other reason. Some of them had helped Moss find Amanda five years earlier. His pain; his aching need for Amanda—whom he might not ever see again—and his sorrow over Hank Stemm's death overwhelmed him; he quietly wept.

• • •

"You've got to get him out of there! You've got to get him out of there before they hang him!" Etta wailed, pacing and wringing her hands. They all stood under a large cottonwood tree, where the mound of dirt was still fresh over Hank Stemm's grave. His body had been found dumped at the barbed wire fence that separated the E.G. and the Crooked "S", where Paul Simpson's men had placed it. Damian Kuntz had ridden into town and casually discovered what was taking place.

"We will get him out, ma'am," Dwight Brady spoke up. "But we can't go ridin' in there without a plan. And they won't hang him right away."

"How do you know that?" she asked in a choked voice.

"The way I figure it, Landers has to have a little time to rile the people up. He won't want no regular trial, 'cause it might come out Moss really was framed, and some other things might come out that Landers would rather keep hidden."

Etta kept her eyes averted from the men. "Yes, I'm sure you all know what my ex-husband is," she said quietly.

Some of them shuffled nervously and Brady continued.

"Well, anyway, I figure he won't want no trial. It's too risky. The questions that would come up—it might make them people start to thinking. So he'll use the next two or three days to talk around town, get the people riled up, call Moss a backshooter, remind them he was once an outlaw and all, remind them he already killed a couple men here, maybe say he went to Simpson's place to threaten the man. There's a hundred things he could say to make Moss look bad. He gets them riled up enough, they'll storm the jail, demand him, and hang him without a trial. That's how I figure it. Then, while they're still steaming, he'll lead them out here to attack your place and that will be the end of it."

She sighed and wiped at tears, turning to face them.

"You men try to get him out of there, and then just keep riding. It's hopeless. I—I'm sorry about Hank Stemm. I didn't want anyone to die over this. And I won't be angry with you if you just ride on and ditch this whole venture."

"And leave you behind to face Ralph Landers?" Sooner asked, pushing his hat back and looking her up and down. "What do you take us for?"

She brushed away more tears. "For good men," she said quietly. "I'll just leave…maybe go East, or maybe back to San Francisco. I'm not sure."

"Looks to me like you're all of a sudden givin' up awful easy," Johnny Pence spoke up. "We ain't the givin' up type, ma'am. What them men did—killin' Hank, beatin' on Moss and draggin' him off—that don't set too good with us. Kind of riles us up, you know? And, uh, ma'am, you've seen us in action, but you ain't never seen us really mad yet. What we done up to now, that was just fun and games for men like us. Now things is a bit serious. And we're madder than a grizzly that's just come out of hibernation and had his food took from him. You gonna deny us the privilege of avengin' Hank's killing?"

"But—"

"No arguin' about it," Slim Taggart spoke up. "We're here to stay till this thing's straightened out for once and for all. Ain't no way Ralph Landers is gonna get hold of you. And there sure as hell ain't no way we're gonna turn tail and run now. No, ma'am."

"But how—"

"We're thinkin' on it," Bullit spoke up. "And I was wonderin' if maybe Damian Kuntz couldn't sneak into town and purchase us a little dynamite."

They all looked at him, and Pappy Lane grinned.

"I forgot you had a natural talent with them sticks," he said slyly.

"A little dynamite could cause a lot of confusion in town," Bullit replied. "Maybe enough to raid that jail and get Moss out of there."

Etta swallowed, trying not to break down.

"You men come in the house," she told them. "I'll have Mrs. Webster fix you something to eat. It's cooler there than in the bunkhouse. You can do your planning there."

"Obliged, ma'am. In fact, why don't you just go on up to your room and get some rest. You look awful tired," Dwight Brady told her.

"I am," she said in a near whisper, turning and walking toward the house. She hadn't slept since Moss left. They all watched her walk away.

"There goes a lot of woman," Brad Doolittle spoke up. There were a few sighs and some of them cleared their throats. Pappy turned to look at Hank Stemm's fresh grave.

"Let's get to the house and make some plans," he said quietly. "Moss will end up just like this if we don't get to it."

"That's a fact," Lonnie Drake replied. "Moss Tucker has got himself in a fix, and he's countin' on us to get him out of it. And if anybody wants to turn tail, you just remember Moss ain't the only one countin' on us. He's got a damned nice woman at home that has already had her share of suffering.

As for me, I don't aim to have to go back down to Utah and tell Amanda Tucker that her man is dead and that we failed him—and her."

Some of them shuffled their feet in anger, others paced: all felt the same way as Lonnie Drake. There wasn't one of them who didn't hold a high respect for Amanda Tucker.

"All right, let's get to it," Lonnie told them. They started toward the house, and Damian Kuntz touched Pappy's arm and held the old man back.

"You think maybe when I go into town I should send a wire to the man's wife—tell her what's happened?" he asked.

Pappy frowned. "No. Don't tell her nothing. I don't want Mandy worrying. Let's wait and see how this thing works out. If we get Moss out okay, then we won't have to tell her nothing. If we don't, well, we'll just wait and I'll tell her in person. But that's one job I sure wouldn't look forward to."

• • •

Three days passed, with little water and only bread to eat for Moss Tucker. His head had cleared, but there was still pain in his back, although it had subsided. He was certain there had to be an ugly bruise there, and he wondered if a kidney had been damaged.

He had slept little, sure his men would come for him, but not sure just how they would go about it, or when, and wanting to be awake and ready. One thing was certain. They would have to come very soon. The crowd outside was building daily, as Ralph Landers used his educated tongue and fancy words to build up a good case against Moses Tucker.

Moss could already see that he would never make it to a public trial. Ralph Landers would make certain of that. The man had a talent for making speeches, and he made them—every day. Moss knew it would not be long before a large crowd of men, and maybe even some women, would come to the jail and demand an end to the feuding by hanging Moses Tucker, a back-shooter. It was all very clear to him. Ralph Landers would make certain he was quickly hanged, and thereby silence the ugly accusations he knew Moses Tucker would make public if he had a trial.

All Moss could think of now was Amanda. Amanda and Becky. How would they fare without him? Why had he ever come in the first place? Had it been a sense of duty? An old, buried desire to be with Etta Graceland again? Or was it simply revenge, a chance to get back at Miles Randall? Amanda had warned him not to go out of pure vengeance. But he had to face the fact that revenge had been ninety per cent of the reason he sat in this jail cell now.

On the afternoon of the third day, the door opened and Ralph Landers stepped inside. Moss had not seen the man since the night after he had been taken from the Simpson ranch. Landers closed the door and walked toward the cell door, holding a glass of beer in one hand and a key in the other. He unlocked the cell door and stepped inside, which surprised Moss.

"Don't get any ideas," Landers said cautiously. "There are four men outside that door who would gladly blow your guts out if you tried to escape." He handed the beer to Moss.

"What's that for?" he asked.

"You. I have a proposition for you, Mr. Tucker. Go ahead. Drink the beer. It's on the house. And, uh, it just might be your last one, you know."

Moss took the beer, unable to resist the frosty glass. He was hot and dirty and thirsty. Landers watched in mild surprise as Moss gulped down the entire contents in a matter of seconds. He handed the mug back to Landers and wiped his lips.

"Start talking," he told Landers.

"Have a seat first," Landers told him. "On your cot."

Moss shrugged and sat down, suddenly feeling slightly dizzy. Landers walked over close to the cot.

"You realize, Mr. Tucker, that I—and only I—am capable of getting you out of this situation," he said quietly. "All I have to do is come up with some story that could clear you. My witness could say he was mistaken. Or I could even aid you in escaping. And I could pay you a lot of money to get out of Wyoming, Tucker. A lot of money. Much more than Etta can pay you, I assure you."

Moss rubbed his eyes and lay down on his back.

"I don't want your filthy money," he replied.

"But think what you could *do* with it, Tucker! Think about your wife. Wouldn't you like to go home, Moss? Wouldn't you like to be with your woman again, and go home with enough money to build her a grand house? Buy her clothes? Help her to live in comfort?"

Moss felt drowsy, and suddenly was more depressed and lonely. Ralph Landers's suggestions sounded good. Home. Amanda. Money. He tried to shake the thoughts from his head. He couldn't understand why they suddenly made sense, or why he was so sleepy.

"I can free you, Tucker," a distant voice was telling him. "I can make you a rich man, and get you out of here. You can even take Etta with you, if you're worried about what might happen to her. And there's only one tiny thing I'd ask of you in return."

"What's...that?" Moss asked drowsily, struggling to stay awake. He felt limp, and seemed to be floating. Then he felt a pressure on his thigh.

"You're a virile man, Moses Tucker," came the whispered words.

The realization that he'd been drugged occurred to Moss through a hazy mist. He fought against the effects now, something in his subconscious telling him not to submit to the drug. Ralph Landers bent over him, and a deep inner fury consumed Moses Tucker.

Suddenly a large fist smashed into Ralph Landers's nose, and the man cried out in shock, stumbling backward to the floor. Moss struggled up off the cot, pulling on all his reserve strength and fury to fight the drug. Landers lay on the floor, holding his nose, blood pouring over his mouth. He was too stunned to cry out again before Moss smashed a boot into the man's teeth.

Landers screamed, and two teeth fell from his mouth.

"You won't be messin' with nobody for a while, you filthy bastard!" Moss growled. The door burst open, just as Moss kicked again, cracking a boot into Landers's face again.

"Hey! Stop that!" a man shouted, pushing on the cell door. But Landers had carelessly closed the door, which locked automatically, and the keys now lay in a corner inside the cell, where they had flown from Landers's hand when Moss first hit him.

"The door's locked! Somebody go find the second key before Tucker kills him!" a man shouted.

Moss paid little heed. He kicked again, this time landing a heavy boot into Ralph Landers's privates.

Landers began crying and screaming even louder, curling up and trying to back away from Moss. Moss was panting now, his whole body feeling like heavy lead. He found the strength to kick Landers again, this time in the ribs, wanting nothing more than to get back at the man for the filthy, dirty trick he had tried to play on Moss. He felt like puking at the thought of what the man had tried to do. And his hatred of the man for being responsible for Etta's tormented mind spilled out of him now. Another kick to the face.

"Get away from him, or by God, I'll shoot you!" somebody yelled at Moss.

Moss just grinned. He tried to tell them what had happened, but his lips wouldn't move right, and his tongue felt thick and useless.

"Hurry up with that key!" someone else shouted. Moss reached down to grasp Landers by the shirt front, but he felt terribly weak and couldn't pick the man up. He stood there staring down at the bloodied and uglied face of Ralph Landers, and he smiled with pleasure. Then there were footsteps behind him. He dropped Landers's body and swung around, but the drug had taken full effect, and he had no strength left. He felt a grueling kick to his groin, then another to his middle. Something hit his face, his head, his back, and he was on the floor. He was sure he tasted blood, and now the numbness from the drug became a blessing, as fists and feet landed into him without mercy.

"If it was me, I'd cut off his other damned arm!" somebody growled.

A horrible memory swept over him, and he was sure he was screaming as hands grabbed at him. Someone threw him on the cot, and he cried out for Amanda. Someone held his arm firmly, and he felt a hot pain in his upper arm. He knew he was screaming, and yet he could not hear himself.

"Come on, Duncan, slice through it!" somebody shouted.

"I can't finish!" someone replied. "I think I'm gonna puke, man. This knife ain't sharp enough to go through bone."

"Jesus Christ, you ass!"

"You do it, then!"

There was silence.

"The hell with it! Let's get Landers to the doc! You've cut him bad enough that he'll lose the arm anyway. Besides, he's gonna hang soon, so what difference does it make?"

The voices faded into blackness.

"Tie it off," he heard faintly. "Landers wants him to feel the noose. We can't let him bleed to death before we hang him."

"Right." Someone fumbled with his arm. Who was it? Was Pappy cutting it off? No! No, not the arm! Not both arms!

"Mandy!" he whispered, before total blackness enveloped him.

Chapter Thirty-Eight

Amanda suddenly awakened from a deep sleep and sat straight up, breathing heavily.

"Moss?" she whispered. She was certain she had heard his voice calling her. She blinked and looked around the room, realizing she was still at home in her own bed. It was late afternoon. The day had been miserably hot, draining her of her strength, and she had intended to lie down just for a moment. But apparently she had fallen asleep for longer than she meant to.

She pushed some damp curls back from her forehead and stood up. She was drenched in sweat, and her heart pounded, her chest feeling heavy. The house was totally silent. She rushed to the door and flung it open.

"Moss?" she called out. Her eyes fell on Buck Donner, who sat quietly at the table going over some books. Buck had been left in charge of things until Moss could return. He looked up at Amanda, putting down his pencil.

"I'm sorry, ma'am. Did I wake you?" Buck asked with concern. She stared at him blankly for a moment.

"No, I…" She swallowed and wiped sweat from her forehead. "I thought I heard Moss calling me."

Buck grinned. "Must have been a dream, ma'am."

The heat and her loneliness and her worry over Moss enveloped her, and to her own surprise she burst into tears. Buck rose from the chair and ambled over to her on long, lanky legs, his spurs jingling and his shirt open almost to the waist because of the heat.

"You all right, Mrs. Tucker?" he asked, frowning and taking her arm.

She wrapped her arms around him and cried against his chest.

"Something's wrong! Something's wrong!" she wailed.

Buck stared down at the top of her head in near shock at her outburst and the embrace. He swallowed and looked toward the door, deathly afraid someone would come inside, see them, and get the wrong idea. He hesitantly put one arm around her, sensing the woman needed to feel a man's strength at that moment.

"Well, ma'am, uh, you shouldn't think that. Ole Moss can take care of himself."

"No! He called to me! I know he did! He's hurt, Buck! Maybe he's…dead!"

She clung to him and wept, and Buck scratched his head, terribly uncomfortable under the situation, yet his manly side not minding being Amanda Tucker's comfort at the moment.

"Ma'am, uh, why don't you come out here and sit down. I'll get you some water. It's just the heat, ma'am. The heat and your worry—it's got you more upset than you ought to be."

He kept a tight arm around her and led her to a chair, making her sit down. Then he walked over to a bucket, dipping out some water and then wetting a rag. He came back and offered her the water.

"You drink this, Mrs. Tucker," he told her. It seemed strange to call someone who couldn't be more than three years younger than himself "Mrs. Tucker." But he didn't feel comfortable with calling her Amanda, even though she had told him it was just fine to do so.

Amanda took out a handkerchief, blew her nose, and wiped at her eyes, then took the dipper with shaking hands. She closed her eyes and drank the water. Buck set the dipper down, then reached up and put the rag to her forehead.

"You put your head back, ma'am, and keep that rag on your forehead. I'll go get a couple of the boys and we'll fill up the tub in the bedroom for you and you can take a nice cool bath and refresh yourself. You want me to get Wanda?"

"No," she said quietly. "She wanted to spend the day at her cabin with her son. He's here from the reservation and she doesn't get to see him often. Is Becky still asleep in her room?"

"Yes, ma'am. Kids seem to be able to sleep through anything, even this heat."

He started to rise and she grabbed his hand.

"Stay just a moment, Buck," she said quietly. "I just need…to hold somebody's hand."

Buck frowned and knelt in front of her. He squeezed her hand tightly.

"He's gonna be okay, ma'am," he told her.

"I heard him, Buck. Believe what you want, but I heard him. It was…like that day…" Her voice choked up and she pressed her lips tightly together.

"What day, ma'am?" he asked quietly.

"The day they…" She swallowed and sniffed. "The day they cut off his arm. I was there. I was in the room. I…heard his screams, heard the awful sound—the moaning, the weeping."

Buck reached up with his other hand and grasped the side of her face firmly, wrapping some of his fingers around the back of her neck.

"Ma'am, you're gettin' yourself all worked up over nothing. Now it ain't good to be gettin' so upset when it's this hot. Ain't nothin' gonna happen to Moss Tucker, and if you don't start takin' better care of yourself, and eatin' better and gettin' more rest, you ain't gonna be fit for him to come back to. And you'd best calm down. What if Becky woke up now and saw you all upset like this? You'd just get her all upset and scared, too."

She clung to his hand and choked in a deep sob, nodding her head.

"I know," she whispered.

They sat there quietly a moment.

"Buck," she finally said quietly.

"Ma'am?"

"Would you…think badly of me…if I asked you to hold me, just for a minute?"

He looked toward the door again.

"Well, ma'am, uh…" More tears spilled down her cheeks. "Hell, what are friends for?" he said with a sheepish grin. "And there's no way I could ever think badly of you, ma'am. Sometimes just bein' held can make all the difference in the world."

"Oh, I don't know what's wrong with me," she cried.

He pulled her forward from the chair and she flung her arms around his neck and clung to him tightly. Buck stood up with her, wrapping his arms around her reassuringly.

"You're just human, that's all," he replied quietly. "And you're used to havin' Moss around. Sometimes it's hard to carry it all by yourself when you're used to givin' it to somebody else. It's all right, ma'am."

He squeezed her tightly, not minding the feel of her against him, yet forcing himself to ignore the baser instincts it brought out in him. He wondered for a brief second just how vulnerable she was at this moment, but his respect for her and his knowledge that Moses Tucker trusted him made him push the thought from his mind. She was like a little girl, and he knew good and well she meant nothing sexual by the embrace. She was lonely and frightened, and Buck knew about her past.

"Do you realize how many bad situations Moss has got himself out of?" he asked her, trying to cheer her up. "Men like him, hell, they go down about as easy as a ten thousand pound boulder. They're tough as that old ornery bull me and the men have been tryin' to corner these last two weeks."

How good it was to feel someone else's strength. Amanda clung to him a moment longer, allowing the strong arms to penetrate her with their strength, to shore up her lagging confidence. She smiled through tears and let go of him.

"It's just that…I heard his voice, Buck," she told him, pulling away slightly now.

"Well, ma'am, maybe you did. I reckon that's how it is when two people love each other like you and Moss. They've got a way of bein' together, even when they're apart."

She looked up at him, now reddening slightly.

"Yes, Buck. And I...love him so much. He's...been my strength, a part of me, for a long time now."

He grasped her shoulders. "It's all right, ma'am. I understand. And I know there ain't but one man you belong to or ever will belong to. Hell, everybody needs to be held now and then."

"Oh, my God!" she whispered, dropping her eyes and putting a hand to her forehead. "What's come over me?"

"Nothin' but the heat and not enough rest and food," he replied, keeping a firm hold of her shoulders. "It's okay, Mrs. Tucker."

"Don't tell anyone," she said quietly, wiping away more tears.

"Why should I do that? Ain't nobody's business. And if you're thinkin' you just did somethin' wrong, you'd best think again. I'm Moss's friend, and your friend. And what are friends for if they can't help each other out? And there ain't a woman west of the Mississippi I respect more than you, ma'am. Now you just sit right back down and I'll get that tub filled. Wouldn't a nice cool bath feel good?"

"Yes, it would," she replied, sitting back down wearily.

"Sure it would," he told her, patting her shoulder. "I'll be right back." He ambled toward the door.

"Buck," she spoke up.

"Yes, ma'am?"

"Thank you. I...didn't mean to put you on the spot. I didn't mean...anything."

"Not to worry, ma'am." He went through the door and stood on the porch a moment, trying to think how long it took to get to Hanksville, the nearest town. He realized it had been a long time since he'd visited the whores there, and he suddenly had an urgent need for a woman.

Inside, Amanda got out of the chair, walked into the bedroom and stared at the crucifix on her dresser. She wiped at more tears and lit the candles on either side of the cross. Then she picked up her rosary beads. She dropped to her knees.

"Holy Mary, Mother of God, help me in my hour of need," she whispered. "Forgive me for allowing another man to hold me, even in friendship. I pray that he understands, and that Moss will understand when I tell him. I just needed…to feel a man's strength." The tears started to come again. "Oh, please, Lord Jesus, I pray to You through the Blessed Virgin and through all the saints. Please, please protect my husband. There *is* something wrong. I feel it in my heart. And I…" She sniffed and wiped at tears. "I have to rely on You to help him. For I cannot be there. Whatever it is, Sweet Jesus, help him. Help him and bring him back to me. Only You know how much I love and need Moses Tucker. You brought us together, Lord Jesus. Don't take him from me now! Not now, when I'm so certain Moss Tucker's seed has taken root in my womb. Blessed Jesus, Son of God, let it be true that Moss's child is finally forming inside of me. And if it's so, then let him live to see his son or daughter. Please, Jesus! Keep him safe from harm. I don't want to have a baby all alone. And I want my child to know his wonderful father!"

She choked on more sobs, looking down at her stomach and running a hand over it. Perhaps it was foolish to have so much hope. It was too soon. When she and Moss had made love before he left, it had been over two weeks since her last period. And now three more weeks had passed. That made close to six all together. She had never gone that long. Yet she was so afraid to believe it could be true. Every time she undressed she was deathly afraid she would see the first signs of blood. Oh, how she wanted a child! But how awful it would be if it finally happened, only to have Moss die and never see his child!

The door opened and she heard men's voices. She made the sign of the cross and rose, clinging to the beads as Buck and three other men came into the bedroom after announcing their entrance and poured large buckets of water into the wooden bathtub.

"There you go, ma'am," Buck told her with a grin as the other three left. "That ought to be enough. You sure you don't want me to get Wanda?"

Their eyes met and Amanda blushed and looked away.

"No. I'd just as soon be alone anyway," she replied, setting the beads on the dresser. Buck looked at the beads and back to her.

"You okay now?" he asked.

"Yes. I—I guess I have to leave things up to the Lord, don't I?"

"Well, ma'am, I expect so. But you just remember all them men that are with Moss. They'll take good care of him, ma'am."

She nodded. "Buck, about the other thing—"

"Not another word, now, Mrs. Tucker. I told you it was all right. I wouldn't say nothin' for the world."

"I know," she replied quietly. "It's just that—I'm just not myself. And I—I think I might be pregnant." She remained turned away, reddening even more. "I thought you should know, so you'd understand why my emotions seem so…mixed."

Buck stood there with his hands on his hips. "Well, ma'am, that's—that's right good news. I mean, that's what you've been wantin', ain't it? You should be happy."

"I am. At least I would be happier if Moss were here. I don't know what I'd do if…" She swallowed. "Especially now."

"Well, ma'am, I expect you'd just keep right on going, 'cause you'd be carrying Moss's kid, and that baby would need its ma."

She turned finally to look up at him. "Thank you. You're a kind man, Buck. And thoughtful. Thank you for the water."

He moved his eyes away from hers, feeling uncomfortable standing alone with her in the bedroom, trying to avoid looking at the bed and envisioning her lying there and doing what needs to be done to get pregnant.

"Sure enough, ma'am. I, uh, I'll be leavin' now. You sure you're okay?"

"Yes. I'll be fine. A prayer and—and a hug from a friend, that's all I needed. Now a bath will get me right back to normal."

"Sure it will," he replied with a grin. "If you don't mind, Mrs. Tucker, I'll be, uh, goin' into town tonight. And it bein' so far and all, well, I don't expect I'll come back till tomorrow."

This time they both reddened and then grinned. Amanda knew full well what he meant.

"You're free to do as you please," she told him.

His eyes took a quick inventory of Amanda Tucker.

"Well, ma'am, I—I wouldn't exactly say that neither."

It took a moment for her to realize what he meant, and she reddened even more, and tears of embarrassment coming to her eyes.

"No offense meant, ma'am. God forgive that I should offend a woman like you. I only meant—well, I think Moss Tucker's got the best wife a man could ask for. You're quite a woman, Mrs. Tucker. And I'm proud to know you, to be your friend. Maybe you'll include me in some of them prayers. I wouldn't mind findin' somethin' like you for myself."

She smiled shyly and finally met his eyes again.

"Well, thank you for the compliment. I will pray for you, Buck."

"Well, I consider that the next best thing to havin' a saint pray for me," he said with a grin. "Say, is it true? Was you really almost a nun once?"

"Yes," she replied, dropping her eyes. "But then I—I met Moss Tucker." She blushed again and smiled. "My plans got changed."

Buck laughed lightly. "Can't imagine why," he told her with a wink. Now she laughed with him. "There, you see?" he told her. "You can still laugh. Everything's gonna be okay, ma'am. Ole Moss will be ridin' in here any day now."

"I hope you're right, Buck."

"I know I am. I'll be seein' you, ma'am. There's plenty of men around to keep watch for the night."

"Fine. Thank you."

He walked to the bedroom door and hesitated a moment.

"Ma'am, you, uh, you're stronger than you think. I mean, with your kind of faith, I expect you're stronger even than most of us men. You remember that, no matter what happens."

"I'll try to, Buck."

He nodded and quickly left. Amanda closed and bolted the door, aching to feel Moss's body next to hers, needing to hold and comfort him and be held and comforted in return, trying to remember the taste of his lips and picturing the glory of taking him inside of herself. How wonderful to love a man and be loved. There was a time, after her rape, when she had not thought that could be possible for her. But Moses Tucker had shown her differently. She undressed, lowering her naked body into the blessedly cool water, and wondered how long it would be before Moses Tucker would see her this way again, touch her in secret places, and whisper her name in the night.

• • •

The loud explosion startled Moss from unconsciousness. He lay sprawled on the cot, his face almost unrecognizable from the beating, his ribs and groin screaming with pain. Yet none of it equaled the pain in his right arm. There was another explosion, and his body jerked. He moaned, the room spinning around him. He could hear running and screaming. But his mind could not comprehend what was happening. He tried to rise, but nothing worked, and a horrid, black pain shot through his arm.

And then he remembered the words: "We ought to cut off his other arm! His other arm! His other arm!" His eyes popped open, but everything was gray.

"Noooo!" he found himself screaming into nothingness. "My God! My God!" Again he tried to rise. The pain! So much like the pain he had had in his left arm before. Was it gone? Was he now a horrid monster without arms? Was he to go home to Amanda that way?

He heard deep, sorrowful moans in the room. Were they his own? There were more explosions around him, more shouting. Now he heard a crashing sound around him. What was happening? He smelled dust—a choking dust.

Pappy and Sooner climbed through the rubble; they had tied ropes to the jail cell window and pulled it out, causing a good deal of the wall to also fall.

"Moss!" Pappy gasped. "What the hell have they—" He stopped short and stared at the half severed arm. "Oh, my God! My God! God, no!" He looked over at Sooner, who had tears in his eyes. "Ain't nothin' to do but get him the hell out of here. We can't help him till we get him back to the E.G." Pappy's voice was choked and strained. They had waited too long. They had failed Moses Tucker. If not for the fact that Moss needed help, Pappy would have shot himself that very moment.

Moss felt someone picking him up. There was gunfire seemingly everywhere, along with screams and shouts. The pain shot through his arm again.

"Mandy! Mandy!" he screamed out. "Don't let 'em cut it off! Help me, Mandy! My arm! My arm!"

"It's gonna be okay this time, Moss," a man's voice was telling him. "We're gonna save it this time! We're gonna save it! I promise you!"

"Mandy!" he groaned. How he longed to hear her soft voice, to feel her lying next to him. If she could only touch him perhaps it would heal him.

His whole body screamed in agonizing pain as he felt himself being slung over a saddle.

"I don't know no other way to do this," he heard a voice saying. "I didn't expect him to be in this condition. Goddamn, all mighty, they beat him half to death! Ralph Landers is gonna pay for this! He's gonna die slow! He's gonna suffer worse than anybody suffered in his life!"

"We'd all like a piece of him," another voice replied.

"And you'll all get a piece: we'll tie him down and each take turns carvin' off a piece of flesh!" came the reply. "And if

Moss loses this arm, we'll cut off his arms—both of them, and maybe his balls too! That man-lovin' son of a bitch!"

"Come on, Pappy, let's get the hell out of here! The dynamite has done its job. Everybody's busy tryin' to put out the fires. This is our chance to get away before they all realize what's goin' on. Let's move!"

Moss felt a terrible jostling, and the blessed unconsciousness surrounded him again.

Pappy and Sooner rode hard out of town, while the rest of the Tucker men kept Landers's men busy in and around the Golden Spur, where they had started to run out when the commotion started. The three men who had been guarding the jail were already dead, and the town hall and the back side of the Golden Spur were blown to bits. Pappy and Sooner had torn out the cell wall and hauled Moss away; the other Tucker men now sat in strategic places, raising long-barreled rifles that flashed in the sun as they took careful aim and kept more men from riding out after Pappy and Sooner.

This was a chance for the small group of hard, lonely men to get some revenge for losing one of their own. Hank Stemm's fresh grave was still in their minds, let alone the fact that Moss had been beaten and jailed. Ralph Landers had totally underestimated the capacity of the Tucker men, not realizing their awesome need for vengeance once they were riled. It brought out a hard meanness difficult to equal, and it gave them the edge they needed. The Landers men were not so emotionally involved as the Tucker men. They were simply men hired to do a job; men who really didn't care one way or another how things turned out. And so they didn't have the spunky fight in them that the Tucker men had.

The firing continued, the buildings blazed, and the local citizens huddled out of range. It seemed an all-out war had broken loose, as guns boomed around them and wounded men cried out. Wood chips, dust, and rocks flew while horses sidestepped stray shots, whinnying and rearing. The entire town was in turmoil, and Slim Taggart grinned, looking across the rooftop at Darrell Hicks.

"That ought to keep them hoppin' for a while!" he shouted. "I ain't had this much fun since that great big posse come after us up in Montana after we robbed that bank! Remember?"

"You bet your ass I do!" Hicks replied with a wide grin. "Let's get the hell out of here!"

He waved his hat, signaling the others. The Landers men had pulled back now, hoping Tucker's men would leave so they could get out on the streets and take care of their wounded. The citizens also hoped it would end soon, so they could try to put out the fires before the whole town burned down.

Ralph Landers huddled with Miles Randall in a stable outside the Golden Spur, watching the saloon burn.

"My papers!" Landers groaned, barely able to move his lips when he spoke. His face was severely swollen from Moss's kicks. His nose was crooked and ugly, and his mouth ached fiercely. He looked hideous, with two and a half teeth missing in front and lips puffed up three times their normal size. How he hated Moss Tucker! He'd waited too long. He should have heated up the crowd faster and had Moss hanged right away. Now his men had him back. And the only way to end the fighting would be to go out and attack the E.G. But he'd lost a lot of men today, and would doubtless lose more. The Tucker men were a heavy match, and he knew some of his men would give up the fight, not willing to die for land that was not even their own. "I'll...kill him...myself!" Landers muttered.

"Give it up, Ralph!" Randall replied, almost in tears. "It's not worth it! Let her have the damned place! He'll kill us! He'll kill us both!"

"Give it a couple of days. He'll die from the beating and from the arm. Then his men will just go home."

"But, what if—what if he doesn't die!" Randall shrieked, shivering from fear. "You don't know what he's capable of!"

"He's not capable of anything now!" Landers hissed, despising Moss with a passion for what the man had done to his once-handsome face. "I tell you the man is going to die. And at the least, he'll lose that other arm! What's he going to do then!" He laughed in spite of his pain. "He'll be a broken, useless man! I'd like to see the look on Etta's face—and his own wife's face—when they see him walking around with no arms at all! When I walked in that jail cell earlier this morning and saw the way it hung there, it just warmed my heart!"

"Listen, Ralph. The shooting—it—it stopped," Miles spoke up.

"Good. It's over. Let's go check the damage."

They both got up, picking straw from their suits. They stepped out of the stable into the sunlight. The Golden Spur was completely engulfed in flames now. They stood there watching it burn, as someone approached them through the alley. Ralph Landers began to pale when he realized it was Lloyd Duncan. Had the man just been a spy after all? Was he coming now to shoot them down? Landers pulled out a small handgun and pointed it at the man.

"Did you have something to do with this?" Landers asked the man. Duncan's eyes opened in surprise.

"Hell, no, Mr. Landers! I told you, I'm on your side. Don't you remember? I was one of the men who helped kick the hell out of Moses Tucker last night. And I'm the one who suggested cuttin' off the other arm."

Landers eased the gun back into his vest. "Oh, I—well, I was in pretty bad shape myself. I don't remember much."

"I, uh, came to see if you was all right," Duncan told the man, studying the horribly beaten face. "And, uh, to tell you an idea I have."

"For what?"

"For gettin' rid of Moss Tucker. It would make things real simple, Mr. Landers, if you could just get the man to leave. It's obvious most of us are no match for his men when it comes to usin' guns."

"I already tried to get rid of him the easy way. I offered him money—lots of it. He wouldn't take it."

"I ain't talkin' about money, Mr. Landers."

"What other way is there to get rid of him?"

Duncan grinned. "He's got a woman back in Utah. He's right fond of her, too."

The two men studied each other, and then light appeared in Landers's eyes.

"Duncan, if my face wasn't so sore, I'd be grinning and laughing right now. Why in hell didn't I think of that!"

"Well, sometimes it takes more than one head to figure somethin' out," Duncan replied. "Ole Tucker, he's right proud and protective of that woman. I seen them together when I went down there with Etta, and he'd go to hell and back for his wife. You can bank on it. I figure if he finds out somebody's gone down there to, uh, harm her maybe he'd hightail it out of Wyoming so fast you wouldn't see him for dust. Then you could just move in on the E.G., arrange to have Etta quietly shipped off, and that would be the end of it."

"It sounds so easy—maybe too easy. And what's in it for you, Duncan?"

"Just Etta. I've got a fondness for your wife, Landers. I want five thousand dollars for the job, and I want Etta kidnaped and shipped up to Canada. Hide her in a cattle car or something. I have a cabin up in Canada where I go to hunt sometimes. I was born there. I want some of your men to hold her till I get there. Then I'll just tie her down and do what I want with her. Once she realizes she's got nothin' left—no money, no friends—she'll come around."

"You're quite a devious man, Mr. Duncan. I suppose you realize that you'd have Moses Tucker after you, if he lives."

"How's he gonna find me? I'll grab his wife and take her down to a whorehouse I know down in Tucson where they drug pretty young girls and turn them into prostitutes. I'll leave her there. By the time Tucker recovers from this beating—if he does—then gets all the way down there to her, I'll be long gone back to Canada, and only you and couple other men would know where I was. Tucker don't even know all your men. So how's he ever gonna trace me? I expect he'd probably go on down to Mexico lookin' for me, never thinkin' I'd head back north. I'll leave today. It takes about eight days to get there. Give me at least four or five before you approach Tucker. Then just let him know what's happened. Him and his men will ride like hell to try and catch up with me."

"Do you really think it can work?"

"Sure it can. Tucker is fond of Etta Landers. But you give him a choice and it's his wife he'd choose. You can bank on it."

Landers looked at Miles Randall.

"What do you think, Miles?"

"It just might work. All this bloodshed isn't getting us anywhere, Ralph."

Landers looked back at Duncan. "Tucker been bedding Etta?"

"Sure he has."

"You planning on doing the same to his wife?"

Duncan shrugged. "As long as I'm gonna do this, I might as well go all the way. It would serve Tucker right, for takin' my place in Etta's bed. An eye for an eye, so to speak. I hear tell Amanda Tucker is real religious. She'd understand an eye for an eye. It's from the Bible, I think."

He and Miles Randall chuckled, and Ralph Landers wanted to, except that it brought him too much pain.

Chapter Thirty-Nine

Etta and Pappy stood watching over a sweating and thrashing Moses Tucker. It had been four days since they had dragged Moss from the jail cell, carried him to the E.G., and sewed and bandaged the arm. In those four days Moss had intermittently screamed Amanda's name, and begged from the depths of his soul that Amanda not let anyone cut off his arm. His mind moved through another time: the gruesome sound of a saw, the horror of the pain, and the awful realization that his left arm had been removed. Now the awful horror was back, only worse. His subconscious mind knew what had happened, and that knowledge came forth in heart-rending screams and tormenting moans. His condition made Etta's heart feel as though it were bleeding through its walls, and she loved him more than ever, not just wanting him there, but truly loving him for the first time.

"What do you think, Pappy?" she asked quietly on that fourth night, dabbing at tears as she sat by his bedside.

"Hard to say. It's infected some, but not like the last time. I don't like that fever, though. Could be a bad sign."

"Oh, Pappy!" she sniffled, horrified at the thought of the possibility of Moses Tucker losing both arms. "What are we going to do! I feel so…responsible!"

"He's a grown man who made up his own mind, Mrs. Landers." He blinked back his own tears.

Moss's eyes suddenly opened and he just stared at the ceiling a moment.

"Pappy!" Etta whispered, rising from her chair. "He's awake, I think."

Moss looked first at Etta, then at Pappy.

"Where's Mandy?" he asked in a whisper.

"She's still down in Utah, Moss," Pappy said, glad to see the man awake. "You're at the E.G. Me and the boys, we got you out of that jail."

Moss swallowed and thought a moment. His lips and mouth hurt. His ribs hurt just from simple breathing. And his arm…He suddenly tried to rise, his eyes widening and filling with horror. Pappy grasped his shoulders.

"You gotta lie flat, Moss! Don't move that arm!"

"You cut it off! You cut it off, didn't you, you bastard! Or—or did they—my arm! They said they'd cut it off!"

"No, Moss! You haven't lost the arm!"

"I can't feel it! I can't feel it! My God! Mandy! Where's Mandy! Don't let her see me like this!"

"Moss, you didn't lose the arm!" Pappy yelled, lifting Moss's arm while Etta struggled to hold him down and called for help. "Look, Moss. Look! It's your hand—your hand!" Pappy shouted. "And if you don't lay still, you'll tear up all our mending."

Lonnie, Max, and Tom came rushing in, automatically grabbing Moss's legs, Tom moving up to take Etta's place in holding Moss down and keeping him from rising. Etta moved back, now weeping openly.

"Let go of me! Let go of me, you bastards! Don't you dare take my other arm!" Moss roared, remembering being held once before. "I'll kill you! I'll kill every last one of you!"

"Goddamn it, Moss, look! Look at your hand!" Pappy growled at him.

Moss gave up the struggling. He was too weakened by his ordeal to fight against four men for long. His breathing was labored and he lay trembling, looking up at the hand that Pappy held in front of his eyes.

"It's your hand, Moss."

Moss's eyes moved from the hand up the arm, and he turned his head to look at the heavy bandage on his upper arm.

"You got any feelin' in it at all, Moss?" Pappy asked him quietly. "You feel me holdin' your hand?"

Moss blinked, and one tear slipped down the side of his face into his ear. He was devastated at the thought of looking weak in front of these men, yet the shock of possibly losing the other arm had thrown him into a terrible depression that he could not control.

"Just…a little," he replied in a weak voice.

"Well, that's a start."

"It's the only arm I've got!" Moss groaned. "And even if I keep it, what if it's useless? How am I ever gonna shoot a gun! How am I gonna…" He looked up at Pappy now. "You can save it, can't you? God in heaven, Pappy, don't cut it off!"

Pappy blinked back tears. "It's infected, Moss, but so far it ain't real bad. But you've got a high fever."

Moss's eyes filled with fiery determination, and their dark irises became almost black with an inner rage.

"Don't you dare cut off my arm—no matter what, Pappy! You hear me? If it gets bad, you leave it and let me die!"

"Moss…"

"I won't go through it again!" Moss growled, a cold look in his eyes that planted fear in all their hearts. "Don't you leave me nothin' more than a side show! I won't go back to Amanda that way. I won't! Don't make me! I'd rather be dead!" More tears slipped down the side of his face. Pappy looked at the other three men.

"I can't blame him, Pappy," Lonnie spoke up. "Once is enough. A man like Moss can't go around with no arms."

Pappy looked back at Moss, his heart so heavy he thought he'd pass out.

"All right, Moss. If it gets bad, we won't touch it."

"Swear it!"

"I swear it."

Moss looked at the rest of them and they all nodded. Tom Sorrells wiped at his eyes. Moss looked back at the bandaged arm.

"Is there…a chance?"

"There's always a chance," Pappy replied.

"I think you've got an edge," Lonnie spoke up. "You've had that woman of yours back in Utah prayin' for you. That can't be all bad."

Moss's eyes flashed back to Pappy's. "You didn't tell her!"

"Nope. We figured we'd wait and see how things turn out."

"Don't tell her anything! Not anything! I don't want her down there all alone worrying."

"We won't say nothing, Moss," Max told him. "That's a promise. But the fact remains she'll be prayin' for you anyway."

"I'm…sorry," Moss said, his voice growing weaker now as a dizziness swept over him. "I—I can't help what…I say… what I do…"

"We know that, Moss," Lonnie replied. "We've been this route before, you know. A man says a lot of things he don't mean when he's in pain."

"Just don't cut it off…no matter what," Moss said, now in a near whisper.

"Whatever you say, Moss."

Pappy turned and quickly left the room, hurrying out of the house and out behind the feed house, where he put his arm against the back wall and wept quietly and alone.

● ● ●

Several more days passed: days filled with pain and fits of unconsciousness, during which Moss always called for Amanda. In his waking moments he cursed Etta Landers, screaming at her to stay out of his room, telling her it was all her fault. She had ruined his life once, now she had ruined the pieces he had managed to pick up. "Why did you have to come back in my life?" he'd groan.

Never had Etta been more miserable and lonely. None of her plans for saving the ranch and getting Moss Tucker back in the bargain had worked out. Now he hated her more than ever, and it hurt. What a time to discover that she truly loved him. He would never forgive her now, let alone have any feelings for her. Not once did he call her name when he was in pain. It was always "Mandy." She grew to hate the name and the woman. If not for Amanda Tucker, Etta was sure she could have won Moss back. She could have finally been happy. But all was lost now; on top of everything else, she would have to suffer the guilt of being responsible for Moss's death or, at best, the loss of the man's other arm—something a virile man like Moses Tucker could never tolerate.

It was twelve days after the injury before Moss awoke without a fever. The room was quiet, and as was his habit, he reached up and ran a hand through his hair upon awakening. His hand reached the top of his head when he realized what he had done. He froze at first, afraid to believe he had actually used his arm. His heart pounded as he slowly lowered it and stared at the hand, which looked pink and healthy. He squeezed his fingers, unaware that that very morning, Amanda had knelt in morning prayer and had prayed for her husband's health and safety. Her earnest prayers had been answered.

"I moved it," he whispered. Great joy enveloped him, and he smiled as tears filled his eyes. "I moved it!" He looked at the door. "Pappy!" he yelled. "Pappy, get in here! Pappy!" He heard voices and commotion somewhere downstairs and he laughed at the vision of the men scrambling up the stairs to see what was wrong.

He held up his arm, ignoring the pain it still brought him, and made a fist. "By God, Ralph Landers, you've had it now!" he growled, a smile of sweet revenge on his face. Killing Landers and Miles Randall would be sheer joy. And he'd get Lloyd Duncan! He was certain now that it was Duncan's voice he heard that awful day, Duncan's voice telling them to cut off the arm. Duncan would pay!

• • •

Amanda wrote the word "New Zealand" on the blackboard, while the five children—three white (including Becky) and two Indians—whispered and wriggled in the background. She wrote the headings "Mountains," "Rivers," and "Lakes" beneath the word, subconsciously realizing the children had suddenly quieted.

"Now, children, who can tell me where New Zealand is?" she asked, putting down the chalk. "I hope you've—"

As she turned around she froze in place and turned white as snow. There stood Lloyd Duncan, holding the barrel of a .45 revolver against Becky's cheek.

"Afternoon, Mrs. Tucker," the man said with a smile.

Amanda felt drained of blood. Lloyd Duncan! What on earth was he doing here! And why would he want to threaten Becky!

"Take that gun away from that child's head!" she said, her frightened voice unable to rise above a near whisper.

"I will. Soon as you get your cape and quickly walk over here to me."

She hesitated, terrible memories of the abduction five years earlier creeping into her mind.

"Whatever for?" she asked. "And where is my husband!"

"Well, he's most likely dead. But just for insurance, you and me is goin' for a little ride together—to make sure Moss Tucker leaves Wyoming."

All she heard was the word dead. No! It couldn't be! She trembled and grasped the edge of her desk.

"What's happened to Moss?" she asked in a choking voice.

"Well, ma'am, it's like this. We tried to cut off his other arm, only we all kind of puked and changed our minds. So now we ain't sure if he's still got it or not, 'cause his men come and got him. So, he's most likely either dead from the beatin' we give him, or alive and armless."

He grinned as he saw every last bit of remaining color drain from her face.

"*Moss!*" she screamed on the inside. "*My God!*"

"Now you step down away from there, or I'll blow a big hole in this pretty little girl's cheek," Duncan growled. Becky whimpered and started to cry. Amanda took the cape from her chair and walked stiffly to his side, suddenly feeling like a piece of stone and not caring what he intended to do, as long as he didn't do it to little Becky.

"Where are we going?" she asked in a cold voice.

"Down south of here to a nice little whorehouse where they take pretty young things like you and make lots of money off them. I gotta say, I'd pay good myself to have a go-round with you."

She looked at him strangely. What did anything matter, if Moses Tucker was dead?

"May God forgive you," she found herself saying.

"Shut up!" Duncan growled, hitting her across the side of the face with his pistol. She screamed and fell to the floor; the children started crying.

The ranch was not far away, and normally at least one man hung around the schoolhouse while Amanda taught. But things had been very quiet; just about every outlaw in the territory knew about Amanda Tucker and wouldn't think of touching her. So she was considered relatively safe most of the time. The one man who had been watching the building, Buck Donner, had left at Amanda's own request, to go to the house and wait for Wanda to fix some lunch for Amanda and the children. It was Becky's birthday, and Wanda made Buck wait longer than usual while she decorated a cake to take back as a surprise so they could have a party at the little one-room school.

"Mama! Mama!" Becky cried out, getting up and going to Amanda, who was struggling to get to her feet. Becky leaned over her mother and cried, then tried to help her up, when Duncan grabbed the little girl's arm and clobbered her hard, sending her flying over two desks. She lay still.

"Becky!" Amanda gasped, grasping a desk and struggling to her feet. Duncan landed the handle of his gun into the back of Amanda's head, and she fell forward, this time totally silent and unconscious. He then herded the children into a small coat closet, throwing Becky's body in after them, and bolted the door. He picked up Amanda and quickly carried her outside and slung her over his horse. He mounted up and wriggled her onto his lap so that she hung over his knees, then dug his heels into the sides of his horse.

"Get movin', boy!" he said quietly. The horse galloped off; Duncan headed for a deep canyon he'd ridden through on the way in, where he knew he could hide easily among its maze of red, grotesquely formed rocks. A trail over rock was difficult if not impossible to find. If he could just get a head start…

At the ranch, work went on as usual, while the children at school huddled in the closet and Becky lay unconscious. Wanda and Buck talked casually, and Buck watched the woman decorate the cake, his mouth watering to taste some.

"Mrs. Tucker will be real surprised," he said with a grin.

* * *

Moss stretched, enjoying the feeling of more strength in his arm. It was good to be alive, good to feel his fingers moving, good to look at his hand and arm and know they were still attached to his body! He was so worked up over the joy of keeping his arm that he couldn't get to sleep. He scooted up in bed and reached over to light a cigarette. He smoked quietly, wondering just what his next move should be. A U.S. marshal seemed the only answer; yet he didn't want to go that route. He wanted to kill Ralph Landers, or at least expose the man. And now he had his own name to clear. Most people still considered him to be the man who killed the sheriff, and Moss was surprised a mob hadn't already raided the E.G. But things had been strangely quiet. Why the delay?

He nearly finished his cigarette when he heard soft footsteps and looked up to see Etta come into the room, wearing a white, flimsy gown that he could almost see through. She stood at the doorway for a moment, the nipples of her breasts erect and making little points through the soft fabric. Without a word she walked closer.

Moss put out his cigarette and eyed her with a mixture of disgust and desire. "What are you doin' here?"

"You know why I'm here. I…need to know you don't hate me, Moss. I never would have wanted them to hurt you that way. I didn't think they were capable of such cruelty."

His eyes moved down and up her body. "You need to wear somethin' like that just to come and talk?"

She walked closer, eyeing him defiantly. "Tell me you forgive me, Moss. I can't live with myself if you don't."

He sighed resignedly. "All right. I don't blame you. I did at first, but that's over now. You couldn't help what they did, and I came up here willingly."

She swallowed and sat down on the edge of the bed. "You enjoyed seeing me beg once, Moss. Now I'm begging again. I love you. I realize that now more than ever. I love you and I want you. And I'm…begging you…to make love to me before I go crazy with the want of you. I know what I am, and that you could never love me again. But you can have me for old time's sake, if you want to look at it that way. You've been without a woman for a long time, and who's to know? The battle is over. You'll leave the E.G. and we'll go our separate ways."

She reached out and brushed her fingers against the hairs of his broad chest, bringing back aches and desires long buried. "The battle isn't over," he answered in a husky voice. "It won't be over until Ralph Landers and Miles Randall are dead."

She met his eyes. "And us?"

Their eyes held for a long time. His own virility, his joy at being able to use his arm, his need for vengeance with Etta Landers—all made him vulnerable. Too vulnerable. He grasped her about the waist and rolled her over onto the bed, needing her strictly for the whore she was at that moment. His mouth came down to smother her own with a heated, hungry kiss as he pressed against her, feeling the full breasts against his chest. She returned the kiss with whimpering passion as his hand moved over her body, feeling the roundness of her hips; then moved up under the gown, feeling the softness of her silken thighs, brushing the soft hairs that hid that place that could bring him great relief.

Their love-making became intense, the kisses not really separate kisses but more like one long, lingering, groaning fit of passion and desire. Her heart raced with wicked ecstasy. Finally! Finally she would have Moss Tucker!

His lips left hers and traveled down her throat as he grasped at the flimsy gown and pulled it away from her full, soft breasts. He tasted a breast hungrily, as though it could give him nourishment, then raised up slightly to move his lips to her other breast. It was then that the crucifix Amanda had given him to wear—and which he never removed from his neck—dangled down against Etta's chest.

Moss froze, staring at it, then trembling with remorse and devastation. Mandy! He could not do this to his beautiful, trusting Mandy! Etta saw the look in his eyes and began to cry.

"No, Moss!" she whimpered. "It doesn't matter! Please don't do this, Moss! I love you! I need you!"

He studied her blue eyes almost apologetically. "I can't, Etta," he whispered, moving off of her and flopping down on his back. "I can't."

She rolled to her side and wept bitterly. He turned and put a hand on her shoulder, pressing it gently.

"Etta, if you really love me like you say, then leave now, before I cheat on the best woman a man ever had. I just—I love her too much, Etta. She trusts me. Why do you insist on makin' it so hard for me?"

"Because I love you, too," she wept.

He felt like his whole body was exploding. Never had he gone through such torment sexually. Not many men would turn down a woman like Etta, no matter how much they loved their wives. There she lay, writhing beneath him, practically begging for it. But there also hung the crucifix.

"We must never let anything—or anyone—come between

us," the letter had said. "What we have is from God...the bed is the loneliest place of all."

"My wife is down in Utah, Etta," he said softly. "And she's got needs, too—same as you and me. Only there's no way she'd lay with a man just to relieve herself. And there's no way I can lay with another woman for that reason alone neither. Why should it be okay for me, and not for her?"

"But that's the way it's always been." Etta groaned, turning to face him and frantic at the thought of losing the battle after coming so close. "No one would blame you, Moss. No one. Do you think those men out there would really care?"

"It ain't them I'm thinkin' about—just Mandy. And who says it's okay for a man to do what he wants? Just other people who want it to be that way. But it ain't that way when you really love somebody—not when they're still alive and well and waitin' faithfully for you to come back."

Her eyes widened with rage and unrequited love. She pushed at him and sat up. Every bone and muscle in Moss's body ached for her, in spite of his decision against taking the woman. The experience had made him long for Amanda to the point of agony.

"Etta, I—"

"I hate you!" she choked out, jumping off the bed to her feet. She whirled to face him, and he pulled the sheet over his nakedness. "How can you be so cruel!"

"How can you be so cruel! I came here to help you, risked my life for you, could have lost my other arm—and you insist on flauntin' yourself in front of me till you just about drive me crazy! You know how I feel about Amanda!"

"I thought you were a man!"

His eyes blazed, and he lurched toward her, grasping one of her wrists. He yanked her to the bed roughly and kissed her hard, hurting her lips. She was surprised by the power in his wounded arm, and she returned his kiss hungrily. Then Moss released her lips and spoke to her through gritted teeth, his jaws flexing in anger, faint bruises still visible through the dark skin of his face.

"I am a man, and what you're doin' to me is as bad as tryin' to shoot me! I would have been your man all these years if you'd have taken me in the first place, Etta! But you threw me out, remember? My 'bloodlines' wasn't good enough for you! My ma was a whore, and I never knew my pa. And when your father had me investigated and found that out, you looked at me like I was filth! Filth! And then your pa had every penny I owned stolen from me! So don't tell me about bein' cruel, Etta. And don't tell me I'm not a man. I loved you. And if you hadn't been so high and mighty that you couldn't let me touch you after you knew I was a bastard, it's me who'd have been in your bed every night all these years. Me! But you didn't want me. And you ended up with that handsome pervert of a husband. Now you want me back!"

He sat up and jerked her up roughly, then gave her a shove. She rolled off the bed onto the floor with a gasp.

"Well, you can't have me!" he growled. "I belong to another woman now! And I'm not gonna break her heart, you hear? You can think what you want of me, but I'm not gonna be untrue to Mandy. There's no other woman I want to get inside of anyway, includin' you! Now get out of here!"

She struggled to her feet and fled the room. Moss rolled over and groaned. He vowed then and there that in two or three days, when he felt good enough to ride, he would go into town and clean the place out—get a confession out of Ralph Landers and Miles Randall, and perhaps kill them both. Then he would get home to his own woman.

He felt weak and breathless in his need, and he found it amazing that he—a man who had known so many women and who had led a life of total abandon for so many years—could be so tightly held now by one small, young woman who spoke so softly and blushed at a kiss. How could a tiny, quiet woman like Amanda have such powers? Etta had the power, the money, the ability to scheme, and yes, she was even more beautiful; yet she couldn't touch Moss Tucker. It was the quiet and unassuming Amanda who could take a big man like Moss and make him submit with just one blush.

• • •

Etta did not come to Moss's room at all the next day. He considered it just as well. Pappy came in and helped Moss dress, as Moss decided he'd been in bed long enough. Pappy argued with him about it, but Moss was getting restless.

"I want to eat breakfast downstairs," he told Pappy. "And bring all the boys inside. I want to make some plans. If I have to be away from Mandy much longer I'll lose my mind."

"Gettin' to you, huh?" Pappy asked with a wink. He buttoned Moss's shirt for him.

"More than you know," Moss replied sullenly.

"Oh, I think I have a pretty good idea," the old man replied. "I know Etta Landers come in here last night. I heard voices and I seen her come runnin' out cryin'. What happened?"

"What do you think? I hope I never have to go through somethin' like that again. The pain was almost worse than my arm."

Pappy chuckled. "I'm proud of you, Moss. Ain't no way on God's earth that you've got a right to cheat on Mandy."

"I know that. She's the best thing that ever happened to me or ever will, Pappy. She's changed my whole life, picked up the pieces and put them all back together again."

"That's right. You're better off to save things for your wife. If everybody gave in to their baser needs, folks might as well not even marry."

Moss chuckled.

"I gotta say, you don't look none the worse this morning, Moss. You're lookin' good."

"I feel good. I have my arm!" Moss replied with a smile, making a fist and raising his arm into the air. Pappy smiled and they walked downstairs.

Outside Etta went for a morning walk, still frustrated and infuriated and hurt. She suddenly hated Amanda Tucker with a passion! How did the woman do it! How did she keep her claws so tightly embedded in a man like Moss! She envied Amanda, wishing she had that certain inner beauty that women like that one had. How jealous she was that Amanda had Moss in her bed at night! She couldn't get the memory out of her mind of how Moss had kissed her, touched her. To have him between her legs would be sheer ecstasy, and she had failed in her final effort! She kicked at a stone.

Pappy called the men to the house, and she watched them go. Sooner walked by her, warning her on his way to stick close to the house and not wander too far off.

"Moss is up and dressed!" Pappy was shouting.

"Hey, ain't that great?" Sooner said to her.

"It's wonderful," she replied with a feigned smile. "I've already seen him."

Sooner hurried on, and she stood there, wondering where to go from there. She walked a little further down past the corral and saw a rider coming. From the distance she could see it was only a small boy, so she just watched curiously without calling out for anyone. The child came closer, and she recognized him as Mrs. Webster's grandson.

"Hello, Tommy," Etta called out.

"Hello, ma'am," the dark-haired child replied. The nine-year-old boy rode proudly on his full-grown mare. "My father was in town yesterday. Grandma told us about Mr. Tucker. Is he better?"

"Yes, Tommy. You mean your family is talking to your grandmother, even though she's working for me again?"

"Father heard from grandma that you meant what you said about sharing the water. He wants to know if it's true."

"It's true," Etta replied. "How did you ride in here, Tommy?"

"The man watching the south gate, Damian Kuntz, he saw me coming and let me through. Father brought back the mail from town, and there were two things for you, ma'am. He said even if he's sore at you, he didn't have any right keeping your mail from you. And one of them is a wire for Mr. Tucker from Utah."

"Well, thank you, Tommy," she replied, reaching out to take the mail. "I hope your father realizes that it was Paul Simpson's fault, what happened to Moses Tucker. Mr. Simpson had no right to do that to Moss, when he went there as a friend."

"Yes, ma'am. Father thinks Mr. Simpson was wrong, too."

"I'm glad. Your grandmother is a good person, Tommy. And so are you. I wish all of the neighbors would realize that I'm not their enemy. I was just afraid to share the water, Tommy."

"I'll tell my dad that, ma'am. Is grandma okay?"

"She's fine. The big house and all the men here keep her busy. She's cooking something for all of them right now."

"Oh. I'll leave then. Bye, Mrs. Landers."

"Good-bye, Tommy."

The boy turned his horse and trotted away, and she saw a glimmer of hope that she could still get along with her neighbors. She looked at the envelopes: a yellow one, the telegram from Utah; and a white one, a letter from the attorney she'd found in Montana whom she felt she could trust. She'd been waiting anxiously to hear from him. She tore open the letter.

> Everything in order. You are officially Miss Etta Graceland again. Your request to place your ranch in both your name and that of Moses Edgar Tucker has also been satisfied. As you preferred, all pertinent papers to this effect are being held at this office for safe keeping. If you will sign the enclosed affidavit, and have Mr. Tucker sign...

"Tommy! Wait!" Etta called out. Someone came to the kitchen door of the house, and Tommy turned his horse.

"Who's there?" Sooner called out.

"Oh, just a little boy bringing some mail," Etta replied. "Everything okay?"

"Fine, Sooner. Go on with your meeting." She turned to Tommy. "Tommy, I'll give you two dollars if you don't tell anyone what mail you brought or where it was from."

"Why, ma'am?"

"Just do it," she replied. "You come around again next week to visit your grandmother, and I'll pay you then."

"Okay," he replied with a shrug.

"Wait just a moment. I want to sign something and put it in this return envelope. And I want you to take it to town and mail it for me, will you? My attorney already covered the postage fee."

"Yes, ma'am."

"Wait." She hurried into a bunkhouse and hunted around for a fountain pen in the desk that was kept there. She breathed a sigh of relief when she found it. She scratched out her name on the affidavit, then wrote Moss's name above the line where it was requested. She changed the writing to make it look as though someone else besides herself had written it. Then she folded the paper and stuffed it into the envelope, running back outside to Tommy.

"Thank you, Tommy," she told the boy. "You can go now."

"You sure this time?"

"Yes, I'm sure," she replied with a smile.

The boy headed out again, and Amanda glanced at the house. Damian Kuntz was far away at the south gate. Two other men were out riding the perimeter again, and the rest were inside the house with Moss making plans. Etta Landers, now Etta Graceland again, had begun her own plans long before she even went to get Moses Tucker. She had been sure at the time, once she heard he was alive and well and living in Utah, that she could easily win back the lower-class man who had once been so infatuated with her. She had thought it would be so simple to walk back into his life, even though he was now married to someone else: so sure that she had gone ahead and placed her property in his name also. What man wouldn't leave a worthless ranch in hot Utah and a plain little wife for a vast estate in Wyoming, with prime beef cattle and a beautiful woman who loved him? She frowned.

"Moses Tucker wouldn't!" she grumbled. "Well, maybe now things will change. I'm handing him a man's dream. He's got to break sometime! If only—if only there weren't an Amanda Tucker."

She looked down at the yellow envelope now, turning it over in her hand. Was it from Amanda? Of course. Who else? She looked toward the house, then back at the envelope. She walked around behind the bunkhouse and tore it open, curious to know what kind of wire Amanda would write, and already determined not to give it to Moss.

"Come right away," it read. Etta frowned, not expecting such a telegram. "Amanda missing. Becky hurt. Out searching. Need you immediately. Sorry. Real sorry. Doing everything we can. Sent out soldiers. Buck."

Etta folded the telegram and looked out over the valley. So, Lloyd Duncan had gone to Utah! There was no other explanation. This was his and Ralph's scheme for getting rid of Moss Tucker quickly and peacefully.

"Well, it won't work!" she said to herself, thinking only of the husband she hated. *"Amanda Tucker can fend for herself! I'll not let Moss and his men leave now. I need them! And if Amanda Tucker dies, all the better for me!"*

She walked around the building and toward the house, shoving the telegram in her pocket. Things were looking up after all. She hurried now, walking into the kitchen with a smile on her face that surprised Moss, after the way he had hurt her the night before. Their eyes held a moment.

"Good morning, everyone," she said politely.

"Morning," came several replies.

"And what do we do next?"

"Make another try with the neighboring ranchers," Lonnie Drake told her. "They can't all be like Simpson."

Etta looked at each man as she spoke. "I'm sure they aren't," she replied. "And I think that's a good idea. I'd like to be on better terms with them anyway. Maybe saving Moss's arm is a sign of good things to come. Don't you think?"

She smiled prettily, and they all felt a pleasant stirring deep inside themselves.

"Maybe so," Pappy said, eyeing her closely. Why was she so cheerful?

Etta walked over to the stove where Mrs. Webster was cooking pancakes.

"I'd like to help," she told the woman. "I'll add a little more wood." She lifted the iron plate and threw the telegram into the flames, watching to make sure it burned completely.

Chapter Forty

Amanda awoke with a terrific pain in her head. At first all she saw was the blurry red of campfire flames, and a hazy figure sitting across from her chewing on something. She groaned and closed her eyes again. She went to rub her head, but realized her hands were bound behind her. Her heart began to beat wildly as the ugly memory came back to her. At first all she could think of was her rape five years earlier, and the cruel treatment of the outlaws who had kidnapped her. She let out a mournful, kittenlike cry that brought Duncan to her side.

"You finally awake?" he grunted, jerking her to a sitting position. "I'm tired of carryin' around your dead weight."

She scooted away from him and pulled at the rawhide straps that bound her wrists, a hellish terror filling her, combined with the awful remembrance that Moss might be dead or armless.

"Why are you doing this?" she choked out, her mouth dry and gravely. Duncan grinned and dragged her back closer to the fire roughly, pinching her upper arm and making her cry out as he did so.

"Stay by the fire. I'm takin' you to a fancy whorehouse, lady, and I don't intend to have you get sick from the cold desert nights before I get you there!" He reached over and pulled a blanket from his bedroll, moving behind her and wrapping it around her shoulders, giving her a hug as he did so. Amanda shuddered and choked in another sob.

"Please don't touch me!" she whimpered.

"We're about the same age, you and me," he told her. "You ever had a man younger than that cripple you married?" He kissed her neck.

"Please stop!" she said in a near scream, feeling the mental horror she had once experienced creeping into her again. "You don't understand! You don't—" She choked in another sob. "Why? Why are you doing this?"

"I'll tell you why, lady!" he hissed into her ear, giving her a jolting hug at the same time and pushing the breath out of her. "That husband of yours was takin' my place in Etta Landers's bed! I'm gonna get him away from her by makin' him come down here to rescue his little wife, and I'm gonna get back at him by havin' my share of you!"

She shook her head and choked in wrenching sobs, trying to sort it all out. It must be a misunderstanding. Moss would never…was Moss even alive?

"You're wrong!" she tried to reason. "Wrong about Moss and Etta!" She tried to remain calm, to think, but all she could envision was her abduction five years earlier. "Holy Mary, Mother of God, help me in my hour of need!" she screamed out, trying desperately to wrench free from Duncan's now searching hands and hot breath. "Lord Jesus, don't let it happen again! Help me!"

Duncan stiffened and pulled away.

"What the hell are you doin'?" He grasped her face firmly in one hand and squeezed. She tightly shut her eyes, her heart pounding so hard it ached.

"Praying." The word came out jerked and strange, through lips he pinched together until she cried out in pain. Duncan hesitated, just staring at her. Then he pushed her hard, making her fall backward to the ground.

"I don't have time for you tonight anyway! I've got more tracks to make before I stop to have my pleasure under them skirts."

She began crying harder, mostly from relief at being spared for the moment.

"Shut up!" he barked. He jerked her back up and threw some water in her face from his canteen, then held it roughly to her mouth and let her drink. She coughed and sputtered and sniffled, her head aching fiercely, her mind whirling with her predicament, combined with the torture of not knowing what had happened to Moss. She could not believe what Duncan had said about Moss and Etta. It couldn't be true. It was impossible. She did not and would not believe it. This man must be crazed with some insatiable love for Etta Landers.

"They'll…kill you," she said in a shaky voice. "My husband…and his men will kill you!"

He laughed sarcastically. "They'll never find me. And by the time they find you, you'll have been bedded by so many men that neither Moss Tucker nor anybody else is gonna want you for a wife."

She felt like vomiting. What kind of place was he talking about? She had to try to discourage him.

"You don't know Moss. You don't know. He has ways. He'll find you. If you let me go now, perhaps I could talk him into not coming after you."

"That won't work, lady. I'll tell you how it's gonna be. You and me are goin' to Tucson. I know a man there who delights in takin' in young women who are innocent and turnin' them into whores. He drugs them." He laughed. "I'll be on my merry way to Canada, where Ralph Landers will have Etta shipped to—tied and waitin' for me to come and show her who she belongs to. It will be easy to move in on her once Moss and his men find out about you and leave Etta to come down here and rescue you. Only it'll be a cold day in hell before they figure out where I took you!"

She tried to shake the grotesque picture that he painted from her mind. If she thought about it too much she'd go crazy. She had to think of the present and Moss.

"Then, my husband…he's alive?"

"Most likely. I checked with Landers when I got to Hanksville. He hadn't heard otherwise. But if he is alive, he ain't got any arms, lady." He snickered. "No arms. That ought to be a sight—a big man like that with no arms!"

Amanda closed her eyes. Her lips began moving as her body trembled and dry sobs made her jerk intermittently.

"What are you doing?" he growled.

"Praying for my husband," she said quietly.

"Well, quit! All that damned prayin' makes me nervous!"

She opened her eyes and looked at him. "God loves you, Mr. Duncan. If you take me back right now, He'd forgive you. He understands how much you must love Etta Landers, and—"

His hand slammed across the side of her face.

"I said to shut up!" he yelled. She cried out and whirled facedown to the ground.

"No more prayin', understand?" he growled. "Tomorrow we'll be far enough south that I don't have to worry too much about soldiers or the men from your ranch! Then I'm gonna test out the merchandise that I'm gonna sell in Tucson!" He adjusted the blanket over her and shoved a jacket under her face. "Sleep tight, my lovely," he told her.

Amanda wondered how long she could go on without completely losing her sanity. She curled up, filled with pain, and the awful sorrow of thinking Moss must truly be armless. But the thought gave her strength, for if she could survive the horrors of what Lloyd Duncan was promising her, then she would be alive to help Moss. Surely he would need her more than ever. Moss. That was what she would concentrate on. Moss. Just Moss. Her sweet and gentle husband who would come for her. Of that she was certain. Armless or not he would come, just as he had come once before.

• • •

Moss poured himself a drink and paced, feeling restless. He felt a heaviness in his chest, as though something terrible were wrong, yet he couldn't understand why. It had nothing to do with matters at hand. He had spent the past two days getting his strength back by riding in the fresh Wyoming air and visiting the other neighbors, who now sympathized with him and

Etta both. They had heard what had happened to Moss in jail, and who had been responsible for putting him there. These were not violent people, and they did not like being identified with people like the embittered rancher, Paul Simpson. And Moss seemed to speak sincerely when he told them they could have water rights. Moss felt things were coming to a head. In a day or two he would ride into town and he would have it out with Ralph Landers and Miles Randall; he would get a confession out of them and clear his own name. If people could only hear the truth Etta would win her battle, especially now that neighbors were being offered water rights.

He should be in fairly high spirits, but a morbid coldness penetrated him, a strange depression. Amanda? Surely if something were wrong, he'd have heard by now. Besides, she was at the ranch, and everyone in the territory knew her. He couldn't think of one man who would harm her. Maybe she was sick! No. They would have wired him. He swallowed the drink, trying to shake the feeling of loss. Perhaps it was just simply that he missed her so much. He heard footsteps and turned to see Etta entering the parlor, dressed in a sleek, black dress with a plunging neckline that revealed deep cleavage and milky-white skin. She smiled with pleasure when Moss's eyes took inventory.

"Do you like it?" she asked, turning around for him. She walked over and closed the parlor doors, then turned to face him again.

"Still at it, I see," he mumbled, pouring another drink and cursing her for her cruel seductiveness.

"You won't be around much longer, I'm afraid. I have to fight to the last straw." She smiled and walked up behind him, putting her arms around his waist from behind.

"Don't do that, Etta. I'm in a bad mood," he muttered.

She sighed and let go of him. "Moss, I'm sorry about the other night. Truly I am. I just—I'd seen you suffer so, and I was so afraid you'd lose your arm and it would be all my fault. It all

419

made me love you so much more, Moss. I wanted to…please you, to do something…nice for you. You'd—"

"Do you have a purpose for comin' in here and interruptin' my drinking, Etta—besides to seduce me, I mean?" He swallowed his drink and took a cigarette from his shirt pocket. He turned to look at her, put the cigarette to his mouth, and lit it. She studied the dark, handsome face, the rugged lines etched into it from the equally rugged life he had led. He stood there, more man than she could hope for, and the time had come for her last try at having him for herself.

"I wish you wouldn't look at me like that," she said, her eyes conveniently tearing.

Moss sighed. "All right, I'm sorry," he said, softening slightly. "I've got Amanda on my mind tonight. I have this heavy feeling, a sad feelin'—like somethin' is wrong. But I know if it was, somebody would have wired me by now."

She quickly turned away, not sure she was able to hide the guilt in her eyes and not wanting him to see if it was there. Her heart pounded with dread that he would somehow find out. But how could he? Of course he could! Ralph Landers must know. Her mind raced, and she felt confused, desperate.

"Moss, I—I've done something to show how much I love you. I came in here to tell you about it. I've been corresponding with an attorney in Montana."

"About what?" he asked, frowning with curiosity. He took a deep drag on his cigarette and walked over to stare out the window.

"About the ranch, you and me."

He turned to face her. "It's the ranch and you, Etta. Not you and me."

She dropped her eyes in disappointment.

"I know that now. Perhaps some day, if you should ever be alone, you'll think of me, Moss."

"Why should I be alone?" he asked suspiciously.

She quickly smiled nonchalantly. "I'm only speaking figuratively, Moss."

"Well, what's this about an attorney in Montana?"

She walked over and poured herself a drink now.

"For one thing, I'm Etta Graceland again. My name is officially changed." She turned to look at him, eyeing him seductively with blue pools of love as she sipped her drink. "Aren't you going to congratulate me?"

He nodded. "Congratulations, Miss Graceland."

She laughed lightly. "I've done something else, Moss. I got the wheels rolling before I even went down to Utah to get you. Actually, at the time, I thought you'd still be free, and that perhaps you'd let bygones be bygones and still want me." She took another sip and set the glass down. She walked up close to him. "I wanted to share my ranch with you, Moss. To make you a rich man, make up for what my father did to you. So I—I've put the ranch in both our names; you own half of this land and all its proceeds, Moses Tucker, which means you are now a rich man."

She smiled, but the smile quickly faded when he did not return it.

"I thought you'd be a little more grateful."

"The two thousand dollars is enough, Etta."

"Don't be foolish, Moss! Besides, the deed is already done. You're part owner of this place, whether you like the idea or not. But I must say, I'm deeply hurt. I've done few decent and nice things in my life. Let me do this."

"What am I supposed to do? Bring Amanda up here so you two can live in the same house together and share me?"

"Well, I—I didn't know when I first made the decision that you were married, and I—"

"I'm not the fool I was eighteen years ago, Etta. Don't lie to me. You did know I was married, and your spoiled little mind just figured that the good old bastard from Illinois would just fall down pantin' after your heels the minute he saw you again! And that he'd leave his plain little wife for the beautiful Etta Landers. Excuse me—Graceland, isn't it?"

"Moss, I hate it when you're angry with me," she whimpered, her lip quivering. She turned away from him.

"Well, I am angry! It only shows what a fool you took me for! And it shows how cold you can be. It wouldn't bother you one bit how much it would hurt Amanda if I left her for another woman. Or perhaps you figured I'd bring her up here with me and let her watch as you paraded around in front of me in your flimsy nightgowns!"

"Moss, stop it!" she said in a near scream. She covered her face and cried. "I love you! Why won't you let me love you?" She stood there weeping and trembling, and Moss rolled his eyes and sighed, deciding it was impossible to know any more when she was serious and when she was acting. He had thought for a while that he had her figured, and that she'd changed a little. He walked up and grasped her shoulders.

"Etta, I do appreciate the gesture but I can't share this place with you, and you know it. It's impossible."

She turned and looked up at him, deliberately remaining close enough that her breasts brushed against his chest.

"Moss, we could be so happy together! We could get married in St. Louis, maybe honeymoon in New Orleans! Maybe we could even go to New York City or Europe! Wouldn't you love to see Europe, Moss?"

His eyes turned cold again, and he stepped back.

"What you don't understand, Etta, is that I could never marry you, even if I did lose Amanda for some reason. 'Cause right now I'm seein' a side of you I could never live with. And I'm my own man, Etta. I make the decisions—not the woman. And I make my own way. I don't go snivelin' after a rich broad like I was nothin' but her prime stud!"

She raised a hand to slap him, but he caught her wrist.

"I'm sorry, Etta. But you've dug your own hole and you're layin' in it. I'm damned sorry about Ralph Landers. But if you want another husband, you'll have to look elsewhere. I came here to help out a woman who had no help and no friends.

And now I'm probably the best friend you've got. Why can't we leave it that way, Etta? Just let it go and let me be your friend."

"Then you might as well know that if you turn down this partnership, you're also turning down gold, Moss Tucker! How many men would turn that away for any woman?"

His eyes narrowed in surprise and suspicion.

"What gold?"

"My gold! Right here on this land!"

He let go of her wrist and put out the cigarette that had rested at the corner of his mouth. He studied her eyes. So this was the ultimate weapon.

"Where?"

"The southeast section where it's so rocky, not far from the stream."

He just stared at her a moment. "That why you wouldn't share the water?"

"I was afraid someone would figure it out, and if Ralph Landers knew about the gold he'd stop at nothing short of murdering me to get this land! Look how hard he's tried already! And he doesn't even know about the gold. Only my father and I knew about it."

"Why didn't you tell me before this?"

She smiled resignedly. "I wanted to win you with my charm, not my gold. But if that's what it takes—"

"You really think that? You think you can buy me? That I'd sell out on Amanda for gold?"

"It's high-grade, Moss. Father never bothered with it. He was saving it for the future, and for me. Then he died. I've never mined it because Ralph has been on my back for this place ever since, and I didn't want him to know about it. Besides, I never had a hired man who was capable of mining it correctly. But you could, Moss. You had a mine once. Think about it, Moss! You—me—five thousand acres of prime Wyoming land, good beef, and a gold mine all to ourselves. With you here, neither Ralph nor anyone else would give us any more trouble." Her eyes lit up as she spoke. "And with the gold, you could buy up more land! We could have ten thousand acres! Twenty thousand! Fifty thousand! Moses Tucker would be one of the richest men in Wyoming!"

He reached out, grasping the back of her neck and wanting to break it. She panicked slightly under his almost painful grip.

"Moss?"

"You've missed the whole point, baby. I'm already rich. One of the richest men in Utah. And my wealth don't lie in land or gold, Etta. My wealth has a name. It's Amanda Tucker!"

Hatred, surprise, anger: they all passed through the blue eyes that stared at him in shock. Then they filled with terrible disappointment, and her lips quivered, and she screwed her face up like a little girl whose doll had just been broken.

"But I want you!" she wailed.

"You're eighteen years too late, Etta," he said softly, suddenly feeling sorry for her. "It's just not the same no more."

"I see," she whispered, trying vainly to put on an air of unconcern.

"No. You don't see at all. And that's the sad part. I'm tryin' to save your land for you, Etta. But there's nothin' I can do about the rest. I—"

They heard running, and a pounding at the parlor doors. They tore their eyes from each other, and Moss hurried over to open the doors. Pappy stood there, slightly breathless. At first he said nothing, looking from Moss to Etta's low-cut dress and the drink in her hand.

"What the hell's the matter?" Moss asked him. Pappy quickly looked back at Moss.

"Riders. About forty men. Comin' into the E.G. Kuntz just rode in ahead of 'em and they ain't more than five minutes away."

"Landers men?"

"He's sure of it."

Moss looked back at Etta. "This is it. You get yourself down behind somethin' and don't come out till you hear me callin' you out, understand?"

She nodded, fear enveloping her. Moss turned back to Pappy.

"Get your ass on your horse and ride for help. I think we can at least count on the Websters and the Tullys to come to our aid. Has everyone else been warned?"

"Yes. The men are shorin' up now. We're down to thirteen. Danny Greene makes fourteen, but he ain't much of a shot."

"Well, our thirteen is as good as twice that many, the way they shoot. Get going, Pappy."

"Right."

Pappy left quickly and Moss turned to Etta. "Come into the kitchen and help me buckle on my gun belt."

"Yes, Moss." He hurried out and she followed behind. They moved quickly now, blowing out lamps as they walked through the house. Moss grabbed his shotgun from the wall near the door, clicking it open with one hand and loading it with nearby shells, while Etta wrapped his gun belt around his hips, buckling it with nervous fingers.

"Hurry up," he said quietly, slamming the shotgun closed with a startling snap.

"I'm hurrying as fast as I can," she whispered. She wiggled it around on his hips. "Does that feel right?"

"It'll do. Tie the leg strap."

He reached for his Winchester and snapped the lever back to load it; she tried to ignore the provocative manliness he exuded when he was tensed up and armed for a fight.

"Does Amanda do it better than this?"

"She's become an expert," he replied with a grin.

"And I suppose you practice a lot," she said, straightening.

"All the time," he replied.

She jumped slightly when he banged the bolt on the rifle.

"You lay low," he told her, as the sound of horse's hooves came closer.

"Be careful, Moss!" she whispered.

"I'll do my best."

"Spread out!" he heard a voice. He glanced back at Etta

again, and they both were surprised. It was Ralph Landers's voice. "I'm going inside and get Etta out of there!"

Moss moved back from the door, astounded that Ralph Landers himself would risk his neck riding into a snare of Tucker men. Etta ducked around the wall into the hallway, and footsteps thudded on the porch outside the kitchen door. One lamp remained lit in the kitchen. Moss waited quietly, knowing his men would wait until he gave a shout for them to start firing. In the meantime, they would all pick a target and be ready.

Landers walked confidently through the kitchen door, brandishing a small pistol.

"Come on out, Etta! You and I are going for a little ride!" he shouted on the way inside.

Moses Tucker rammed the end of his Winchester into Landers's belly, and the man froze in shock, turning gray.

"What the—"

"You lost your mind, walkin' into Tucker territory like this?" Moss asked. He gave the rifle a nudge, making Landers grunt. The man dropped his pistol, beads of sweat breaking out on his forehead; Moss enjoyed looking at his crooked nose. But he was confused as to this sudden and brazen attack on the E.G.

"You!" Landers gasped. "You're—you're not supposed to be here!"

Moss wanted to laugh out loud. "You disappointed I didn't die, Landers? Sorry. But I not only didn't die, I can even use my arm—see?"

He shoved the rifle hard this time, remembering the hideous act the man had attempted on him in the jail cell, and realizing it was this man's fault Moss took a beating afterward.

"You scummy pervert!" Moss sneered. "Speak up and tell your boys to sit tight. Tell them they're surrounded. We might be outnumbered, Landers, but right now there's thirteen guns on your men, and they're gonna have a piss poor time decidin' which one of your men to take down first! And there's more help coming!"

"I…" Landers' breath came in short gasps. Etta came from around the corner, smiling wickedly, enjoying the look on Ralph Landers's face.

"Tell them!" Moss growled. "You and me are gonna talk about how you're gonna clear my name and leave Etta alone!"

A trembling Ralph Landers moved a little closer to the door.

"Sit tight, boys!" he managed to holler out. "You're surrounded. Something…went wrong." His voice cracked slightly. Outside his men just looked at each other curiously.

"You heard him!" Moss roared. "Everybody stay real still. In a few minutes you can all go back to town, without nobody dying!"

Rifles seemed to be clicking everywhere, as Tucker men now made themselves visible from behind rooftops and barrels and wagons.

"What's the word, boss?" Sooner shouted, holding a shotgun on a Landers' man from a distance.

"I'm okay. We're havin' a little talk in here. Seems Landers figured Etta was all alone out here!"

"He figured that one wrong!" Sooner shouted back.

Moss grinned and looked at Landers. "Looks like you're up to your ass in Tucker men, Landers. Why don't you sit down to that table, and Etta will get you some paper and a pen. Then you can write down as to how I'm not guilty of killin' that sheriff."

"You bastard! What are you doing here! Why aren't you with your wife!"

Moss's face drained of all color, and Etta's heart froze. Moss jammed his rifle into Landers's chest and rammed the man up against a cupboard.

"What the hell are you talkin' about!" he growled.

"Didn't you get a telegram or something? Duncan wired me four days ago that he was—"

Moss began to tremble so bad he looked ready to fall apart. His jaw flexed and his finger seemed to tighten on the trigger.

"Duncan! Has he hurt my wife?" he roared. The men outside could hear, and Lonnie looked at Darrell.

"My God!" he said quietly.

Landers swallowed. "He—he was supposed to go down to your ranch and kidnap her, take her to Tucson. He wired me he was there. I even threatened the man at the telegraph office to find out you'd gotten a telegram telling you to come to Utah, so I knew the deed was done. That's why I—I thought you'd all be gone. Duncan said you'd choose your wife over Etta! How could you—"

"I never got no telegram!" Moss growled.

"But he said he gave it to the Webster boy to bring out here."

Moss moved back so that he could see Landers and Etta both. He shifted his eyes to Etta.

"Did I get a telegram?" he hissed.

"I—"

"You knew!" he roared. "I can see it on your face! You knew and you didn't tell me!"

"Moss, I—I needed you here! You have men down there to look after her. I needed you here to protect me!"

"You bitch!" he hissed through gritted teeth, his eyes filling with tears. "You bitch!"

"Moss, don't! Please don't! Oh, God, Moss, I'm sorry!" She burst into tears. "I didn't want you to go! I didn't want you to go!"

Landers saw his opportunity. He pushed hard on the Winchester, shoving the barrel away from himself and toward Etta. The sudden movement caused just enough pressure on the trigger, where Moss already had his finger arched, and the gun went off. Etta screamed and fell to the floor, and Landers started running for the door. Moss stared at Etta, a black sorrow sweeping over him. What had happened to Mandy!

This was all Ralph Landers's fault. All of it! The door slammed, and Moss fired again, blowing a hole through it.

"Don't let him get away!" he shouted, heading for the door. Outside all hell broke loose. Guns fired from every direction, horses whinnied and men screamed and fell from their horses. More Landers' men dismounted and began running for cover. Moss threw down the Winchester and grabbed his shotgun, catching a glimpse of Ralph Landers ducking into the feed shed. Moss bolted outside, diving for the ground and rolling amid flying bullets, tasting dirt in his mouth and gripping the shotgun.

"Get the hell out of there, Moss!" he heard Darrell Hicks shouting. Something stung his left side, but he kept rolling until he reached the feed house, then ducked inside and plastered himself against the wall. He was certain he'd seen Landers enter the building. He could hear his own men moving around on the rooftop, where they held their positions and kept up the gun battle outside. But inside there was only Moss and Ralph Landers—somewhere. There was no other exit from the building.

An all-out war seemed to be taking place outside, as Moss raised his foot and pushed the wooden door, shoving it along its runner and closing it so that no one could leave. It creaked and banged shut with a thud; with the insulation of bales of hay, everything was suddenly quiet, except for the dull pinging sound of bullets hitting the side of the building.

"Come out now, Landers, and I might spare you!" Moss growled.

There was no sound or movement. Moss made his way around a tall stack of straw bales, his eyes taking in his surroundings, including the rafters. He was almost sure Landers was now unarmed.

"You don't have a weapon, Landers! Don't make me shoot an unarmed man. Come on out!"

Still nothing. Moss kept a tight grip on his shotgun, moving toward the back of the building. His side burned where a bullet had grazed it. But he ignored the pain and the blood that now stained his shirt. All he could think of was Amanda. He had to find Landers and he had to make the man tell him what Lloyd Duncan had done with her! Mandy! Mandy! His chest felt tight and painful. His head throbbed with the horrible realization that he had again failed the only person who had ever mattered to him besides his little girl. She'd never survive another abduction and rape. Her mind wouldn't be able to take it.

"Landers!" he roared in desperation. He heard a noise behind him and whirled, just in time to feel the searing pain in his upper arm: pain caused by a heavy bale of hay shoved hard against him from a position to his right and slightly above him. The jolt knocked him to the floor and caused his gun to fire. But only one barrel went off. Moss rolled on the floor a moment, the pain in his arm excruciating, as delicate nerve ends had been reawakened by the blow. He groaned and grunted, having to use the same arm to help get himself back up. But when he reached a sitting position he caught Ralph Landers before him, poised with a pitchfork and ready to ram it into Moss's middle.

There was no time to hesitate or to allow the awful pain in his arm to stop him. It all happened in a fraction of a second. Moss had kept hold of the shotgun, and now he managed to raise it with the almost useless arm and fire just as Landers threw the pitchfork. Moss rolled away at the same time he fired, not even sure if he hit Landers. The fork caught his shirt near the spot where he was already wounded in the side, one prong piercing the flesh. Moss cried out, literally pinned facedown to the dirt floor now, the pitchfork sticking out behind him. Then, all was silent.

Moss cursed himself for having shot Landers without getting the information; yet to fire had been his only recourse. He tried to rise, but fell facedown again, screaming out from the combined pain of his arm and his side. He lay flat, envisioning Etta lying in the kitchen—probably dead from his own bullet—and Amanda, desperate and alone somewhere in the deserts of Utah or Arizona. He cursed the cruel turns life often took, and cursed himself for ever having come to Wyoming. He gritted his teeth, growling in pain and desperation, wanting to let go and weep loudly over the thought of Amanda being hurt again.

The door finally slid open, amid gunfire, and Moss half expected to now take a bullet in the back. But in the next moment Sooner was bending over him.

"Jesus Christ!" the man mumbled. He yanked out the pitchfork, and Moss cried out again. Then he reached down and lifted Moss around the chest.

"Amanda!" Moss groaned. "Duncan's got…Amanda."

"Here, sit down on this bale of hay," Sooner told him. Moss sat down, panting and putting a hand to his side, feeling more pain in his arm as he did so. He looked down at Landers, who lay on his back with half his neck blown away. Then he looked at Sooner, who was kicking at the body.

"He won't be givin' Etta no more problems," the man said quietly.

"Etta's…dead," Moss moaned. Sooner looked at him in surprise. "Landers…pushed my gun. She's dead…by my own gun." Moss blinked back tears. "I know by where the bullet hit…she's dead…or at least dyin'. And Mandy's been kidnaped by Lloyd Duncan." Moss bent over and groaned out her name.

"Take it easy, boss. We'll finish cleanin' out this mess and we'll get that wound taken care of and get down to Utah. We'll find her, Moss. We can find anything, you know that."

"It'll be too late," Moss groaned. "Too late."

Both men were brought back to matters at hand as two Landers' men rushed inside for cover. Sooner raised his rifle and fired, and one man screamed out and fell. The other turned to fire back, but Moss's handgun was out in a flash, in spite of the painful arm, and the quick bullet caught the man in the forehead before he could get off a shot. Seconds later there was the sound of galloping horses, as what was left of the Landers' men rode off. Then silence.

Sooner grasped Moss about the waist and helped him walk outside. What they saw was nothing less than a virtual battlefield. Landers' men and even some of their horses lay everywhere. Some of the windows of the house were broken from bullets. Moss looked around stunned, as some nearby ranchers rode in now, ready to do battle. Tucker men came out from hiding places, Lonnie Drake holding a wounded shoulder and Dwight Brady tying a neck scarf around his wounded thigh.

"We lost Max," Johnny Pence said quietly. "Took a bullet right in the brisket."

The ranchers and Pappy Lane dismounted, and the group of men were strangely quiet, all watching Moss, waiting for their next order. Moss swallowed, still holding his side.

"Etta's dead, shot with my own rifle," he told them brokenly. "Landers shoved the barrel. She's in the kitchen."

Slim Taggart rushed inside to check. Moss looked around at the neighbors who had come to help.

"It's all over now," he told them. "And I'll be leavin' right quick. Landers said—he said one of the men went down to Utah and they've taken my wife as bait to get me away from here."

Several of the Tucker men cursed under their breath.

"We're sorry, Tucker," one rancher told him. "We don't believe that about you shootin' the sheriff neither."

"Why didn't they wire us about Amanda?" Pappy asked heatedly.

"They did," Moss replied. "Etta took the wire. She never showed it to me. Didn't want me to go."

"Good God in heaven!" Johnny Pence hissed. "How could she—"

"I don't want her cursed now," Moss groaned. "She...had reasons for the way she was. I can't curse her now. We'll get things straightened around here, ride into town tonight, and get a confession out of Miles Randall. He's gonna tell us who shot the sheriff and what Duncan's done with Amanda! Then we're ridin' south!"

"We're with you, Moss!" Tom Sorrells spoke up. "And we'll find her! Don't you worry about that! And Lloyd Duncan will scream for mercy before we get through with him!"

Moss eyed them all. "Some of you boys were with me before. I still owe you for that."

"Ain't nothin' due us. Not when somebody like Amanda is involved," Johnny Pence spoke up. "We rode with you once to find her and we'll do it again, even if it means goin' back down into Apache country!"

The statement brought a temporary silence. Moss had not even considered that going to Tucson would mean riding through Indian country. Most were on reservations now, but the hills were full of renegade Apache who refused reservation life. And Duncan would have to ride alone. He wouldn't be able to stick to towns and trains until he got to Tucson—not when he had a prisoner along. He'd know the law and soldiers would be searching for him. Johnny immediately was sorry for presenting the obvious new danger there would be for Amanda.

"Hey, maybe Duncan didn't even get away with it," he suggested. "Maybe Amanda is alive and well right now, just sittin' on the porch waitin' for you. She is well guarded, you know."

"We'll check when we get into town," Moss replied. "Maybe there's another message. I don't even know what the first wire said for sure. Maybe…" He blinked back tears and furiously wiped at his eyes with his shirt-sleeve, suddenly feeling tired and weak and desolate. "Maybe, uh—"

Taggart appeared at the kitchen door. "Moss, you'd better come in here. Etta's not dead yet, but she's in a bad way. She's askin' for you."

Moss looked toward the door with mixed emotions. Etta Landers Graceland had betrayed him in the worst way; yet now she lay dying, and the fact remained it was his own bullet that had wounded her. The fact also remained that he'd loved her once. He walked wearily to the door, assisted by Sooner. Outside, men began checking bodies for life.

Moss stared down at the beautiful woman he'd once almost married. Her skin was even whiter now: pale, deathly. An ugly red hole gaped from between the deep cleavage, and blood ran profusely over the full breasts, trickling off her shoulders onto the floor. She looked up at him with blue, vacant eyes and blinked. He knelt down close to her, reaching behind her head with his hand and ignoring the pain in his arm. She tried to smile.

"It's…yours now…" she gasped. "The ranch. My safe… in my bedroom…papers there. It's all…legal. You…bring… Mandy here. She'd…like it here."

"Etta," he groaned, tears running down his face openly now.

"Not…your fault. Tell me…you loved me, Moss. You did…still love me…didn't you?"

He choked in a sob and bent closer, pressing his face against hers.

"I love you," he whispered in her ear.

"I…knew it," she whimpered. "I knew it."

She let out a pitiful gasp and grasped his arm.

"Moss!" Her body arched, and Moss clung to her, feeling the last breath of life against his neck as she exhaled. The hold on his arm weakened. Then her hand fell to the floor. He kept hold of her and wept, the broad shoulders shaking as he hunched over her, remembering for a moment another time and another place.

Slim and Sooner looked at each other in sorrow and resignation. The battle was over, and no one had really won.

Chapter Forty-One

Amanda strained at the rawhide that bound her wrists to the trunk of a tree, her arms stretched over her head. She closed her eyes and tried to control her panic, wriggling to get the sharp point of a rock away from her back where it poked into her and hurt her through her dress. She was weak, tired, and hungry, and worst of all, she was near insanity from the rough treatment Duncan had handed her.

So far he had not raped her, but only because he'd been in too much of a hurry. She was sore and feeling ill from the countless hours on horseback and the constant struggle to keep away from his prying hands; her wrists bled badly now from the leather straps that were never removed. The hair that had been in a bun when he captured her was now hanging long and loose, tangled and dirty.

They were somewhere in the deserts of Arizona, headed for the dreaded house of prostitution he had spoken of, and she continued her endless prayers to be rescued from such a fate. Always she tried to concentrate on Moss. Was he dead? Was he armless? What horrid thing had happened to him up in Wyoming? Had it been the day she awoke to the sound of his voice calling her? Perhaps she had been right after all to think then that something terrible had happened.

"Oh, Moss!" she whimpered, wondering where she found any more tears to cry, considering her terrible thirst. What horror it would be for him to feel someone cutting into the only good arm he had. It was almost a worse torture than the thought of being sold to a pimp in some house of filth in Tucson.

She pressed together lips that were cracked and swelling.

Everything hurt, and she was grateful at least for the shade Duncan had managed to find for her. But she was also worried. He sat nearby, drinking. For some reason he had apparently decided it was time for a day of rest. But she didn't want him to rest. It gave him too much time to sit and look at her, and think about his manly needs.

Duncan took another slug of whiskey, wiping his lips and watching her lie there whimpering. And then he pictured Moss in bed with Etta, taking what belonged to Lloyd Duncan. If not for her love for Moss, Etta would still be in love with Lloyd. Perhaps he'd have even been married to her by now, sharing the riches of the E.G. Instead, Moss Tucker had not only outdone him in a fist fight with only one arm, but he'd apparently outdone him in bed also; Lloyd Duncan burned with jealousy. He kept watching Amanda—young, still fresh. She'd never had a child yet. And she was Moses Tucker's woman. Young, fresh, pretty, and Moses Tucker's woman. And right now he needed a woman himself. What difference would it make to the man who would buy her in Tucson?

He got up and walked over to her, and she suddenly stiffened when he came near, ready to kick him, scream, and struggle the best she could. This man was not only responsible for trying to cut off Moss's arm—and possibly for his death—but his treatment of her could very likely cause her to lose the precious life in her belly. She had begged with him, told him about her tender pregnancy, hoping it would touch something inside of him and make him take her back. But nothing had worked. She was more certain than ever that she was with child, and the thought of losing it was overwhelming, making her cry all the more—and making Duncan clobber her for her simpering. So long! So long she had tried to get pregnant! To have it end this way—to lose Moss, lose the baby, and to suffer the horrors of a house of prostitution—she could not help but wonder why God would allow her to suffer this way after all she had been through. She and Moss had found such happiness together. Surely God meant for it to last longer than this! Surely He would hear her pleadings.

Duncan bent over her, his eyes glittering from whiskey and desire. She tossed her head, pleading with him with her eyes and mouthing the word no. But he only grinned and unbuttoned his pants. She closed her eyes, refusing to look upon another man, and she heard him chuckle. He viciously ripped open the front of her dress, and she kicked upward with her knee, managing to jolt him but not with much force. He raised up and punched her across the cheek with his fist, and everything began spinning. She heard more tearing and felt her body being exposed to the air. She knew she was screaming now, tortured at the thought of another man looking at her, wanting to fight him but too weak to do so. She kicked again, slamming her foot into Duncan's middle and sending him reeling backward, surprised at the fight she had left in her.

Duncan crawled back toward her, cursing and brushing dirt from his face. She felt a heavy weight on her stomach and smelled whiskey on the breath close to her face. Then there was a strange jolt and near her ear a terrible scream from the mouth of Lloyd Duncan. She felt more pressure on her, and she opened her eyes, looking beyond Duncan to a circle of renegade Apache Indians.

She shook with worse fear than she had known to this point, thinking only of the horror stories she'd heard about Apache torture and rape. Moss had told her it wasn't all true, but as she looked at the tangle-haired, dark-skinned and wild-eyed men who stood around her now, it was difficult for her to think otherwise. And it had been Apache who'd caused Moss to lose his arm.

One of the renegades bent down and grasped Duncan's lifeless body, throwing it aside. Amanda looked over at it and saw a tomahawk protruding from the man's back. She let out a desolate moan and wept, praying at the same time.

Now the Indian came closer. He remained standing at first, straddling her naked body and staring down at her with bloodshot eyes. His bronze, muscular arms glistened with oil and sweat. He wore only a loin cloth, and his legs and thighs were powerful. An apronlike piece of material hung at the front and back of his loin cloth, and a maze of silver and turquoise beads and necklaces draped the broad chest. He wore enough weapons for an army, and a red band was tied around his forehead.

He went to his knees, his dark eyes capturing hers, filling her with the worst dread she had ever known. This man would not only likely rape her, but his friends would take their turns as well. What physical torture might they devise for her?

Her devastation knew no bounds as he reached out and took her face in his hands; yet his touch was strangely gentle. He sat straddled over her belly now, and she expected him to drop the loin cloth and perform a hideous act, but he only pushed some hair back from her face.

"You are...lovely," he said in an unexpectedly gentle voice. Did he intend to try to seduce her, rather than beat her into submission? She trembled violently, sure she would vomit any moment if he touched any other part of her body. She automatically began to struggle, and he tightened his grip on her hair with one hand, while with the other he pulled out a huge, ugly-looking knife. Her eyes widened, and she made a sound like a wounded animal.

"Don't hurt me! Please don't hurt me!" she whimpered.

He laid the knife against her cheek and bent close to her face.

"And do you think Apache bucks are cowardly like the white trash who was beating you?" he hissed.

She just stared at him, not knowing what he wanted her to say, trying to think.

"My husband...tells me the Apache men...are the bravest he has known," she managed to choke out. "To take a woman against her will...is not being very brave."

If not for his fierce, unkempt look, she could have sworn a smile passed over his lips.

"You are clever with your words, white woman," he said in a near whisper, still straddled over her belly. "And perhaps..." He looked down at her breasts. "Perhaps you only say you have a man, and you only speak highly of the Apache because you think it will save you."

"I never lie," she found herself saying, wondering where she was finding the courage to speak at all. "My God does not allow me to lie...as yours does not. And you've...heard of my husband. He's considered a brave white warrior by the Apache. His name is Moses Tucker...and he has only one arm. One of your own kind...planted a hatchet in his other arm five years ago and he lost it."

He ran one hand over her breast and she grimaced.

"I know of Moses Tucker. We allowed him to go free once. And he is brave. But he is also white!" he spit out through teeth that seemed extra white against his dark face. "The Apache nation is dying because of the whites! Why should I do him another favor by not harming his woman!"

She swallowed. "Because if you rape me...and hurt me... you would be just like that white man over there," she said in a stronger voice, glancing at Duncan's body. She felt as though someone were putting the words in her mouth. "Is that what you want? To become the kind of man you detest? To be like a cowardly white man?"

This time a very faint smile crossed his lips, and he ran the knife lightly under her chin and down her chest, not cutting her but just frightening her.

"And," she went on, "because my husband is not like that man...and he respects the Apache...and because I am with child."

Her breath came in short gasps as the fear that had waned momentarily began to grow again when he casually circled her breast teasingly with the tip of the knife. When she spoke the last words, he moved the knife away from her skin and leaned closer again.

"I am Chano—what the white man calls a renegade. And

I like the way you speak. I think maybe you are as brave as your one-armed husband. Another white woman would have screamed and kicked and spit in my face, called me names!"

"I would not fight something my God sent to me."

He frowned, amused.

"I prayed to my God…for help. And you came. Would my God send me someone who would turn around and harm me?"

He snickered, sitting up straight again, still straddling her. He turned and said something to the band of renegades who rode with him, and they all chuckled. Then he barked some kind of order. One of the men ran off, and Chano bent over Amanda again. He studied her closely with flashing, dark eyes, resting the knife on her nose, then grinning a little. Amanda wondered why she didn't faint.

"We will take you to our camp and we will decide there what to do with you," he told her. He leaned farther forward and in one quick flash he cut the leather straps that bound her wrists. She closed her eyes and breathed a sigh of relief for at last having her hands free again. He cut the straps completely off her wrists and rubbed them gently, barking another order. Another man ran off.

The first man returned with a blanket. Chano moved off of her and laid the blanket over her, and she broke into tears at the relief of finally having their eyes off her naked body.

The second man returned with a pouch, and Chano dipped his fingers into it, coming out with something greasy looking on them. He rubbed the substance onto her wrists, and though it smelled bad, it made them feel much better. He pulled her blanket up a moment and rubbed some onto the scratches and cuts on her legs. She was too weak to object. He rolled her onto her stomach and rubbed more onto her thighs and buttocks and back, then wrapped the blanket completely around her and picked her up in his arms.

"You shouldn't cry. Your God sent us, remember?" He laughed again, but it was not a cruel laugh. He seemed to be more amused than anything else. He hoisted her up on his spotted horse and eased his way onto the horse's back in one swift motion. He barked another command, and they were off, to what destination or fate, she did not know.

• • •

"No! No!" Miles Randall screamed, writhing on the floor. Moss Tucker's knee was in his gut and the man's .45 jammed against his throat. "Get him off me!"

Tucker men, a few Landers' men, and miscellaneous ranchers and townspeople alike stood around in the lobby of the hotel, where Tucker had thrown Randall to the floor after rousting him out of bed and kicking him down the stairs. It was now two o'clock in the morning, and the sleepy Miles Randall was at first confused, just now beginning to realize what must have happened. Moss's arm ached furiously, and his side was still bleeding through the quick bandage job Pappy had done.

"Help me! Somebody help me!" Randall whimpered, staring at the wild-eyed man who held him down.

"You're gonna talk, Randall, or, by God, you're gonna suffer!" Moss growled, ramming his knee harder into Randall's belly. Randall whimpered.

"Where's Ralph? What have you done with Ralph?"

"Your lover's dead, Randall! And you're gonna be dead if you don't tell me what Duncan's done with my wife! And tell these people I didn't kill the sheriff!"

Randall's face paled and tears welled in his eyes.

"Ralph's…dead?" he asked.

Moss smiled. "You break my heart, Randall!"

"But he…" The man choked in a sob. "He loved me!"

"My God!" someone muttered. A few others gasped and some left the room. Sooner turned purple with rage at the thought of the simpering Miles Randall being partially responsible for what had happened to Amanda. He grabbed one of Randall's arms and yanked it over flat against the floor, stepping on the man's wrist with one foot and stomping on the palm of his hand with the heel of his boot.

Randall screamed out in the terrible pain, and a few men had to look away. But not a single Tucker man averted his eyes or even winced. Sooner knelt down at Randall's head and grasped the man's hair tightly, while Moss continued to hold the .45 to his throat.

"Mister, you talk fast 'cause I'm half Indian, and it would do my heart good to slit off your balls and cram them in your mouth—after I scalp you!" Sooner hissed. "And then it would still be Moss's turn to have his piece of you! Now you tell these people here who shot Sheriff Tillis!"

"Ralph! Ralph shot him!" the man screamed out. "He did it to frame Tucker! Please! Please don't hurt me again!"

There were murmurs in the crowd, and their anger began to build.

"And where's my wife!" Moss growled.

Randall's breath came in short, terrified gasps.

"D-Duncan—he was supposed to…kidnap her and take her to…a whorehouse in Tucson!"

Moss began to tremble, and the room quieted.

"Which one?" Moss asked in a desperate whisper.

"I—I don't know! He said the owner—he buys young women and drugs them until they're broken in! I—I don't know which house—I swear!"

Moss was visibly shaken, and sweat broke out on his forehead. He suddenly and viciously slammed his gun barrel across Randall's face, splitting open the man's cheek. Randall screamed in horror as blood spilled over his face and down his throat. Moss got up off the man and turned to look at the crowd.

"You do what you want with him. My name's cleared. I'm headin' for Tucson."

He stumbled and grasped the reception desk, enveloped in the horror of what Randall had told him. Even if Duncan didn't make it to Tucson, he was susceptible to being caught on the way by outlaws of the wrong nature—or by renegade Apache. Either way, Amanda's fate could be nothing but torture and death. If she did make it to Tucson, the humiliation of what would happen to her there would break her completely. And what of Duncan himself? He was an angry and jealous man. It was likely he would use Amanda for some of his own revenge.

"Let's hang him!" someone shouted.

The crowd began to mumble among themselves, and more agreed with the first man. Sooner let go of Randall's hair and the man began trying to crawl away, crying, weeping, and begging with the crowd. Someone grabbed him and jerked him up, then shoved him over to another man, who shoved him to another and yet another. They began taking turns at hitting and kicking the man, while another went for a rope; Randall screamed and pleaded with them. Minutes later they were dragging out a bloodied Miles Randall to string him up to the nearest rafter, and Moss enjoyed the man's screams.

Outside there was a din of voices now, and even laughter, mixed with shouts of anger and vengeance. Some of the Tucker men remained inside with Moss, who took out a telegram he discovered had been sent him that very day, and that still lay at the telegraph office.

"Where are you?" it read. "No reply from you. Have searched everywhere for Amanda. Becky okay now. You're the best tracker in these parts. Need you." Moss wadded up the telegram and threw it to the floor.

"When's the next train?" he asked Pappy in a strained voice, reaching into his pocket for a cigarette.

"About six hours yet," the man replied.

Moss lit the cigarette and took a deep drag, and the others stood around nervously, wishing they knew what to say to the man.

"String him high!" someone shouted outside. More screams from Miles Randall. Moss looked toward the doorway. His revenge toward the man who had once embezzled his little fortune was not as sweet as he thought it would be. The price had been too high.

"Don't forget you've got Becky," Pappy spoke up. "She loves you, Moss."

Moss stared at him with bloodshot, tired eyes.

"Man like me can't raise no daughter alone. She needs..." He swallowed. "She needs a woman." He took another deep drag, almost choking in his efforts not to break down in front of the men. "The E.G.—it's mine now." He smiled sadly. "That's a laugh, isn't it? What the hell do I care about the E.G.! What good is anything without her!"

The last words were growled, and he kicked viciously at the bottom portion of the boxlike reception desk, knocking a hole right through it.

"Take it easy, Moss, you're wounded, you know," Darrell Hicks spoke up.

"Who gives a damn!" he roared. "If I don't find her—or even if I do and Duncan has done what he said he'd do, or if the Apache got her—it's not gonna make a hell of a lot of difference if I have one arm or no arms, or if I'm alive or dead!"

"You don't know nothin' for certain," Lonnie Drake reminded him.

"Well, what kind of odds would you give her! Duncan was jealous and mad! And the Apache! Jesus Christ, there's no way to predict what an Apache renegade will do! If they put a mind to torturin' her..." He closed his eyes and leaned over the desk top, covering his eyes with his hand. "Jesus!" he whispered. His shoulders shook.

The others sighed in anger and frustration, looking at each other, each hoping the other would know what to say. Finally, Johnny Pence walked up and hesitantly put a hand on Moss's shoulder.

"You're forgettin' a few things, Moss. You're forgettin' there's somethin' special about her that shines right through, somethin' that could even make an Apache think twice. She's braver, now that she's been around you so long—learned from you, and she's stronger—and she's a smart woman, Moss. Maybe even smart enough to fast-talk her way out of a bad situation. You know the Apache better than any of us. If she gets caught and stays calm, tells them who she belongs to and all..." He shrugged. "Who knows? You shouldn't be thinkin' the worst. And remember the faith of hers. You think that God of hers is gonna let somethin' bad happen to her twice?"

Moss rubbed his eyes, then wiped at them with his shirt-sleeve.

"I don't know what to think any more. All I know is the Apache are as unpredictable as the wind. You can put two of them together and reason with one, while the other one is plannin' how long he'll take to cut your guts out while you're tied to stakes. There's no way in hell to be sure what they'd do. And there's no way in hell to be sure what Lloyd Duncan would do, but I've got a pretty damned good idea! Let alone that whorehouse!"

Miles Randall's screams were louder than ever now, and were followed by a strange gagging sound. The crowd had quieted, and for a moment there was no sound at all.

"Let's all get a drink!" someone finally shouted. "Maybe we can get some law and order back in this town after tonight. And to hell with our debts to Miles Randall!"

There was more cheering, and most of the crowd wandered away, leaving a strangled, dangling Miles Randall, whose feet were still kicking.

The rest of Moss's men came inside the hotel lobby, along with the owners of two ranches that adjoined the E.G. One of them stepped up to Moss and removed his hat.

"Mr. Tucker, uh, I know things didn't all work out too good. We, uh, the others and I—we hope you find your wife and all. And we're sorry about Etta Landers."

Moss studied him a moment, then looked away and paced.

"You had no hand in what Lloyd Duncan has done," he told the man. "And you had every reason to hate Etta Landers." He turned to face the man. "The E.G. is mine now. Whether or

445

not I come back to it depends on what's happened to my wife. But if I sell it, I'll be sure that water rights are a stipulation."

The man looked down at the floor and fumbled with his hat.

"We're real grateful, Mr. Tucker." He raised his eyes to Moss again. "We, uh, we'd be glad to keep an eye on the place while you're gone. Mrs. Webster could stay there and tend the house, and I reckon among all of us we can spare a few men to keep the chores done and all."

"I appreciate that," Moss replied. He paced again. "I guess we have to wait for that damned train. It's faster than riding, but it's gonna be a long damned six hours till it gets here."

Chapter Forty-Two

Buck Donner looked over at the doorway of the Tucker cabin as Moses Tucker filled its frame. He looked away again, taking another drink of whiskey and leaning forward in the homemade wooden rocker, staring blankly at the fireplace and waiting for the physical pain that he was sure Moss Tucker would inflict upon him, and which he was equally sure he deserved.

"Becky's stayin' with Wanda over at her cabin," he said in a distant voice.

Moss looked around the familiar room. Every part of it spoke of Amanda Tucker: every ruffled curtain, every vase, every neatly set piece of china in the heavy wooden cupboard. Buck remained turned away. Moss said nothing at first, but lumbered toward the bedroom, needing to see it—needing to see her clothes, to smell her perfume. He walked through the bedroom door and slammed it shut, and Buck Hanner put his face in his hands and cried like a small boy.

In the bedroom Moss shed quiet tears of his own. He'd already heard the news of the wire from Tucson. He had sent his own wire from Rock Springs before leaving, telling Buck to send someone down to Tucson to check out every whorehouse there. But none of them had turned up an Amanda Tucker. It seemed now that she had simply disappeared, and there was only one conclusion any of them could come to. Apache!

Moss sat down wearily on the bed, then stretched out on his back. It had been a long, grueling trip home; he'd stopped for nothing but a bite of jerky once in a while, other than sleeping no more than two or three hours at a time between rides that lasted sixteen to twenty hours. The man and the horses

447

both were spent. His side ached, and his arm still ached. It was still bandaged, and still prone to fits of numbness.

He closed his eyes and rolled onto his stomach, and stared at the pillow beside him. He pictured her lying there the way she had looked that morning he'd made love to her twice in a row. He heard her light laughter as she teased him about being late and embarrassing her. He could feel the softness of her hair, smell her light perfume, taste the sweet, young lips, and he could see the slender thighs that opened for him and let him come inside to a place she would never willingly allow another man to enter. He remembered her telling him he shouldn't go to Wyoming just for vengeance. She'd been right. He'd sworn that was not the real reason, but down deep inside he knew it was. Amanda had been right to warn him, but now she was the one who had suffered because of his own stupidity. Why did men do such stupid things? Why were they so prone to live by their temper and animal instincts? Yet she had not complained nor tried too hard to interfere with his decision. Because he was her husband—the man of the house—and she loved him.

He closed his eyes, groaning out a long breath of desire for his wife, whom he'd pictured lying there beside him, waiting for him to come, but who was now gone. The pain it brought in the pit of his soul seemed unbearable, and he realized how easy it would be right now to put a revolver to his head and pull the trigger. Amanda had been the only really good thing that had ever come into his worthless life, the only thing to give it purpose. Yet there was still Becky: his golden-haired little girl, the child he had decided to fiercely protect from any suffering the very moment he picked her up and held her in his arms. But he'd had Amanda then. He'd found a woman to be a mother to his child. How could a forty-three-year-old ex-outlaw and poorly-educated man raise a little girl alone? And how could he ever find a woman to replace Amanda? She was dead. He was sure of it. Yes, he would continue to look for her. But he had to face the fact that there was little hope of finding her alive.

The grief and his total exhaustion converged on him to force him into a much-needed but fitful sleep.

• • •

A few hours later Buck Donner walked hesitantly into the bedroom. He stood for a moment and stared down at Moses Tucker, hating himself for the agony the man must be suffering. He hated to wake Moss, but there was no choice. Soldiers had come. Besides, Moss hadn't wanted to sleep too long. His intention was to rest a while, visit with Becky, and be off again in search of his wife. Donner bent down and nudged Moss's shoulder. Moss stirred and moaned, and Buck nudged him once more.

"Boss? You gotta wake up."

Moss moved slightly, trying to rouse from a deep sleep brought on by the shock and overexertion of the past several days. He reached over to the other side of the bed and pulled the pillow to him.

"Mandy?" he mumbled.

A pain shot through Buck Donner's chest. He shook Moss harder.

"Boss, you gotta get up. There's soldiers here."

"What?" Moss turned onto his back and looked up at Buck, his face haggard and more aged.

"Soldiers. They found something."

Moss bolted out of the bed and charged through the door into the main room, where an army captain stood in his blue uniform, holding a bundle of clothes. Moss froze in place, glancing down at the clothes.

"I'm Captain Fallows, Mr. Tucker," the man said, almost apologetically. "My men and I—we've been searching also. We found these clothes. I wasn't sure if they belonged to your wife. We continued our search, but to no avail. I'm afraid, Mr. Tucker, that we simply have to give it up, sir. There's nothing more we can do."

Moss rubbed a hand across his chest as though in pain. He stepped closer to the captain and reached out for the dress, which was in shreds. There was no doubt that it had been ripped off a woman's body. He let it fall full length, and Buck Donner turned away, trembling with rage. It was Amanda's.

"Where'd you find it?" Moss asked coldly.

The captain swallowed. "Down in Arizona, Mr. Tucker, in a remote canyon. There was a dead body next to it—a man's body with an Apache tomahawk in his back."

"Oh, God!" Buck moaned, running a hand through his hair.

Moss laid the dress across the back of a chair, noticing some blood stains on it.

"Where? I mean, exactly where?" he growled at the captain.

"Mr. Tucker, you can't go there. It would be suicide."

"I'm already dead, mister!" Moss barked. "So that part don't matter! Now I want to know exactly where you found them things. I have to try. I have to at least try to find out what happened to her. I have to know for my own peace of mind!"

"But, Mr. Tucker, we've already searched and searched. You know how those renegades are. They melt right into the rocks. They're—they're like ghosts. There have been many times when we've sent hundreds of men in search of two or three Indians, and they come back empty-handed. And there have been other times when soldiers have ridden where they think it's safe, only to suddenly discover they're completely surrounded by Apache who seem to literally rise up out of the ground. It's no use, Mr. Tucker."

Moss lurched at the man, grabbing him by a lapel and jerking him forward.

"You tell me where you found that dress!" he roared, his eyes looking like those of a crazy man.

Captain Fallows stared at him in shock for a second, thinking how useless it was to search.

"All right, Mr. Tucker," he replied calmly. "Let go of me, please."

Moss released him and the captain straightened his jacket.

"I'm sorry," Moss told him. "But I have to try, captain, even if it means I'll get myself killed. Besides, I've had experience with the Apache. This stub of an arm is testimony to that."

The captain looked at the arm and frowned. "Then you know the odds, Mr. Tucker."

"Better than most."

The captain nodded. "All right. It was down past the Painted Desert, south of White Mountain but north of the Salado River."

"Thank you," Moss told him. "You go on back to wherever you're stationed. I appreciate your efforts. But I have an edge."

"Oh? And what is that?"

"Them renegades would never show themselves to soldiers. But civilians like myself—that might draw them out, whether for friendly reasons or to kill us. But at least I'd have a chance to talk to some of them. If they show themselves to us, maybe I can at least find out for sure about my wife. If I don't go down there and find out, I'll always wonder. And that's as bad or worse than knowin' she's dead. She could be a slave to some Apache buck, or they could have sold her to the Utes, or the Mexicans. God only knows. And to go on livin' and not knowin' would be to live in hell."

The soldier sighed. "I understand, Mr. Tucker." He put out his hand. "Good luck, sir."

Moss shook the man's hand and nodded. "Thanks. God knows I'll need it."

"You'll let me know if you find her? You can wire me at Fort Defiance."

"Sure. I'll let you know."

"Good. Good-bye then, Mr. Tucker."

Moss nodded again and the soldier went through the door. Moss turned to Buck, who had his hands braced against the fireplace mantle his head hanging down in remorse. Both men stood silent for a moment.

"Why don't you shoot me or beat me—have me whipped

or something?" Buck asked in a strained voice. "I deserve it. I'm the one who was supposed to be keepin' an eye on her that day."

Moss studied the man a moment and then walked closer to him, putting a hand on the younger man's shoulder.

"Buck, when I first heard I wanted to kill every last man I'd left behind to take care of her," he said quietly. "But then I remembered five years ago, when Rand Barker got his hands on her. It was me that supposed to be watchin' out for her then, Buck. Me! But one of Barker's men fooled me and had a gun in her side before I could blink and realize what was happening. And I failed her, Buck. I failed her. How can I blame another man when I've made the same mistake myself? Besides, I should never have left her. She didn't really want me to go, but I went anyway. I've got nobody to blame but me, Buck. Nobody else. And there's no way in hell I'd believe you didn't do your best."

Hanner made a choking sound and threw his head back, fighting tears. "I, uh, just stayed at the house...a few extra minutes, Moss! Wanda was decorating a cake...to surprise Becky with for her birthday."

Moss sighed. "You comin' with, Buck?"

"If you want me."

"I do. I'm goin' to wash my face and change my shirt and go see Becky. And then I'm gonna head out."

He lumbered back toward the bedroom.

"Moss?" Buck spoke up.

Moss turned. "Yeah?"

"I love that woman."

Moss frowned, unsure how to react.

"Not like you think. I mean I love her, you know? Every last man jack out there loves her. And if you find her, you'd better keep treatin' her good or you're gonna have about twenty men tryin' to take her away from you."

Their eyes held, and then Moss grinned a little.

"I expect I'd better walk easy then, hadn't I?"

Buck wiped at tears and smiled himself.

"I expect so, boss." He swallowed and looked at the floor.

"You leavin' somethin' out, Buck?"

The young man bit his lip nervously. "Yeah," he said in a near whisper. "I am. Your wife was—she was pregnant, Moss. She told me herself before—before she disappeared. Leastways she was pretty sure of it."

Moss closed his eyes and looked as though someone had plunged a knife into his chest.

"My God!" he whispered. "She wanted that for so long!"

"I'm sorry, Moss. Goddamned sorry."

Moss took a deep breath and opened his eyes.

"Go round up the men. Tell them to be ready to ride yet tonight. We need fresh horses and plenty of food and water. We're ridin' into Apache country, and we're gonna find Amanda Tucker or die trying!"

Buck grinned a little. "Yes, sir! Ain't one man out there who'll not want to go along."

Buck rushed out the door and Moss went back into the bedroom. He stared at the crucifix and the rosary beads she kept on the dresser. He reached out and touched the crucifix lightly.

"Don't you fail her again," he said in a choked voice. "She's been faithful to you, a good servant. It's not right you should fail her. And if I find her dead or worse than dead, I'll curse you for the rest of my life!" He choked on a sob, gritting his teeth and grasping the crucifix tightly, then tossing it to the floor.

• • •

They rode in a long, silent string, their shirts stained dark with sweat, their thighs displaying revolvers, their rifles loaded and ready, all with one purpose in mind: to find Amanda Tucker. There were ten now: Darrell, Pappy, Johnny, Tom, Bullit, Buck, Dwight, Sooner, Lonnie, and Moss. Brad Doolittle had stayed behind at the ranch, and Slim Taggart had gone home to his wife and two children, after much objecting. It wasn't that he didn't long to go home. It was only that he, too, was fond of Amanda. His own wife was a former prostitute, but she was a good woman, and she and Amanda had become very good friends. Amanda had given Wilena Taggart a certain pride in herself that she had never had before. Moss knew Wilena would surely want Slim to stay, however; for he'd been gone long enough, and Moss felt Slim had done more than his share by leaving to go to Wyoming in the first place.

Those who were left were the same shiftless, homeless men who had gone to Wyoming with Moss, and four of them—Darrell, Pappy, Johnny, and Lonnie—had been among the original men who had helped Moss search for Amanda five years earlier.

There was a strange and understanding silence among them. What Buck had said was true. They all loved her. And because of Amanda they all knew that at least once in a while they had a home at the Red "C". For they were always welcome there when they passed through. There was always a meal and a kind word, and they all fantasized that someday they, too, would find a woman like Moss Tucker had found. And yet they knew it was unlikely they would ever have homes or families of their own. Perhaps it would still happen for a few of those who were still relatively young, but it was not likely for the older ones. They all knew, and Moss himself knew, that Moss Tucker was simply one of the lucky ones. Women like Amanda did not cross a man's path every day, let alone pay attention to men such as they.

Their loneliness was something they would seldom admit to. All protested the idea of being tied to a woman's apron. All gambled and drank and whored around, laughing and often breaking the law, pretending life was nothing but fighting for the next dollar and not caring where it came from, sleeping with easy women and calling the entire "big sky country" their home. There was a certain freedom they were after, yet in spite of the way they lived freedom seemed to elude them, and they secretly knew it was men like Moss—who had a woman like

Amanda—that were truly free. For then they no longer had
to pretend to be happy. And the fact remained that the law of
nature demanded that a man should have a good woman at his
side. For now, they all considered Amanda Tucker their woman
in a private, special way. And to lose her would not be a loss
just for Moss, but a loss to all of them. To lose Amanda would
leave a vacancy in all of their lives that could probably never
be filled again. For to look at her meant to hope for something
better for themselves.

"Storm coming!" Darrell hollered from behind.

Moss studied the ugly dark clouds ahead, as he had been
for at least the last hour.

"I see it!" he hollered back. "Keep goin' till you feel the
drops. The Little Colorado is up ahead a ways. We'll camp
there by the water."

It sounded good to all of them. They could bathe, and
Moss had promised that this time they would sleep five hours
instead of two or three. A half-hour later, as the sun's light
faded behind the ominous black cloud, their horses splashed
through the Little Colorado, and some of them jumped off and
literally fell into the cool wetness. Horses and men alike took
long drinks. Then there was a loud crack of thunder, and they
quickly prepared makeshift tents, four each in two tents and
Moss and Buck in a third.

The thunder rumbled and lightning split the blackness
of the sky while rain pelted the canvas over Moss and Buck's
heads. Buck stirred the fire, but they kept it low and near the
entrance to the tent to avoid the smoke as much as possible.
Moss sat quietly on his bedroll, staring at a trickle of water that
began to flow inside and smoking a cigarette.

"We in Apache country yet?" Buck asked him.

"Have been for quite a ways," Moss replied.

"Think there's any out there?"

"They're there—just waiting. From here on we've got to be
damned alert. These are renegades, not the ordinary Apache.
And ordinary is bad enough. But these men, they're the ones

that have fled the horrors of reservation life. They're the ones who've lost families, had their women raped, their villages burned to the ground, their children butchered in front of their eyes. These are the ones full of hate and violence. So that makes them that much more dangerous. But they're still honest men—brave and proud men—and if they're treated with respect, it's possible to reason with them."

"You think she'd be capable of reasoning with them?"

Moss sighed. "Hard to say. She's not one to ridicule anybody or speak bad to them. That could give her an edge. She always told me the Indian deserves to be loved as much as anybody else. We're all God's creatures."

"God creates some real monsters sometimes."

"He don't create them. They become that way. Who knows what the reasons are. Sometimes they're legitimate."

Buck stirred the fire again.

"Moss, there's something—something maybe I should tell you, to save her the trouble. I'm sure she'd be the type to think she should tell you."

Moss moved his eyes to meet Buck's and puffed his cigarette quietly, waiting for the man to go on.

"I, uh, well, this one day I was in the house. And she was takin' a nap. She woke up real bad upset. Came to the door and looked like she was gonna pass out, cryin' and carryin' on about how she was sure something bad had happened to you. I mean, it was you she was hurtin' for, you know?" He moved his eyes away from Moss's and looked at the coals. "I felt sorry for her. I walked over to take her arm, 'cause I was sure she was gonna pass out or something. I mean, it was hot—awful goddamned hot—and she looked pale and was shakin' bad. And when I got close she just—just up and hugged me around the middle and cried against me. And then she…asked me to hold her for a while."

He swallowed, and Moss remained silent, taking inventory of the broad-chested Buck Donner who had two strong arms and was a good ten to fifteen years younger than Moss.

"She—she didn't mean nothin' by it, Moss. I mean, she was just feelin' damned scared for you and lonely. And she'd been carryin' the burden of that worry all alone, and knowin' she was pregnant on top of it, she just needed to give it over to somebody—to have somebody stronger than her hold her for a while. I felt real funny about it, but she was so—I don't know, pitiful, I guess you'd say, like a little girl, you know?" He finally met Moss's eyes again.

"I know," Moss replied. "God knows I've seen her that way many times."

"Well, I—I just thought you should know. I didn't mean no offense. And she—she felt real funny about it afterward. I know she worried about it, tried to figure out how she'd tell you about it."

Their eyes held in understanding.

"Thanks for tellin' me," Moss said quietly.

Buck swallowed nervously again, as though he was afraid Moss Tucker would swing the powerful right arm any moment.

"Well, I, uh, ain't the kind to move in on another man's woman or nothin' like that. I mean, she's special, you know? I felt sorry for her. I figured what are friends for? If holdin' her a minute would help, why not?"

He looked at the coals again.

"If I thought you meant somethin' else by it, your face would be restin' in them coals right now," Moss told him.

Buck glanced up at him, at first in fear, but he saw the teasing smile on Moss's lips. Moss put his hand out and Buck took it. They shook hands and continued the grip for longer than normal.

"Fact of the matter is, I'm glad you was there, Buck," Moss told him. "But don't ever let me catch you with your arms around my wife again."

They both laughed lightly and released hands.

"Hell, you old son of a bitch, once we find her there ain't nobody gonna be able to get near her!"

"That's a fact," Moss replied. "And I'll never leave her." He sobered and tossed his cigarette outside. "I don't know what I'll do if I don't find her, Buck. I just don't know what I'll do."

Buck reached over and grasped his shoulder. "We will find her, Moss. You'll see. We will find her."

Moss sighed and lay back on his bedroll. And the rolling thunder outside and the lonely raindrops only added to his desolation.

• • •

The storm had ended sometime during the night, and by the time they arose, the arid Arizona air had dried the tents. They all cursed the fact that the rain had not seemed to help anything. It was already hot when they packed their gear, and the ground was so dry that it seemed the storm must have only been an illusion.

They started to mount up, but Johnny Pence suddenly cried out. Everyone whirled to see an arrow sticking out of his shoulder.

"This is it! Find some cover!" Moss shouted, grabbing his horse's reins and yanking the animal behind a boulder with him. Arrows sang through the air and rifles were fired, but as yet they couldn't even see the Apache. Darrell Hicks bravely dragged Johnny into a gully with him, and it was then that a band of about twenty renegades charged toward them, yipping and howling with delight at finding someone to do battle with—let alone the weapons and supplies and horses they would take as bounty once the white men were dead.

"Make your shots count!" Moss hollered out, whipping out his .45 and taking aim himself. He fired, opening a hole in the dark-skinned chest of the warrior in front. The Indian yelped and fell from his horse.

"Right in the brisket!" Buck told him, cocking his own rifle. For the next few moments the gunshots were almost deafening, as they echoed over and over, the sound and bullets bouncing off rocks and multiplying the noise. Moss's heart pounded at the thought of wild-eyed renegades such as these coming across a soft white woman like Amanda. To think they might spare her was foolish. And it made him angrier. He fired again and again, each time making his shots count.

"Look out, Moss!" he heard Buck holler. "Behind you!"

Moss whirled as Buck fired, and one of the three Indians coming up behind them lurched forward, his face a bloodied mass of nothingness. The other two came at Moss. He fired twice, reacting fast and hitting his targets. But then three more were upon them, and Moss's gun was empty. With only one hand there was no way he could reload fast enough. Buck was busy shooting at more who came from the front again. Moss grabbed his Winchester and cocked it in midair, firing it with one hand and killing one more Apache. Then there was no time for any more shooting, as the other two came at him with hatchets, bringing back sickening memories; Moss Tucker knew for sure that he'd not let them get near his only good arm. They came fast, leering joyfully, their white teeth looking like fangs against the dark skin, black hair wild and tangled, bronze arms shining in the sunlight.

Moss pulled a knife from his boot and hunched over slightly, waving the knife and waiting for the two men to pounce. One swung at him with the hatchet, and Moss ducked, running head-on and unexpectedly into the man's belly. There was a loud grunt and a flash of steel, and Moss's blade struck deep into the soft flesh of the Indian's groin. It all happened in only one or two seconds, yet it seemed an eternity. Moss shoved the body hard, yanking the knife out as he did so and whirling to see the other Apache gleefully raising his arm to strike down with the hatchet. Moss tried to duck, lashing out with the knife at the same time and cutting a deep gash into the Indian's forearm. The movement made the Apache's blow falter, and the hatchet came down Moss's left side, skinning a piece of flesh off the stub of his missing left arm. The horror of having had his arm partially severed by an Apache in almost the same manner five years earlier only brought new rage to Moss, who quickly took advantage of the Indian's sudden imbalance and plunged his knife into the Apache's neck.

Moss backed up, panting and staring down at the five Apache he'd killed in a matter of seconds, and with only one arm. His rage at picturing Amanda with these men, combined with his memory of fighting them once before, kept the adrenaline flowing, and he whirled with gritted teeth, ready to face his next attacker. It was only then he realized that things had quieted. He looked over at Buck.

"What's goin' on?"

Buck turned and momentarily gaped at the dead Apache near Moss, who stood over them with the huge blade that dripped blood.

"Did you kill all them?"

Moss gritted his teeth. "With pleasure."

Buck looked back out over the boulder. "They left."

"They'll be back," Moss replied. "Stay low, men!" he hollered louder. "What's the damage?"

"Just the arrow in Johnny's shoulder!" came the shouted reply. "We're gonna pull it out and pour some whiskey on it!"

"Nobody else!"

"I lost the top of my ear to a bullet!" Tom Sorrells hollered. "Goddamn, I was bloody ugly enough to begin with!"

There was light, nervous laughter.

"You should see how many Moss got!" Buck bantered. "At leave five! Two or three with his knife!"

"That one-armed bastard has all the luck!" Lonnie Drake shouted from behind a rock somewhere. All of them needed to joke at the moment, sensing the dangerous situation they were in. But it was worth it if somehow they could find out about Amanda this way.

There was a heartrending cry, followed by a long groan, as Darrell Hicks yanked the arrow from Johnny's shoulder and poured whiskey into it. And then there was silence, as the long wait began.

They nestled down into their hiding places, smoking,

sweating, thinking their own thoughts, but mostly thinking about Amanda and wanting to puke at the thought of her being in the hands of men such as these. These were desperate men. Who knew how long they'd been entrenched in the torturous canyons and among the grotesque rocks of the Arizona deserts and mountains? And how long had they been in hiding without the softness of a woman? Just how far did their honor and bravery go? In spite of their ruthless fighting capabilities and their murderous raids, Moss held a certain respect for these red men who were fighting for a small piece of the vast land the whites had grabbed away from them. They were a desperate, deprived people, with nothing left to call home, and nothing to look forward to but death.

The long afternoon dragged, and Moss was nearly asleep from the heat of the sun when Buck nudged him.

"Look up there," the man said quietly. Moss moved his eyes to see a grand-looking Apache warrior, sitting on a rise not far off and wearing a headdress of many eagle feathers. He sat on a painted pony, holding a stick with a piece of white cloth tied to it.

"You have a one-armed warrior among you!" the Indian shouted.

"Don't nobody shoot!" Moss ordered his men. "This one knows something!"

"We do!" Sooner shouted back at the Indian.

"We wish to know if he is called Moses Tucker!" the Indian called back. Moss's heart pounded with hope and fear combined.

"I'm here!" he called back.

"You have guns, Moses Tucker!" the Indian hollered down to them. "And ammunition! Food and supplies! You will give them to us!"

"Come down here and try to take them, you son of a bitch!" Moses shouted back. The Indian grinned.

"You will give them to me, Moses Tucker!"

"In return for what?" Moses shouted.

"For your woman, Moses Tucker! Or do you not think she is worth trading for?"

Moss looked down at Buck, his feelings torn. What had these renegades done with Amanda?

"Come out from your hiding places and give up your weapons!" the Indian commanded. "Or you will die where you are and the woman will belong to me!"

Moss stepped forward, wondering if he would simply end up with an arrow in his chest or back. His men followed suit, appearing out from behind rocks and holding their weapons in the air. Perhaps they would die, but if this was the only way to find out about Amanda Tucker, then it would be worth it.

"Lay your weapons on the ground!" the Indian commanded, enjoying the hold he had over this group of brave white men. The small woman who had been his captive apparently had much power to bring men such as these to surrender their weapons. More warriors appeared and moved in, to collect the guns of the lonely men.

Chapter Forty-Three

Moss approached the Apache leader, who remained on his horse, smiling in his victory.

"What have you done with her?" Moss asked through gritted teeth.

The Indian's jaws flexed, showing the anger that lay beneath the smile.

"Why is it, my white friend, that the white man thinks it such a horror for an Indian to claim a white woman, yet he thinks nothing of raping and torturing and murdering Indian women!" The smile left the Apache's face, replaced by hatred. Moss's chest ached, and Sooner made a move toward the Indian.

"Stay where you are, Sooner!" Moss ordered. "They'll kill you sure as you're breathin'!"

The Indian smiled again. "The white man speaks the truth."

"Then I'll tell you somethin' else!" Moss hissed. "I've never laid a hand wrongly on any Indian woman, and there's not a man with me who has, either! There are some white men who hold women in the same honorable position as any of their own women. Only a coward would take his pleasure in a woman against her will, no matter how full of vengeance he is. Is that what you are, my Apache friend?"

The Indian lost his smile again.

"It is sometimes difficult to remember honor, when you have seen children butchered before your eyes!" the Indian snapped. "And when you are chained to a wagon, and forced to watch white men grovel in the dirt with your woman and then cut out her privates!"

Moss paled and his stomach churned. Somebody behind

him cursed. The Indian strutted his horse in a circle, as his warriors formed a tight circle around Moss and his men.

"However, Moses Tucker," the Apache went on, "when I saw this white woman tied and struggling with the while filth who was bent over her—and I remembered what happened to my own woman—I saw that the white man seems to have no preference for color when he has trouble controlling his man part. This seems to be a trait with many white men."

Moss studied him, his mind whirling with confusion, still racing with the slim hope.

"I did not like the pitiful sounds the white woman made, and I took out my vengeance on her attacker." The Indian dismounted and stepped up close to Moss, their eyes holding in what was beginning to be an understanding.

"I thought about finding out what a white woman is like," he went on, "as I stood over her naked body. And I thought about more vengeance. I also thought about how much she would be worth to the Mexicans. Many things passed through my mind as I stood there looking at her."

"Stop torturin' me with your words and tell me what you've done with her!" Moss growled, clenching his fist and longing to hit the man—or better yet, murder him. The Indian grinned a little again.

"Chano is not like the white coward who attacked her," he said quietly. "And I watched her eyes. They were wise, like a shaman—a medicine woman, a woman of faith. And do you know what she told me?"

Moss swallowed, daring now to hope that perhaps she was not harmed after all.

"She told me her God had sent us to help her!" The Indian snickered. "She looks straight into the eyes of an Apache renegade and says her God sent me to help her!" He laughed more and said something in his own tongue to his men, who all then joined in the laughter. Moss didn't know whether to smile or hit the man. The Apache continued seconds later, still smiling, "So, how can a man sent from God harm she who has prayed for him to come? I cut the rawhide that bound her wrists, and I took her to my camp."

"How do you know it's my woman in the first place?" Moss asked.

"She said you would come for her. She did not fail to tell me many times. She told me her husband was the white warrior who had lost one arm to the Apache. And she said you would probably kill me when you came, if I harmed her."

"She spoke the truth," Moss said flatly. The Indian grinned.

"I am sure she did. You and your men fight well, as brave as any Apache. When we attacked you, it was for your supplies. But then one of my warriors said there was a man here with one arm, and I knew the white woman had been right. Her man had come for her. It takes a brave man to walk into the nest of Apache renegades—or a man who thinks highly of his woman. I think she must be worth much to you—perhaps worth all of your weapons?"

"I'll give you anything you want if she's alive and well and I can take her home," Moss said quietly.

"Mmmm. I thought you would, Moses Tucker. And she is alive and well."

"And do I have reason to kill you?" Moss asked coldly.

Their eyes held.

"She is not like other white women, who stick their noses up at an Apache buck as though he were a rattlesnake," the man replied. "She is soft and good, like my woman was. And I would not hurt my own woman, would I?"

"You sayin' you made my Amanda your woman?" Moss hissed.

"I told you I am not a coward. She belongs to you only. And I will trade her—for your guns, and any whiskey you have, and most of your food. We are starving, Moses Tucker. But we will not go back to Bosque Redondo. We will not live on the reservation ever! We will die first!"

Moss put a shaking hand to his head and took off his hat, rubbing his sweaty forehead before putting it back on.

"Where is she?" he asked almost brokenly. "For God's sake, take me to her!"

"I will tell you that I spared her not just for honor. I spared her because she told me who her man was. Do you not remember me, Moses Tucker?"

Moss studied the man more closely. "Remember you from where?"

"Five years ago, your arm was half cut off by Apache warriors. The two warriors that you spared ran off. They came to me to tell me about the very brave white man who had killed six others. So we let you go free. But then the white outlaws found you—the ones who had paid us to attack you—and they did a very cowardly thing. They tied you and whipped you when you were bleeding to death and unable to fight them. I saw then that they were the cowards and they were the ones who deserved to die—not you. We saved you from death, Moses Tucker. And we learned that the outlaws had raped your woman and that was why you had come to Apache country to search for them. We allowed you to kill them yourself, and we allowed you to leave Apache country alive."

Moss frowned. "You? You were the one?"

"Ai. I am Chano."

"I was in so much pain. I don't remember the faces."

"You fight bravely and with honor. And you spoke the truth that day. Your woman is also brave, and speaks only the truth. She has not been harmed."

"She was pregnant."

"She is still with child."

Moss blinked back tears and looked back at the others, who were grinning. He turned back to Chano.

"You'd better be tellin' the truth!" he said brokenly. "Or you're a dead man, whether I've got one arm or not—even if I don't have any weapons!"

Chano grinned. "You and I are not so different, Moses Tucker. Except that you are white—and free. And I therefore request one more thing in exchange for your woman." He sobered, and his eyes filled with a sorrow that even Moss found himself sympathizing with.

"If my woman is truly unharmed and well, I'll do anything you ask, Chano. And I'll be forever indebted to you." He was struck by the fact that there actually seemed to be tears in the eyes of the wild Apache renegade. The man blinked and swallowed.

"I am not a fool, Moses Tucker," the man said in a strained voice. "There are only two roads now the Apache can travel. He must either live on a reservation—which is humiliating and unbearable—or he must live the life of a renegade, which only ends in starvation or death in battle. Either way, there is no future for the Apache among his own; yet most cannot hope to live in the white man's world."

"I don't get you, Chano."

Their eyes held.

"I have a son who has no mother, and no future," the man said quietly. "Your woman has taken a fondness to him, and he to her. And you are one of the few white men brave enough and strong enough to raise a son to be a man of courage and honor. There is nothing left for my son. Perhaps if you would take him…"

Moss could not hide his surprise and near shock. Nothing was more important to an Apache man than his sons. To give one up could only mean he held Moss and Amanda both in the highest regard. This was a totally shocking and unexpected turn of events. He studied the terrible pain in Chano's eyes, and his hatred of the man vanished.

"You want me to take your son?"

"His name is Lipan. He is only six summers, but he is good and already very brave. And he is quick to learn. Already your woman has taught him the white man's letters, and he writes his name in the sand, like a white man writes his name. To lose him will be to tear out my heart, but to keep him with me—knowing the kind of future he will have—is worse."

Moss rubbed his chin and turned to look at his men.

"That's the craziest thing I ever heard, Moss," Darrell spoke up. Moss looked back at Chano.

Chano's eyes were tired and desolate, the life seeming to have suddenly gone out of them. Moss tried to envision himself in the man's place, picture Becky living the life little Lipan was living. And he remembered a time when Becky's real mother had died and he himself was on his way to California to find a home for the child he loved but felt he could not care for. Then he'd met Amanda.

"My wife?"

"She is fond of the boy. And she has the wisdom and gentleness that he needs. She is not like other whites I have known. She has a love for all mankind."

Moss smiled lightly, blinking back tears and longing now more than ever to see her.

"That she does," he said quietly. "All right, Chano, I'll take your boy—if I find Amanda is all right."

"I want him to be a man—to learn to hunt, and shoot, and fend for himself. I want him to be of courage, to be honest. You will teach him these things?"

"I will."

"He must learn the white man's tongue well—learn to write it and read it. He must learn to live among the whites, but he must also never, never forget that he is an Apache! And he must never be ashamed of what he is!"

Moss put out his hand and they grasped wrists. "There is much to be proud of in being an Apache," Moss told him as they held a firm grip. "He will not be ashamed. Nor will he be allowed to forget his father. He will understand how much his father loved him by doing this thing."

The Apache nodded. "Get on your horse. I will take you to your woman."

• • •

They rode the rest of the day, deeper into the confusing maze of rock formations surrounding White Mountain. Finally, darkness came upon them, and they had to make camp. Moss and Chano sat near a fire and talked well into the night, and Moss could see that there was far too much hatred and bitterness within the heart of the Apache leader for the man to ever go back to a reservation or accept white men. And he knew that even his own life still hung in a delicate balance at the hands of this renegade, whose temper often flared as they talked about the coming of the white man, and the deprivation of the Indian. It was the loss of freedom that hurt most of all. Chano could not understand why the white men seemed to think land was something that could be purchased and fenced. The land was put there by the Great Spirit, and filled with wild beasts for hunting and survival, and it was there for all to share. But the white man didn't know how to share.

"I do not want my son to lust after gold and land as the white man does. I want him to care, and to learn to share what he has."

"I understand," Moss replied, smoking quietly and staring into the campfire flames. "I have to tell you, Chano, I own property myself. Some in Utah, and now some up in Wyoming. But I don't lust after land like you're talking. What I had in Utah—it's just enough to get by on. The land in Wyoming, well, it's a pretty big spread, and it was willed to me. But I don't have no desire to take more. And Mandy, she's not the type to care much about a lot of possessions herself. But it's a real pretty spread up there, Chano. Lipan will live where there's plenty of green grass, cool shade, enough water, and a fine house. I gotta tell you, I'll make him work hard. A man with only one arm needs a lot of help."

"It is good that he works. It will make him strong, responsible. Will you share this land with others?"

"The only thing on it that needs sharin' is the water. Yes, I share the water with the nearby ranchers."

"Good. You are not selfish like the others."

Moss thought for a moment about Etta, realizing how

poorly she would have fared with men like these Apache. And then he thought of Amanda, his heart racing wildly at the knowledge that sometime the next day he would see her! And he knew that sleep would not come easy to him that night.

"Is she really all right, Chano?" he asked quietly.

"She is well. She is thin, because we do not have much food to share. The first night there was much arguing among the other bucks and myself. They are all just as full of hatred as I. But it touched me when she said that her God had sent us. I saw the faith and trust in her eyes. And I convinced them that to abuse her would be to offend the Great Spirit. She was badly bruised and shaken—scratched and dirty. I allowed her to rest, put bear grease on her cuts. There are only three women with us now. One of them gave her a tunic to wear. She was very frightened the first few days, and then she came to trust us. And she and my son became fast friends. The things she teaches him—they interest him, excite him."

Moss took a long drag on his cigarette. "The, uh, white man you found with her. Did he rape her?"

"Not the day we came. He was beating her—doing vile things to her—but he did not get the chance to put his man part in her. I do not know for certain if he had taken her before that. It is a question you must ask her yourself."

Moss closed his eyes and sighed. "Yeah," he replied in a near whisper. "I couldn't repay you enough, Chano, if I spent the rest of my life trying."

"You will spend the rest of your life trying. You will be raising my son."

They looked at each other and Moss smiled a little. "You want me to try to get word to you once in a while?"

Chano lost his smile. "No. Once he is gone, it is better I never see him or hear about him again. It will be easier that way, for both of us."

"Does Lipan know what you plan to do?"

"We have talked about it. He honors his father. He will do whatever I ask of him."

Moss rubbed his forehead. "I'm sorry, Chano. Sorry it has to be like this for the Apache. If it were up to me—"

"You do not need to explain. If there were more like you, there would be peace among us."

Moss took another deep drag and tossed the cigarette into the campfire.

"Why didn't you try to get word to someone that she was okay? You could have turned her over to the soldiers or something."

"And have them find us?"

"Yeah. I guess that's a pretty stupid idea."

"And there were no white men I could trust. How could I be sure white men I did not know would care for her and take her home? Perhaps they would treat her as the other one did. I decided the only man to whom I could give her was her own man. She kept saying you would come, so I believed her." He glanced at Moss's right arm. "But she said perhaps you would have no arms at all. She was much worried about that."

"Duncan must have told her what they did to me." He looked at Chano. "She must have wondered if I was even alive."

"She did. I think she was afraid that if you did not come, she would never see her white world again—and perhaps she would not have." He grinned a little. "I almost wished you were dead, Moses Tucker. Perhaps in time, as the affection between her and my son grew, she would have learned to have affection for me, also. She would make a good woman for Chano."

Their eyes held a moment. "She's the best," Moss replied.

"It was not easy for me to be near her so much—to watch her with my son and not claim her for myself. But she would not have been willing. It was too soon. And I would not have wanted to hurt her. There was too much trust in her eyes."

Moss smiled. "Yeah, she does have a way of gettin' to a man."

"Even an Apache," Chano replied. Then he sobered again. "She tells me you have a daughter about Lipan's age. She was very worried about the child and prayed for her often."

471

"Her name's Becky. She's okay now. She's a damned pretty little thing. I fathered her by another woman before I met Amanda. Her ma was blonde, and Becky's blonde. She's got the sweetest smile I've ever seen, and she kind of teases me with her eyes like her ma used to do."

"Your daughter and my son—they will grow up together. Perhaps one day there will be a little half-breed grandchild, no?"

Moss's eyebrows went up. "Who knows? Only thing I know is a strong, young Apache man couldn't make a bad husband."

"If she grows up to be like your woman, she will be easy to love," Chano told him.

Moss nodded. How he missed her! "Yes, she'll be easy to love if she's anything like Mandy," he answered, staring into the flames of their campfire.

"We will sleep now," Chano told him. "Tomorrow you will see your woman. It has been a long time, no?"

Their eyes held in understanding. "Yeah. It's been a long time."

"As it has for me. I think one day I will sneak down to that reservation and seduce a young Apache woman into coming here with me. It is lonely for a man without a woman."

Moss thought of his own men, and of himself before he'd met Amanda.

"I know exactly what you mean, Chano." He moved over and stretched out on his bedroll, filled with the luxurious knowledge that come the next night, he would not be sleeping alone. Nor would he ever again, if he could help it.

• • •

They came upon a rise and looked down into what seemed another world. Below them was a valley, surprisingly green. A few tipis sat near a small stream, and they could hear a waterfall from further down the stream. Thick pines surrounded the valley, and it was a spot that Moss was certain no soldier had ever seen. He wasn't even sure that he could find his way back out of the myriad of rocks and hills and mountains through which they had ridden to get to this spot.

"I must have your word that you will tell no other white man about this place—the word of you and all your men."

"My men are as truthful as I am, Chano. No one will tell. I'll make up a story as to how I found her. And I'll figure out some way to explain the boy. When my wife explains how much she wants to keep him, I'm sure the authorities will allow it."

They headed the horses down a steep embankment, ducking under pine branches. They could barely be heard approaching, as their horses' hooves padded against fallen pine needles.

White men and Indians alike approached the small camp, and then he saw her! He was certain it was Amanda. She wore a tunic, and her long, brown hair was tied into two tails at her shoulders. She was squatting down near the stream, laughing with two other women and trying to catch a fish, and a little boy was in the stream trying to chase the fish toward the women.

Moss stopped his horse and just stared a moment. The little boy screamed with delight, holding up a large bass in his bare hands, then handing it to Amanda. She squealed and dropped it when it wiggled, and the little boy put his hands to the sides of his face in exasperation. Amanda laughed. How good it sounded! She actually laughed! She picked up the little boy and swung him around, and it was then she saw them.

Her laughter stopped, and she slowly put the little boy down. They stared at each other transfixed. The Tucker men also sat and stared, all in love at the same time.

"Hell, she looks like an Apache squaw!" Pappy finally spoke up.

"Ain't she a sight!" Johnny said. He let out a war hoop, and Moss nudged his horse forward. Buck kept his face turned away from the others, not wanting them to see his tears.

Moss rode closer, while the others hung back. She watched him, studied the handsome face and the lean body she had wondered if she would ever see again. Oh, how tired he looked! He came close to her now, and their eyes said it all. She knew he had not touched Etta Landers. He had been true to her after all. Words stuck in her throat, where a painful lump seemed to choke her. She swallowed, and her lower lip quivered.

"I knew you'd come," she whispered.

"It's a long story, baby. I have so much to tell you."

"Your…arm." Tears streamed down her face. "Lloyd Duncan said…"

He reached the arm down toward her. "Good as ever," he told her.

"Oh, Moss!" she whispered, her tears coming harder now. He bent down and swept her up onto the horse in one swift and powerful motion, and she sat sideways, curling up her knees and embracing him. His own tears flowed freely, as he breathed in the clean scent of her hair and held a hand to the small waist.

"Mandy!" he whispered. She turned her face up to his, and each relished the taste of the other's lips. Such a long time it had been! He released the long and hungry kiss and she kept her face nuzzled in his neck. "I'll never leave you again, Mandy! Never!" he whispered.

She kissed his neck and clung tightly to him.

"Down the stream," she whispered in his ear. "There's a beautiful waterfall. We can be alone there. We can…talk. There's so much to talk about, Moss!"

"I know. I know all about Lipan. And I have things to tell you. I'm gonna take you to live in a grand house, Mandy! With real shiny wood floors—two stories high and six bedrooms for all them kids we're gonna have! And real indoor plumbin'. And—"

"Moss!" She leaned back slightly to look up into the handsome dark eyes. "What on earth—"

Their eyes held. "I'll explain it all later, baby. Let's go find that waterfall."

She felt the lovely stirring in her groin.

"The grass is soft there," she told him. He grinned.

"And we have some catchin' up to do…on a lot of things."

"I'm all right, Moss. I'm okay. I still belong to you."

He kissed her lightly. "Let's go put a seal on that, Mrs. Tucker."

"I think that's a good idea, Mr. Tucker."

They rode off into the thick pines, headed downstream, and the lonely men watched in envy and joy. Sooner scratched his chin.

"I don't know about you boys, but I've got to get back north and find me an easy woman 'fore I go crazy."

They all snickered. "I'm with you," Lonnie replied.

Then they all tore their eyes from where Moss and Amanda disappeared into the trees and looked around at each other. Not an eye was dry.

"I reckon most of us will be headin' back up to Wyoming eventually," Buck put in. "Chances are somebody up there is gonna be needin' some ranch hands, wouldn't you say, boys?"

Pappy grinned. "I expect so," he replied. He wiped at his eyes with his shirt-sleeve. "Too much dust down here in Arizona. Gets in your eyes."